TAKE INK & WEEP

ELIZABETH GUY

FirstRider Publishing

Contact:
Sign up to Elizabeth's newsletter on her website:
www.elizabeth-guy.com
Keep up to date with what Elizabeth is doing:
Instagram @elizabeth__guy | Facebook @elizabethguy01

Elizabeth Guy was born in Australia and currently lives part of the week in Sydney's inner city and the rest, in the Blue Mountains. She is a full time writer and a part time tutor and education consultant. *Take Ink & Weep* is her first historical fiction to be followed by *Abandoned by God*, set in the tumultuous year of the Russian Revolution. Elizabeth's doctorate was awarded by the University of Sydney (*The Poetics of the Nation State*). Elizabeth is also the author of *The Alchemy of Poetry: A Reader's Guide to Understanding Poetry* (2020). She has worked and travelled extensively throughout a number of places, including Russia and South America.

To
Madelaine,
my daughter,
who is the reason for everything.

The newspaper boys shouted hoarsely,
Evening Paper! Italy! Germany! Austria!
And in the night, starkly outlined in black
Crimson blood poured and poured in a stream.

Vladimir Mayakovsky

Chapter 1

November — December 1914

She told herself, *this is what I want ... Sofia's mouth on mine ... this is what I want,* as the chilly Russian night made her eyes water and her gloveless fingers burn.

Sofia pressed Marina hard against the brick wall as night revellers passed about them on Italianskaya Street. Her fingers moved up Marina's face and into the thick blunt cut of her hair. She stroked Marina's neck and teased her ear lobe with feint bites. Sofia's hand moved up Marina's thigh, across her hip and slowly made its way to her breast. Marina felt reckless and opened her lips to Sofia, whose kisses tasted like abandonment.

A cab pulled up and its horse snorted. A tall svelte female moved out of the doorway, a metre or so from where they were kissing, and strode towards the cab.

Marina watched her.

As the passenger stepped up into the cab her tight cloche skirt pulled high, exposing her impossibly long calf.

Sofia tugged at Marina's hair playfully.

The woman's skirt slipped above her knee and then … *God help me*, thought Marina … the start of her thigh.

Sofia moved her soft full mouth across to Marina's ear and said, "Where are you?" It hadn't sounded like a question.

The woman in the cab was bending over something in her lap. A letter? An address? Money? And the outline of her fur ushanka was just discernible in the inky darkness.

Sofia opened her mouth and pushed her teeth against Marina's neck.

The door next to them unbolted again and strains of music and light spilled across the doorway and there stood a man, quite still, watching the woman in the cab.

"Anna," he said faintly as if he didn't want her to hear.

Then the cab driver grunted something to his horse and Marina heard the man in the doorway whisper again, "Anna."

The horse clopped off.

Marina unbuttoned the top of Sofia's woollen overcoat, unravelled the scarf at the base of her neck and undid the silk tie at the collar of her shirt. Sofia stopped kissing and held her breath.

Marina closed her eyes and slid her hand under Sofia's cotton chemise which was damp and warm, and toyed with a hardened nipple.

Sofia groaned.

Marina knew this was what she wanted, right here, several hundred kilometres from Moscow ... from her home, from her husband and from his insistence that their daughter has a sister or brother.

Marina loved her husband, Sergei Yakovlevich Efron. She loved his impossibly beautiful face. She loved the way she wanted to be mother and daughter to him. She even found their two year old endearing. Little hands and large eyes that seemed to watch her at a distance. And yes, her husband cared for her and needed her and wanted more than anything to be everything for her — but that was just the thing — she didn't want everything to be just him, in their sour apartment with the dirty Kremlin walls beyond the window.

That can't be everything, Marina told herself fiercely.

Marina and Sofia had only just arrived at Nicholaevsky Railway Station, St Petersburg, a few hours beforehand. On the long train ride north, they had planned to work on Sofia's poetry but Marina was too caught up in the rush towards her future. Marina had packed her beloved copy of Alexander Blok's poems. She didn't need to pull it out of her bag because she knew many of his poems by heart, but it was there nonetheless, should she need a break from Sofia's intensity.

The train pounded onwards.

As she watched the race of landscape and rain, Marina found herself reciting Blok:

The streetlamps barely glimmer
And I can see the morning rays,
Beyond the Neva ...

Sofia heard the recitation and, not recognising the composer, wondered if this poem was for her, if Marina was truly for her.

Marina looked out the grimy window of the second-class compartment and continued:
... the awakening blaze
Conceals the nearing resurrection,
Of dreary, melancholy days.

It wasn't the first time Marina wondered why she felt the drama of language more intensely than life itself. It was strange. It was as if she was outside herself, looking in, always writing or reading the moment.

"Is that your poem, my love?" Sofia asked as she snuggled closer to Marina.

The train charged alongside dachas closed for autumn and the oncoming winter.

"Blok." Marina addressed her answer to the window, "Alexander ... Blok" and her mouth remained open.

A little later, after the guard had checked the passenger tickets and the girl had brought around the samovar and jam-filled blinis, they were fighting.

"... but fate has brought us together," Sofia's whisper was fierce. "We must surrender to it or die!"

Marina hissed back at her, "As I have said before — now that Efron has volunteered to fight I cannot commit to more than a few weeks away from Moscow. Everything is so dependent on the goodwill of his sisters." She thought about their devotion to her daughter and ignored the frustrated exhalation beside her.

Efron was a cadet in the officer's academy when Marina met him in the Crimea. Slender, handsome and a face filled with tragedy. He was haunted by his family's heritage of sedition, treason, illness and suicide. It was no wonder Marina's family shunned their marriage, which was also aggravated by the fact that he was a Jew.

"Well, I'm not going to wait around for you to decide! Why can't you give me what I am offering you?"

Why can't you give me what I want? thought Marina. But instead, she responded tiredly, "Can we just enjoy our time together?"

It was Marina's idea to head north for a few weeks to St Petersburg or rather Petrograd — most Muscovites had more pressing concerns than to remember a name change. Efron had been gone for a few months and every Russian knew the war would be over by Christmas, so what little time they had was precious.

The train's whistle screamed and Marina looked away from Sofia's anger and out into the crossroad of some small township through which they were flying.

The whole reason she wanted to go to St Petersburg was to abandon herself to the heady atmosphere of

nightclubs and literary soirees where music and read-
ings and conversation and bodies comingled with the
sole purpose of pursuing one's desire. It would be here,
in this tumultuous city of poets, that Marina's secret
self, her shadowy other-self, could be completely un-
encumbered by the roles of mother, daughter and wife.

"The problem with you, Marina," Sofia's voice was
thick with emotion, "is that men like Efron can only
love the idea of you — whereas, a woman like me can
love the real you."

Marina admitted to herself that she loved having
sex with a woman. With Sofia. Pleasuring a woman was
wildly instinctive ... doing to her what you want to be
done to you. Her hands and fingers and tongue and lips
knew exactly what to fondle or suck or bite or slap.
The sex was delicious and yet as their affair had progressed so had the fighting. It always felt as if Sofia
wanted to mould her into a version of herself.

She heard Sofia say next to her, "I won't keep asking
you to move into my apartment."

Marina knew Sofia was hurting and that she should
turn to her, kiss her, hold her hand — something —
but instead, she thought about Efron. She had cried
when he joined the Reservists, although, she was unsure if she cried because she felt forsaken or because
she feared freedom.

"I can't live up near the Belorusskaya Railway Station with you when just a few blocks away my sisters-in-law and daughter are waiting for me to come home!" She knew that some passengers nearby were glancing across at them because every Russian considered the business of others to be theirs.

"Oh — and I suppose you want to be there when Efron has furlough!"

God give me strength, thought Marina and closed her eyes but after a while, she heard Sofia clearing her throat and sniffing. Marina took her hand and pushed it to her heart, which, at that moment, felt completely empty.

The train roared harder into her destiny.

Two hours later they climbed down onto the platform at St Petersburg and the hot urgency of humanity seethed about them.

Scurrying porters and civilian passengers pushed against each other trying to either leave the station or clamber onto the trains, clutching their dirty bundles of luggage and their precious travel certificates. Soldiers leaned about smoking, their rifles slung across their backs, indifferent to the screech and steam of the locomotives.

Marina felt giddy with the sea of people roiling about the edges of the little island she and Sofia made, as they stood together craning their heads this way and that trying to see how to exit the station.

"This way!" yelled Sofia, and Marina found herself being hauled past the quiet infantrymen.

She, like many Russians, did not initially believe the rumours of the devastating losses at a battle near Tannenberg, but as summer gave way to autumn it was confirmed in the *Kommersant*.

"Keep up!" called Sofia but her assertive little chignon was bobbing further and further away from Marina who felt cast adrift in the memory of that shocking roll call of a dead generation. How had it all happened? The Tsar had given his assurance that the war would be over in six to seven weeks and that God would grant them victory.

A boy of about nine pushed past Marina and despite being shoeless he had the bluster of someone in authority. Under his arm he carried a stack of newspapers and pinned to his front and back was the headline banner which he cried out in a sing-song swagger, "RUSSIA DECLARES WAR ON THE OTTOMAN EMPIRE!"

She saw Sofia waiting for her impatiently at the exit gates and as she reached her Marina said breathlessly, "It's hard not to feel patriotic!"

"Those in power have abused and exploited Russians since antiquity —"

"Yes, but all I'm saying —"

"It's what rulers do here in Russia. And they are always men ..." As Sofia turned to move off, Marina heard her add, "And never Jews ..."

Marina knew that she should let it go but Sofia's teacherly tone was exasperating, "Princess Olga of Kiev," Marina raised her voice over the din, "was a powerful female ruler — quite merciless, actually —"

"And the Christians canonised her!"

And somehow that is supposed to be my fault, Marina thought to herself and hurried along behind Sofia's stiff departing back.

Marina's sister had promised to send her driver who would wait for them outside the station. They were staying in Anastasia's one-bedroom apartment that was crammed up against the Obvodnogo Canal, she and her husband were looking forward to their visit.

"Shall we have tea at my sisters and freshen up before we go out tonight?"

"No," said Sofia briskly. "We'll send our luggage on without us so that we can get out and about in St Petersburg!"

Sofia moved swiftly behind the porter, their luggage piled perilously high, as he wove his way through the human mass. They spewed out past the passenger gates and into Ligovsky Prospect. Marina stood on tip-toe to survey the city that promised escape.

An afternoon downpour had turned St Petersburg into a watercolour palette with its raw umber, burnt sienna and bone black.

Marina and Sofia were found by her sister's taciturn driver. He was a bear of a man with a beltless smock hanging low over his trousers. His coal-black beard and long hair framed his light watery eyes. He immediately took charge of the luggage, throwing it high over the side of the cart while the horse waited patiently. Then he turned his attention back to the two women, expecting them to climb up and be away.

Sofia gave two kopeks to the porter and then said to the driver, "Tell Anastasia Ivanovna Tsvetaeva that we will be home later tonight."

His hefty body was surprising agile as he climbed up into the cart and with open curiosity took in the two women beneath him: one in trousers, a suit coat and tie, the other in a dress with her hair out, no headscarf.

Marina thought she heard the driver scoff, *Pff Muscovites* but when she glanced at him he responded neutrally with, "As you wish."

Then without even looking back over his shoulder at the oncoming traffic he slapped the reins against the rump of the horse and was gone.

Sofia bustled Marina through the melange of horse-drawn trolley busses, electric trams, army trucks and flustered pedestrians pouring west from Nevsky Prospect and north from Ligovsky.

"Anastasia," Marina commented, "will disapprove of us dashing about the city before going first to her apartment." She thought of her younger sister with both affection and rivalry. She hadn't seen Anastasia for more than a year. Her book, *King's Musings* had already been published and even the brilliant Boris Leonidovich Pasternak had praised it as a stellar debut.

Sophia took Marina's arm and linked it through hers as they pushed their way along the early evening crowd on Nevsky Prospect where the tricolour was flying from every lamp post.

"In what way would she disapprove?" Sofia's tone made Marina look across at her quickly. Her impish expression and jaunty pace made Marina feel she was in a Valentin Serov painting. She still hadn't got used to Sofia's mercurial changes of mood.

"That you have left your tiresome husband?" Sofia asked coquettishly. "And that you love the taste of my skin?"

People pushed and shoved, ran for trams and trolleybuses, darted across roads or into noisy shopfronts, and the two women clung to each other as they were joyfully dragged along in the crowd.

"I'm *here* in St Petersburg!" Marina cried, "No rules, no obligations — just me!" Then with her arms out wide she spun around and around into the oncoming foot traffic.

"And me," murmured Sofia.

2

Lidka was fed up with the cook's foul mouth and filthy eye. He shambled about the kitchen yelling orders, slamming knives into the mackerel or red peppers or tomatoes as if they were the Germans themselves. Lidka was the newest wait staff to Kolobok's, a restaurant that had seen better days, just off Nevsky Prospect along the Fontanka River. The cook had been working for Kolobok's for the past 12 years and had seen his fair share of ugly waitresses so it was a pleasant surprise for him to examine the latest hire. She was tall and slender with fair hair that was cut a little too short, but then again, she had come up from Odessa.

The cook looked hard at her small breasts and adjusted his crotch as he leaned back against the chopping bench.

"Whadya call those then? Not much for a man to get his hands on."

He used the rolling pin to emphasise his point by shoving it towards Lidka's chest. She gazed back at him.

A mangy old chook who thinks he is the cock of the walk, thought Lidka.

The cook dropped the rolling pin and with the subtlety of a moron and asked, "You got a boyfriend then, or what?"

"I'll work the tables," she replied dismissively and left the stench of his body odour behind her.

"I'll be watching you ..." His departing words were lost as she pushed through into the dining area.

Lidka had not been in St Petersburg for long. Her aunt had managed to get her into the boarding house where she lived and together they shared the same bed. It was bearable. Her aunt snored and occasionally farted but so far they saw little of each other, with Lidka's hours at the restaurant differing to those at the Putilov Factory, where her aunt worked. It had taken Lidka over a week to get to St Petersburg and she was determined to make money so that she could send it home to her mother, who was caring for her son.

Lidka believed there was no point in staying in Odessa after hearing her husband had been killed. At first, she had hoped he had been taken prisoner by the Turks after they torpedoed the gunboat he was crewing, right there in their harbour. She would never forget that black morning at the end of October, where every man, woman and child in Odessa woke to the bombardment. Later, the names of the dead were stuck on the town hall windows and, sure enough, there was the name of her husband.

Lidka realised three months into the war and one month after her husband had been blown to bits, she, herself, was as good as dead. War was a quiet ending to her 20 year life. She did not feel she was herself anymore. She didn't know who she was but she certainly wasn't that young woman who made love to her husband, or walked to the railway each day to sell her famous khinkali dumplings or chatted with friends about Russia's new future. They all knew sacrifices would have to be made, God knows, they were Russians, sacrifice was in their blood. She had believed in her husband; she had believed in the war. Back then her heart used to pump. Her blood used to flow. Now she was numb. Now she believed in nothing.

The head waitress gestured to the table where two women were waiting for their order to be taken. Lidka adjusted her short black headscarf and tightened the apron over her long skirt. She moved effortlessly between the square tables where cheap cigarette smoke rose to the ceiling. The two women looked up expectantly. One, in what appeared to be a man's dark suit with trousers, shirt and tie, and the other in a sleeve-less navy-blue dress with a lace blouse beneath.

"Good evening Ladies," said Lidka and kept her wide green eyes downcast.

"Potato pancakes, the Buko cheese, red caviar and smoked salmon —"

"Sofia, what about the solyanka — just one bowl," Marina purred. "We'll share."

"The solyanka," Sofia repeated. "And the adzhika."

"Certainly."

Lidka took their menus and tried not to notice the way the one in the dress looked at her. Hungry and watchful.

"Oh and lavash!" Sophia added.

Lidka nodded acknowledgment and moved back to-wards the kitchen.

Sofia had led Marina to Kolobok's, assuring her the food was worth the walk. After the cramped train ride from Moscow, they relished the evening exercise. It was only November but they had noticed the chill hardening, especially by the time they got to the Anichkov Bridge. Marina had been enthralled by its arches galloping across the Fontanka River but it was the sculptures of the horse tamers on the four points of the bridge that brought her to a stand-still. She had reached up and touched the hoof of one horse and then stroked the tamer's slender calf as he knelt before the magnificent beast. Here was an attempt to tame muscle and sinew into marble. *Oh, to make art this beautiful, this everlasting, this true*, thought Marina.

She had read that Pushkin composed one of his poems right here on the Anichkov Bridge but she was careful not to recite out loud the lines she remembered:
I loved you once
and I could love you once again.
Love hasn't faded fully in my heart.

St Petersburg was an enormous inhalation of breath. Seeing this city for the first time was like recognising a lover, even though you had never met before. Eventually, Sofia had dragged Marina off the bridge and around the corner, past the red exterior of the Beloselsky-Belozersky Palace and into a private courtyard where they found the restaurant Sofia had promised.

Hours later, Kolobok's was thrumming. Lidka and the other girls moved swiftly back and forth from the dining room to the kitchen: avoiding the cook's hands, carrying large bowls of steaming borsch or refilling glasses of vodka, collecting plates, wiping tables and picking up the rare tip. Kolobok's attracted theatre-goers and officers, as well as moneyed locals who enjoyed the occasional night out. Socialising was a national pastime especially as it was lubricated by alcohol. Nonetheless, the Tsar had banned the sale of vodka in a patriotic effort to back the Russian troops. But all Russians knew that the armies marched on vodka and so in the spirit of supporting their troops, civilians drank shots.

Lidka was bringing dessert to the two women when an overcoat draped giant flopped down at their table. The woman dressed in a man's suit looked fit to burst, but the other threw back her head and laughed.

"Vlado!" Marina's voice was full of joy as she leaned across the table to hug and kiss his enormous head.

He returned the affection with one arm stretched away in an effort to protect his cigarette.

"What's this? Coffee?" he asked and his deep gravelly voice caused Lidka to pause.

"Oh, Vlado! I can't believe it's you! I haven't seen you since forever!" cried Marina with her hand affectionately resting on his arm.

"Vodka," he told Lidka who nodded as she unpacked the tray and then turned to fetch the glasses and vodka.

"We are having coffee and honey cake." Sofia's assertion reminded Marina she needed to make introductions.

"Oh my dear Vlado!" exclaimed Marina again, but he was reaching out to shake Sofia's hand, a glint of amusement in his deep-set eyes.

"Vladimir Vladimirovich Mayakovsky," he said.

Sofia moved her cigarette to her left hand and shook his.

"Call me Vlad." He added, "Or comrade!"

Hard lines bracketed Mayakovsky's generous mouth and a furrow dug permanently between his dark eyebrows; everything about him was too much — his nose, his ears, his legs, his hands — then Sofia realised who he was.

"Yes! I've heard of you. I'm Sonya Yakovlenvna Parnok. How do you do?"

"Call her Sofia! This is Vlado he is the most outrageous poet. Aren't you, my darling! He's from Moscow!" Maria added like it was the most extraordinary coincidence.

At that moment Lidka reappeared. When Mayakovsky took the bottle from her, his cold fingers made her flinch, despite the ceramic tile heater stretching from floor to ceiling in the alcove nearby. He looked up briefly but by then she had turned her back on the party and was moving swiftly away.

"And how is Efron, Marina?" Mayakovsky directed his question at Sofia as he poured their drinks, "Still writing his heart-breaking verse to you?"

Sofia felt her neck flush and her face burn.

"Don't be annoying," Marina pouted at Mayakovsky. "He finished up his time with the ambulance corps and is now with the Reservists. Because of the TB. Anyway, I'm so glad you insisted I come to St Petersburg to visit! You know we are staying at Anastasia's — you've met her, yes? Published last year!"

She is utterly exhausting, thought Sofia.

"I do want to see everything!" Marina continued, "Moscow is so boring and tired and walled in!"

He chuckled and winked across at Sofia as he said, "I see you are in the right hands!"

Soothed and admired, the three of them reached for their glasses.

"Nostrovia!" Mayakovsky boomed across the table.

"To your health," they replied and drank back the clear liquid.

Mayakovsky reached for the bottle, once again.

"You know, Marina, vodka comes from Moscow." His smile was slow and lazy as he looked directly into her adoring eyes, "Some fucking monk came up with the recipe." He took a drag on his cigarette.

"Really?"

"Chudov Monastery."

Marina smiled and held his gaze. Mayakovsky hit the table with his giant fist and laughed.

He is incorrigible, magnificent, Marina thought.

Could she have slept with him? Sofia wondered.

The talk spilled about between Marina, Sofia and Mayakovsky. Lidka watched them out of the corner of her eye as she attended to the other guests. It seemed like yesterday, but also a million years ago when she and her husband decided on a night out at Odessa's Yellow Table Café. The place was buzzing with artists and writers and musicians. A group of young poets was billed to be the star attraction that night, they had been touring the country with their wild anarchic poetry. She found a table up close to the make-shift stage and sat there spellbound while these men, not much more than boys really with their top hats and canes, were completely and absolutely iconoclastic. They declared, *We alone are the face of our Time ... The past is too tight ... Throw Pushkin, Dostoevsky, and Tolstoy overboard.* These young poets had been unstoppable — despite the howls and boos of the audience.

That poet, Vladimir Mayakovsky, was at the center of it, his monumental body like abandoned scaffolding left on the stage. The audience loved him. His troupe of poets called themselves the Futurists and, although Lidka didn't understand much of the mayhem of their verse, she, like everyone around her, knew a door was opening.

He and his comrades smashed the old world of their parent's generation and trumpeted in the new. But there was more — he was queer and he didn't seem to care who knew. Every so often, he and one particular fellow Futurist would kiss or touch or whisper in a way that seemed lasciviously angelic. Lidka had found their halo of lust liberating.

When Mayakovsky left Kolobok's, Sofia ordered more coffee. The two women promised to join him a little later at the art cellar on Italianskaya Street. Even though Sofia had lived in this city on and off over the years, and had even written on the poets who Marina aspired to meet, she too felt the infectious vibrancy in the air. It was as if everything and everyone could be born again.

Indeed, Sofia's generation would make the older generation see that whether you were a Jew or Christian, afflicted with a disease or had the body of an ox, loved women or men — there was a place for everyone. The new Russia was being born: beautiful, glorious and free! *Look at Mayakovsky*, thought Sofia as she sipped her coffee, *openly proclaiming his right to love men or women!* This was Russia where anything was possible.

As they paid the bill, gathered their coats and pushed out into the night-filled city, Marina was a whirlwind of chatter and Sofia filled up on the delight of her. They headed along the side streets which would take them to the art cellar and Mayakovsky, hugging their coats against the gaunt cold that dug into their bones. Marina talked on excitedly about Mayakovsky and the Futurists and any other poet or painter or musician who popped into her mind.

The strange thing is, Sofia thought, *Marina's poetry is fierce and nothing like her indulgent self.* And she suspected, as they huddled arm in arm alongside the canal, that she was in love with Marina Ivanovna Tsvetaeva, the poet.

3

Earlier that night at the infamous Stray Dog Café —
the bohemian art cellar, the belle époque dance basement, the den of iniquity — the crowd had called out
for Boris Leonidovich Pasternak to recite one of his
poems. It had only just turned midnight and so there
were a few chairs and bar space available if one could
find them behind the thick veil of Turkish cigarette
smoke and dim lighting. It was a common occurrence
that one of the talent would be asked, either by the
owner of the café or the adoring dilettantes, to show-
case their latest work — a poem or short story or ballet
or musical score or play.

The crowd had watched Pasternak saunter in and
take a table close to the bar, the one reserved for the
poets or musicians or dancers. After his publication of
Twin in the Clouds, an astonishing collection of poems,
Pasternak had become the talk of St Petersburg, de-

spite being a Muscovite. Rumour had it that the daughter of the Jewish Wissotzky Tea Company had refused Pasternak's offer of marriage and so the Adonis heart-throb had turned up in St Petersburg. Needless to say, every woman, single or otherwise, had her cap set in his direction.

Pasternak stood up and the crowd cheered. Chairs shuffled, glasses quieted and the shushing curbed the conversations.

Oh, February. Take ink and weep!
To weep about it, spilling ink,
While raging sleet is burning hot
Like in the blackness of the spring ...

When he had written this poem earlier in the year, the icy cramp in his fingers had run up into his heart so that he was all claw and anguish as he wrote about the shock of rejection, his marriage proposal rebuffed. He had told himself over and over that from this wintery darkness, spring must emerge.

... To rent a buggy. For six grivnas,
Amidst the church-bells, clanking wheels,
To steer it where a shower drizzles
Much louder than ink or tears ...

The quiet poem moved into the corners of the cellar. A poem about writing and sadness and a Russian winter. His conflation of romance and rejection was a lament of frustration known to every Russian.

... Where thousands of rooks fall fast,
Like charcoaled pears to their demise
And as they hit the puddles, cast
Dry sadness to depths of eyes ...

Rooks always signaled the start of spring. And when he wrote this poem Alexei Savrasov's landscape, hanging in Tretyakov Gallery, had flown into his mind — a painterly moment still wet and unpredictable — with its rooks tracking the soggy skies and casting their image in the shadowy puddles below.

... Beneath — thawed patches now appear,
The wind is furrowed by the yelling.
New poems are composed in tears,
The more unplanned, the more compelling.

Pasternak's intense gaze, high cheekbones and wide mouth remained motionless as the audience clapped and roared for more of his deep sonorous voice. He looked into the crowd to see if she had arrived; the unconquerable Anna Akhmatova.

As he eventually took his seat, with the clamour of congratulations, salutations and drinks still ringing in his ears, Pasternak wondered why he had chosen this particular poem to read on this particular night, of all nights. The wintery world always gives way to life in spring, he once again reassured himself, and as spring will nudge its way into the landscape, an entirely different poem will be born.

He hadn't expected to be asked to recite tonight. His mind had been aflame with plans to leave St Petersburg and travel into a new life. He and Anna would make good their escape. Rather than remain downcast because the army had rejected him, Pasternak had decided to offer his sweat and toil to the war effort as a labourer in a chemical factory in Vsevolodov-Vilve, the Ural Mountains. She would come with him and together they would write poetry about their beloved Russia — which was her, which was him and more than the sum of each other. She had said she loved his devotion ... to music, philosophy, poetry, Russian classics and her mind (he had added boldly, *and your body!*). She had said his sensitivity and brooding was not of this world. About himself, he felt he was full of restraint and over scrupulous responses, in his ardent worship of the feminine.

He looked up and across the crowded sea of revellers at the Stray Dog Café he saw her move towards him in that languid sexy way she had as if no one in the world existed except him. And as usual, all eyes turned towards her. She was statuesque but moved willowy and fluid. And everyone watched that hot-wired body. Her hair, a sheath of raven black and her dark blue eyes, saw everything and nothing. She was an electric current and he was her cross wire.

"AKHMATOVA!", "QUEEN OF THE NEVA!" and "ANNA AKHMATOVA!" The crowd called because they had forgotten him and were fawning over their true beloved.

Pasternak watched her. She was gypsy, whore, goddess, saint, daughter and beloved but always and every time, indifferent.

People begged for her to sign their napkins or shake their hands or accept a glass of Dom Pérignon as she tried to make her way to where Pasternak sat. She waved a hand away at their calls for her to recite her poetry as if batting insects of no consequence. But a metre or so from Pasternak she eventually succumbed.

With her deep throaty voice and holding her head slightly downwards, in that way she did, she gave them a few lines:

All of us here are hookers and hustlers.

We drink too much and don't care.
The walls are covered with birds and flowers
That have never seen sunshine or air.

And just like that, she kept moving. The crowd roared and saluted her, not bothering to hide their fantasies to have her and be her.

Although she wasn't looking directly at him, he knew she was coming to him. He had caught the uncatchable. *They all love her and want her*, he thought, *but only I have her!* He could barely contain his incredulity. He had read her poetry, of course, and heard about her (who hadn't?) well before he met her. Indeed, most of last year, Mayakovsky had tried to get him to come north and visit the Stray Dog. If Pasternak had known this was Anna's favourite haunt, he would have left Moscow in a heartbeat. As it was, he met her seven weeks ago and his life changed forever.

Anna, at last, folded herself into the chair beside him and pushed up against his leg. He leaned into her and breathed in her body. And without touching him she moved her own nose close to his neck and drank him in.

They had been lovers for a short while but he knew she was his and, unlike her husband, Pasternak could never be indifferent. Her husband, Nikolay

Stepanovich Gumilyov, was away. He was always away. Previously it had been in Somaliland and Abyssinia, but more recently he had been fighting at the Front. Pasternak thought Gumilyov was jealous, not of her lovers, but of the reputation she was acquiring as a poet, one that far outstripped his. Anna thought Gumilyov was disinterested, not in her poetry, but in her body, heart, and soul. There was an underlying sadness in her that was both compelling and mystifying and Pasternak devoured her, loved her, adored her.

Most nights after their love-making, the sheets twisted in an exhausted mess, Anna and Pasternak smoked and talked. She would lay for hours naked and without any self-consciousness. Her body was hard and muscular and lean. Her legs, impossibly long, her thatch of pubic hair, decidedly thick, and the wide areolas on her upturned breasts, a succulent wonder to him. Anna would pull away from his endless hands and tongue and snatch up a book or a poem in progress and read to him. Together they would talk on and on about anything and everything. Poetry was the world. Poetry was sex. Poetry was food and drink. Poetry was Russia. And as poets, hungry and driven, they both knew their destiny was to give witness to the flesh and breadth of Mother Russia.

Pasternak poured Anna a drink and bent his head to hers.

"Everything is in place," he murmured. "I have our tickets for the Urals. Moscow ... Vladimir ... Nizhniy-Novgorod," he recited the cities like a holy litany, "Kazan ... Perm ..."

Around them, the laughter and chatter bounced off the cellar walls.

Anna seemed more distant than usual, so he explained quickly, "You know how unpredictable the trains are, so the sooner we report to the railway station, the sooner we can queue for our seats."

He watched her smoke slowly, her dark blue eyes scanning the seedy cellar.

"I suggest we pack lightly. We won't need anything by way of bedding or kitchen utensils." He knew he was rushing but he could not find the brakes, "The manager of the chemical factory said our rooms would have good amenities ..."

Anna looked at him momentarily, her eyes puzzled and yet he had told her that he had secured work in a chemical factory so that they would have an income to live off.

"Oh, and the travel certificates arrived today — so ..." He pulled her hand to his and kissed it because soon they would be leaving St Petersburg and travelling into their future.

She raised an eyebrow and from the bar, someone darted across with a fresh bottle of vodka. She watched the random devotee pour the alcohol and then offered him a smile that would flutter about his heart long after he returned to the bar.

"Imagine, my love, clean air, the mountains, the lakes ..." Something about her made Pasternak unable to stop, "The meadow flowers in the Urals, the space, the time ..." He knew he wasn't expressing himself as clearly as he had rehearsed, "A home with you. Just the two of us. Together ..."

Anna sipped her drink as she pulled a violet silk scarf from her beaded purse and proceeded to wrap it around her long pale neck.

Pasternak wanted to hold her in his arms and reassure her that she would be loved forever, and he wanted to reassure himself that his dream was hers and together they had paved a way for the greatest poetic love story ever imagined.

He looked at her exquisite profile as she watched the hot melee of bodies fill the cellar. The dim lighting cast shadows about her long aristocratic nose, wide eyes and mouth. Pasternak knew he was locked in a love greater than himself.

At last, when Anna turned slowly and looked into his eyes, he saw it.

"Anna, please ... What is it?"

She was already gone.

"Has something happened?"

He saw she was not getting on their train to the Urals, but rather, she was hurtling towards her own future. One without him. And although he wanted nothing more than to hold her and crush her in his arms, he felt his limbs grow weak.

"I am sorry, my darling," she spoke her words to him like she was reciting one of her poems.

I will never write again, he thought. *Without her I am dead.*

He tried to catch her hands but they were tucked beneath her crossed arms. He searched for her eyes but she would not look at him and when he tried to cup her face in his hands, she jerked it back and moved her gaze to the drunkards and whores — her adoring public.

Pasternak felt his throat constrict. "This isn't possible — I *love* you ..." But this was not what he wanted to say at all. He hadn't seen this coming, he never thought this night, of all nights, would be the end of his life.

Near them, oblivious to his howling heartbreak, an inebriated couple danced a jig while their friends clapped and hooted, and Pasternak noticed the way Anna watched them. It was as if she had forgotten him already. He thought of the lines he had recited earlier, *spilling ink, while raging sleet is burning hot.* And a part of him knew that her icy heart would shape the poet he was to become.

Pasternak could have slapped her hard across her face, in front of all these adoring acolytes, but he was already dying.

She was standing up. She was pulling on her fur ushanka. She was moving towards the cellar exit. In a few short steps, she was yanking her coat off the hook at the door.

He lurched out of his seat and bumped his way through the inebriated dancers and reached her just as she was tying the belt on her coat. She would not look at him. He caught her by the arm and into her gloved hand he shoved her train ticket: the one he had bought to start their lives together, the one she was supposed to want, the one that would take them away so they could write what Russia would never forget.

She pushed past him and dashed up the steps leading out of the cellar — then stopped.

One hand on the door.

He called to her, "Anna."

She held back a single hand with its palm upwards, her head and body facing the door. She was absolutely still.

Then he heard her say, *"I've just put on my right hand my left-handed glove."*

And she was gone.

The moment she pushed through the door and stepped out into the gelid night, a cab was pulling up.

She moved in one swift motion across the pavement, past revellers on Italianskaya Street and lovers fondling at the door of the Dog. Her tight skirt rode high as she threw herself into the cab but she did not care. If the world thought this was who she was, nothing but a body, breasts, legs, eyes — an object of love to be possessed, to be managed — then the world was a fool.

She looked down at the train ticket. By the time she looked up, the driver was already moving along the Konyushennaya Ploshchad.

She was numb with the pain of liberation.

4

Trooper Nikolay Stepanovich Gumilyov of the 8th Hussar Regiment, attached to the Russian 2nd, drank his bitter coffee in the gloam. It was far too cold for mid-November. At night men moved about restlessly in an attempt not to freeze to death.

Their bivouac clung to the skirts of Łódź in Polish Russia. Meanwhile, snow and mist caused poor visibility. To add insult to injury, the Russians were running dangerously low on ammunition.

Łódź was a bitch.

For the past two weeks, the Russians had been engaged in a game of cat and mouse with the Germans. Sometimes they were the cat, other times the mouse, and all the while it was becoming more and more frustrating. Russia's wireless messages, about their impending invasion of the mineral-rich region of Silesia in Germany, had been intercepted. As a consequence,

Germany's military commander, Paul von Hindenberg, ordered his armies to carve a corridor down the centre of Polish Russia, through Łódź, to divert the Russians away from Silesia.

Gumilyov's regiment had been recently attached to the fated Russian 2nd, the very one which had been routed in Tannenberg a month or so beforehand. The 2nd was now a patchwork of Divisions, Brigades and even Reserves. They were commanded to defend Łódź. A slumbering giantess, its factories quiet, its people in-doors. There was a wariness, a disquiet in Łódź as if she was uneasy about the protection Russia offered. The memory of Russia invading Poland some hundred years earlier was still written on her body. For many of the Polish Russians, invasion was invasion — be it Russian or German.

As an attack on Łódź was imminent the Hussars huddled around their night fires, waiting to be dis-patched as sentries or, in the case of Gumilyov, to lead a reconnaissance team beyond Łódź.

Gumilyov's mouth tasted acrid. He spat. The recent success of Russia at Galicia, where the spineless Aus-trians were defeated, was enough to fill every Russian with the hope that soon they would be returning home. Even the Grand Duke Nicholas Nikolaevich had proclaimed that they were the Russian steam roller de-stroying the enemy — all the way to Berlin.

Gumilyov made an involuntary snort of contempt for his foe and held his frozen hands up to the flames but a part of him knew that Russia's brouhaha harboured a deep-rooted fear of Germany.

He could still hear the shouts and cheers of St Petersburg back in August, *FOR FAITH, TSAR AND RUSSIA!* He and thousands of Hussars had ridden past the Tsar and Tsarina who blessed them from the balcony of the Winter Palace. *FOR THE DEFENCE OF HOLY RUSSIA!* the world had roared.

When they first arrived at Łódź they had been ordered to patrol the vast countryside beyond the town, but as the days grew frostier and the Germans moved steadily closer, they had begun to employ tactics to deny the enemy information. Routing German scouts, surprising their sentries and chasing down their messengers. *It's a bloody business*, Gumilyov thought. But he knew he would rather move swiftly among light horsemen than be the poor sod marching into cannon fire — often without a rifle and boots but singing anthems of love.

The night grew still and he heard some of the horses nicker, then a cadet murmured and quieted. The fire before them grew cold.

It was time.

Tonight's plan was to pick off a scout from a German reconnaissance team and bring him in for questioning. Gumilyov's mind went immediately to the thick woollen coat he knew the German would be wearing.

Gumilyov and three other men from his squadron set off on their horses in single file.

They had decided on a south-easterly direction past the bridge and into the forest; then circle back into Łódź by 0300, which gave them approximately two hours. The hard cold had a spite in it. They moved swiftly across terrain that was familiar to them now, even in the dark and snow. After they reached the side of the forest they dismounted and led their horses on foot. About 100 metres in Gumilyov tied up his horse and his men did the same. Each man had left his lance, carbine and revolver back at camp, as instructed. Their sabres were at their side and their daggers in hand. Gumilyov led his men deep into the thicket. The night was filled with shadows. He steadied his own breathing, all the while straining his eyes to see.

Then a sound so quiet he was sure he must have heard nothing.

Gumilyov gripped his dagger tightly.

He and his men melted into crouched thickets beneath the aspen trees, silent and still. He waited. How many were approaching? Could they take one alive? Would the enemy cry an alarm to his countrymen?

Then Gumilyov heard a crunch underfoot maybe four or five metres away. He felt his heart race up to his throat. He merged hard against the freezing shadows.

Like a spectre, a German uniform appeared a metre from Gumilyov. He waited. There would be more. The German seemed unsure of himself but after a second another German stepped behind the first and together, they moved forward. Gumilyov let them pass and listened for more. Just two? It was too good to be true. He forced himself to be still. He knew his men would not budge until he did. Sure enough, there was a third German making his way into the Russian ambush.

Then in the distance, so far away it didn't seem real, a horse whickered.

The Germans froze.

Like a ghostly horror story, the thickets around the aspen stood up and their icy bulks moved with killer instincts.

Gumilyov caught the soldier closest to him from behind and with a grunt of surprise the German felt the hot blade as it plunged into his throat. He slumped to his knees. In his peripheral vision, Gumilyov saw Rad drive his huge fist through the side of the head of the German who had last appeared. Gumilyov dragged the weapon across the jugular of the one he had captured; the German waved his hands in front momentarily as if attempting to protect himself from a fall then slipped into a tired dead mess on the forest floor.

Stani and Borislav had downed the other German with a frenzy of knife wounds. *The men need to let off tension*, thought Gumilyov. He, himself, felt nothing but a slow icy numbness. The captured German was already being bound tightly by Rad. Gumilyov looked on and wondered why he felt no elation in their success.

After the men had quickly and quietly stripped the dead Germans of their boots, jackets and hip flasks, they made their way, with growing urgency, back to the horses. Rad's prisoner was young. Obviously a conscript and, now, fearing for his life. Rad threw him over his horse as if he were a young buck, then pulled himself up onto the saddle.

Their return to the campsite was rapid.

Gumilyov took the prisoner directly to the makeshift interrogation centre in the damp basement of Łódź's town hall. The fact that they were surrounded by Germans meant that captured prisoners could not be transported east to Warsaw, as per standard interrogation procedure, so they were now questioned in a makeshift Headquarters at Łódź. It wasn't the first time Gumilyov had successfully brought back a German for question and he and his motley crew were starting to get a bit of a reputation for swift and incisive reconnaissance trips that often resulted in live information.

The prisoner remained bound and gagged but his eyes were bulging with terror. He was shoved before the two captains, Kalugin and Vlacic, who were seated alongside an attendant secretary at a typewriter, and a corporal on standby. The chilly basement was drowning in cigarette smoke and as Gumilyov turned to leave, Captain Kalugin told him to stay.

This is a first, Gumilyov thought as he took out the hip flask, taken from one of the dead Germans, and took a shot. Schnapps.

Everyone was watching the young POW.

"You are a prisoner of the Imperial Russian Army. If you answer all our questions you will be treated correctly as a prisoner of war. If not, you will be shot. Do you understand?" Captain Kalugin's voice was hard and empty.

The German looked frantically from one captain to the next and then swung round to the corporal behind him. At last, he saw Gumilyov and his eyes stopped at the hip flask in his hands.

The corporal stepped forward and roughly pulled off the gag. The German looked even younger.

"Name. Rank — we can see you are cannon-fodder," said Captain Kalugin. Then he repeated for effect, "*Kanonenfutter!*"

The corporal chortled. The room waited. Captain Vlacic stood up abruptly and his steel chair scraped loudly on the cement floor, "Take this prisoner out and shoot him!"

The corporal, with a cigarette still in the corner of his mouth, moved towards the German.

Fearing the worst, the prisoner pleaded, "*Nein! Ich verstehen nicht!*"

The corporal did not hesitate and began manhandling him away from the captains.

"*Bitte!*" pleaded the prisoner and he began to cry.

They had all seen this before, men crying in the interrogation room, in battle, in their sleep, in their quiet moments of letter writing.

"We speak German," said Captain Vlacic. "And French — Oh and Russian." He smirked but swapped to German, "So, we understand you, you cowardly piece of shit."

The German was shivering. His pale skin, brown eyes and thatch of blonde hair, made him look like a child.

"My mother is French," he cried out desperately.

The Russians watched on impassively.

The prisoner's shoulders slumped and he hung his head, "Walter Schafer."

The clack of the typewriter followed.

"Rank," barked Captain Kalugin in German. "Regiment or Battalion?"

Walter continued quietly, "21st Landwehr Infantry Brigade." He was not thinking about the Russian men in front of him or the death that awaited him, but rather he thought about his mother and Heike, his sweetheart, in the kitchen back home in Saarbruken and the way they would busy about in the morning light.

"What were you and those other foot-shufflers doing out there in the forest?" Captain Vlacic was going through the motions because he pretty much knew what he would receive.

"Reconnaissance," Walter answered miserably

What does it matter now, he thought, *I will be dead before morning*. If he closed his eyes, he could just about smell the fragrance of the sablés biscuits his mother and Heike would bake and the way the taste of buttery shortbread melted in his mouth.

"What day will your brigade make its incursion into Łódź?"

Walter's brown eyes opened and he looked directly at Kalugin, "They are not, there is no activity ... No orders."

The Russian captains looked at each other.

"Your army is planning to invade Łódź. We know it is commencing from the east of Łódź. This is where your brigade is positioned." There was no disputing Captain Vlacic's information but the German looked from captain to captain in a state of increasing bewilderment.

"No. There is no assault planned that I ... that we, that I know."

Captain Vlacic gave a nod to the corporal who immediately moved forward and took the prisoner by his bound ties and began to shove him towards the steps leading out of the basement. The prisoner struggled and twisted around frantically but the only Russian watching was Gumilyov.

To him, the German cried, "Please, my mother is French! My platoon knows nothing about an assault on Łódź!"

The corporal began hauling him up the wooden steps but still, Walter shouted, "There have been counter strikes from the Russians in the south — it's too dangerous yet for ..."

The room went quiet except for the struggling prisoner.

"Bring him back," Captain Kalugin ordered sharply and the corporal pushed the German back to the captains.

There was a renewed spark in the room.

"This is your last chance," Kalugin's eyes were fierce.

"I just don't ... it's just I'm not sure ..." The room seemed to fizz and spark, "There are skirmishes, continual skirmishes. The Russians are attacking us from the south. Outside of Łódź. Since Tuesday ... or Wednesday — for the last two days ..."

Walter looked frantically at the typist who had paused with the other men to watch.

"Most of the platoons have been moved down south to head off the Russians who have just arrived — there's only a few of us positioned up here in the north ..."

The clacking of the typewriter filled the basement and every Russian in that room was thinking that hope had arrived.

"Trooper!"

Gumilyov came out of his own euphoric thoughts of salvation.

"Take this prisoner to the internment quarters."

Gumilyov gathered up the boy.

"Well done," added Captain Kalugin and gave Gumilyov a curt nod.

When Gumilyov stepped out of the town hall basement the pale feckless sun was just beginning to light the square. It gave off no warmth. The German slumped against the wall as Gumilyov lit a cigarette.

"Will I be shot?" Walter asked quietly in French as he watched the Russian with his wide Slavic features and quiet eyes.

"No," Gumilyov smoked his cigarette and thought of his two year old son back in Bezhetsk, not far from St Petersburg. *I might be home soon*, he thought, and he would visit his mother who looked after Lev. Gumilyov liked the idea of getting back to St Petersburg and catching up with everyone, maybe even seeing Anna.

He finished his cigarette and without really knowing why, he said to his prisoner, "I lived in France."

The German looked at him confused.

"Sorbonne." Gumilyov offered, "I was a student there, with many other Russians, learning French." He laughed without any trace of humour and stamped his feet for circulation.

"You studied at the Sorbonne?" Walter was incredulous. How could this peasant have been to his mother's beloved homeland for the purposes of academic study? Even Walter had not had the opportunity to study there or anywhere. He had completed primary school as most Germans, but it was only the wealthy who could send their sons to secondary. And since his father had died that was not an option and so Walter worked on their landowner's small farm until he had been recruited.

Gumilyov didn't bother to answer but moved across the square, slippery with ice, with Walter in tow. The sky was heavy with grey mist and snow clouds but for the first time since the entire Russian 2nd had been surrounded here at Łódź, not by one but two German armies — Gumilyov felt light! Help was on its way. *Russians will not leave Russians behind,* or so he would like to think. It might be a different thing before the war, especially back in St Petersburg. Then, the division between the rich and poor had been growing ever wider; indeed, the only way the workers could be heard was to strike. Now Russia was at war, and defending the Motherland was the beginning and the end of what mattered.

Just as Gumilyov and Walter got to the POW camp, set up temporarily in one of Łódź's old single-story cotton factories, Gumilyov looked up at the low glittering sky and recited, almost to himself:

I'm in the days' embracing limits,

Where even skies are ever grey.
Look through the ages,
Live in minutes,
And wait for Holy Saturday.

Walter thought of Heike at Mass and the murmur of the rosary before the service commenced. He remembered the warmth as he knelt close by her.

"*And wait for Holy Saturday,*" Walter repeated and for a moment he had forgotten he was a prisoner and then he added his realisation "... Resurrection ..."

Gumilyov looked at him and nodded.

"In another life, I was a poet," said the Russian.

5

Three days before, the Russian 5th had been ordered to abandon their preparations for an offensive at Silesia and leg it north to Łódź. Lance Corporal Aysen Manchari was a Yakut, an Indigenous Siberian, and had been conscripted to the 1st Siberian Rifle Division that was attached to the Russian 5th.

As the second son, Aysen had been working for his father, moving furs from their trading post in the capital, Yakutsk, to Tynda, the most important railway junction, then all the way down to Vladivostok.

He had met Sayaana in the city of Ussuriysk. Her mother was Yakut but her father was an ethnic Russian, originally from Vladivostok. Probably because Sayaana's father wasn't Yakut meant they had bypassed the complicated and time-consuming marriage arrangements that would normally have entailed gifts of animals and furs. Aysen's father had provided a significant dowry, so Sayaana and her parents were more than happy with their new son-in-law who was a significant cog in the machine of Manchari Fur Traders. One of the biggest, if not the biggest, fur traders in Yakutia.

Although he and Sayaana were living with her parents in their two-bedroom apartment, Aysen was still moving up and down Siberia collecting pelts from his father's extensive network of hunters, meeting the transport that would take their furs all over Russia and handling the ever-increasing paperwork for the multitude of certificates needed to run their family business.

In the few short months of their marriage, Sayaana had travelled with him to see his beloved Lena Basin — the meadowlands and verdant grass plains that his family had for centuries inhabited. She had met his parents and younger sisters but his oldest brother had been working up in the Arctic rim during the summer months, horse rustling, so she had yet to meet him.

Sayaana's wide-open face, high cheekbones and dark slanting eyes made her a spirit goddess in Aysen's mind. She would whisper and chuckle and tease him in bed, her lovely brown naked body made his heart race and his cock harden. Aysen could recall every aspect of her compact legs, tight buttock and small breasts. But for the most part, he kept his thoughts away from the warm frenzy of their lovemaking when he was unable to be with Sayaana. It was just too debilitating, otherwise.

He and two cousins, Kaskil and Tuyaara, who had taken over a week to get down from Yakutsk, had reported at the Ussuriysk barracks. All three of them had been conscripted. When Germany declared war on Russia, the Yakuts knew what history had already taught them — that their land, horses and fur trade would be coveted — so fight they must. The Yakut cousins were excited nonetheless for the places they would see and things they would do.

When Aysen, Kaskil and Tuyaara completed their four-week rudimentary training at Ussuriysk barracks the cousins were invited to doss down in the living room of Sayaana's parent's place before they moved out with the Siberian Rifle Division. Everyone knew that no one was a better shot than a Yakut, and no one tired of saying with great whoops of laughter, "May the gods help those Germans!"

Kaskil and Tuyaara had brought down from the north rifles and knives for the three of them and in addition, Aysen's father had sent long wide pelts of fur to line their boots and coats. A winter in Yakutia could plummet to minus 70 °C so they would easily cope with whatever Germany threw at them. Having said that they packed the fur lining anyway. No one spoke about fear.

The night before they left Aysen and Sayaana's lovemaking was fierce.

The three cousins had heard there were a few other Yakuts scattered throughout the division and when they were moving west on trains to Moscow and then to Warsaw, they sought each other out in the way Turkic people do. From Warsaw, the Russian 5th moved southwest to the border of Polish Russia and Germany.

Here, they had waited for a few days, preparing for the offensive on Silesia. Aysen was surprised at how many Russian soldiers, especially those from the cities, criticized the Russian military leadership and its inability to make a decision that wouldn't leave millions of them dead. Then the orders came through to abandon their preparations for an attack on Silesia, consequently, there was considerable frustration. Up until this point, there had been much talk of teaching the greedy Germans a lesson or two about keeping their hands off Russia. But needs must, and there was a Russian army surrounded by the enemy up in Łódź and the Russian 5th was to be their rescue.

Aysen noticed that on the long march from Silesia to Łódź, many of the Russian soldiers smoked too much and drank too little. They talked and argued and laughed and complained along the way. They made so much noise. When they were all permitted to rest, the other Russians would lay on the early winter floor and try, without success, to sleep. The Yakuts walked in quiet, their minds patient, their bodies closed. The natural forces of the mountains and the rocks and the lakes and the trees spoke to them as they passed by and when they came to rest, they would crouch against the ichchi spirits in the rocks and be restored.

The Yakut cousins tucked their fur lining into their boots and coats, which had come all the way from their land on the Arctic Sea. They did this not because they felt the cold in the same way as the other men but because the spirit of the animal still lingered in the fur and so it entered their skin and kept their hearts still.

The Yakuts tried not to think about what would happen if one of them was killed in battle and a horse, steer or reindeer was not sacrificed to help them travel to the land of the dead, which was skyward and filled with the promise of life eternal. On the other hand, their rifle skills were legendary. The truth was they had centuries of refining the muscle memory of hand-eye coordination. Yakuts could distinguish a target in a whiteout, but more importantly, they understood shamanic spirits in certain animals and ichchi spirits in rocks and trees, so they could navigate through unknown terrain as if it was their own. The ethnic Russians remained respectful but wary of the Yakuts.

It took two days and two nights of walking to reach the outlying countryside of Łódź. By this stage, their officers had confirmed rumours that they were to fight the German 8th and 9th Armies in an attempt to save the Russian 2nd, which was encircled at Łódź. A tired *HURRAH!* was sent up by most and they were promised an eight-hour rest. The ground was too frozen for dugouts, so most men huddled together in stink and filth, trying not to freeze to death before the abundant German artillery would kill them the next day.

Instead of finding a place to sleep alongside the rest of their platoon, Aysen, Kaskil and Tuyaara each tore a small strip from their fur lining and discretely placed their sacred offerings beneath an al lukh mas, the largest tree close by. Aysen sang softly:

With the great mountains,
With the great rocks,
With the great trees,
All of you see me.

The Yakuts then joined their platoon and slept.

Within hours, German reconnaissance reported back to command that the Russian 5th had suddenly got them in a pocket, the initial reaction was disbelief. There was no rail or direct roads from the southern border of Germany to the outskirts of Łódź. How could several thousand men have moved in two days? The German heavy artillery was immediately turned away from the trapped Russian 2nd inside Łódź to face the newly arrived Russian 5th camped in the forested outskirts to the southeast.

So it was only four hours after the Russians had walked 117 kilometres in 48 hours that they awoke to the earth seizing and writhing beneath them in an ear-shattering German artillery bombardment. The deep double boom of canons, the howling of mortars, the explosion of shells and the roar of fire ripped open their world.

Aysen knew immediately that if they laid there any longer, the only sleep he and his comrades would get would be the sleep of the dead. All around him, men hugged the ground waiting for the barrage to stop but it went on and on and on.

Aysen could not see more than a few steps ahead of him; the black stench of smoke and thick soupy mist added to the men's terror. Aysen's hearing was smashed. Everything around him rang or vibrated in muffled sounds. It was as if he was deep underwater and above him the world no longer made sense. Men sobbed, smoke hissed and the thin icy daylight darkened. Time lost all meaning as the horror became more and more indescribable.

But the bombardment was not sufficiently spearheaded because the Germans were unsure where the Russians were, exactly.

Finally, it ceased and Lieutenant Bobrinsky roared like an ox to *GET THE HELL UP!* Aysen hauled himself out of the runnel. The acrid air stung his vision as he shuffled low towards the bridge. He crouched amongst the aspen at the edge of the rugged forest, and moved his Mosin Nagant into position, loading the clip of five rounds and checking the steel sights. He still couldn't hear but he could see the others around him readying their aim.

The Germans were already moving across the bridge towards them, about two kilometres away. In the distance, Aysen could see the outskirts of Łódź.

"HOLD FIRE!" screamed Bobrinsky.

The Germans poured closer and closer and when they were about 500 metres from Aysen, his platoon was ordered to fire.

The riflemen unleashed their thunderous onslaught forcing the enemy to run the bridge, like a swarm of ants, stumbling over their fallen comrades.

Meanwhile, Aysen's platoon was taking fire from the German gunners on the other side of the river. The sharp *tzing tzing* of bullets sprayed above and beside Aysen. Lying a metre to his left was a dead Siberian, a bullet clean to the head. In amongst the sound of weapons discharging Aysen could hear a screaming rifleman behind him, dragging his mutilated torso back down into the forest where the medics were running.

In between assaults Aysen and the others reloaded their rifles. With only a limited supply of ammunition, distributed before the battle, they knew every bullet had to count.

The bridge was now littered with bodies of the German dead and dying. Aysen then saw another wave of Germans charging across which was met with a fresh rain of bullets. German machine guns responded by tearing up the trees and ground all around Aysen's platoon.

Two Russian medics ran up behind Aysen and began hauling a wounded rifleman onto a stretcher, his shoulder and arm a gape of blood and shattered bone. Then one of the medics raised up on tiptoe, flung his arms out in cruciform and with a startled look spasmed beneath a volley of German bullets, paused, tipped back onto the stretcher with the wounded soldier, and the three of them rolled and skidded down the small rise into the gully below.

Aysen's rifle burned with heat as he fired again and again. He could see the bridge was now heaving with corpses.

"THE RIVER!" yelled Bobrinsky.

Aysen took aim.

The Germans were rushing neck-deep into the water. By the time they reached the middle of the river, the Russians opened fire. Russian riflemen and gunners were relentless until the river swirled a pearlescent greyish pink. Despite this, although it was impossible to fathom how, some Germans began scrambling up the embankment towards Aysen's platoon.

More and more of the enemy arrived. As if by sheer force of numbers they had become a wall of Germans, tottering ever closer.

Aysen could see their faces.

Many of the Germans walked in formation without firing. Aysen began to shoot at the officers and bigger soldiers. The ones in front dropped and some of the ones behind turned and tried to flee. But the bulk of the incoming forced most of them to turn around and push on towards the Russians.

Aysen watched their pale faces march ever closer.

He aimed and fired, aimed and fired, aimed and fired, aimed and fired, aimed and fired.

Reloaded.

Aysen lay firing on a small rise at the end of the forest. The bridge with its carnage was to his left and the river swirling in blood directly ahead of him. He was in his body and yet he knew he had left it. His shooting was exact, and he did not falter. He was killing. Not wounding or defending or drawing fire, but accurately and effectively killing. He stopped thinking. He lay, shifting slightly this way and that, watching the enemy move into his sights. The mist and smoke in the immediate drop of the forest in front of him made the whole scene otherworldly.

He was there but he wasn't.

He considered how the enemy no longer seemed threatening. Their feldgrau tunic made them the same. Some still wore the pickelhaube helmet, offering their heads little protection, while others had long since lost it. Somewhere in Aysen's mind, a long way from the machine he had become he thought faintly: *Someone's husband. Someone's brother. Someone's son.* But none of it seemed real. There was too much sound. Too many bodies. Somewhere he knew there was the juggernaut of weapons firing, men yelling for help or worse ... just begging.

He forgot why he was there. Why he was shooting. How he got to this strange world made no sense. The madness didn't even look real. Somehow Aysen knew, in the back of his brain, that soon it would end and the dead men lying in front of him, those he and his platoon had killed, would stand up and walk back across the river and the Russians would also return home.

Aysen had forgotten why the Germans kept coming.

Still, he kept aiming, firing, killing.

Aiming, firing, killing. Aiming, firing. Aiming.

Slowly at first, it seemed as if there were less and less of them hauling themselves out of the river and heading to die a few hundred metres from Aysen, but then strangely, as if the yawning maw of time was satiated, the Germans just stopped coming. From where Aysen lay he could see Mauser rifles with bayonets attached and a raised arm with a Luger pistol still gripped in hand.

All this, Aysen thought to himself, *all this ... for what?*

"HOLD FIRE!" screeched Bobrinsky.

Aysen pushed his back up against the aspen and looked away from the carnage. Beyond the forest, he could see the white sky. A light snow had been falling, but up until this moment, he hadn't noticed.

Aysen moved his spirit into the quiet of the snowfall and let it slow his breathing and touch his face. He wondered if he would ever find all of himself again and be put back together, whole. He thought about the Lena River in Yakutia, a thick creamy expanse of snow where in summer the river ran. Some days not even the wind swept the soundless earth of the Yakut. Pale blue skies above, stippled in gold. The alder, birch and willow would begin to shake the bridal mantle of winter as it turned to spring. Nestled about would be the call of plover, sandpiper, geese and sniper.

The snow drifted onto his lips and nose and cheekbones.

He mouthed the words but there was no sound:
And you, Day
And you, Night
All of you see me
One with the world.

Aysen looked about him and saw Kaskil and Tuyaara. They, too, were facing the snow-covered forest.

Later, after they were told to fall back, the red-faced Bobrinsky moved amongst the platoon and spoke quietly to this one, patted the shoulder of another and pointed to the canteen miming it was time to drink. The men watched him. He was an ethnic Russian from Ussuriysk and even spoke a little Turkic. He was trusted by the men.

After a while, he came over to his lance corporal.

"Move the men back to camp. Get them fed." Bobrinsky looked haggard.

Aysen could see other divisions moving in and he knew that their platoon would be relieved.

"The pork-eaters are fucked," added Bobrinsky, although Aysen wasn't sure the lieutenant believed his own words.

Aysen collected his platoon, which was now down to 20, and moved them back out to the company's bivouac set up earlier that day. He then selected two of his men and made their way several kilometres through the forest to the field kitchen. Parcels of black bread, cold cooked sausage, pickled beets and vodka were handed over, and by the time they returned to their platoon some of the men were sleeping, despite the ongoing crack and fire of battle that could still be heard some distance from the Front.

Aysen didn't mind the meat, it was usually reserved for special occasions back home, but he missed real food.

His cousin must have been thinking the same, "I'd give your right arm Aysen for a cup of kumys," laughed Tuyaara as he threw back his ration of vodka.

"What are you chinks wanting?" asked one of the other men in the platoon.

"Fermented mare's milk," Tuyaara shot back and Aysen's mouth watered.

"Fuck that," was the light-hearted reply.

The platoon ate their food slowly. Their minds trying to erase memory. Their stomachs were accustomed to hunger.

The snow was falling more heavily and the noise of the battle had subsided. Bobrinsky appeared and told the men to head back to camp which they did, many of them surprised by the sting of blisters they had long forgotten even though it was only yesterday they had nearly wept with relief to shuck off their boots and end the long march north.

Back at camp Bobrinsky spoke quietly to the platoon and told them that tomorrow they would be moving northwards and then entering Łódź to help evacuate the Russian 2nd trapped in the city if all went to plan. The men didn't take much of that to heart because the so-called plan often changed on an hourly basis, which was never the lieutenant's fault. The cold was becoming heavier and the men moved into the tents that had been set up. Some slept or stared into the darkness. Others wrote letters because they had been told there would be a postal dispatch the next morning.

Aysen took some brown paper from his pack and sharpened his pencil with his knife:

Sweetheart Sayaana —

Are you well?

Are the days getting shorter out there in Ussuriysk?

Your parents have spoilt you with those electric lights in their apartment. Are you still carrying books back from the library to read at night? I hope you tell me what you have been reading.

Kaskil and Tuyaara are here with me. It is getting colder, but we are doing fine. Today we had meat for our dinner! I know you want to tease me and ask if it was fresh elk or bear — which I love — or even squirrel which I have been known to eat. But no, it wasn't. We were talking about how good it would be to have some cheese or milk from home. But we are fine.

I hope you give my love to your parents and tell them to keep an eye on you so you don't get yourself into mischief!

Love Aysen

I just wanted to add … look up at the night sky because I will be looking up at that same moment. I am thinking of you, Sayaana, looking at that same sky, your face turned up and your eyes smiling. I am looking too, Sayaana.

My love.

The men's letters were collected in the morning. There was no mail for Aysen but it did not worry him. He would rather not think about her as they started moving northward with Łódź in their sights.

6

While being holed up in Łódź, Gumilyov had not received any letters. The last was from his mother, who lived in a small village 30 kilometres northeast of St Petersburg where she cared for his son. She sent tit-bits about the child's progress: *He is sleeping well now ... he loves to eat jam with a spoon right out of the bowl ... he can count his numbers up to six ... he wants the big shaggy house cat to sleep under the bedcovers with him each night ...*

Gumilyov found these morsels deeply consoling even though he had little contact with Lev in the past, having been away in Africa the year before the war began. It was his mother who had suggested to him that he ask his wife to bring her grandson to stay, especially because Gumilyov would be away with the Hussars. So, Lev was brought along — a bundle of arms, legs and trembling lower lip. It was best this way. Now both Gumilyov and his estranged wife, Anna, could get on with their lives and see Lev grow up well in the arms of Gumilyov's mother.

Instead of writing to his mother and saying nothing, which was what he had been saying to her for most of his life, Gumilyov decided to write to Mandelstam, although even that decision was made with a certain degree of reluctance. He had met Mandelstam at the Sorbonne years ago and he was immediately drawn to his mix of vulnerability and charm. Indeed, Mandelstam's honesty had the capacity to disarm the well-dressed students around them who all spoke in accents a la mode. Mandelstam was from Warsaw but his family had moved to St Petersburg where he eventually converted to Methodism from Judaism, in order to enroll at the university there.

If there was hesitancy in writing to Mandelstam, and there was, it was only because Gumilyov knew he could not lie to his friend, not here, not ever. No one could.

It was not yet dawn but there would be no more sleep. He got up from his stretcher and moved across to a bench close to the embers of a fire. In the last week or so, his squadron had moved into a small local schoolhouse in Łódź.

He lit a cigarette, tore a page from his book of writing paper and drew ink into his pen:

How is my dear friend, Osip Emilyevich Mandelstam? I am missing you and all our friends in St Petersburg. What have you been up to lately?

Here, the days are getting shorter and the winter beckons. There is not much sitting around but when we do, I try to write or at least read a little. Some of the lads have brought a book or two with them and we swap our stash about a bit.

He thought of the collection of Turgenev stories he had acquired because the young Hussar who lent it to him never returned from an assault.

How are our friends at the Dog?
Do you see much of Anna Akhmatova? Are you still in love with my wife or have you strengthened your resolve and turned your back on her!

Gumilyov's relationship with his wife staggered and faltered. It has been so long since he had any feeling for her. So strange to think that there had been a time, twice in fact, when he had attempted suicide all because she refused to marry him. He realised long ago he did not love her or want her, although he could never put his finger on why.

Listen my friend — take some advice — there is an emptiness in Akhmatova, she will do you no good! You would be better off returning to your Georgian princess, Salomea Andronikova! Hah! What a beauty!

Mandelstam's heart was broken into a thousand pieces when he had found out, what they all had known, Salomea was already sleeping with the poet Sergey Rafalovich while trying to end her affair with Mandelstam. But Rafalovich was an inferior poet to Mandelstam, everyone knew it, including Rafalovich.

I was thinking of you and our days strolling the Seine, talking philosophy, poetry, love, language and Russia — always Russia. We were two love-sick boys for the motherland.
I expect you to be writing great poetry for all of us.
I must say farewell now.

Nikolay Stepanovich Gumilyov

Courage,
Brothers, as the cleft sea falls back from our plow.
Even as we freeze in Lethe, we'll remember
The ten heavens the earth cost us.

He knew Mandelstam would smile when he saw lines from his own poem scribbled here in the post-script. Its uncanny prediction, written a few years before the war, had come true. Well at least, that was what Gumilyov believed. He sent off his letter with a cadet as the men were stirring in the sharp frost of dawn.

Final preparations were underway for the strategic withdrawal from Łódź. Over the last few days and nights, they had been hearing the assaults and counter-assaults between the Russian 5th and the Germans on the outskirts of the city. Meanwhile, the Russian 2nd trapped inside Łódź had been instructed to prepare to leave and not engage in any skirmishes, as their ammunition was at an all-time low. Indeed, the General had sent word to all divisions that infantry was to empty weapons of ammunition and to fix bayonets. The Hussars preferred lances and sabres anyway, but even their carbines and revolvers had been collected by offices until they reached the defensible lines of Warsaw.

Needless to say, the men were feeling edgy.

In the last 24 hours, most of the Russian 2nd had moved up to the northern end of Łódź in preparation for the withdrawal. Gumilyov, and those around him, knew that they would be facing a bloody melee.

It was not only the Russian 2nd that was moving out, with its various divisions made up of over 3,000 men but carts, trucks, pack horses, equipment, catering corps and other support units. The withdrawal also involved evacuating civilians and POWs. They had been informed that some of the platoons from the Russian 5th had been ordered to enter the city and assist with the evacuation of civilians and POWs.

Gumilyov thought of the German prisoner he had brought in recently and how he had given the captains vital information. Gumilyov wondered how this day would go and if he would become a POW of the Germans before nightfall. Perhaps he would be dead — better that than wounded.

Whatever the outcome, Gumilyov took strength in the fact that his squadron would be moving rapidly out in formation, flanking the right of the infantry column. In battle, the charge of the Hussars struck terror in the enemy.

Scouts had estimated that from the northern exit of Łódź to the forest it was approximately three kilometres; after that, apart from a few predicted scuffles and sniper attacks, it was a mere two day march east to Warsaw. He, like every other man in the Russian

2nd, had mulled over this scant information again and again. *The defence of Holy Russia*, Gumilyov thought bitterly, *is becoming more and more about self-preservation.*

Indeed, the whole effort to defend Polish Russia against the Germans had been a debacle and when Gumilyov thought of the Łódź civilians with their half-hearted effort to welcome the Russian 2nd — closed shops and inns, empty streets with most of the inhabitants in hiding — he wondered why the Generals had bothered. Even when the evacuation was announced, rumours began spreading that many of the citizens would take their chances with the Germans. Some of the Russian soldiers had been openly scornful of the Łódź people, especially the Jews who were said to own the factories. Their loyalty was not to Mother Russia. Or so most of Russia believed. No wonder they would not leave.

Gumilyov couldn't help wondering at the irony of these assumptions, considering the fact that any Jew, take his dear friend Mandelstam for one, could recount cruelties towards them and theirs which had been a national sport for Russians over the centuries. But for the most part, Gumilyov kept his own counsel.

Not long after, Gumilyov was on his white, eight year old Orlov gelding with sabre in hand. In a few short minutes, they would be leaving the city of Łódź.

The cadets moved on foot, between the Hussars, attending to the bridle of this one and readjusting the stirrups of another, according to the last minute orders from the Hussars. His own horse stamped and snorted, impatient to be off and charging. The noise behind Gumilyov's squadron was growing and the bite of the snowy morning made him long to be thundering across the countryside.

The exact location of the enemy lurking in the mist beyond Łódź was, at this point, still unknown. They had been given vague assurances that German heavy artillery had been relocated to the southeast of Łódź and not up here in the north.

The smell of dung and piss and fear hung in the frost.

Still, they waited.

Then one of the officers, in his rich baritone voice, began singing the Imperial Anthem which was taken up by what seemed to be the entire Russian 2nd standing behind:

God save the Tsar
Mighty and powerful
Let him reign for our glory
For the confusion of our enemies
The orthodox Tsar
God save the Tsar.

The order was then given for the Russian 2nd to commence their strategic withdrawal and run the bloody gauntlet of German artillery fire across the three kilometre passage between Łódź and the forest. Russian soldiers and riders kissed the holy medals they wore or the small icons they carried.

For the Hussars theirs was a special devotion to Saint Martin of Tura and alongside his brothers, Gumilyov found himself making the sign of the cross as they began to move out.

"HOLY RUSSIA WILL NEVER BE DEFEATED!"

"GOD SAVE THE TSAR!"

"FOR THE GLORY OF MOTHER RUSSIA!"

And over a thousand voices shouted up to the grey sealed heaven above: "HURRAH!"

7

Aysen felt the sound of the Russian Hussars long before he heard them.

The Siberian riflemen had been positioned some several kilometres further north and it had to be admitted that the din of the Russian 2nd evacuating was more like a stampede than a strategic plan.

Bobrinsky had ordered his platoon to enter Łódź and then move out the remaining POWs and citizens.

Heads down, rifles ready, they jogged across the open countryside leading down to the city. As the mist swirled around them and the snow churned underfoot, Aysen anticipated the enemy mid-charge with bayonets sharpened.

Any moment he expected to hear the *tat tat tat* of a German gunner start up or the *tzing tzing tzing* of bullets whizzing past.

They ran on.

The rattle of packs and weapons chinked and clanked as his platoon ran harder. Aysen kept low and watched the ground beneath him undulate and flatten. He emptied his mind of everything so that it was just him racing across a vast steppe. In his mind's eye, he followed the arctic eagle, with its black underbelly and white tail, soaring overhead — while all the time urging him on faster and faster and faster.

Then the shapes of factories and buildings emerged above the mist about 500 metres away.

Aysen's chest was pounding and his breathing was ragged. He had never run so hard and so desperately in all his life.

Bobrinsky was up ahead somewhere, Aysen could hear his muffled boom urging his men onwards. And then there was stone underfoot, wooden sheds alongside him, a street signpost and he knew he had made it!

Bobrinsky was already dividing the platoon into three groups while the riflemen were hitting each other on the back making quips about their newfound métier as huskies, desperately trying to catch their breath.

Aysen moved over to Lachkov, his sergeant, who was directing them to an old cotton factory, where the POWs were being held. They were to round them up and return across the exposed countryside that they had just crossed and escort them to Warsaw. They had to hurry. The only reason his platoon crossed unseen was a combination of the weather and the fact that the Germans were busy fighting the Russian 5th southeast of Łódź.

Aysen hated the thought of mustering and guarding POWs. He had seen how some of the officers allowed their men to shoot German POWs. This was because Russian officers, and many of the soldiers of the 2nd, had recounted tales of the Germans killing not just the wounded Russian POWs taken at Tannenberg but the fit and walking. Meanwhile, many of the Russian soldiers complained to the sergeants, and even some of the officers, that keeping alive German POWs while killing German soldiers, who were the aggressors and invaders of Mother Russia, was just bullshit.

Bobrinsky wouldn't take any of that from his men, but Aysen was not so sure about Lachkov. He was a mean bastard.

They moved quickly towards the cotton factory. Aysen was surprised how many of the civilians had no intention of evacuating as they went about their business and even stared defiantly at the Russian soldiers trying to evacuate them.

Aysen realised maybe he had landed the better task.

The streets were rutted with snow and muddy slush where the soldiers and carts of the Russian 2nd have pushed through en masse earlier.

Eventually, they arrived at the POW camp located inside the disused cotton factory, with much of its machinery dismantled and rebooted into the multiple needs of other factories throughout town. There were two guards waiting anxiously inside the makeshift prison. No doubt they were concerned they may have been left behind and were wondering when to make their run.

Lachkov was brief in his instructions, "MOVE THESE PRICKS OUT!"

Aysen realised the sergeant was worried.

The Russian 5th could only draw fire from the German 8th and 9th for so long. As soon as the Germans realised the Russian 2nd had withdrawn from Łódź they would be charging the city. It would be a strategic capture in Polish Russia with its industry and close access to Warsaw.

Lachkov knew that they too could be caught and by the look of the motley crew before them, half-starved, half-frozen POWs, there would be retaliation on the minds of the incoming Germans.

The sergeant was yelling at the guards and the platoon as if his life depended on it. The Russians started shouting at the POWs who were scrambling to their feet and helping those too weak to get up. In the distance, Aysen heard a huge explosion to the south and knew it was the Germans softening up the south end of the city before they entered.

Amongst the POWs was Walter Schafer. He had only been a prisoner for two nights and, more importantly, he had retained his greatcoat.

Many of the prisoners' possessions, except for the uniforms they wore, had been immediately stripped by the guards. The prisoners watched glumly as a series of interactions had taken place between the various Russian guards and soldiers conducting what appeared to be a complex level of barter and exchange over the items stolen from every POW.

For the two hungry days Walter had been held here, he had kept his head down. He had no interest in escape because he had no desire to return to his regiment or the army itself. Escape was what the other 20 or so prisoners had talked about in low grunts or when the Russians were occupied with their business.

Why bother, thought Walter, *we will be dead soon.* Besides, even if he did escape and find his way back to the army he would be interrogated and most probably punished, if not shot, for the information he had given the Russians.

Last night he had decided he must erase the thoughts of his mother and his sweetheart from his mind. Soon he would be lost to them forever. He closed his heart to the memories of his mother chatting and Heike baking ... the aroma of cinnamon, cardamom and anise, luring him in from the farm.

Walter's stomach gnawed away at itself.

All the while, Walter kept pace with the other POWs as they were trundled along between several Russian soldiers to the edge of the city. Their original guards had simply vanished as soon as they emerged from the factory in which they had been held. Now a bunch of thuggish-looking Russians with rifles and knives seemed to be intent on pushing them out beyond the confines of the city. These captors were different from the other Russians he had so far encountered. They were shorter men with Asiatic features, not at all like the Slavs of European Russia. Furthermore, they spoke little but when they did their rhythms of speech, inflections and possibly even the words they spoke were different from the Russian that he had heard.

When the city seemed to end and the countryside, covered in a sea of snow, reached out before them, the POWs were ordered to stop. Up until this point, the POWs had marched, or rather, shambled in formation with three abreast and several lines deep.

The Russian sergeant began yelling more orders, but there was either confusion from his soldiers or some level of hesitation. Swiftly the sergeant raised the back of his rifle and brought it down with a crack on the nose of the Russian closest to him, who staggered momentarily, then righted himself. Immediately, the other soldiers pushed through the German formation and began shoving the POWs into a shambolic circle around the Russians.

Of course, thought Walter, *we're to be a human shield.*

There was some sort of bleak justice in the knowledge that he was probably about to be shot by the Germans themselves as they ventured across the open terrain in front of them, leaving the protection of the city behind.

Ahead, Walter could just discern the straggly tail ends of carts and civilians staggering through the snow. The mist was lifting above them. Easy targets. He heard artillery explosions somewhere behind them in the city, but it was still quite a distance away.

A prisoner behind Walter was reciting the Lord's Prayer:

"Valter under im Himmel,

geheiligt werde dein Name."

"HEADS DOWN! SHUT THE FUCK UP! MOVE IT!" yelled the sergeant bringing up the rear.

The POWs lumbered through the snow.

"Dein Reich komme."

Tzing tzing tzing. The German prisoners and Russian soldiers fell as one into the soft snow.

"STAY DOWN! STAY DOWN!"

More whizzing of bullets. The prisoner in front of Walter had fallen awkwardly across him and was not moving. He shoved him hard and his ruined body rolled to the side, his eyes staring at the white sky blanking above.

"Dein Wille geschehe."

"FIRE YOU FUCKING CHINK MORONS!" screamed the demented sergeant.

The soldiers were already positioned, some laying spread-eagled on the snow while others were kneeling, all with rifles aimed and they returned fire with deafening speed.

Walter heard the Russian rifleman kneeling close to him cry out and collapse forward. His face lay in the snow close to Walter. One of his eyes was a sharp gutter of black and red ooze.

While the bullets showered across him, Walter looked at the white of the snow against the brown skin, the scarlet blood and the grey brain-muck of the dead soldier that was soaking into its palette.

Behind him he heard the German continue the Lord's Prayer:

"Wie im Himmel so auf Erden ..."

Someone was crying.

"Unser tägliches Brot gib uns heute —"

"UP! NOW! YOU FUCKING SHIT KICKERS AND MOVE!"

The sergeant hauled the nearest POW onto his feet and aimed his rifle at another prisoner.

In the firing lull Walter joined the others and half crouched, half crawled onwards, their destination seemed to be the forest opening just a few kilometres up ahead.

Snow began falling and he heard:

"Und vergib uns unsere Schuld ..."

Walter breathed heavily and kept as low as possible, knowing the smack of slaughter was about to hit them once again, and all the while the snow feathered about him.

"Wie auch wir vergeben unsern,"

Another prisoner across from Walter had joined in the prayer.

The riflemen jostled the POWs across the snow.

Walter pushed on and up ahead he saw the trees, distinct and heavy with the burden of snow and ice, *not much further* he thought.

The prisoner next to Walter jerked back under a shower of machine-gun fire and Walter found himself buried, once again, face down in the snow. The ice burned his nose and ears, as the sound of gunfire reverberated above him. Walter felt himself squeeze the frozen slush beneath him, then his fingers locked in a vice grip. He laid like the dead and waited. He heard someone cough and then gurgle deeply.

"UP ..." the sergeant's voice scraped across the litter of bodies, the dead and dying and breathing.

Then Walter heard, faintly,

"Und führe uns nicht in Versuchung."

And for some reason, Walter thought he would sob. He wanted to look behind and see the man who somehow believed he was more than just himself, here in this place of so much beauty that God had forgotten, here amongst the wounded whom God had abandoned.

A few of the riflemen attempted to drag their fallen comrades into the forest edge — tantalisingly close.

"Let the dead bury the fucking dead," spat the sergeant.

And at his command, the riflemen dropped the scruffs of their comrades and slouched hurriedly across the next 200 metres to the start of the forest.

All except one.

He continued to drag the dead body of a fallen soldier. There was something in the face, in the whole body of this one man carrying his brother onwards, which made the others look away and pretend it was not happening.

Then they were shoving and sliding onto the shores of the forest edge, its dirt and sludge showing the tracks of cartwheels and feet that have passed through earlier. The soldiers and POWs moved into the thicket of safety and as they did Walter heard the German behind him pray:

"Sondern erlöse uns von dem Bösen"
Some of the Germans answered:
"Amen."

Chapter 2

January — February 1915

The night was still early but already he knew it would be quiet. Boris Pronin anticipated that many of his paying clients, who had families to go to and even churches to attend, would not be visiting the Stray Dog Café tonight. *This is the price one pays on January 6*, thought Pronin, *Christmas Eve!* He looked at the huge mirror, speckled with age hanging above the bar and saw his business partner, Mikhail Kuzmin. His perfectly manicured head of hair bobbing up and down as he straightened the chequered tablecloths in reds and purples and yellows, draped across the small tables. A few customers chatted idly. Kuzmin was supposed to chase up the ordinary mortals who wandered in and charge them three roubles, but he was now busy pouring himself a drink.

Pronin never charged an entry fee to the talent and often waived their bar tab. Of course, Kuzmin regarded himself as one of the great talents of St Petersburg, being queer and a poet and just generally fabulous — or so he thought. *You had to love him*, sighed Pronin. The fact was Kuzmin's indecent liaisons often led to useful outcomes for the Dog. Pronin leaned back and gazed up at the vaulted ceilings which were covered with Sergei Sudeikin's mosaics — a menagerie of birds and vines and light and bodies and flowers and trees. No dogs. Sudeikin and Kuzmin had been lovers, but this ended when Sudeikin's first wife caught them in flagrante delicto. Pronin allowed himself a chuckle. After that, Sudeikin had moved on to another handsome poet, and Kuzmin had moved on as well, supposedly helping Pronin run his enterprise in the basement of the Dashkov mansion: the Stray Dog Café ... cabaret cum art cellar cum night club cum seedy glamour.

Pronin's vie de boheme was the lifeblood of St Petersburg, or so he liked to think. It was here that he was the superlative stage manager, producer and artistic performer, in this glittering moment in time. Pronin worked his alchemy on the artists, musicians, dancers and poets. It was only a few months ago that the Firebird herself had danced here! Pronin would never forget the silence when La Karsavina stepped onto the huge mirror they had taken off the bar wall and placed on the floor, she moved into a crouch, hands splayed on either side of her exquisite face and looked heavenward. Tamara Karsavina, the Prima Ballerina for the Imperial Russian Ballet, had danced here at his establishment. Pronin smiled. The composer of Firebird should have seen it. Igor Stravinsky had distorted traditional techniques of his composition in order to disturb the audience's emotions and moods, so much so, Pavlova had declined the lead role and the rest, as they say, was history.

La Karsavina was magnificent. It was as if she was brushed with a silver salt. The monochrome memory of the evening would be exposed and processed over and over again for many years to come. A wolf hunger had swept through the crowd as her dance became the song of a fantastical bird, and just for a moment, Pronin knew that his cellar was the beginning and the end of the world. Unforgettable.

Even without Nijinsky, La Karsavina was unearthly. No one could have anticipated her magic. The collaborator of Firebird, Sergei Diaghilev, had joined them that night at the Dog and watched. Afterward, he kissed his fingertips to Karsavina and drank on in Pronin's cellar, with top hat askew, telling anyone who'd listen that he, Diaghilev, had broken with Nijinsky, his ex-lover. *The great Nijinsky and Diaghilev are no more*, he had blubbered. By midnight he was asleep behind the bar. Sure enough, Karsavina's danseur noble did not attend her cameo that night.

The dapper-dressed Pronin, with his pink and white striped silk necktie, tailored suit and buffed shoes, felt an icy draught and looked over his shoulder expectantly. Two of the talent descended into his cellar. The vagabond genius, Mayakovsky and the goddess, Anna Akhmatova. Although only a dozen or so were in the bar at the time there was a roar of greetings. Pronin couldn't make up his mind about Mayakovsky as he stepped towards them. Prophet or charlatan? As for Anna, Pronin's heart was aflutter.

"Dear friends!" Pronin cried, extending his arms in welcome.

Both Mayakovsky and Anna, bent low to receive the gift of hospitality from this elfin proprietor. He found them a small table tucked in towards the bar. Pronin gestured and Kuzmin languidly delivered a bottle of vodka to the table with some clean glasses.

"Welcome, welcome my friends, and may I wish you a cheerful Christmas!"

Anna and Mayakovsky joined Pronin for a drink. The two poets seemed to want to be alone but unperturbed and, because he considered himself a worldly man of the theatre and of life, Pronin pushed on.

"You have both been coming to my cellar for a few months — or maybe longer," he smiled and waited.

Neither of his two new guests replied.

Pronin gushed, "Forgive me, but how can I put this?"

Anna pulled off her silk scarf and a fragrance of jasmine wafted towards Pronin.

"Would you do us the honour of a reading? A short poem? Perhaps later ...?"

"We are only here for a minute or two," Mayakovsky's big grin stretched about the room.

Charlatan, thought Pronin.

Then Anna looked up and with a soft doe-eyed wink said, "Of course, B.P."

She used his nickname as if only she and he were on the most intimate terms, and Pronin felt himself morph into hot putty.

"Thank you, Anna," he said as he bent over her hand, kissed it, then moved off.

"Did he actually click his heels?" teased Mayakovsky.

Anna rolled her eyes and drew Pasternak's letter from her beaded purse.

"So, as I said before, it's over with Boris. I love him. I will always love him. And I wish him well. But I can't ..."

She handed the thin two-page letter across to Mayakovsky and sat back in her chair. Around the walls were black masks behind which glowed electric lights. Pronin was particularly fond of this addition to the cellar.

"My Darling, I have found —"

"Please don't, Vlad. Seriously, if you insist on reading his letter out loud, I will leave. I don't need to hear it." She lit a cigarette and lowered her gaze at Mayakovsky.

"What's got you so hot under the collar?" he asked but read on quietly.

The letter had arrived about ten days ago and Anna already knew the sorts of declarations Pasternak would make. A part of her didn't want to open the letter. Why go through it all, again? At least he hadn't threatened to kill himself. She lit her cigarette and thought how she would always love Pasternak for not making the tedious mistake of trying to bind her to him through a sense of guilt. Gumilyov, on the other hand, had attempted suicide a number of times when she fought off his many offers of marriage over the seven years he pursued her.

Marriage to Gumilyov had been a revelation she thought as she blew smoke above Mayakovsky's bent head. As soon as Gumilyov had her, his passion dissipated. She inhaled deeply. His original mind did not extend to great poetry and his philandering confirmed his lack of sincerity. She stubbed out her cigarette.

Theirs had been a battle of wills but she would never surrender the gift Gumilyov had given her: a passport out of parochial Russia into the literary world of St Petersburg.

Anna watched the revellers in the cellar. Loud and frank, they gave voice to their joie de vivre intensified by the fact that they need not fulfill obligations of family and church on Christmas Eve. No strict nativity fasting for these sinners just a bit of caroling and fortune-telling.

How strange, she thought, *the contretemps with Pasternak must have happened at this very place. Surely not this actual table ...*

Mayakovsky looked over the letter directly at her, "Why does he write about last year's flood in Perm? The one that nearly destroyed the city? Oh wait," his face full of mischief, "it's a metaphor for what happened between the two of you ..."

"I know it's a metaphor," Anna replied curtly. "I've actually read his letter, Vlad —"

"So it's his way of saying that you just about ruined him. Listen to this!" And before she could stop him Mayakovsky read aloud: "*... rushing water tore through* *the veins of the city, ripping open the wooden structures of homes and churches and shops, so that those left standing could do nothing but watch as the torrential body of river drowned all they had ever known ..."*

Mayakovsky looked at her closely as he reached for her newly lit cigarette. He took a drag then handed it back. The truth was he loved Pasternak, being poets from Moscow, albeit from very different sides of the tracks, Mayakovsky loved him. Despite the fact that Pasternak's own father had expelled Mayakovsky from The School of Painting, Sculpture and Architecture a few years back. *What can you do?* Mayakovsky had later remarked to his fellow Muscovite poet. But that was just the thing about poetry and art: it brought together the truth in people and this alone defied all barriers.

"I have to say, dear Anna, you have treated my friend, Pasternak, badly." His smile was slow, "What is it with you and the men who fall for you?"

"Oh, Vlad." For a moment he thought the impossible was about to happen and he would see Anna cry, but then she added unconvincingly, "Give me back his letter ..."

She knew Pasternak would have been brooding over their break-up. What he would never come to accept was that she had no drive other than to write. And yet how was it possible that a woman would want to dedicate her life to poetry and her audience? She did not want another husband and child and obligations that would nail her to a sinking ship. She wanted freedom. Was that so much to ask? She wanted freedom in order to become the great poet she knew she could one day become. All this accolade up to now from people in and around St Petersburg, for her last publication, was endearing, but at the end of the day what ignited her will and burned through her veins was the fire to write. To be a writer. To be a poet. To be the voice of Russia.

Mayakovsky turned to the second page and read on. She didn't really mind. She wanted Mayakovsky's careless insouciance when it came to love. She didn't want her own veins to thrum with passion the way they did. She wanted her body to be quiet so she could hear words. Her words. The verse she was composing, every moment, every day. Why did men always want to fill her head and her body with their words, their desires and their world? Besides, a passion that ripped up the wooden structure of one's soul was a waste of energy. She knew. She had learned. Now she had no faith, no belief in the religion of love.

Her pagan heart twitched as she said, "You know in Kiev we still believe in the deities and spirits …"

Mayakovsky looked up at her and responded, "That's a non sequitur."

"Yes, but it's Christmas and I was just thinking …"

"Oh, I know — you are a rusalka washed up in the flood that haunts Pasternak!" His big laugh barked about the room as he imagined Anna as a drenched mermaid.

"God, you're tiresome. Give me the letter, I mean it!"

He handed it back across the table and as she shoved it into her purse she said, "I have to go, I actually feel like getting some fresh air —"

Mayakovsky's response was soft and full of love, "Anna."

He had that way about him where one moment you could be the butt of all his jokes and the next, he was your fierce protector. She felt her eyes prick with tears.

"Anna, he loves you. He will always love you." For a second she thought Mayakovsky was referring to Gumilyov but then he continued on, "I've known Pasternak for a while now and everything is all or nothing for him — you know that. You must have known that when you two first got, well first got into whatever it was you got into —"

"Sex."

"Anna, this is me you're talking to. It was never just sex — not even for you. It will be fine, my little rusalki, it will be fine."

At that moment Pronin caught Mayakovsky's eye.

"Look let's go! We can catch a cab, maybe go to a church service and make fun of the fanatics. And afterward, we can stroll back to your apartment ..."

Anna shook herself and looked around at Pronin.

"Yes. Alright then, but I did promise ..." She raised her eyebrow to Pronin who beamed adoration and devotion across the room to her and began moving amongst his clientele announcing Akhmatova would recite and would they like to purchase one more bottle before she began?

"By the way let me please introduce you to Marina Tsvetaeva, you know, the poet I told you about from Moscow?"

Anna was moving out of her chair and answered distractedly, "I don't mind ..."

"Please Anna, she's very talented. She wants to meet you. She's here in town with Sofia Parnok — she used to work on the —"

"Oh, I know Parnok." Anna leaned down to the ashtray and stubbed out her cigarette, "She wrote on my poetry a while back. She interviewed me."

"Yes. Well. Tsvetaeva wants to meet you," said Mayakovsky distractedly as his eye wandered over to Kuzmin, a notoriously pretty chap with a legendary libido, and no further thought was given to a newly arrived poet from Moscow.

As Anna took a few steps into the centre of the cellar, all eyes were upon her. The crowd burst into cheers and then settled down almost immediately. She was the darling of St Petersburg and her poetry was cutting edge, or so they told one another in snatches beforehand. And so her recitation began.

Sunlight fills my room
With hot dust, lucent, grey.
I wake and I remember:
Today is your saint's day.

It was true, she had remembered Pasternak's saint's day after they had broken up and she knew in the morning sunlight that, if she wanted to, she could call him back and he would come running. She looked out to the crowd and continued.

That's why even the snow
Is warm beyond the window.

But she steeled herself. She thought about how this dead wintery ache inside of her — for Pasternak — would pass and new love would spring.

That's why sleeplessly,
Like a communicant, I slept.

The crowd was on their feet applauding, their faces alight with adulation and joy, and she thought to herself, *Poetry will be my greatest lover.*

2

Forty minutes later they were riding through the hard, cold evening in a horse-drawn cab along the Griboyedov Canal. The slate grey water thwacked and caroused against the canal walls.

"Driver, stop here."

They climbed down and Anna handed over the fee. The driver clicked his tongue and the horse moved off up ahead.

The night wrapped itself around Anna and Mayakovsky. She watched the cab move between the park and the Church on Spilled Blood, all the time growing smaller and unfamiliar. She had walked this route a thousand times but tonight it was sharply focused as if she had readjusted the lens.

She slipped her arm through Mayakovsky as they walked. The Church on Spilled Blood was an explosion of hard lines and curvaceous afterthoughts. Rationalism and sensuality. The stonework a nod to the West, the minarets a nod to the East. It *was* Russia. A monument to suffering and salvation blocking her path, unable to be ignored.

They moved to the right, where a towpath meandered between the church and the park. Groups of families and friends hurried ahead into the warmth of the church and its breath-taking interior that promised beauty to their otherwise drab lives. Rather than feel overwhelmed by the church looming in the darkness beside her, lit up by a thousand lights from within, Anna felt strangely protected by a narrative that existed long before her and would remain long after she had gone.

"Let's go inside Anna — I'm freezing my balls off out here!"

She laughed and walked a little faster. She loved Mayakovsky's irreverence and the way he had never fallen in love with her.

A couple pushed past sharing a cigarette and the lines of a poem she had written years ago came to her:

I meant it all in fun.
Don't leave me,
or I'll die of pain.

She tried to push Pasternak out of her mind but letting Mayakovsky read his letter tonight had brought it all back. She did not want to be alone, not tonight. And if she was honest, not ever. She had seen what abandonment had done to her beautiful mother: poverty, fear and rapid ageing. The year Anna's charming goodlooking father had walked out was the same year her adored sister had died of tuberculosis and it was the same year she had lost her virginity to a university student ten years her senior. She had been 16 and knew that being of aristocratic blood would mean nothing unless she hauled herself out of its destitution.

Mayakovsky was talking about Christmas Eve with all its reliquary and pagan ritual. *What a dear friend*, she thought as he strode along beside her and she realised he was the perfect antidote to that unbridled passion she had allowed to surface for Boris Pasternak, who never seemed to need the glittering literary milieu in the way she did.

At the entrance of the church, they pushed open the huge double doors and a riot of chanting and colour and incense and chatter drew them inside. It was a medieval fairy-tale, with its Old and New Testament mosaics colliding in a vertigo of cerulean, cobalt, indigo, sapphire, jade, emerald, crimson, cerise and gold stretching impossibly high above them. While chandeliers cast the upper regions of the church in shadows.

Anna thought, *excess and fear.* She turned around slowly ... *romance and darkness.* She moved across into the huge belly of the church and couldn't help but believe Russia would be saved.

She watched how every believer who entered this church walked past the site where the grandfather of the Tsar had been mortally wounded. The ciborium, a shrine beneath an ornate onyx canopy, indicated the exact spot where Alexander II, who had abolished serfdom, had been blown up. A case of too little, too late. It was a grenade-throwing protestor from The People's Will — because Russia and revolutionaries have always been synonymous. Indeed, right here, in the Church on Spilled Blood, was the redemptive quality of dynamite. The gift of the 19th century.

The crowd within the church moved about like great clouds of evening starlings, following this priest and that to various altars tucked into the sides of the church, singing prayers and mumbling recitations that were instinctive. Anna and Mayakovsky followed. People either bowed their heads and prayed or mooched about chatting quietly to one another, as was customary. The unwashed body heat within the church was oppressive.

"It's a sauna in here!" exclaimed Mayakovsky as he dragged her deeper into the throbbing mess of people.

It was at this point that he stopped in front of a young slender blonde who was arm in arm with an older, thinner woman.

"Good evening." Mayakovsky seemed delighted, "Lidka! May I wish you a cheerful Christmas." He kissed her, "And you must be her aunt?"

Lidka beamed, "Hello Vlad, this is my aunt. Yirina Matveyevna Sokolova."

Mayakovsky shook hands vigorously and introduced Anna. He boomed over the voices around them about how he had become firm friends with Lidka, a waitress at Kolobok's. He added for the aunt's benefit, but certainly not for Anna or Lidka, that this was a favourite restaurant of his and he always seemed to manage a couple of free drinks and even a bowl of borsch. Mayakovsky was explaining to the aunt that he had actually met Lidka's husband when he and some other Futurists had been on a tour down south and visited Odessa. The aunt nodded politely. Anna watched on with a ghost of a smile.

The church was thick with incense and the desperate pleas of priests and milling congregations insisting that the birth of the Christ meant salvation was at hand. The four decided it was time to join the frigid night air and so they pushed out into the evening's darkness. They walked together the few metres to where Mayakovsky and Anna were to turn down Konyushennaya Ploshchad. The aunt was now chatting amiably with Mayakovsky about her work in the Putilov Factory and true to form, he was deeply engaged in her views concerning the power structures operative at work and the ways this could be realigned to represent the needs of its workers more effectively.

"Would you like a cigarette?" asked Anna.

"Thank you." Lidka realised the evening had certainly run a different course to what she had originally anticipated as she accepted Anna's offer.

The match flared and Lidka inhaled. Anna watched her calmly as if she had always meant to arrive at this point, on the crossroad where Lidka stood.

"Do you live close by?"

"Yes," answered Lidka. "To the left of the Teatralny Bridge. My aunt and I share a bed at a boarding house."

Lidka's pale skin and wide green eyes shone in the glow of her cigarette but there was a desolation about her that Anna found beautiful.

"How is it working at Kolobok's?"

Lidka didn't know how to respond but in the end, she said, "It's a job. I am grateful for a job."

Her answer made Anna think of the unquiet Moyka River up ahead and how some of the prostitutes had a tochka close by. So many women had arrived in St Petersburg from the rural areas looking for work while their husbands were off fighting at war. But work was hard to find.

Meanwhile, Mayakovsky and Yirina were emphatically agreeing on the revolutionary future for Russia, one that believed in the destruction of the ruling elite. Anna loved Mayakovsky but she believed in patriotism. Turning upon fellow Russians, especially during the war, was not the way.

"The cook is a right prick," Lidka's words cut across Anna's thoughts but made her smile.

She was starting to like this young waitress with her southern accent.

"They all are," laughed Anna.

Her voice is deep and lovely, thought Lidka, and she noticed Anna had a way of ducking her chin and lowering her head when she spoke.

"I haven't been there long," Lidka offered as a way of explanation, "I lost my —"

She didn't finish her sentence because she didn't know where it had come from, this desire to tell this tall quiet woman about her dry hard grief. How could she finish that sentence? Grief was an expansive desert, her only country, and one where she was both lost and found.

"I know. It's hard," said Anna and placed her long fingers on Lidka's frozen hand.

Lidka felt disorientated by Anna's kindness.

"And you are from Odessa," said Anna and a willow brushed against the river of her own childhood memories. "As am I."

And for a moment Anna was filled with the scent of cherry blossoms and the long hot walk to the edge of Bolshoy Fontan and the Black Sea where, unlike the other girls who wore corsets and petticoats and rubber shoes while splashing the seawater on themselves, she hurtled herself into its greenscape in a silk chemise that fell past her thighs and swam for hours at a time.

"We must go comrades!" Mayakovsky scooped his huge arm through Anna's, kissing Lidka and her aunt farewell.

Anna drew out a train ticket from her pocket and on the back of it she scribbled down something with her pencil.

"This is my address. Close by." She handed it to Lidka and added, "Come and have tea with me tomorrow. A few friends are dropping by for Christmas."

"Yes! That's the idea! Wonderful!" Mayakovsky was already pulling Anna in the direction of her street and waving emphatically.

"Thank you, we will!" Lidka called back as she and her aunt hugged each other close and moved swiftly onwards to their boarding house.

3

Anna's apartment on Konyushennaya Ploshchad was entered via a small garden filled with daylight and the quietude of frozen aspen. Mandelstam crunched across the winter snow and opened the front door to her building. A wave of fried onions and the honeyed spiced Christmas drink of zbeetyn greeted him. For the past few years, he and others had made their way to Gumilyov and Anna's apartment for a Christmas meal. *So much has happened since*, he thought, as he began the three-flight ascent. Gumilyov had been fighting at the Front and his wife Anna had enthralled Boris Pasternak.

Mandelstam paused at the landing and fumbled in his pockets for a loose cigarette.

His own love affair with the Georgian princess, Salomea Andronikova was well and truly over.

He found a cigarette, slightly bent, and struck a match against the window sill.

Salomea had received Anna, Gumilyov and himself as her guests at one of her swanky soirees — she had an appetite for poets and devotees of her beauty. They had all loved her and the delicious salons she would host in her apartment near the Winter Palace. Anna's latest collection of poetry had been dedicated to Salomea, for God's sake!

Salomea declared she had loved Mandelstam as an exile might. He was her home, for a time. Her need for him was ferocious and he basked in that love. But Mandelstam instinctively knew Salomea had a diasporic soul.

He continued up the staircase, smoking his cigarette with a slow sensual pleasure.

Of course, Salomea found another poet and threw him over. Gumilyov and his other friends thought he was bruised because she chose Sergey Rafalovich over him. He snorted in derision at the thought. Rafalovich was nothing. They had ended their affair because Salomea, in all her porcelain beauty, knew Mandelstam wanted another woman, a different woman. He wanted Anna. He had always wanted Anna.

Mandelstam rested against the banister.

At the time, Gumilyov said good luck to him if he wanted his beautiful-bodied wife who was all brain and no passion.

One more flight, Mandelstam assured himself, and with a sharp drag of his cigarette he pushed on.

The irony was, of course, he hadn't actually slept with Anna until after the Salomea affair was well and truly over. It had happened in this very apartment when Gumilyov was away on one of his trips. In fact, he realised with a start, it had happened just before Germany declared war on Russia — that was six months ago.

"Come in! Come in! Anna is in the kitchen. Heard you climbing the stairs. What took you so long?" Mayakovsky pulled Mandelstam into his huge body and hugged and kissed him as though they hadn't seen each other for years.

"Mandelstam is here!" Mayakovsky roared across the living room to the kitchen as he helped him out of his oversized greatcoat.

Anna appeared in the doorway between the kitchen and living room, her hands were held upwards, caked in pastry. She blew Mandelstam a kiss and returned to the kitchen. Mayakovsky was already explaining his night on Anna's couch and the family next door who woke him up well before daylight with their squealing kids and barking dog.

In amongst all this bustle, Mandelstam was handed a glass of zbeetyn, pushed into an uncomfortable armchair with a spring that dug into his lower back and shown a new poem Mayakovsky was currently writing.

Mandelstam sighed and read it to himself, slowly:

There's no grandfatherly fondness in me.
There are no grey hairs in my soul!
Shaking the world with my voice and grinning
I pass you by — handsome
Twentytwoyearold

"What is this?" Mandelstam shook the scribble at Mayakovsky.

"Read on. Read on!"

If you wish —
I'll rage on raw meat like a vandal
Or change into hues that the sunrise arouses
If you wish —
I can be irreproachably gentle
Not a man — but a cloud in trousers.

Mandelstam wished he hadn't come. Or that he had but it was only to be Anna and himself here in the warmth of her apartment with her cooking in the small kitchen.

"So, what do you think?" Mayakovsky's face was all smile.

Mandelstam ignored him and continued reading.

I refuse to believe in Nice
I will glorify you regardless —
Men crumpled like bed sheets in hospitals.

And there it was. The line snagged at Mandelstam's heart. He read it again:

Men crumpled like bed sheets in hospitals.

Fucking bastard Mandelstam thought, but said aloud, "Yeah, it looks like it is coming along."

"I won't be long," called Anna. "The pastry is breaking and I just ..."

The men smiled at each other. Anna had no interest in food and had never learned to cook. Mandelstam was sure the contents of the pie, which he could smell frying on the stove, had been thrown together by Mayakovsky, who loved food and cooking. He assumed she was only left to roll the pastry but even that was proving to be a challenge.

"What news of Gumilyov? Any? I should be out there fighting! Look at me? The Germans would run as soon as they looked at me!"

"Well I know I do," responded Mandelstam dryly.

Mayakovsky laughed and offered a toast as if this was his home and he was not just once again crashing at Anna's place. Mandelstam knew he should find Mayakovsky endearing, everyone else did, especially as this bombastic larger-than-life Georgian was poor like him, self-made like him and often cold and hungry like him.

But they were fundamentally different in their politics. Actually, most people, including Anna and Gumilyov, not to mention the enormous Easter Island statue, Boris Pasternak, thought Mandelstam to be insufficiently patriotic.

"News — well it's not new, but yes I have had a letter from Gumilyov and —"

"Anna!" boomed Mayakovsky — *can the man never speak?* thought Mandelstam — "He has a letter from Gumilyov!"

They heard the oven door crunch and then she was there filling the room in all her stillness and grace. Mandelstam was up and out of his armchair offering her Christmas wishes, which they both found amusing, and kissed that warm delicious cheek dangerously close to her mouth.

"Osip, my love ..." Her vague fingers fluttered about his face momentarily.

And there in the snug of her living room, with Anna and Mayakovsky sitting alongside each other, both somehow languidly alert, Mandelstam read the letter, or most of the letter, aloud. When he finished with Gumilyov's citation of Mandelstam's poem, all three of them were quiet.

"He does love you," she said and looked across the room into his eyes and down into his soul.

Mandelstam thought to himself *If you could put your hands into my heaped-up heart* — but then Mayakovsky was stretching across the room with a bottle of vodka to top up Mandelstam's now empty glass.

"The Seine, huh?" asked Mayakovsky nonchalantly reflecting on the contents of Gumilyov's letter.

"Yeah," Mandelstam's answer was on alert.

Anna felt the room tighten and so added, "You know Vlad, Gumilyov and Osip met at the Sorbonne, back in ... when was it, Osip?"

"That's right," Mayakovsky was now pouring Anna a glass, "I heard about that. So, they take Jews there?"

Anna was taken off guard but Mandelstam had seen it coming. It was always coming.

"Yeah. Even the Jews from Warsaw."

Voices and footsteps interrupted the moment and then there was a soft knock. Mayakovsky threw open the apartment door as if he was the host and a slim tall blonde with a darker woman in her forties, a basket slung over her arm, exchanged Christmas salutations and offered goodies to the hostess. Mayakovsky swept up the basket, bumping about the small living room into the kitchen while Anna introduced Mandelstam to Lidka and her aunt, Yirina.

Later, when the table had been pulled away from the wall and set up in the middle of the living room, with its mismatched chairs assembled, some from the kitchen and some on loan from next door, Mandelstam helped Anna bring in the mushroom meat pie, the vegetable blinis, heavy black bread, jam and a large bowl of onion soup with herbs. The guests were delighted.

Anna scooted back to the kitchen mumbling she had forgotten the rice, returned and plonked a small bowl of uncooked rice on the table.

Glasses were topped up with the zbeetyn or vodka, but in Mayakovsky's case both, and Anna asked everyone to make a wish. There was laughter and teasing.

The rice bowl was passed around the table, and each person made a wish as they placed their hand into the bowl. The game was to count the number of grains left clinging to one's hand; an even number meant one's wish would come true. Anna completely unfazed, counted seven, to shouts of dismay, Lidka had six, her aunt had four and the two women smiled at each other, Mayakovsky couldn't quite get his hand in and struggled to pull it out and then there was a commotion because he tried to flick off the ninth grain to skim down the count to an even number, but in the end, there was a great deal of amusement and fun.

"Osip Emilyevich Mandelstam," said Anna as she dragged the bowl towards him. "Make your wish, dear one."

Ten grains! Cheers all around the table helped him forget, just for that moment, that Anna would never take him back as a lover.

Not much later, everyone was caught up in the conversation as the meal progressed, with Mayakovsky brandishing his own passionate views about the modern Russia that must be forged in the fire of workers' rights and never surrender to the corruption of the masters. No one believed more ardently in the revolution than Mayakovsky.

"If it wasn't for the Putilov Factory, hundreds of thousands of workers would still be toiling a 12 hour day for despicable wages!" Yirina's eyes flashed. Her wiry frame belied her enormous appetite for the discussion concerning the liberation of the workers not just in St Petersburg and Odessa but all across Russia.

"But surely, this is the time to put all workers' disputes aside?" Anna was equally stirred up, "We are at war and we must stand united against the Austro-Hungarian Empire's insatiable desire to expand its empire —"

"And the bloody Germans!"

"Yes, Vlad that's right, so you must agree that Mother Russia needs to be defended and we are all called to protect her against —"

"With respect, Anna, she is no mother to me." Yirina spoke quietly but there was no missing her bitterness, "What I know about being mothered by this country is that people like me have been abused and forgotten and if wasn't for the revolutionaries led by —"

"Aunty, please —"

"Led by the brave workers of the Putilov Works, who were then gunned down —"

"Yirina we are guests —" pleaded Lidka but everyone at the table knew that this story was as much hers as it was theirs.

Undeterred Yirina pushed on. "Gunned down by the troops of *Father Tsar*," she said with heavy sarcasm.

"All because the workers partitioned for an eight-hour day and a basic set wage!"

"I agree with Yirina! No one will forget the Revolution of 1905!" cried Mayakovsky.

"Oh really," added Mandelstam laconically. "And where were you? Still in Georgia? In breeches? Squalling for your mama?"

Mayakovsky didn't miss a beat, "The revolution is the only path forward for a truly modern Russia —"

"So why did you try to volunteer for the war? Were you just wanting to help the Tsar slaughter his own people?" Mandelstam's comeback hit the mark and for a moment Mayakovsky sat brooding across the table.

Demanding revolution while offering himself at the Front, did not make Mayakovsky an enigma, because it was a paradox for many Russians who were deeply involved in strikes one moment and the next, patriotically marching off to war.

Mandelstam felt deeply ambiguous towards Mother Russia, but in a way that went beyond the clean contradictions expressed by Mayakovsky. Mandelstam had lived in a nation blatantly anti-Semitic, so Russia as homeland remained suspect. Furthermore, the Bolsheviks demanded that all artistic contributions should be a voice for the State and this was anathema to Mandelstam. He believed in the French poet, Theophile Gautier's axiom of l'art pour l'art. That was true revolution. That was true liberation.

"What are your thoughts?" Anna asked Lidka.

The table looked at her and Anna noticed that Lidka's pale skin seemed almost translucent.

"I don't know. I used to care. We ... I used to talk about it all back in Odessa but ... I don't care now."

Mandelstam realised the others seemed to know something about Lidka that he did not. Mayakovsky had explained to Mandelstam when the visitors arrived how he had met Lidka at Kolobok's and they had struck up a friendship.

"Well, I still believe we have to focus on the war and, really, only our patriotism will defeat the invaders. Russia is ours and cannot be ripped away from us." Anna's words were a benediction over the table scraps and empty plates.

"I read," Lidka's voice was soft, "that the dancer, Nijinsky, was struck by a Cossack at the Winter Palace that day. In 1905. He was just a young boy with his mother in the protest."

Her eyes filled with tears as she thought about her own son back in Odessa. No one spoke. Anna placed her hand to her throat and looked away because she too was thinking of her son on Christmas day.

"We know him," said Mandelstam quietly across the table to Lidka. "Nijinsky." And then he added because he realised there was something deeply attractive about her emptiness and grief, "You should come along with us, one night, to the Dog, he often — well sometimes — drinks there. Many of the Ballets Russes dancers come in and —"

"I've heard Nijinsky is in Budapest," interrupted Mayakovsky. "And there are rumours the Bolshoi and Mariinsky are closing down, now we are at war."

Mandelstam ignored Mayakovsky and held Lidka's gaze, "You should come, one night. It's on Italianskaya Street."

As evening nudged its way into the living room, the conversation turned, as it always did if Mayakovsky was around and there were newcomers to impress, to May last year when he had stayed at Korney Chukovsky's dacha, in Kuokkala. This was where he had met the great artist, Ilya Repin.

Anna moved about turning on shaded lamps, closing the thick curtains and setting up the samovar on the oak sideboard.

Meanwhile, Mayakovsky was giving details about the sittings he had done so far for Repin and how the great artist had told him what a magnificent head he had. The table laughed but Mayakovsky was unstoppable — Repin had shown great interest in the epic poem Mayakovsky was writing and asked him what he meant by the phrase, *a cloud in trousers.*

"Did you tell him that's all you have in there?" asked Mandelstam and the women laughed.

Mayakovsky held an imaginary paintbrush high in the air and explained how it would take Repin a number of sittings, as well as months of labour in his studio before the portrait, would be complete. Mayakovsky beamed at the guests who seemed to be gathered there just for him.

"Oh, and I had many conversations with Maxim Gorky," he added as an afterthought.

"Really?" asked Lidia leaning into the table.

"Derelict genius."

Mandelstam snorted at Mayakovsky's summing up of the most significant writer of their day.

"Well I knew Chukovsky, years back," said Yirina. "When he was working for the *Odessa News* —"

"Oh, I didn't know he worked there," interrupted Anna.

"Yes — he really was —"

"Ah, that reminds me," Mayakovsky was not going to surrender his centre stage that easily. "You all must meet a friend of mine, a wonderful poet from Moscow. Marina Tsvetaeva ..."

But by this point, Anna was passing around the sugar and even Mayakovsky seemed more interested in sweetening the final cup of tea.

"Thank you!", "Wonderful Christmas dinner!", "I must go!", "Let's meet at the Dog in the next few weeks!", "Anna, my love!", cried the guests as they gathered their limbs and checked their walking legs to join Mayakovsky in the great exit.

Anna could not say she felt disappointed. These social occasions seemed to take so much out of her. She longed for loving friendship yet felt replete almost as soon as people arrived. Privately, she was glad Mayakovsky hadn't asked her to stay another night. She needed some peace and quiet, not to mention the fact that there was hardly any food left after his recent stayover. Besides, she felt sure he was braving the dark winter night to satiate another sort of appetite. She may not see him for weeks, as was often the way.

She kissed her new friends, Lidka and Yirina, to whom she had formed a surprising attachment and they assured her they would be hosting afternoon tea for her, one Sunday soon, in a café close by. At last, she farewelled Mandelstam. She realised, as he hugged her, how she had forgotten the crush of his arms and the scent of his skin. He was the dearest soul and she would always love him. Then Mandelstam moved away from her and hurried after Lidka down the staircase, leaving Anna feeling, as she stood there alone, just the slightest twinge of regret.

Anna did her best to tidy up, but she would leave most of it to one of the girls who came around in the mornings for housekeeping. Just like her mother, she was hopeless at keeping house. She flopped down in her armchair and pulled her legs up under her, despite her woollen dress and stockings she felt cold to the bone. She sipped a thimble glass of fortified wine and pushed her head back up into the crown of the chair.

She looked across the room.

Above the couch was Amedeo Modigliani's drawing of her. It wasn't really her. It was more a rendition of the way their love had never lifted off the page. Anna sipped her wine and for some reason, perhaps because he remained the only reason, she thought of Amedeo.

"Ahh me de oh," she whispered his name to the cold filling up her living room.

And she remembered how he laughed at the way she always exaggerated the first syllable as if she had made a discovery.

Amedeo Modigliani *was* her discovery. Her honeymoon in Paris a few years back was filled with the wonder of romance and desire. Not with Gumilyov, her husband, the one who had pursued her when she was a schoolgirl only to lose interest in her days, hours, minutes after they were married, but with the Italian artist living in Paris.

Her body woke up the moment Amedeo touched it, never had she known love like this before. His tousled dark looks, peasant body and ferocity in bed were just some of what it was. She had met him days after they had arrived, he rented the apartment upstairs.

Meanwhile, her husband made his own amusement there in Paris, catching up with friends and lovers. At the time Anna thought her husband's abandonment would not affect her — but that was back then.

Left to her own devices Amedeo and Anna had mooched about the streets of Saint-German ... ducking into le Jardine de Luxembourg to kiss, ordering patisseries at Pierre Herme and sheltering in the Eglise Saint-Sulpice from the occasional summer shower.

But mostly they lay on the mattress in his one-room apartment surrounded by blockwork or canvasses morphing into figures. Their own bodies a fascination of flesh and bone and sinew. He was obsessed with her long thighs, neck and nose that made her look, he said, *like a heroine from a Greek tragedy*. She was his Phaedra, which made her laugh because, as she used to point out, that made him Hippolytus who had in fact rejected Phaedra. *No, no, no*, he had said, denying her version and insisting she stick to poetry because she knew nothing of the Mediterraneans and their passions.

Anna returned the following spring to Paris and on her second evening invited Amedeo to dinner. He stayed two months. But by then his addictions were becoming legendary, and although she knew later what he was hiding, with his weight loss and blood-stained coughing fits, at the time it just felt like abandonment.

She went back to St Petersburg, her marriage and the obligation of giving her husband a son. Her Hippolytus had crashed and burned.

But all this was a long time ago.

4

After the battle at Łódź they had their doubts.

Not just Gumilyov and his fellow Hussars but most of the Russian 2nd were now talking amongst themselves about the incompetence of the aristocrats and courtiers appointed to high command by the Tsar and the way they continued to make spectacularly ridiculous decisions.

Grim fatalism was beginning to freeze their hearts.

After the Russian 2nd was decimated in East Prussia, five months ago, Gumilyov's regiment had been one of many assigned to rebuild it. No one would confirm or deny, but rumours had it that 100,000 Russians had been killed and 90,000 taken prisoner in August last year at a battle the Germans were now calling Tannenberg. Some men said the numbers were too high. Gumilyov kept his own counsel. There were a handful of soldiers he had met who had been there at this battle, mostly in Supply. He didn't count the Orthodox priest assigned to his regiment, who was a drunkard and a fool. These survivors spoke about the fatigue and hunger, the lack of communication, Supply in chaos and Artillery mired — and that was before the battle began.

Five months later and Russia could not seem to move forward. Gumilyov had read in the newspapers that General Alexander Samsonov, leader of the Russian 2nd, had ridden out into the forest after Tannenberg and shot himself through the head. A noble and proper ending. But Gumilyov and other soldiers talked amongst themselves about people higher up in the Stavka, commanding blind, applying strategies outdated and deadly. Everyone must have known that the Russian colossus was militarily unready and crippled by incompetent leadership. At Łódź, every soldier in the Russian 2nd had known this to be true when, once again, Stavka had left them surrounded.

Despite all of this, the newspapers were reporting that the battles so far in the war had been a victory for Russia because they had successfully distracted Germany from their lunge at Paris. *What a price to pay,* Gumilyov thought sourly.

January 31, 1915, and Gumilyov was back at the Front.

The Germans were in Bolimów, a railway town between Łódź and Warsaw, central Polish Russia, and they were softening up the Russian 2nd before an attack.

The shelling had started in earnest around 6 am and had gone on for hours. The men up ahead in their dugouts hunkered low. Gumilyov and the other Hussars were already saddling their horses alongside cadets who were making jittery and unhelpful efforts.

Being quite some distance behind the trenches the Hussars mounted and waited for their orders. *Shellfire comes quickly*, thought Gumilyov dryly. Trench mortar, on the other hand, would spiral upwards performing some strange ballet, each man watching its slow arc and then when it reached its apex it would turn downwards and unhurriedly descend, as every man huddled in horror.

The horses stamped and shook their heads, the men pulled their papakhas low over their ears and tucked their fists up under their armpits. The hard-icy wind seemed to be blowing all the way from Siberia and hopefully into the faces of the enemy. The Frontoviks in the trenches had been given a bashing but the machine gunners on both sides had quietened.

An eerie stillness settled.

Lieutenant Zheleznyak emerged out of the mist presumably to give orders.

"At ease men!" Zheleznyak's waxed moustache remained perfectly in place while he spoke across the heads of his squadron.

"Gas shells, men! They were sending us a present of gas!" The men shuffled anxiously before the lieutenant, "But they didn't explode!"

"HURRUAHH!"

"The Germans are nicking off with their tail between their legs!"

Relief exploded in laughter. The men couldn't believe their luck. They had heard about tear gas used by the French on the Germans last year. Grenades had exploded and gas burned the enemy's eyes and skin, making them gag and stagger about in terror until they ran out of the trenches and were mowed down by gunners.

So, their attempts to gas us didn't work, thought Gumilyov happily, *and now the enemy is running back, maybe even all the way to Germany!* At last, maybe they could regain some of the precious Polish Russia they had so far lost to the invaders.

"What happened, sir?" Rad was never bothered by etiquette and his enormous physique somehow made his superiors ignore the fact that he should not be asking.

"Too fucking cold! That's what happened Trooper. The shells exploded but the gas wouldn't vaporise."

The lieutenant was enjoying himself because he added, "Some of the shells did release something but the wind hauled it right back across enemy lines!"

The men cheered and threw a few papakhas in the air and even Gumilyov who didn't quite believe Zheleznyak appreciated his efforts to raise their spirits.

At that moment a messenger arrived with a letter. While the lieutenant read its contents, carefully, the men smoked or talked quietly. Gumilyov inhaled on his cigarette and thought about the last time he had seen Stani alive. When they charged out of Łódź that morning, protecting the flank of their infantry from enemy attack, he heard nothing but the thunder of hooves and the war cries of his fellow Hussars. He never heard shots, but he knew men all around him were being killed mercilessly. It was not until they got through to the forest that he realised Stani was dead. His horse rode on gallantly without its rider for some time.

"READY YOUR HORSES!"

Zheleznyak's voice cut through Gumilyov's reverie and Hussars all about him began stubbing out cigarettes and tucking what was left of them into their pockets.

"NEW ORDER JUST IN, MEN!"

Gumilyov had no faith in orders from above, he only had faith in the brotherhood of Hussars around him.

"WE ARE TO GIVE THOSE COWARDS A RUN FOR THEIR MONEY!"

Zheleznyak paused as if anticipating a cheer but then hurried on pretending he hadn't noticed the quiet.

"A COUNTER-ATTACK HAS BEEN ORDERED!"

He stopped yelling and turned to the sergeant, "Lava formation, Sergeant Drugov. Lava formation on my orders — get the men ready!"

Drugov stood high in his stirrups facing the men: "ON MY ORDERS! WALK TO THE CLEARING AND MOVE INTO LAVA FORMATION!"

They began moving northeast.

Trotting in extended formation the 8th Hussar Regiment crossed several kilometres of farmed land to the town of Bolimów. They skirted around it and saw that the enemy, who had been fleeing, were now scurrying about their howitzers preparing to fire. Gumilyov had already seen enough of the German artillery power to know that this would mean high explosives, shrapnel and smoke rounds. Meanwhile, several Russian infantry divisions were setting up their machine guns and phalanxes of riflemen to offer a counter-attack. Gumilyov already knew the outcome.

Then down through the Hussar formation, the word was passed: *LAVA!* Again, their belief in each other and their own horses far outweighed their faith in command.

At some point out front Zheleznyak must have yelled the order because Gumilyov saw Drugov stand high in his stirrups, his sabre pointing to the hard impassive sky, and heard him scream "CHARGE!"

Other squadrons followed suit and Gumilyov found himself in the midst of 600 Hussars swarming towards the enemy as artillery mowed them down with reckless abandon. To their left Russian infantry divisions were running into the rain of shells and bullets.

Onward he rode amongst the Hussar brotherhood who were trained to close ranks 50 metres from the enemy and then break through enemy lines.

Then a furious hot whirlwind hurled past Gumilyov, throwing him violently off his horse and under the stampede of the cavalry. He lay stunned while the snow and earth and offal smashed about. There was no thinking, only instinct *to get the hell out!* Oncoming horses narrowly missed Gumilyov as he half staggered, half crawled across to an old stone wall of an outer farmyard. Something whizzed viciously past and sliced into the wall — a piece of jagged steel about 40 centimetres long. The scream of the guns and the charge of the horses pounded along his arteries and into his heartbeat. His left arm seemed useless. He felt his shoulder and even without looking he knew it was a tangle of blood and bone. He kept trying to slow his breathing but the terror of the smoke and noise and screams of battle kept him desperately gulping air. As he lay up against the wall in the icy snow, he felt his body burn. The battle raged on and on until the cold took him like a mother's warm embrace.

Later, he came to as he was thrown over Rad's horse. It seemed darker now. How much time had passed?

Rad kept up a long stream of curses and swearing, mostly aimed at General Gurko who had apparently come up with the brilliant idea of a Russian counter-attack. The one thing the Russian High Command did well was to offer their own men as fodder for the German guns.

"Headquarters is full of fuckwits," Rad stated flatly. "All of them suffer from useless gallantry and foolish ineptitude because they fucked their own mothers from an early age." Rad was taking a circuitous route back to camp as night fell.

"Fucking disaster," he repeated over and over again.

No one knew how many they had lost in the regiment but Rad estimated that only a dozen of their own squadron had survived.

"Borislav is dead," he said as he led his horse with Gumilyov's body into the forested camp. "A fucking disaster."

And that was the last Gumilyov heard before he passed out.

5

"Dear Mama

I am in Warsaw at the moment taking some rest and recuperation."

Gumilyov watched the nurse deep in concentration as she scribbled down the letter he was dictating. She was deliciously curvaceous with red hair.

"I hope you are well and little Lev is not being too much of a handful for you."

The nurse looked up at him, her dark round eyes smiled, and dimples appeared in her cheeks.

"I was wounded in my shoulder recently, but the nurses at Saint Stanislaus Hospital are taking wonderful care of me."

She blushed as Gumilyov, handsome, square-jawed and smoky-eyed, dictated lazily.

"In fact, you should meet this very one, her name is —"

"Stop!" she giggled. "Your mother doesn't want to know your mischief!"

"But I haven't done any ..." he said as he reached out and stroked her cheek. "Yet."

"Nurse!"

The red-headed nurse jumped visibly.

"Get on with that letter then come here immediately and fold these bandages before the next lot of wounded arrive!"

She nodded to her superior.

"You will get me into trouble," she whispered and made a show of holding the pencil ready.

"The wound will heal, so don't be fretting, Mama. Soon I hope to be home with you and Lev —"

The nurse looked surreptitiously across the room and then asked the Hussar, "Where is your wife?"

"Gone. She left me." His smile was too much for her and she giggled again. "I want you to help me get onto my feet," he said quietly and tugged at the letter she was holding, "I want to stretch my legs and have some time with you."

The nurse glanced around but no one seemed interested in them.

"Maybe, tonight, I can check on you and ..."

"Yes, tonight!"

"Nurse! Finish that letter and come here at once!"

Without missing a beat, Gumilyov lent back in his bed with his right hand behind his head, his left arm and shoulder tightly strapped:

"So, I send you my love and give a kiss to my brave little Lev.

Affectionately,

Your Son."

She finished off the letter and scribbled down his mother's name and address. Outgoing mail was to be dispatched that afternoon.

Hours later Gumilyov was pressed up against her in an office she had found just off the kitchen. It was warm and clean, and he had done worse. At first, he thought she might have needed a little more persuading but then he realised she knew all along he was right-handed and could have written the letter himself.

She had found a copy of Mandelstam's *Stone*, published two years back, in Gumilyov's pack. Somehow in a world that threw up only illiterate peasants, this nurse had discovered a good-looking Hussar who read poetry. At first, Gumilyov tried to chat about poetry but most of all he wanted to feel her heavy breasts that could not be hidden under her nurse's uniform and apron.

Once they were ensconced in the office near the kitchen Gumilyov pushed her against the desk and began massaging her breasts with his right hand. His cock throbbed almost immediately and she furtively began unbuttoning her uniform.

She could be sacked for this if caught, but she ached with her own wet hunger to be loved.

He pushed his mouth onto her nipple and sucked, and she grabbed the back of his head; with his good hand, he reached down and rucked up her dress and petticoat and moved his fingers up into the break between the woollen stocking and her cotton underwear.

She lent further back on the desk and opened her legs. He felt along the line of her thigh and then paused. She pushed his face towards hers and kissed him passionately. Then he pressed two fingers into her and she moved her thighs even further apart, half leaning, half lying on the desk behind. She had unbuttoned his trousers and just as she began the first tremor of coming, she raised her knee and guided him into her, stockings askew, up high on the desk. He moved his right hand down to her backside and thrust again and again and again.

He felt her body shudder as he came deep inside her. She clung to him and he clung to her, as if they were trying to survive.

"What's your name?"

"Jula," she replied softly.

6

Kaskil had checked, but Aysen had no intention of joining them. The sergeant had told them they were pulling out of Warsaw tomorrow and heading back to the Front, so a bunch of the men had decided to visit a brothel down on Jerozolimskie.

Sergeant Lachkov had lectured them, before they left Moscow, about visiting brothels. They were told to check the worker's certificate and to have one of their own Division doctors check them afterward.

A necessary evil, Lachkov had called it.

The men joked amongst themselves that having one of the doctors manhandling their eggs and sausage was actually the greater evil than a little clap, which, let's face it, most of them dealt with periodically anyway, especially as most had visited the brothels up around Polonez in Moscow as soon as they knew they were leaving for the Front.

So, they set off in the gloom of the February evening, full of muck and bravado.

En route Kaskil thought about Tuyaara, who had been dead for two months. Unlike Aysen, Tuyaara would have come to the brothel just for the hell of it. Everyone knew in their platoon that Lachkov was pissed with Aysen because he had defied orders at Łódź and carried his dead cousin out of enemy fire and into the forest. Kaskil and Aysen had buried Tuyaara deep enough to touch permafrost and shallow enough to be seen by the spirits. Their Yakut faith taught them how to let Tuyaara's soul travel skyward to the lush green heaven promised above.

Kaskil and Aysen had not wanted to be haunted by his trapped soul on earth. The last few months of war had shown Kaskil that the world was riddled by the malevolent spirits of many trapped souls. They knew it was impossible to sacrifice a horse or reindeer to help Tuyaara travel to the land of the dead but Aysen had taken his pencil and on the back of one of Sayaara's love letters he had drawn a fairly good horse. Short, muscular and ready to gallop away. He had placed it in Tuyaara's hands as they buried him in the forest outside of Łódź. He had a long way to travel homeward.

Lachkov had threatened to report Aysen to the lieutenant because *the Imperial Russian Army would not tolerate the irregular abuse of their dead soldiers* ... blah

blah blah ... *and the orderlies were collecting the dead and wounded and Tuyaara had to be accounted for like everyone else ... blah blah blah ... and Aysen and Kaskil were superstitious untrustworthy chinks, as bad as Jews ...*

At the time Aysen and Kaskil had not cared or responded to the sergeant's vitriol. They, along with everyone else in the platoon, including Lachkov, knew if a Yakut was killed, his brothers would perform the sacred ritual — no matter the consequences.

Twenty minutes later, Kaskil and the others had arrived at Jerozolimskie Avenue, which threw its arms open in a wide and expansive gesture. There were bars and cafés and offices and tram stops littered down either side. People were scurrying out of the snow to get home as if there was no war. Groups of khaki-clad men in greatcoats and papakhas moved about purposefully. Some even had their bashlyk, drawn up over their fleece cap, so they looked like medieval monks moving determinedly to the east end where the brothels were located.

Kaskil was being led by Yuri and Smirnov who were all talk about their visit three nights ago. Kaskil had been to brothels before, both in Moscow and Ussuriysk, when he and Tuyaara had come down from Yakutsk to report for duty.

Sometimes Kaskil wondered whether any of the Yakut boys, not just Aysen and himself, would ever again see the Stanovoy Mountains or the Aldan plateau where they once hunted. Aysen shared his letters from his wife, but other than that Kaskil had only received one letter from his own father. Unlike most of his comrades, Kaskil could read and write because he, like Aysen and Tuyaara, had worked alongside their fathers in the family fur trading business where they moved pelts from their hunters and trappers down to the train junction at Tynda and then across Russia. All of which involved an enormous amount of paperwork.

Kaskil and the other men jostled to a stop outside a shopfront with the word *Tochka* painted on the window and a red lantern at the doorway. They had passed a few similar places but the lantern had been yellow and Yuri, the source of all knowledge or so he thought, had explained to the other men that was for officers only.

This tochka certainly looks pretty swanky, thought Kaskil.

He had heard that the Polish Russian whores were ambitious and generally pretty. He jangled his roubles unselfconsciously.

A large matronly woman greeted them and offered a small glass of vodka, and the men threw back their drinks as one. The over-powdered madam eyed the men closely and then drew them to a cluster of small photographs on the wall. At the corner of each was written a number. The men leaned in and were asked to select a number and the madam would then show them this worker's passport which had the stamp and date of the latest VD examination.

Yuri did not hesitate and called out a number. He diligently checked the passport he was handed, repeated the room number the madam told him and strode off down the dark hallway.

As if on cue all the men started calling out numbers, jostling for whatever sepia photo promised energetic sex or clean skin or simply the smell of a woman.

By the time it came for Kaskil to choose he had no idea who was taken or who was still available. He looked at the madam and she handed him a passport. Instead of checking the details of the VD examination, he gazed at the photograph of a young face attached to the passport. The image showed a thick white scarf tied low over her forehead. She had a flat chest, he noted.

Room 5 was like a dormitory with six or seven mattresses lying on the floor, each mattress was divided by heavy drapes that were hooked from the ceiling above.

Kaskil followed the wall down to the furthest mattress, gingerly stepping over discarded uniforms and coats and backpacks and boots, glancing into the cubicles as he passed, with their strange discombobulation of limbs and agitated movement. His comrades in various stages of undress. Sex workers in various pretences of interest. Kaskil felt himself buzzing as he got to the end of the room.

A young thin girl stood up from the mattress, black stockings pulled up past her knees and a smock top that she lifted immediately to show him her dark pubic hair. Kaskil, shunted off his greatcoat and unbuttoned his fly, then sat at the base of the mattress and began pulling off his boots. He smelt vinegar and turned around to watch her crouch over a small bowl soaking a flannel, she then handed it to him and gestured to his cock and balls. He rubbed himself vigorously with the cloth and dumped it amongst his clothes somewhere. He turned back to her and she deftly pulled off her smock and laid down on the mattress.

Kaskil knelt in front of her. Then she pushed back her elbows and sat up, gazing at him. He watched as she slowly parted her thighs and raised her knees. Kaskil scrambled across the mattress, his trousers snagging. She raised herself to him and he pushed inside her; one hand gripping her buttock and the other rubbing her small breast.

She listened to the grunts and shouts and slaps of the other men on the other mattresses; he smelt her musky odour and wanted to fuck her forever. She could hear some of the other girls murmuring encouragement and offering little gasps and exclamations as if they too were in the throes of ecstasy. He watched her mouth open slightly, she took his hand from her breast and sucked on one of his fingers.

He ejaculated his hot seed into her and groaned.

She stopped sucking and laid still for a few seconds. He found himself slouched over her tiny body, nose up against her sticky skin. She absently played with a few strands of his dirty hair.

Kaskil thought about the meadows in summer in the Lena Basin and the smell of grass so thick you could eat it. He remembered the way the sky would move constantly when you laid on your back in the summer clover and buttercups and lupines.

She slipped out from under him and began pulling on her underwear. He could hear the other men putting on their boots and coats. Someone farted and laughed. He sat on the mattress with his back to her and began redoing his trousers and pulling on his boots. They had left their money on the counter after the madam had invited them to down a glass of vodka. The business was done.

So it surprised him when he felt her small body push up against his back just as he was about to lift himself off the mattress. He remained still and put his hand on the arm she stretched across his chest. He looked down into her little upturned hand, a sweaty gesture of hope. He dumped a few roubles into her quick closing fist.

But the greatest surprise was the butterfly kiss to his cheek and then she was gone — pushing past him and the other mattresses and out the door of Room 5 with the other girls before the next men arrived.

7

The following day Kaskil and Aysen, along with their platoon, moved from Warsaw to Augustovo. From there they marched up through the forest until they got within sight of Lake Serwyn.

It was February 15.

They had been reassigned to the 3rd Siberian Riflemen Division in the Russian 10th Army which had sustained great losses.

According to some of the original survivors, the battles up around the Masurian Lakes had all come to a grinding halt a week ago when the Germans sent over a deafening offensive during a major snowstorm. The Siberian 3rd was the *only* Division holding off the entire German 8th Army. It had taken the near decimation of the Russian 10th before General Sievers sent through the command to retreat.

But just as they were pulling out, General Ruzsky, *a fuckwit of the highest order*, according to one of the Siberian Riflemen recounting the horror, rescinded the command to retreat and ordered them to counter-attack.

Their own lieutenant ran from phone to men to phone to men, desperately trying to convey the fuckup to anyone who would listen, until the line was cut.

By this stage, the snowdrifts were a metre high and none of them had any idea why they were fighting, except for the promise of one meal a day. At least they had their winter uniforms. The Germans they had shot or captured were still in summer uniforms, and all of them were riddled with frostbite.

"If you are going to die, at least die warm and drunk," the Siberian Rifleman had added.

No one chuckled.

After a while, Kaskil offered, "We have come up from the battle at Łódź." He then added, "But before that, we marched from Silesia to Łódź. In two days. 120 kilometres."

"Shit! When was that?"

"Late November."

The soldiers nodded sagely at each other, recognising the way Headquarters treated them like animals.

The tide felt like it was turning, and the Germans were throwing everything at the Russians. No one commented on the irony that they themselves had invaded Poland just 100 years ago. What they did comment on was Russia's success in September at the battle of the Vistula River when they had defeated Germany's attempt to seize Warsaw.

"There was something in the newspaper in Warsaw about a battle at Bolimów," said Kaskil.

"I heard it was a bloody massacre," said one.

"Fucking Germans," added another and the rest of the men agreed.

"The enemy will push on until they have all of Polish Russia and then Russia!"

You can always count on an ethnic Russian to state the obvious, thought Kaskil.

"They'll never take Warsaw," added someone else with little conviction.

"Fucking generals. They know fuck all!" said a rifleman next to Kaskil.

One of the Siberians from another platoon added, "General Sievers is now in Grodno."

"What!?"

"Yeah, giving orders to us, while he sips cognac in his dining room in Belarus."

Some of the men spat.

"So, who's in charge here?" asked Kaskil incredulously.

"Belolipetsky."

In the blinding cold of February 16, Aysen and Kaskil, along with several hundred other men, were led out from the forest in a morning temperature that was just hovering around freezing. There was a stiff breeze blowing from the south which made it feel five degrees colder.

Around Sersky Lake it was mostly wooden houses and barns, long since abandoned. Colonel Belolipetsky's mission, according to Aysen's lieutenant, was to take back Mahartse from the Germans. This village, nestled amongst the Masurian Lakes and Augustovo Forest, led to a vital crossroad that would secure a withdrawal route for the Russian 10th Army. So when Aysen and his platoon had been redeployed to join the Siberian 3rd, they realized with dismay that they were there to help with a strategic withdrawal.

"Once again — we have come all this way to retreat. Sounds like another order from Grodno," Kaskil muttered.

"Shut your mouth chink!" Sergeant Lachkov's cadaverous face was all beak and claw.

"MEN," Bobrinsky's voice rose above the platoon's frustrations. "FOLLOW MY LEAD AND KEEP LOW!"

"CHECK BAYONETS! LOAD RIFLES" screamed Lachkov.

Aysen, like all men in the Division, had been given 30 rounds of ammunition which he had secured into each of his two leather cartridge pouches as well as an extra 40 rounds packed in the top of his haversack.

"YOU HAVE BEEN ON THE MOVE FOR DAYS BUT THE ENEMY HAS BEEN SITTING IN THIS MISERABLE COLD!"

There were chuckles all around at lieutenant Bobrinsky's comments.

"BESIDES, WE ARE RUSSIANS! THEY ARE PUSSIES!"

The men cheered.

Dawn crept over the forest tops and a light drizzle mixed up visibility from clear to hazy then back to clear. Bobrinsky and then Lachkov started moving ahead, and Aysen with men all around him joined them towards Mahartse.

About 400 metres out Colonel Belolipetsky had ordered three artillery batteries to move up the line with the infantry; so that, under cover of morning mist they could let off a deafening good morning to the Germans.

The Russian gunners and the 76.2mm field guns got into the action with roaring effect.

The men watched as Mahartse was pounded with shrapnel and high explosives, suppressing any return fire from the German outposts.

The fuckers won't fire and show their positions, thought Aysen, but before he could worry about that he heard Bobrinsky's distinct roar, "TO THE VIL-LAGE!" and he joined the charge across the snow-covered field as if his life depended on it, because it did.

Machine gunfire from the enemy lines opened up and the men in front of Aysen threw themselves down onto the soft snow. Above his head, he could hear bullets flying. Minutes later Aysen was scrambling to get up and move forward. The snow was thigh deep. He blundered on and then the roar and rattle of the German gunners was on them again.

Aysen buried himself in the slush and slurry of ice. He brought up his rifle, drew back the bolt and checked the sights. A few others were doing the same.

What followed was a barrage of return fire from his platoon.

"FORWARD!" cried Bobrinsky as he hauled himself up and ploughed on.

Aysen and the others followed but the village seemed to be moving further and further away from them.

A shock of light — a deafening BOOM!

Aysen was thrown against Kaskil and they landed entangled in limbs and rifles. Aysen was dizzy and his ears ran. He looked up and saw the two German outposts were being bombed. Bricks and smoke and fire threw up screams.

Another explosion, followed by shockwaves. Aysen saw that the remnants of the outposts were only 20 metres away.

Kaskil was already scurrying over the snow towards the rubble where the German gunners had been silenced. Aysen and a few others from the platoon crawled after him and took shelter against the stone slabs that had once formed the outpost. Breathing heavily Aysen reloaded his rifle. He carefully assessed the position of the enemy who seemed to be retreating into the village.

A staccato rain of rifle fire from the Siberian 3rd followed them.

By the time they made it to the village of Mahartse, Aysen realised all they had to do was find Bobrinsky or Lachkov.

Aysen yelled, "Malik, how much ammo do you have? You too Kaskil — we need to double-check."

The three of them checked their pouches and haversacks.

"Twenty," responded Malik.

"Yeah — about 20," from Kaskil.

"Me too," agreed Aysen. "Now we need to find the lieutenant or the sergeant. Keep your eyes out for snipers."

Aysen peeled himself off the wall and slid up against the side of a building at the start of the street. Kaskil and Malik, pulled in behind him, all the time watching for friendlies, especially their own platoon members, and in particular Bobrinsky and Lachkov.

At the end of the building, they were exposed to an open square. Aysen crouched low, and like all the Yakuts, took his time. He watched the square and seemed to be determining not only where a sniper may lay in wait under camouflage, but also where the exit points could be for the hunter and the hunted. Kaskil, crouching behind Aysen, was studying the buildings with slow determination. Malik was just grateful he had hooked up with the Yakut boys.

Enemy fire ricocheted around them.

Aysen pushed back into Kaskil and made a slight gesture with his left hand. Kaskil nodded, stood abruptly, aimed high and began firing. Aysen did the same.

Malik heard the thud of bodies and boots running ... then nothing. Both the Yakuts discarded the used shells quickly.

"Down and low," Aysen said and left, followed by Kaskil, then Malik.

They ran to the nearest intersecting street of the town square and into a wooden building. Inside they saw it was a bar. While Malik seemed relieved he was no longer exposed to enemy fire, Aysen and Kaskil remained as cautious and quiet inside as they were outside. They kept low, scanning the room and the exit points, checking ammo. Malik did the same. When they remained still, so did Malik, and when they began moving towards the back of the building, so did he.

No words were exchanged. Aysen opened the back door ajar. Again, a slight gesture to his cousin. Kaskil nodded then swiftly kicked the door wide. Aysen threw himself on his belly and let lose the crackle and thud of rifle fire.

Kaskil was down beside him and joined in the assault at the unsuspecting enemy.

The reverberation of their Mosin Nagant rifles filled the bar until Aysen rolled back and swung the door shut. It was then that they heard groans and urgent German and again boots retreating and then nothing.

The Yakuts watched the door quietly before one of them opened it gradually.

The small courtyard, which had a passageway at the rear, was littered with half a dozen bodies. Some of the dead had no greatcoats, just their feldgrau uniform. A lone pickelhaube helmet was still rocking between the cobblestones.

Aysen said, "Grab a rifle and the ammo."

Scattered across the bodies of the dead were their German Gew rifles. Aysen, Kaskil and Malik slung a few quickly across their shoulders and grabbed the bounty of ammunition.

Aysen led them out of the courtyard and down the passageway. In the distance, the three of them could hear gunfire. They waited. Inside the maze of wooden houses, shops and larger structures, they knew this could be a trap with snipers perched high above. But on the other hand, the gunfire was fading, and it sounded as if the Germans were retreating.

They moved out unhurriedly. All three had their rifles pointing upwards in different angles covering the various structures they passed. Around them the day swirled on in dirty white mists of poor visibility. In the distance occasional gunshots could be heard and the rare *RATATATATA* of a machine gun. At the end of the passageway, with no loss of their own ammunition, the three Russians emerged.

In the distance, they saw a rundown warehouse area where some of the Division clustered. They jogged across the slush and muddy snow.

When they got up into the shelter of this area, they noticed a surprising number of German POWs and many were without greatcoats.

Aysen got thwacked on his shoulder by Bobrinsky who appeared out of nowhere, "No problem?"

The lieutenant was not really asking a question so Aysen shrugged.

"Good men."

The lieutenant managed to thump Kaskil and Malik's backs and move them towards some of their flagged-out platoon members clustering at the edge of the warehouse, trying to get out of the cold.

"Hey Malik, what happened to you?" one of them asked.

"Had to look after the Yakut boys," answered Malik.

The soldiers chortled.

After a moment when cigarettes were passed around, matches struck and the smoke inhaled, Malik leaned across and shook Aysen's hand and then Kaskil's.

There was a splutter of talk as the men exchanged information and rumours and questions between each other.

"Lachkov can't be found," said one of their platoon members.

"Yeah? No kidding."

"Bastard."

"Such a prick."

"He'll probably crawl out of a hole, you wait!"

Laughter.

After a while, someone started snoring and another started rooting around in the POWs haversacks that have been tossed close by. But most of them were too numb, too tired and too cold to do much else. Aysen looked across at the prisoners who were being guarded by another platoon. The POWs had been pushed back into the corner of the warehouse and were sitting or lying about in various positions. No one would want to be in charge of them.

Aysen closed his eyes.

He remembered the walk out of the forest beyond Łódź after they buried his cousin Tuyaara. They had a dozen or so POWs. One of them spoke softly in his own language to Aysen. Someone else had said the POW was asking why Aysen had carried a dead comrade into the forest with them.

No one answered the POW.

Aysen saw the way this POW watched him on the journey back to Warsaw. People usually gave Aysen a wide berth so it felt strange having this young fair-haired POW keep him in his sights. On their arrival into Warsaw, two days later, the POW had approached Aysen and asked him, in a smattering of French, German and broken Russian, where he was from and why, if he wasn't Russian, was he fighting?

Aysen had not answered but one of the other platoon members had overheard and explained to the POW that Aysen and his cousins were *Yakut. Siberian. Chinks.*

Nowhere did Aysen hear the word, *Russian.*

Aysen opened his eyes. There was a buzz amongst the platoon as they watched Bobrinsky striding towards them.

"Lachkov is still unaccounted. Lance Corporal I want you to write down the names of the platoon members who have turned up."

Aysen moved to his feet and took the pencil and notebook Bobrinsky handed him and began to write, occasionally looking up at someone but never asking them to call out their names as Lachkov would have.

Meanwhile one of the platoon members asked, "Sir, what's happening? Any news?"

"Now men, it seems there is some good news," even Bobrinsky sounded as if he believed it. "Apparently some of our boys have come across a frozen lake and snuck up on the other side of the enemy — taking them by surprise!"

The men cheered and shoved each other in friendly comradery.

"And there's more," Bobrinsky smoothed his black moustache and pushed his hand through his thick beard. "Some of the scouts have reported that the Germans have abandoned Mahartse and their guns!"

The men responded as though they had momentarily won the war. Cheers were heard amongst other huddles as the various officers were doing the same and sharing the good news.

Aysen handed a completed list to Bobrinsky.

"So, no one saw Lachkov?"

The men looked away from the lieutenant's enquiry.

"Right men. Be alert. Anything could still happen, but we have had a good day."

"Sir," it was Malik. "What about Supply and our meals and gear? The weather's coming in."

The men glanced out of the warehouse entrance at the roiling grey skies.

"So, I can see," responded Bobrinsky and moved away into the huddle of officers.

In the end, they had taken 1000 German prisoners and several field guns, but rumour was that the road out of Mahartse to Fracki had been blocked by the enemy. The morale flagged as the afternoon set in. Despite Bobrinsky's quiet encouragement, every Russian huddled in the warehouse suspected that the promise of backup was a lie. The hard cold settled in beside them as the afternoon began to turn dusky.

And then to the surprise of no one, but with bitter disappointment, they were ordered to return to the forest where they had left that morning. In other words, they were to abandon Mahartse. The strategic village they had seized that very day would now be given back to the Germans. It was all for nothing.

The men began the trudge back. Some mumbled that at least they were moving and at least Supply might be waiting in the forest. But considering the roads were impassable, others decided this was unlikely. At least guarding the POWs had not been a short straw drawn by Aysen's platoon.

On the third day after the battle at Mahartse Aysen woke in the forest and knew no help was coming.

He watched Bobrinsky and the other officers, including the Colonel, trying to keep up morale, but by this stage, with the Division reduced substantially and whole battalions missing in attempts to push past the German blockade on the other side of Mahartse, everyone knew it was hopeless. They waited. There were no rations and the dense forest meant that the captured guns had to be abandoned.

As yet, Aysen's platoon had not been rostered for POW duties. Bobrinsky had reminded the platoon when they had returned to the forest that it was in their interests to treat the POWs well, should the tables be reversed. He didn't need to add any more detail; every Russian could see that it was hopeless.

"Fucking generals," said someone when Bobrinsky had left.

"Yeah — where the fuck are they now?"

On Thursday morning, February 18, Bobrinsky spoke to his men, "Colonel Belolipetsky needs a message taken to General Sievers in Grodno, Belarus. It's our only hope, lads."

He looked around at the pinched faces and said evenly, "We need the General to know we are still alive and with POWs. Then he will be forced to send reinforcements."

The men could not look the lieutenant in the eye and show their lack of faith.

"The Colonel believes that when General Sievers gets this message he will send reinforcements."

The men looked away from Bobrinsky. He was doing his best but even he knew it was useless.

"So, men. Are there any volunteers amongst you who would —"

"I'll go, sir."

The men looked across to where the Yakut stood but Bobrinsky ignored Aysen and continued speaking, "It is about 100 kilometres through enemy lines but it is the only way we can get word to Headquarters ..."

Aysen watched the lieutenant who at last looked directly at him.

"Me too, sir," Kaskil shuffled up alongside his cousin.

Bobrinsky looked hard at the Yakuts.

"Well men, if you are sure," he paused because he certainly didn't want to lose his best men.

"There's a local boy who has been working with the Colonel. He will go with you. He has a route that hasn't been tried or tested by one of us but nor has it been by the enemy."

Both Aysen and Kaskil began gathering their gear.

8

Valentin Ivanovich Gavrilov was from Augustovo.

He had no memory of his father who had fought and died in the war against the Japanese, in 1905. Valentin, who hated to be called Valia, was 12 years old and was waiting impatiently to turn 14 when he would be accepted as a junior cadet in Vilna's Yunker school. He would go on to the military academy of Vilenskoe. His mother said she always knew her sons would have this destiny, but she cried each time Valentin mentioned he wanted to fight and die for Mother Russia. *Why not live for your own mother instead*, she would sniffle.

Valentin's older brother, Fyodor, was already about to graduate from Vilenskoe and was applying for a commission with the Guards. Their eldest brother Alexander had died at Tannenberg, he had been a lieutenant with the 22nd Infantry, the same Division as their father, who once was a captain in the Battle of Mukden.

Valentin wasn't scared of dying. In fact, his brother Fyodor, who was the bravest person he knew, would say that you had to die one day, and it was better to die for Mother Russia. Valentin agreed completely. He was going to apply for a commission in the Guards, like Fyodor, just as soon as he finished his cadetship.

Initially, the Colonel was surprised when Valentin had volunteered to get through the German cordon and deliver a message to Headquarters in Grodno. But this enterprising 12 year old had managed to slip into the forest with a message from Supply saying they were unable to move past hostile fire to reach the trapped Russian 10th. So, he had already proven his courage and ingenuity. Eventually, the Colonel had agreed to send him through to Headquarters.

Valentin was deeply familiar with the Augustovo forest and the surrounding lakes. For years, he and his mates had hunted for boar or roe deer while pretending to hunt for bison or moose or even a wolf. For the most part, they just caught corncrakes and white storks, which were too little to eat anyway.

He wasn't happy that the two riflemen were also coming with him, but the Colonel had handed *him* the letter for General Sievers, so it all worked out well in the end. Besides, Valentin had a reputation to uphold. He was proud of the fact that he had been a runner for the Russian forces in September last year when they went head to head in a battle on the Vistula River. He even had souvenirs: a pickelhaube and a Gew rifle with ammo and a pair of leather marching boots from a dead German! The boots were too big, but he stuffed them with straw. Besides, that was how most Russians wore boots in winter.

That morning, February 19, he led the way through the forest. The two strange Siberians were surprisingly silent behind him. The three of them had set out before dawn and were headed northeast through the woods, keeping Lake Serwyn to their right and the village of Tobolovo to their left.

They had been walking for two, maybe three, hours.

The snow underfoot squelched occasionally and the occasional dump of heavy ice and powder from the larch and fir trees made a soft thud.

As they came up to a rise, he saw the Siberians slink into the undergrowth and load their rifles. He paused and crouched low.

Listened.

Nothing.

The flutter of misty wind drifts curled about the crest of the rise. One of the Siberians shuffled even lower, elbows sunk in the snow with his eye glued to the steel sights of his rifle. Valentin could hear nothing but there was something about the rifleman that reminded him of a fox.

They had about 100 kilometres to go so Valentin didn't want to stop and start continually.

After a few minutes, he began pulling himself out from behind the bush and that is when he heard them.

Germans.

He pushed himself back down into the undergrowth. To his left was the Siberian with his rifle fixed and ready, to his right he saw the shine of a long sharp dagger in the hand of the other Siberian.

Neither of them moved or even looked towards Valentin.

He could hear the soldiers' voices getting louder and he could smell the stale scent of tobacco. He drew his own dagger from his belt.

And waited.

The crunch of boots across the snowy ridge up ahead paused. German voices chatted on amiably and one laughed.

They sounded young. Valentin did not move and it was as if the Siberians had completely disappeared. *When are they going to attack the enemy?* wondered Valentin as he contemplated charging and killing one of the Germans just ten metres away. He tried not to think about how he had never killed a human being before. Valentin thought about Fyodor and what he would do, but he couldn't seem to concentrate. His mind was filled with thoughts of his mother and the way she would pray and kiss the icon of The Lady of Sorrows.

The crunch of boots.

A flicked cigarette.

Someone coughed.

Then the punch of footfall moving back down the other side of the rise.

Valentin realised he was holding his breath and looked across at the Siberian with the rifle who continued to remain absolutely still. Valentin turned his head. The other Siberian was no longer there. He looked ahead to the rise and there he saw him on his belly, alongside a rocky outcrop, watching the descent of the Germans.

A short time passed before the boy and the Riflemen moved on.

Later, when the watery sunlight seemed to be slipping and their legs were aching with trudging through thigh-high snowdrifts, they decided to rest. The two men and the boy had found a section of thick entangled tree roots which served as a shelter.

"We could have killed those Germans," said Valentin sullenly. He'd had quite a lot of time to consider the heroic drama that could have been.

The Siberians seemed to ignore him and dug through their packs for rations of dried fish. Valentin wished he had some venison jerky, but he took an onion and ate the fish along with the Siberians.

"That is not our task," said Kaskil softly as he took a swig from his canteen.

"Where are you from?"

Kaskil smiled at the non sequitur, "Russia. And you? Ahh, you are from Poland."

The two Siberians chuckled quietly.

"I am Russian. My father was a captain with the 22nd Infantry!" Valentin spoke vehemently as he broke off some black bread and chewed.

Then out of his pack, he pulled a slim book with a dark green cover. He opened it to a well-worn page and proceeded to read. The Yakuts watched the forest around them.

After a few minutes, the boy spoke, as if in answer to a question, "I am reading poems by Tolstoy." And to make his point as clear as possible to the Siberian Riflemen, who did not seem Slavic at all, "He is a Russian. Like me."

Kaskil took the small volume from Valentin and looked at the name on the flyleaf: *Ivan Sergeyevich Gavrilov.*

The boy pointed to the faded ink signature, "This book was my father's but now it is mine."

And then, holed up in the forest with the two eternal enemies of Russia, Germany and winter, the boy recited quietly and deliberately, as if measuring out careful footsteps:

We were slashed with sharp scythes.
They scattered us in the middle of a meadow.
They separated us far apart from one another

There is no defence for us …

Valentin paused and concentrated hard on the cross-hatching of tree roots and undergrowth that protected them.

In our eyes, there are black crows
In our eyes, eclipsing the stars …

He paused and then rushed to the end.

Oh eagle eagle hear out lamentations
Strike them from the heavens
So that they are strewn about
So that upon the wide steppe
The wind disperses them far far away.

He couldn't help himself and a smile stretched broad across his smudged face.

Kaskil placed a hand on Valentin's shoulder. Warmth and love and protection for Mother Russia flooded the boy's body as if the Yakut had sent a river of courage through him.

Then he heard Aysen speak for the first time, "Tolstoy fought in a war, just like your father and just like you."

Valentin blinked back sudden tears and sat quietly alongside the Riflemen.

Not much later they pulled on their packs and slunk their rifles over their shoulders. Valentin was finding the Gew rifle a little heavy to carry but he would never give it up. It would be a couple more hours before they arrived in Fracki and so they pushed onwards as the light began to fade.

In the end, it took two days to walk out of the forest, get to Fracki, cut across to Belarus and arrive at Grodno. They encountered a few patrols but the track the boy had devised led them well away from the German blockade. When they rested, Valentin talked quietly and only to Kaskil, who humoured the young boy with stories about the first Cossacks who were brave enough to enter Yakut country some 400 years ago. Valentin was particularly interested in the urasy, the conical tents, which Kaskil told him the Yakuts would use in summer during their hunt for bear. The bounty of food and fur.

The boy didn't believe Kaskil when he told him that some of these Yakut tents could fit more than 100 people inside, but he kept his doubt to himself.

Besides, he loved tents in the summer.

On the evening of February 21, they scrambled down from a Supply truck, after hitching a ride into Grodno, and followed the driver's directions to Headquarters. The letter with Colonel Belolipetsky's seal got them into the General Sievers' office but only to be told that it would be delivered when the General was free.

It was the boy who surprised them.

Valentin stood toe to toe with the secretary and said he would not relinquish the letter until the General himself took it from his hands. The secretary looked at the stinking Siberians with their slanted eyes and filthy hair and thought it better not to argue.

He then left the room, and the men and the boy waited.

After a while, they heard a commotion beyond the doors and then General Sievers stood before them. His thinning hair and fashionable moustache seemed a disappointment to the two men and the boy who had risked their lives to deliver a message of such urgency.

Valentin handed the letter from the Colonel to the General, who tore it apart and read it closely.

"You have come from Colonel Belolipetsky? How is that possible?"

"We walked, sir," Aysen spoke slowly.

"Walked? Through the enemy lines?" He looked closely at the men and the boy.

Then the General said decidedly, "It's too late. I'm afraid Belolipetsky's men have surrendered to the enemy."

"No!" the boy's shout ricocheted around the room. "They would never surrender!" Valentin looked around desperately at the Yakuts who were still and watchful. The 12 year old spoke urgently, "The Colonel has sent us to tell you they need help! Send help sir —"

"Get this ragamuffin out of here!" General Sievers commanded.

His intelligence was that Russian forces were now being mobilised to protect Warsaw. Therefore, Russian troops needed to fall back.

How the hell did Belolipetsky's men get left behind? Sievers wondered angrily.

Belolipetsky was a rogue and his popularity irritated Sievers. He also knew that Colonel Belolipetsky would never surrender.

Let honour be his last breath, thought Sievers dispassionately.

"There has been *no* surrender," Aysen spoke quietly and directly to General Sievers.

"Who the hell are you? State your name and rank! You — you could be spies or worse!"

Kaskil spoke up, "Siberian 3rd Rifle Division. Now with the 10th Army, sir. My cousin Lance Corporal Aysen Manchari. I am his cousin, Kaskil Manchari."

The General looked at them and then asked, "Buryat?"

"Yakut, sir."

"Ah," the General seemed to be pleased with his guess. "And this thing?"

"One of the locals, sir, from Augustovo —"

"My father was a captain in the 22nd Infantry," Valentin's thin chest seemed to expand.

Aysen placed his hand on the boy's shoulder.

The General glanced at them once more, then instructed his secretary to have the Yakuts billeted until further orders were delivered. Without another look, and knowing that his decision to not send help was the right one, Sievers strode out of the office.

Chapter 3

March — April 1915

Lieutenant Efron had arrived 30 minutes early. He had packed for the long-haul east, glad the bitter winter was thawing but worried his leaving Moscow coincided with the very day his wife, Marina, was returning from St Petersburg.

He was to report to Captain Chudov to assist with the removal of POWs from Belorussky Station, recently renamed Alexander Station, and march them across town to Kursky then escort them east. Efron was quite pleased that at last he would be involved in something a little more interesting than the endless drill and training he had to oversee in barracks.

Efron pushed through the throng outside the station; horses, carriages, electric trams, pedestrians and troops were swarming across Tverskaya Zastava Square. In the last couple of months, as Russia's successes and advances gave way to failures and retreats, Efron had noticed the growing tension in the streets of Moscow and heard that it was worse in St Petersburg. He had written to Marina a number of times urging her to come home and care for their daughter who lived with his sisters in their apartment while he was assigned to barracks. He was worried about Marina, for so many reasons.

He saw his platoon assembled alongside others to the left of the station. He made his way towards the batches of men smoking and talking in various states of incorrect uniform. It was getting harder and harder for lieutenants to get uniform supply; including adequate footwear, the gymnastyorka and the peaked cap. Then on the other hand he was grateful that the young recruits were no longer involved in the time-consuming task of sewing their own uniforms and making their own boots.

"Lieutenant Efron, of the 56th Reservists, reporting for duty, sir."

Captain Chudov's florid complexion and stout body belied his reputation as a disciplined officer who would not hesitate to use harsh punishment on any of his men who did not serve with feverish nationalism. Chudov had encountered Efron a number of times and was impressed with his love of Mother Russia as well as his frustration in being diagnosed with tuberculosis which precluded him from service at the Front.

Chudov nodded acknowledgment and then addressed all officers gathered about him, "As you know we are to march the POWs through the streets of Moscow to Kursky Railway Station. From there we will be guarding the POWs to Perm, at the base of the Ural Mountains."

Chudov looked beyond the lieutenants to where their various sergeants were milling about the platoons, "Your men are to be alert and on guard at all times. This is the enemy and they will take any opportunity to steal our weapons, take our lives and rape our women!"

The Captain's cold grey eyes beneath red whiskery brows searched the faces of his lieutenants until Efron believed wholeheartedly that Marina, his daughter, and his sisters would be safer here in Moscow than anywhere near this moving plague of POWs. Besides, the prisoner camps in Perm would make them regret being captured.

"But remember, they are prisoners of war." Chudov added, "As such, must be afforded the treatment outlined by the Hague rules."

The officers nodded to indicate they were well versed in the regulations.

A whistle screamed from within the station.

"Right. The train on arrival will be emptied and cleared of the wounded, troops on furlough, citizens and refugees." The captain seemed to spit this last category out of his mouth as if every patriotic Russian should die fighting the enemy rather than become a refugee. It was no secret that Moscow was being over-run with refugees, their tents and their begging.

"Then we are to move the POWs off the train and assemble them here in the Square. Loaded guns and mounted bayonets at all times! Questions?" Chudov looked away from the officers and into the grand Renaissance railway entrance with its stunning two floors of arched windows, roaring high chimneys and ornate stucco above the gates.

Whether there were questions or not, Chudov had no interest.

2

At that very moment, Nurse Jula Stolinski who had been travelling with the wounded soldiers on the train pulling into Belorussky Station, was relieved the ordeal was over. Since they had left Warsaw she had spent her days moving among the wounded and the sick, making sure they were not in need of water or more blankets or assistance to use the filthy latrines. It had taken them four days of travelling from Warsaw to Minsk then on to Smolensk and finally Moscow.

Sometimes, she thought of her sweetheart Hussar, with his sharp cheekbones and smoky eyes. He had been convalescing from a shrapnel wound to his shoulder and arm but, still, they had managed to find a place for lovemaking. Fierce and passionate. Jula had nursed him back to health and now he was gone — back into the jaws of battle.

Meanwhile, her sister had already moved to Moscow and urged Jula to join her. Rumours were now circulating that Warsaw would soon fall to the Germans. The four-day journey had been brutal for everyone and at one point Jula, herself, had contracted a fever. But the doctor had given her a tincture, which tasted mostly of French brandy, and it had helped her into a deep sleep and afterward, she did feel refreshed. Perhaps it was just exhaustion.

The brakes screeched, the train shunted and then shrieked to a final stop. Steam and smoke filled the carriage even though she had closed the windows securely, before arrival. The men were stirring, those who could, and those in charge were issuing instructions to soldiers, doctors and nurses. Jula leaned across one soldier who was still sleeping and peered through the dirty window to the platform of Belorussky Station.

She had never seen so many people.

Women in long dresses and gloves and ostrich feathered hats, men in beautifully cut suits and waxed whiskers with gleaming pocket watches. Infantry troops sat or stood about with rifles and open coats and cigarettes at jaunty angles from their mouths. A wave of dark-skinned people swept by in colourful headscarves and homespun coats, carrying large parcels that appeared to contain their entire lives, alongside them ran children rickety and bawling.

Already the wounded from the carriages next to them were being unloaded. Stretcher after stretcher glided past, carried by orderlies; then men with bandages and crutches and slings were assisted by nurses. Jula pulled back away from the window.

From her own carriage, they were hauling the wounded off one by one through the narrow corridor of beds, passing the maimed, sick, ambulatory or stretchered out the doorway to orderlies waiting on the station. At last, Jula grabbed her own small suitcase and exited the carriage.

"Nurse!"

She looked across to the elderly doctor beckoning her into Carriage 3.

"Assistance please!"

Everyone had been told to avoid Carriage 3 because typhus was contagious.

She paused, but only momentarily. And then she handed her suitcase to one of the nurses and ran along to the doctor, but he had already moved back inside the infectious carriage. She stood on tiptoe peering into the fetid darkness beyond the doorway.

All of a sudden, he reappeared and held out his hand to help her climb up.

His eyes had the kindness of a grandfather.

"There are just a few soldiers here who need our help."

He was already tying a rudimentary mask across his mouth and nose.

Surely, he has not been wearing this for the past four days, Jula wondered to herself. He handed her a similar napkin and she began pulling and tugging it across her own face and securing the ends.

Inside was quiet and still.

The blinds were drawn but the sunlight slicing through the chilly platform station found tears and holes to light up particles of dust and disembodied mounds beneath grey blankets. The doctor pointed to a small body that she thought was dead. Then she re-alised the soldier was alive and his Asiatic eyes were watching her calmly.

"Hello, I'm Nurse Stolinski. I will be helping you off the train —"

"He needs to be moved to Lefortovo, Military Hospital," the doctor said.

Jula had no idea where this hospital was in Moscow and didn't know whether the doctor was telling her this information or the typhus victim.

"Can you tell me your name?" she asked.

She thought she heard *Aysen* but his lips did not seem to move.

"Where are you from, Aysen?" But he had closed his eyes and turned his head away from her.

She took his pulse and felt his forehead. Instead of a fast heart rate and signs of fever, she was surprised at his quietude. Now the orderlies were lumbering into the carriage and moving out the poor souls who had not survived the journey. Jula got up to help the few who had made it; some were still rattling in their febrile thin bodies, murmuring for something to stop the pain in their bones and joints. Their putrid breath made her realise that homemade alcoholic concoctions that sent them into the arms of Morpheus were all that was offered for the insufferable train journey to Moscow.

Jula had seen cases of typhus in Saint Stanislaus Hospital. Her superiors had explained that it was transmitted by lice and that the uniforms of the infected soldiers should be stripped and washed in boiling water. They tried their best but many of the laundry workers avoided collecting, let alone washing, the uniforms of the infectious. The fever of the typhus victims would rage over 40 degrees and their bodies were covered in a nasty red rash. Delirium, body pain, the sweats and, then after about three weeks, death. Those who pulled through were few.

As she stepped off the train the orderlies passed down the soldier on the stretcher to whom she had been speaking. He opened his strange dark eyes and looked up at her. Without another thought she placed her hand on his blanketed shoulder and walked ahead briskly to where the entourage of the wounded was moving — beyond the hot throng of porters and passengers and infantrymen and refugees, not to mention the small portable mountain of bags and baskets and boxes being dragged along the platform. Jula then spied the trucks waiting to take her and the typhus-infected soldier to Lefortovo, Military Hospital.

3

Efron watched a petite sonsy red-haired nurse walk purposefully across the square to where trucks were being loaded with the wounded and sick soldiers.

While they had been waiting for the station to clear, Efron and the other lieutenants had spoken to their corporals and their platoons about the orders. Everyone knew they were to escort the POWs east but hadn't known it would be Perm. The men had mumbled about the long train ride ahead and Efron had ignored them. Besides, it was sure to be longer than anticipated, with the stoppages and breakdowns. The POWs had already been processed in Warsaw and registered at Kozhukhovo before they made their journey into Moscow, so at least the tedious paperwork had been completed.

For the POWs themselves they had been travelling further and further east into enemy territory, the vast interminable countryside was going to become ever more expansive as they moved across Russia and into the Ural Mountains.

The wide platform of Belorussky Station had been expanded a few years back in the anticipation of war and was filled to overflowing with hundreds of POWs.

Gefreiter, the term for the German foot soldier came unbidden into Efron's mind.

Some still sported the leather pickelhaube, but most wore uniforms in disarray with the brass buttons gone or tarnished and the red piping no longer visible under mud and grime. Some wore greatcoats despite the fact that it was well into spring.

When the station emptied one of the Captain's assistants dashed across to where the company of Reservists were waiting and spoke hurriedly to Chudov.

"FORWARD, MEN!" Captain Chudov cried as if they were about to launch an attack on the enemy.

Minutes later, he was bellowing orders to both the Russian soldiers, who had escorted the POWs from Warsaw, and to the Moscow Reservists, who would soon relieve them of this burden. Already, Efron noticed, despite Hague rules, the German officers were being singled out and treated with indifference rather than abuse, which was how the rank and file POWs were treated.

The prisoners were haggard and wary but what hit Efron was the stench that seemed to hang off them. It smelled of defecation, vomit and despair. In the square, the German officers were put at the head of the march and the 300 or so motley crew of *Gefreiter* moved into formation behind them. Efron, his platoon and all the other Russian Reservists ordered to guard the march were stationed along the sides of the phalanx, with bayonets fixed and rifles ready.

Chudov said something to one of the German officers who seemed particularly decorated, Efron watched as the German then turned and called down the ranks of POW countrymen behind him: "*VOR-WÄRTSMARSCH!*"

There was something in the way this German officer lifted his chin and stared high above the sea of men behind him that told Efron, and the other Russians, that despite appearances they were not a conquered people.

As they set off, Efron heard the crunch of their boots in lockstep as something vaguely menacing.

The march took the POWs along the Boulevarde Ring, which was once Moscow's ramparts built in the 16th Century to keep the Tartars out. This route curved towards the Kursky Railway Station. Meanwhile, Russian civilians stood beside the road and watched, impassively. Here in their city was the pathetic parade of German invaders who attempted to take their beloved Motherland and kill their heroic soldiers.

Mothers in headscarves stood beside their thin children and hard face men, as the German POWs, marching in step, passed by. Some onlookers spat, some pointed and grimaced but most watched on silently.

This was Moscow — after all — with the red obdurate Kremlin.

One hundred years ago after the Battle of Borodino, and immortalised in Tolstoy's *War and Peace*, Napoleon had marched into their city and installed himself in their Kremlin. But that night, Muscovites set the city alight and abandoned it to the invader. The next day Napoleon dragged his army back to France through a zero winter. Europe's greatest conqueror could not take their city.

So Muscovite shop keepers and factory workers, doctors and lawyers, tram drivers and street sweepers, women and men, children and elderly stopped to watch these filthy beleaguered POWs pass by.

An elderly woman, hooped over and gnarled, pushed through the onlookers until she was a metre or so from the lice-ridden prisoners marching by. When the last POW moved on, she stepped out and threw the contents of her bucket over the road upon which they had marched.

Dirty dishwashing water sloshed and slewed, behind them.

On they trooped through the inviolable power of Moscow.

At the eight-storey high Afremov Building, an impressive Art Nouveau skyscraper, the POWs and their guards turned left towards the Kursky Railway Station.

Efron was proud of his city with its architecture and grandeur; his people with their belief in Russia for Russians; and his platoon with their determination to protect their nation from the marauding enemy. It was as if the Reservists led by Efron himself had gone into the Front, plucked these savages from the battlefield and marched them all the way to Moscow.

The façade of the Kursky Railway Station came into view, grand and foreboding with its marble edifice and Doric columns soaring above the two-storey high entrance.

Efron had never travelled further than Koktebel, a beach in the Crimea where he met Marina. So, he had to admit, a part of him was filled with the excitement of seeing more of Russia in the train ride east to Perm.

Like every railway station in Russia, Kursky was packed beyond bursting with cartloads of covered supplies lining up patiently outside the station. Indeed, queuing had become a national occupation. The railway officials seemed to have no authority whatsoever and mayhem ruled supreme. The POWs were herded onto a platform while Chudov roared at whatever bureaucrat got in his way. As this was happening, there were civilians and refugees, from Poland and Belarus and Lithuania and Armenia and Georgia and Serbia, all desperately attempting to board any train heading east or northwest.

Efron watched as the train from St Petersburg pulled in and then disgorged with passengers and infantry and refugees and cargo; while at the same time, desperate travellers attempted to haul themselves on board.

It was pandemonium.

Army suppliers were dragging their cargo onto certain trains only to be pulled off by other personnel. Arguments erupted and announcements were constantly made and updated and overruled.

The POWs looked on in disbelief.

Efron had heard about the German efficiency and organisation, he imagined they had never seen anything like this.

"Sergei!"

Efron knew it was Marina even before he turned around.

"Sergei!"

He was immediately torn. He didn't want Chudov or the other officers and men to see him greeting his wife on a railway platform as if he was Pushkin's Eugene Onegin clutching the beautiful Tatyana, but on the other hand, he had longed for Marina's return for the past three months.

He blushed as he moved towards her.

"Marina," his voice sounded more subdued than he meant and already her face was a moving spring sky — first brilliantly lit and then covered with shadows.

"At last." Efron returned her kiss, "You have come home!"

It was then that he saw, standing directly behind, that woman.

Marina swung around and grabbed Sofia Parnock's wrist, "Yes Sofia has been so unwell, we thought it best to come home."

Efron ignored the pale-faced woman with her bulging brown eyes and looked intensely into Marina's coquettish face, "How was your sister? How is her husband and will they be returning to Moscow soon?"

"Oh yes, Anastasia and Boris are coming back. How is —"

"Ariadna misses you," as he named their daughter he looked sternly at the woman standing as his wife's sentry.

He had heard rumours about what they had been up to and even his sister-in-law had written revealing her disquiet but still ... he could not believe it. Of course, like everyone he knew that the Russian upper class was fully immersed in the sexual liberation of their times, and, the Tsvetaevas were from a more well to do lineage than the Mandelstams. But Efron also knew that his need for Marina was enormous and she wrote to him every other day, always affirming that their love would endure everything. He and Marina had been inseparable from the very day they had met strolling along the Black Sea, she 18, he 17, where he plucked a carnelian stone from the shoreline and handed it to her as if the burnt orange nugget was a diamond itself.

Just at that moment, the POWs were being made to shuffle towards the train. Efron realised Marina must have disembarked from the very train that would now take him and the POWs east.

A stab of pain ran through his heart and for a fraction of a second he thought he would throw himself at her feet and beg her to hold on to him, as a mother might her only child so that the train would pull out without him.

"Are you leaving? Where are you headed, Sergei?"

Her face looked genuinely worried but that was how she was: full of love and hate and desire and resistance and hunger and disdain, all at once. He had loved her the first sun-drenched day he had met her.

"I ... we ..." he looked towards his corporal and men pushing POWs into the carriages usually assigned to horses or cattle.

"I have to go," Efron said abruptly. "I am delivering this lot east. I will be back home soon."

Marina caught his sleeve as he added, "I need you, Marina, I —"

"I know," she interrupted him. "I will be here."

And then he was swept up into the great heaving mass of bodies and found himself strangely comforted by the job he must do over the next few weeks.

4

The Military Hospital in the old palaces of Lefortovo was surrounded by a wild and overgrown garden. She had only been there a week but already Nurse Jula Stolinski was grateful her surname was more Belarusian than Polish. People in this strange city of Moscow seemed ambivalent about the fate of the Polish Russians. When she first arrived from Warsaw, she had no idea if she would ever feel at home. Everything felt foreign. Often, she would have to ask her colleagues to repeat what they had just said, so bewildering was their accent. Her sister who worked for the Army Administration had organised a permanent position for Jula. The fact Jula was a nurse, qualified and experienced, made her more than eligible for the Military Hospital in Lefortovo Park. The nursing quarters, barracks, Army Administration, Church of St Peter and Paul as well as the petite chapel, of Our Lady of the Holy Virgin, made up Jula's world of Moscow so far.

Even though it was still early spring and a lot cooler than Warsaw, some of the wounded were brought out to the enclosed garden behind the surgical rooms. There they would either sit in wicker chairs or lay on temporary mattresses placed on rusty bedframes that seemed to have been outdoors since the start of the war. Jula had not seen a practice such as this at Saint Stanislaus Hospital. One of the older doctors, who before the war had worked in a hospital on the Black Sea, had said this was best convalescent practice.

Jula was instructed to clean out the wounds when the soldiers arrived, even if the tag tied to the soldier's arm indicated that wound cleansing had already been done. She would lay gauze soaked in saline over the worst injuries or simply leave the wound open to the elements, as instructed. Jula, like all the nurses, had little to give the soldiers for their pain. There was morphine, but that was kept for the worst cases. The doctors in surgery used chloroform and ether but the nurses had little other than water, salt and words.

The wards in Moscow's Military Hospital in Lefortovo Park were originally grand palace rooms. The cold morning light would pour in through the extravagant stained-glass windows and when the men opened their eyes they would look up at the froth and fancy of Baroque murals, painted high on the domed ceiling.

Regardless, the cots were packed alongside each other, row upon row upon row.

There was no running water in these wards. Much of the nurses' fatigue was caused by running up and down the innumerable stairs to fetch and carry. On the top floor were those with infectious diseases and shell shock; while the surgery rooms, kitchens and laundry were on the ground floor. What made no sense at all, to Jula, was that the floor between contained mostly the wounded who would have to be assisted to climb down the staircase daily in order to reach the convalescent area outside.

There were many who were too ill and too close to death to do anything but lay in their cramped cots. No one called out, except some of those on the top floor, but everyone knew that the shelling had affected their minds.

Part of the nurses' duties included taking the dead across to the cemetery. The orderlies were supposed to do this job, but if they couldn't be found the superiors would ask two nurses.

Jula didn't mind too much.

They would carry the stretcher between them and cross the narrow towpath until they got to the tented area behind the chapel. There they would leave the body with the grave workers — always women and always speaking in a tongue Jula could not understand. One of the other nurses told her they were Romani women from the Caucasus whose men were Cossacks fighting in the war.

This made Jula think about her own Hussar, who wasn't hers. Where was he now? And even though she had written to his Regiment and told him where she was headed she had no faith that a letter from him would find her.

"How did you manage to get down here to the garden?" Jula stood over the small, dark Yakut man she had assisted at Belorussky Station just over a week ago.

Patients from the infectious disease ward were not meant to be brought outside but she was not surprised he had made his way unnoticed to the outdoor convalescent area.

Aysen smiled up at her and stretched his legs wide.

"I might have to report you," she grinned, her dimples appearing.

He responded quietly, "Outdoors, even in Moscow, is good."

Jula agreed but made a show of tucking in the grey army blanket about his legs and chest, "You are still recovering so you must be careful. The doctors ..." she buttoned his greatcoat across his chest, at least he had dressed warmly, "... said you were very lucky to have pulled through. Typhus kills many soldiers."

He had a way of looking at her that made her feel as if her heart was slowing down.

"Any more headaches? Pain in your muscles or joints?"

He looked away from her questions and into the wild mass of trees and overgrowth.

"No vomiting ... the rash gone ...?"

She knew he was getting better day by day. Even though she was working with the wounded she had ventured upstairs a few times to visit Aysen in the week they had both been here. She didn't know why, but she thought of him as someone who knew her.

The doctors at first feared more would arrive with typhus and that they would have to quarantine a section of the hospital for an endemic onslaught. News had reached Moscow that typhus was wiping out much of Serbia and medics were already jumpy about carrying whole trainloads of the infected through Russian towns. However, in Aysen's case, the doctors were surprised and curious that he had already survived the worst of the fever and delirium well before he had arrived in Moscow. The tag tied to Aysen's arm had indicated that his cousin had brought him from Grodno to Minsk with permission from General Sievers and that he was to be taken to Moscow's Military Hospital. The orderlies who had boarded the train in Grodno said that Aysen, his cousin and a kid, had snuck through the German lines to bring vital information to Head-quarters.

Apparently, he was some kind of hero.

Every time she heard about the Germans in Polish Russia Jula's heart raced. She couldn't believe how close they were getting to Warsaw! She had left behind friends and neighbours and wondered if they would ever get away.

"My wife is coming to Moscow."

She had been daydreaming and had forgotten Aysen and the other patients sunning themselves in the garden. She looked about her but luckily the other nurses were too busy to have noticed.

Jula bent down to straighten up Aysen's blanket, "Really? How lovely," and it somehow made her feel winsome for her Hussar.

"It was in her letter. She has already left Ussuriysk."

Jula didn't know where that was but Aysen had told her he was a Yakut from the Lena Basin. There were no maps to be found these days, but she had a vague idea that it was high in Siberia. He had also told her about his wife and how she would read books from the local library.

She sounds smart, thought Jula, *but how could that be if she is from Siberia?* Everyone knew that only people in the cities could read and write, but Jula had noticed once or twice when she had gone to see him, that Aysen had been reading the well-worn newspapers that got passed from patient to patient.

"Well. It will be very hard to get on a train. You know, the newspapers are all reporting that the bottleneck is caused by civilians filling up the trains — while soldiers and supplies are left waiting on the platform."

She stopped herself abruptly. What had caused her to be so insensitive? Here was a soldier who had left his beloved homeland and travelled for God knows how many weeks to defend Polish Russia against the Germans.

She bit down on her lower lip.

Aysen said nothing but reached out and held her hand. His skin was warm and his fingers strong.

She was surprised, not by his kindness, but by the tears she had to blink back.

Sayaana's letter had been delivered to him yesterday. Aysen thought he was still hallucinating but when he tore it open and read the first few lines, he realised Kaskil must have written and told her where he was.

Aysen had little memory of what happened after the battle around the Masurian Lakes. Just flashes of making it through the German lines with his cousin and a boy, whose name escaped him, then arriving at Grodno in a truck. He also had a slightly deranged recollection of talking to a General begging him to send reinforcements to those they had left behind in Augustovo Forest.

The General had refused.

In her letter, Sayaana told him that Kaskil had insisted Aysen be moved from the Regimental Aid Base in Grodno to Moscow, apparently the General agreed, and this was how his cousin had saved his life.

Sayaana's letter was nestled inside his shirt-tunic.

I am coming to you, Aysen, my love.
My father has booked my train ticket and I leave tonight.
I might even get there before my letter does!
I am coming to you.
Sayaana xx

Aysen stretched back in the chair, shut his eyes and smiled quietly up into the milky white sunlight of Moscow.

5

It had been over a week since Marina bumped into her husband at the train station and she was still finding it hard to settle back home after the three months in St Petersburg.

Strange times, Marina thought, as she looked out the grubby window of the landing. Her apartment, 6 Boris and Gleb Street in Old Moscow, was in sight of the Kremlin walls, but most days she didn't see them. Although, today, when spring coursed through her veins on the way home from shopping, she paused to look at the ancient red walls, a fortress inside a city.

A boarded-up heart.

Marina sighed, it had taken six and a half hours to get some of the provisions they were desperate for this week: black bread, onions, carrots, cabbage and a little milk.

It is getting harder, she thought, as she hefted her basket and continued up the stairs. Just the other day she had read in the newspaper that the queues were getting worse in St Petersburg as well. What about Moscow? Every day the lines were endless no matter how early she joined them. Shopkeepers were always saying that supplies coming into the cities were being blocked — meanwhile soldiers on leave were growling about the lack of provisions going out to the Front.

She felt her heart skip at the thought of her husband becoming undernourished. She loved his soft dark eyes, his poetic intensity and his abject devotion to her.

She also knew she should feel guilty, but she just felt tired.

Marina shoved the key in the door and was glad she had convinced Sofia to remain in her own apartment now they were back in Moscow.

On a rug in the living room, Ariadna and one of Efron's sisters were playing cards. They both looked up.

"Mama!" Marina's three year old held up her cards triumphantly, "Aunty teaching me Durak!"

Her wide eyes and dimpled smile made the fatigue in Marina's back fade and she thought, *I will never be like my mother, a dominating tyrant. No, my daughter and I are to be friends.*

She dropped her basket on the bench and sat down on the floor. Ariadna immediately climbed onto her lap and Marina looked closely at her cards.

"Hmm ... you know you are supposed to get *rid* of the cards ... to make Aunty lose, so you can win."

Efron's sister, Alena, was laying on her side, legs crossed at the ankles and one elbow propping up her hand of cards. She was 16 and had the softness of her brother but lacked his intensity. Marina enjoyed Alena's easy-going manner. Efron's other sister, Irina, also lived with them in this one-bedroom apartment.

"Irina not home yet?"

"Not yet," answered Alena and slammed down three or four cards on the pile.

"I hope she was lucky enough to get some fish." Marina gathered up four of the cards from Ariadna's fat little fist and plonked them on top of the pile, "I got the bread and a few carrots —"

"Yum! Carrots," interrupted Ariadna.

"Have you heard any more news?" Marina knew Alena was asking about Efron.

"No. No news," said Marina and pushed her nose into Ariadna's dark hair and felt her own restlessness fill the small apartment.

And not for the first time she thought, *I need space to write.*

It had been over a year since her second collection of poems had been published and she felt as if time was racing on without her. Even Efron had recently published his dear little monogram of poetry. What she really wanted to do was to break into the literary scene of St Petersburg, as Mayakovsky had.

Marina moved to the kitchenette to put away her meagre groceries. *To think, only a year ago, we had servants to do it all*, she thought, *not to mention nannies to take care of my daughter.* She dampened a tea towel and wrapped it around the black bread and popped it on the stove, still warm from this morning. The practicalities of life bored her.

Sofia had said that all concerns should be subordinate to writing.

Marina knew she was right. *Why should I feel guilty for doing what men before me and after me have and will always do*, she thought.

She and Sofia had visited the Dog a number of times and Marina loved the atmosphere and met composers and ballet dancers and poets and writers and actors. In the end, Marina had only caught up with Mayakovsky once or twice and had never set eyes on the elusive Akhmatova nor another poet she had heard a great deal about, Osip Mandelstam. Sofia, on the other hand, had decided early on that the Dog was a pretentious café and that they would do better staying in Anastasia's apartment on the canal and get on with their writing. Sofia was a wonderful translator of poetry, being a beneficiary of a liberal education.

Sofia pushed and challenged her in a way that Marina had never known before. Their lives were about writing, not domesticity. Of course, there were sparks between them but there was never ever boredom.

Marina sat in the kitchenette, warmed by the easing sunlight, and found herself thinking about Sofia's fingers tracing her damp naked body and the way she would slide her leg between Marina's so that she was forced to open. Right there, Marina's breath caught audibly in her throat.

She couldn't remember a time when she wasn't consumed by Sofia. She picked up her pen and began writing.

Where does such tenderness come from?
These aren't the first curls
I've wound around my finger —
I've kissed lips darker than yours ...

In St Petersburg, Sofia found it harder and harder to be out and about because of her health. So, in the end, they settled down to a routine of writing and reading in the morning, then a stroll in the afternoon that would more often than not end in coffee and cake at Baba Yaga Café. In the end, Marina agreed to return home to Moscow — Sofia had Graves' Disease and wanted to be near her doctors.

The kitchenette was just off the living room and her daughter's squeals punctured the quiet as Alena and Ariadna played on. It seemed everyone was used to Marina's ability to secrete herself away. The light was watery and fading with the onset of night. She sat at the table, pen and notebook before her.

The sky is washed and dark
(Where does such tenderness come from?)
Other eyes have known
And shifted away from my eyes.

She thought about Anastasia's welcome when they first arrived in St Petersburg. Her sister seemed un-comfortable, watching Sofia closely and asking her whether she kept in touch with her ex-husband. Sofia was not fazed but at the same time, Marina knew how vulnerable she was. Then there was that awkward mo-ment when her sister had said it's best if Marina sleeps with her (God knows where her husband Boris was sup-posed to sleep!) and for Sofia to take the sitting room. For God's sake, what was her sister thinking?

I went to St Petersburg to be free! To escape asphyxi-ating conformity, thought Marina. She bent her head to her notebook and wrote.

But I've never heard words like this
in the night
(Where does such tenderness come from?)
With my head on your chest, rest.

Marina sucked the end of her pen and gazed, without seeing, at the frugal kitchenette in which she sat. She had written to her sister about her nascent and exciting new affair with Sofia before they went to visit, she had spelled out the implications of her love.

Well, maybe she didn't quite spell it out — but why should she have to? This was the dawning of a new Russia! This was their time and she, for one, knew that the old rules could no longer apply. Well of course there had to be some things that still held true, as Efron would say, but those truths were only in poetry and art and music.

Marina wondered to herself why other people seemed to make everything so much more complicated than it had to be.

It's just attraction.

It's just a wildness of the heart that can't be tamed.

She wrote the last few lines slowly.

Where does this tenderness come from?
And what will I do with it? Young
Stranger, poet, wandering through the town,
You and your eyelashes — longer than anyone.

6

Pasternak stood on the platform in amongst the crowds and trolleys and felt his body sway and chug as if the ten-day rail journey east from Moscow would never end.

There had been heavy snow throughout March and its white thickness covered the red brick minarets on the Church of the Ascension, making it appear like frosted gingerbread. The Karma River flowed purposefully from the Ural Mountains in the distance, alongside the railway line, to eventually tip out into the Black Sea.

Pasternak took hold of his suitcase and looked around at the rather impressive Perm railway station. Naively he hadn't expected so much cosmopolitan bustle. There were soldiers and refugees and POWs; locals and out of towners and Russian ethnic minorities; sellers and traders and pickpocketers. He didn't really know what to expect but it certainly wasn't this colourful mayhem.

The journey out had been endlessly contemplative. Somehow, he felt immune to the cacophony of the other travellers. He stopped hearing the clacking of the train journey, the intermittent throaty screech of the brakes and the shrill whistle announcing Nizhniy-Novgorod, Kazan, Izhevsk and finally Perm. There was a part of him that could have gone on and on and on across the Siberian plains and eventually into Vladivostok. But he had given his word to the manager at the chemical factory, owned by the widowed millionaire Zinaida Rezvaya, that he would take up his kind offer of work. This would primarily be clerical duties for a factory that manufactured acetic acid, acetone and chloroform. Zbarsky, the manager, had written explaining he would be in Perm when Pasternak arrived and together, they would take the slow rail journey to the small village of Vsevolodov-Vilve, some 200 kilometres north.

As he moved towards the exit gates, Pasternak checked his coat pocket for Sibiryak's collection of short stories that he had been reading in preparation for his coming to Perm. In his other pocket, although he had no need to check, he had a book of Rilke's poems, which he more or less always carried about.

Mostly, though, he had been writing about *her* in his notebook, secure in his bag. His writing was filled with *her. She* was everywhere.

He felt he was at the crossroads of his life. Anna Akhmatova had rejected him out of hand and his plan to move to Perm with her to write and live had simply evaporated.

Who would have guessed? Obviously not he. Didn't she know that without him as a friend, lover and husband, their futures would be bleak, their writing meaningless?

He had believed they were each other's destiny.

A pain opened up in his heart and he realised he wanted to copy a fragment of one of her poems and send it back to her:

I don't think of you often at all,
I'm not interested much in your fate,
But the imprint you left on my soul
... won't fade.

Yes, this is what I will do, he thought calmly. This was it. She will hear me because she herself wrote these very words. She will recognise their truth. She will, at last, know our love cannot end.

Pasternak wondered why this plan sounded so right but at the same time, in the shadowy room of his heart, he knew he would not write this letter.

The wide-open face of the Railway Station clock indicated that it was 11. He looked around for a café to wait for Zbarsky who would not be here till noon. A tired old canteen presented itself to him as having the only outdoor seating and, after being enclosed in a train carriage for over a week, Pasternak lumbered across, sat down and gave his order.

A few minutes later he was sipping his sweet tea and wondering whether the borsch with sour cream and beef would actually contain meat. While he waited, he smoked a cigarette and looked upon the bustling city of Perm moving about its business at a frontier pace.

The façade of the railway station gleamed in the mid-morning sun; indeed, its 19th Century architecture painted in red, green, and white looked like a celebration. The busy waterways of the Kama River behind the railway station moved resources from the north and east into the anxious south and west of Russia.

What a town! thought Pasternak as he considered its metal, paper and phosphoric factories. A city with steamboats and trams and trains and carts pushing and shoving Russia to win the war. The borsch arrived and Pasternak picked up his spoon and dug in as the waiter returned with a small plate of dry black bread.

It was good.

When he had decided to make a genuine effort to support the war, he knew he wanted to go to the heart of Russia, to toil amongst the workers in a chemical factory. His father's solicitor had gently suggested Pasternak initially teach on-site, so that, like many factories, he would be a staff member offering courses in which any worker could enrol.

Initially, Zbarsky seemed flummoxed that a university graduate from such a distinguished Muscovite family would actually be coming all the way to Vsevolodov-Vilve and so he had offered his own home for accommodation and thought it important to mention that Perm, which was only 200 kilometres away, had an opera house. Pasternak accepted the manager's offer but indicated in his last letter that he would teach as well as work as a labourer in the factory so that his full skills could be utilised.

Pasternak tore the bread into slabs and sunk it into the soup and ate on.

Before long the borsch was finished. He wanted another bowl but lit a cigarette instead and called for a second glass of tea. Pasternak pulled out the Rilke poems. When he was just ten years of age, he met the great Bohemian poet who was brought to his home by Tolstoy.

His parents often had wonderful visitors. The handsome and sensitive Rachmaninoff who would play occasionally but never persuade Pasternak's concert pianist mother to perform; the diminutive Scriabin, who had enthralled young Pasternak and encouraged him to pursue a career in piano; and the erudite Shestov, who was the reason why Pasternak ended up studying philosophy in Germany.

He turned his attention to Rilke's poems which offered comfort with their focus on the permanency of objects. He preferred the muscularity of the German edition. After a while, Pasternak looked up and as he watched POWs spilling out into the square he thought, *we are all exiles.*

7

The German POW, Walter Schafer, had learned enough on the train ride from hell to last him a lifetime.

When he was first taken prisoner, outside Łódź back in November, he was secretly relieved. He had been ordered to join a small reconnaissance team, which had, except for himself, all been slain.

He didn't know why he was spared and for a long time afterward, he had no interest in his own survival. He longed for the bullet or piece of shrapnel with his name written on it.

As a POW he had gone for days and days and days without water or food or shelter when forced marched to Warsaw; he had endured the overcrowded train wagon carrying nearly 50 men with a stove in one corner and an infested latrine in another, throwing out the dead at various stations as they rambled from Warsaw to Minsk to Moscow; he had borne the humiliation of being paraded through Moscow from one train station to another, the peasants watching on in ignorant silence, and he had somehow survived the ten-day rail journey with its vermin and filth to this godforsaken town.

Some of the other German prisoners had told him they had heard the Russians would look the other way if they attempted to escape, but Walter knew it was the seduction of suicide speaking.

In Kazan, about three days into the journey heading east, the guard had rolled open the door of their wagon for the prisoners to climb down and collect the supplies organised by the Red Cross; most of the supplies had been so badly fleeced by the Russian rail workers that it was hardly worth the trouble, but Walter had clambered off anyway, grateful to be out of the fetid wagon while the train stopped.

It was then, Walter recalled, that one of the prisoners from his wagon scurried under the train and bolted across the train lines.

The Russian guarding them moved swiftly.

He leapt onto the iron coupling laid between the wagons.

Took aim.

Fired.

The escapee fell.

The Russian lowered his rifle and stood perfectly still for a moment, then he stepped back onto the platform and pointed to Walter and a prisoner beside him to go with him to bring back the dead POW.

No one looked at them as they trudged around the front of the train, jumped off the platform and crunched across the dirty snow to the deflated body of their dead countryman.

Walter felt nothing, he was done living a life that was no longer his.

Later when he was inside the wagon shunting ever east along with several hundred other POWs, he had heard that many Russian towns had no idea what to do with the influx of prisoners who often outnumbered the townsfolk.

Nothing surprised Walter, anymore.

The first 19 years of his life he had lived on the same farm where he had been born but in these last 12 months he had seen Berlin, where he reported for training; Polish Russia, where he nearly saw combat; Łódź to Warsaw, where he was made to march with other POWs through a freezing winter; Minsk to

Moscow by train, where many died but for some reason, he survived; and now on to the Ural Mountains.

He tried not to think about his mother with her warm hands always busy in the kitchen and who, for the most part, spoke French to him all the days of his life. As for Heike, his sweetheart from next door — well, as far as he was concerned, all promises were off. He had no hope left in his heart that he would ever see or hear from her again.

Mostly, Walter found the world bewildering.

He kept his distance from those German prisoners who were constantly plotting to escape or forever talking about the *Vaterland* and patriotism. Most of them, he noticed from their accents and the way they expressed themselves, were from wealthy or educated families.

Now that he was ensconced in Russia, love of the *Vaterland* seemed irrelevant.

At last, they arrived at their final destination.

"MOVE OUT! MOVE OUT!"

The Russian soldiers assigned to guarding the POWs yelled and banged the wagon doors, even though the prisoners themselves had no way of rolling open the doors from the inside. They had been sitting at the station, which someone had announced was Perm, for the past 20 or so minutes. Voices from the platform had subsided and Walter guessed the Russians in charge were just waiting to clear away the crowd before the POWs were herded out.

"EVERYONE OUT!"

When the doors opened, the wagon's putrid stench transformed into icy daylight. The men stood stunned, momentarily, until the prisoner closest to the doorway was hauled down onto the platform with a thump.

The other prisoners scrambled down as quickly as they could, some assisting those suffering from injuries and sickness. A thin, scruffy, and ill-dressed crowd began to grow on the platform as wagon by wagon along the railway track POWs disembarked.

"STAY IN YOUR ASSIGNED GROUPS!"

"ASSEMBLE TO THE RIGHT!"

"KEEP TO YOUR ASSIGNED GROUPS!"

Walter followed the men in front of him. The station was cold after the hot stinking wagon of the past ten days.

They were shunted through the railway station. A few locals stared openly at them and the women pulled their headscarves to cover their noses. The soldiers guarding the group to which Walter belonged seemed both lackadaisical and watchful. He did not doubt that the Russians would show no mercy to the POWs.

"HALT!"

Walter and the others in his group bumped to a stop outside the railway station, its lurid façade of red and green and white dazzled in the sun and made him think Perm must be deep in Central Asia.

He looked up at the clock on the domed frontage of the station and noticed it was noon. They were fed once a day. Walter and the others seemed to be thinking the same and looked about expecting a Supply cart to come by with some food and drink.

But time slowed down and after a while, the POWs began to slump about like filthy garbage filling up the railway square.

Walter's group was near a tired café and he noticed a tall young man, who could have been Walter's age, sipping his tea, smoking a cigarette and reading. There was a bowl of something in front of him.

Walter's mouth watered.

He couldn't put his finger on what was so odd, but then he realised the Russian was reading Rilke with a start.

In German.

We read the same poets to make sense of our lives, thought Walter, *and then we kill each other.*

The young Russian man reading Rilke, who was rather well dressed, stood up and paid the bill. Walter found this country to be unsettling. Up until this point he had thought of Russians as backward, dirt poor and ignorant. He knew they were viciously brutal, sometimes to each other and certainly to invaders. The Germans, on the other hand, were educated. Walter didn't know of any German who hadn't completed compulsory schooling. They were civilised and organised and disciplined.

It was curious though, that since Walter had been taken prisoner, he had met Russian soldiers who had gone to university and Russian poets who willingly joined the war to defend their nation. Russians had a type of religious devotion to their country as if she was a giantess made of flesh and blood.

Walter was drawn out of his quandary when a short stocky man appeared at the café and approached the young Russian who had been reading Rilke. This was followed by handshaking and kissing, they then moved off together to a horse-drawn cart just down from the café.

Walter wondered if he would ever be in control of his own destiny.

"FORWARD MARCH!"

The soldiers guarding the POWs pushed and shoved them into some sort of order, but the Germans themselves had a proclivity for keeping in file and so the several hundred shambolic prisoners marched out of the railway square and up into Pokrovskaya Ulitsa and through the main part of town where factories and shops and boarding houses seemed to shove up alongside each other. Down they marched through Kungurskaya Ulitsa, past an impressive synagogue and out beyond the town until a large group of them were corralled into an empty barn around which several log barracks had been hastily assembled.

They were then ordered to sit down.

Walter took in the smells of home as he sat amongst the manure and hay and rusted troughs. He had often worked alongside Heike and together they would help the neighbouring farm tend their dairy cows or dig potatoes. He shook his head and hoped the kaleidoscope of fractal memories would disappear. This world had no need of his sweetheart. Walter turned up his face to the white sunlight above and shut his eyes. He willed himself to think of nothing.

Around him, he could hear some of the prisoners grumbling about the Russian pigs who were guarding them and how they were always eating the POW supplies or selling them to other Russians. The prisoners were lucky to get whatever leftovers could be scrounged.

Walter didn't care.

Russian food was inedible anyway. Besides what would it matter if he starved.

8

Lieutenant Efron moved around speaking to members of his platoon who were guarding their assigned POWs. All he could see of this farm compound was a draughty barn and some log barracks.

Captain Chudov had let his officers know that, unsurprisingly, the soldiers replacing them had not yet arrived and so, after a ten-day train trip east, they were now expected to continue guarding the POWs.

The Supply carts hadn't met them off the train as planned, and he knew the POWs were hungry. Efron assumed the town was scrambling to meet the needs of this giant influx of newcomers.

On the long journey east, the captain had said that the POWs were exactly what was needed to ensure that the factories and mines could remain open while Russians were off fighting the war. A huge percentage of the Russian Army was made up of illiterate Russian peasants and factory workers, so it only made sense that these POWs would be put to use.

Efron wondered how long he would be expected to stay in Perm.

He called over his sergeant and asked him to bring back a report, quick smart, on what equipment existed within the barn and the barracks.

Efron would have been more inclined to stay on in Perm if he hadn't seen Marina on the Kursky platform the morning they were boarding the train.

She put a tremor through his heart.

"Sir," the sergeant was incredulous. "There are bare bunks — no blankets in the log barracks. Each has a stove. But in the barn, nothing. Straw only, sir."

Efron looked at him and realised his platoon had enjoyed Moscow and its comforts for too long.

"The barracks will be for the POW officers, as per Captain Chudov's instructions," Efron saw the sergeant's face fall. "The rest will be housed in the barn until they dig their own huts."

"Zemlyankas?" asked the sergeant in disbelief, he was a gnarly old thing with his dark whiskers and a missing right eye.

"Yes. Zemlyankas. It won't take them long. There's a birch forest across the field — look you can see it from here. That's a good start."

They were interrupted by the rumble of carts and when the POWs saw Supply approaching, they stirred to their feet.

"SIT DOWN! STAY WHERE YOU ARE!" screamed the sergeant who had also perked up at the sound of food.

Walter opened his eyes and looked beyond the approaching Supply carts to the wide-open fields and in the distance, he heard the rustle of birch trees as if they were impatient for spring.

9

Nearly 3,000 kilometres away, Trooper Gumilyov had been redeployed to the Russian 11th Army siege lines surrounding Austria's fortress town of Przemyśl.

While he rode his horse through the surrounding forest, he found himself thinking about the blue and yellow tit bird, and the way it flittered around the woodland as if it had time to spare. As a young boy, Gumilyov would sometimes watch these little guys soar sporadically through the sky, build a nest with great busyness and most interestingly, feed spiders to their chicks. Even in winter, these sturdy little perching birds would be completely undaunted by the cold. Their whistle chirp was throaty, they were hardy and indefatigable, *like Russians*, Gumilyov thought, and shifted his reins to let his horse walk on through the budding deciduous trees.

The Austrians had been preparing for the Russians to attack Przemyśl since the 1855 Crimean War.

So, little by little the Austrians had built their web.

At the centre of the web was the town of Przemyśl, surrounded by barracks, magazines and interconnecting roads; from this, nine forts spiralled out; then an infantry fortification wall encircled; followed by reinforced trenches as well as the construction of more barracks and more artillery placements. And then beyond the Przemyśl fortress, 41 entrenchments formed an outer defence line to this snare.

The Russians were the blue and yellow tit bird wanting to snatch the spider — the Austrians — in order to feed its chicks. This dangerous sticky web had to be crossed by the Russians if the Motherland was to have its morale fed and triumph restored.

Gumilyov knew this would be a greatly needed victory for Russia, not just because it would make easy access to Hungary and allow them control of the Carpathian Mountains but, more importantly, it would mean that the inordinate losses Russia had sustained, could be arrested.

Gumilyov allowed his horse to pause so he could listen to the tick and swish of the forest around him.

It was spring but the fortress at Przemyśl didn't know it. The Russian 11th had surrounded this stronghold for the past six months and no longer were the Austrians attempting to break out. After Russia's victory in the Battle of Galicia last year, the Austrians had been trapped in Przemyśl and left 160 kilometres behind enemy lines.

Indeed, those left behind in the besieged town were without hope.

A part of Gumilyov felt sorry for them.

But only a very small part.

He had seen action at Łódź, which later had been referred to in the newspaper as a *strategic withdrawal.* Gumilyov knew there was nothing strategic about it. Then he was in the debacle at Bolimów, where General Gurko, a name he would never forget, had masterminded the massacre of hundreds of thousands of his own Russian troops. The gas sent over by the Germans had failed to work and instead of allowing the Germans to retreat, the Russians had been ordered to attack.

The pain in Gumilyov's shoulder from the injury he had sustained would never leave him. At least it meant he got a few weeks off convalescing in Warsaw, nursed by a Rubenesque red-head.

Gumilyov softly pressed his heels to his horse and it walked on. He was glad for the forest and the quiet. His regiment had been sent along to Przemyśl to support the Kiev Hussar Division fighting under General Selivanov. Their orders were to outlast the Austrians cowering in their fortress until they surrendered or starved. Selivanov had ordered the Hussars, Cossacks, Cavalry and Dragoons to conduct reconnaissance to ensure the siege lines were not broken by either the blockade runners attempting to bring supplies in or Austrian desperados attempting to get out. Many of these hungry escapees had been either shot or taken prisoner.

Gumilyov had arrived in early March and been part of the successful attempt to break through the outer lines of defence. The blockade runners had ceased but not before those captured admitted that the morale within Przemyśl was rock bottom. Ammunition, food and water were dangerously low. Horses had been eaten.

Automatically Gumilyov patted the neck of his own mount.

Thirty thousand horses. *Hopeless*, he thought again. Przemyśl had been surrounded by the Russians since September last year. It was already turning out to be one of the longest sieges in military history.

Gumilyov abruptly pulled on his reins when he saw a rider with the distinct red breeches of his regiment, coming towards him through the forest.

Lieutenant Zheleznyak appeared.

"Sir!" Gumilyov's salute was resolute.

"At ease, Trooper."

Like most Russians, the lieutenant wore his peakless cap pushed back on his head. He seemed to respect his men, primarily because they were from the same class and educated at military school or university.

"So far nothing to report, sir," Gumilyov volunteered.

He didn't mind Zheleznyak, with his inflexibly waxed moustache. Most of the men sported a long moustache and played the role of the swashbuckling hero — dashing, reckless and brave. Hussars were great horsemen, hard drinkers and relentless womanisers, or at least, that's what they told each other. Part of the legend was of course what appealed to Gumilyov but whether it was his years abroad before the war or his loveless marriage or his intolerance of Russian command, he no longer was enamoured by the military.

"No doubt there may be more attempts to escape the garrison," responded Zheleznyak. They both glanced up in the direction of Przemyśl, despite it being obscured by the forest, "And the Austrians may well try to send more supplies."

Gumilyov doubted that very much, especially as one of the Austrians taken prisoner yesterday had admitted no more help would be coming.

The pounding of General Selivanov's guns could be heard in the distance.

"That'll be us smashing the inner line of defence!" announced Zheleznyak looking pleased with himself.

Gumilyov thought about the ground around Przemyśl; pockmarked earthworks riddled with barbed wire. Extraordinary the way men just clung on and on and on.

"Won't be long now, sir."

"That's right Trooper. We are evenly matched, or so intelligence says." Gumilyov watched Zheleznyak's face for any sign of irony. "After breaking through the line at Malkovise, we are all itching to put those poor bastards out of their misery."

Six days ago, Gumilyov had been part of the Russian thrust forward. They had bombarded the outer defence line of Przemyśl, at Malkovise, ceaselessly and without mercy. The Hussars and another cavalry then charged what was left of the retreating enemy.

It was a short fracas.

Now it was March 19 and the Russian artillery was shelling the inner line of the Austrian defence.

"The noose is tightening — won't be long now!" said Zheleznyak enthusiastically.

There was another thunderclap. They looked up above the tree line at the enormous fountain of black smoke spewing forth, followed by clods and clods of soil raining through the treetops.

Then Sergeant Drugov rode up out of the trees and called to Zheleznyak, "Sir, enemy approaching on foot! To our west!"

Drugov swung an arm in the general direction and then added in a voice that could not hide his own surprise, "Tens of thousands, sir."

"What? Surrendering?"

"No, sir. They are making a charge against our lines!"

"Emboldened by hunger, I'll bet! Right. Sergeant, round up our squadron and have them meet me directly west, at the edge of this forest. Now!"

"Sir!" Drugov galloped into the forest and Gumilyov rode quickly after Zheleznyak through the trees.

As they got closer and closer to the edge of the forest, Gumilyov heard the screams and cries of men interspersed with exploding shells, machine-gun fire, and rifle bullets. Even though Gumilyov had long stopped asking himself what would compel men to run into enemy fire, the answer always being *orders*, he still looked on amazed.

Thousands and thousands of Austrians were swarming out of Przemyśl and attempting to cross the Russian line. Gumilyov watched on as the Russians mowed them down.

It was a massacre.

Pushkin whispered dry and unbidden in his soul.

Now with purpose dread
Like men in mutual loathing bred,
Each plans ... the other's downfall in his heart ...
But worldly hate, like worldly fame,
Shrinks at the breath of worldly shame.

The other Hussars from Gumilyov's regiment jostled their horses alongside him and waited. The chink of bridle and stirrups washed up with the smell of shit and sweat. All were impatient for the instruction to charge. But the spectacle before them was a tempest of slaughter, where wave upon wave upon wave of enemy combatants surged into the relentless whirlpool of death.

Now come together!
Calmly, coldly
The combatant's four steps advance,

Four steps to death ...
Still forward moving o'er the green
The other likewise first began
To raise his weapon, fix his man.

Gumilyov looked on grimly. Something seemed to pass from Hussar to Hussar, mounted side by side on their horses; not the usual rousing hurrah and lust for battle but rather fatalistic despair at the carnage before them. Here was not the noble fight they had once dreamed. Here was not the thunderous charge of sabre and lance. No wonder Pushkin's duelling days of yore crashed about inside his heart.

And there he lay!
Beneath his breast, the ball had pierced him,
The smoking blood ran down apace,
Thence, where, a few brief moments past,
The pulse of life was bounding fast,
Where hate and hope and love were strong,
And warm emotions won't to throng.

Gumilyov heard the nicker and whinny of the horses around him as Hussars watched, expressionless, across the 20 kilometres between the edge of the forest and Przemyśl's fortress. He could hardly see whether the Austrians were still attempting to run the Russian lines, so thick was the smoke from the constant machine-gun fire and shelling. He looked across at Lieutenant Zheleznyak's profile, motionless and patient beside him, and he thought about how the deaths of these Austrian bastards weighed more heavily than any other he had witnessed so far in this godforsaken war. At least they were not dying for an ideal — it was the desperation of hunger that had given them something to die for.

The heart is now a house bereft
Of former inmates — every floor
Is dark and still forevermore,
With dusty panes. The host has left:
And wither went he? Who shall say?
His very trace is swept away.

Two days later, Austrian General Burgneustädten surrendered and opened the gates of Przemyśl.

When the triumphant Russian 11th marched into the fortified town they were met by the ragged war-torn survivors. Many of the civilians who had been left behind were Jewish and well aware of Russian anti-Semitism. They waited with dread for what would happen next. The Russian military command reported that 120,000 prisoners had been taken; including nine generals, nearly 100 officers and 117,000 soldiers. To Gumilyov it was clear that Przemyśl's morale had been crushed and the end of the siege had meant a blow from which the Austro-Hungarians would never recover. For 113 days Russian troops had been tied up in this struggle for the strategic gateway to the Carpathian Mountains, that would open up a route to Hungary.

When the Hussars rode into the vanquished city of Przemyśl, Gumilyov couldn't help think that since the days of Classical Antiquity besieging a town was the surest way to destroy its identity, drive and spirit. For this moment in time, Russia was the invincible Ancient Roman Army with its fluttering flag of the two-headed eagle.

10

It was a surprisingly dusty morning in April when Gumilyov realised that although he had seen the Tsar on a number of occasions, he had never seen the Commander in Chief, Grand Duke Nicholas Nikolaevich.

Gumilyov stood to attention in Przemyśl, alongside the Kiev Hussar Division. The motorcade drove swiftly past and the soldiers saluted. The few civilians left standing attempted a half-hearted cheer, as if to say, this was always what they had hoped.

On seeing the Grand Duke for the first time Gumilyov understood the ambiguity of this monumental human being. Standing nearly two metres tall, with military experience and a belief in the common people, the Grand Duke was a formidable presence to both soldiers and civilians throughout Russia. On the other hand, after witnessing some of Headquarters' catastrophic decisions played out on the battlefield, Gumilyov believed the Grand Duke was incompetent, like all bureaucrats and politicians who pretended to govern. It was difficult to reconcile this feeling because Gumilyov, like most, badly wanted to believe that the carnage and horror of the war were worth something.

Gumilyov loved his country but he was more and more disturbed by the infallibility of the military command, not to mention the holy emperor himself, Tsar Nicholas II. But until the enemy was beaten, he couldn't see any other way except to rage against the invaders who were desperate to rape and pillage Mother Russia.

A little later after the motorcade had passed, Gumilyov rode on to Przemyśl's town square with the other Hussars who were to form a ceremonial guard on either side of the raised platform built specifically for the purpose of the Tsar's visit today. The Cossacks were already positioned and by the time the Hussars took up their place, the square was rapidly filling with the Russian 11th.

There was some enthusiasm amongst the men because General Selivanov had announced that after the ceremony all members of the Russian 11th would be given vodka and meat.

Gumilyov could see above the Russian soldiers who managed to squeeze into the square and looked upon the ruined fortifications of what had once been an invincible Austro-Hungarian stronghold.

The choir stood to the right of the platform and their voices soared heavenward.

God save our noble Tsar!
Great be his glory!

The Tsar blinked out at the crowd. Benevolent, if not slightly bewildered. The Grand Duke stood beside him, tears shimmering in the sunlight.

Growing in power and majesty
Tsar! May good fortune
Be showered upon thee!

All eyes were on Russia's holy emperor and the sea of men enthralled before him joined in song. Their own eyes glistening with the love of country as fingers of roiling cloud moved majestically across the hard-blue sky above.

God save thee still, Our Noble Tsar!

A deafening clamour rose up as thousands and thousands of men knelt on the cobbled square. The

Tsar raised his hand in blessing. Every head bowed and many covered their eyes and wept.

After receiving their blessing, the men remained kneeling for the Tsar to bestow the St George Cross on the Grand Duke for his achievement in ensuring Russia's victory.

The Grand Duke knelt in front of the Tsar but even so he soared high above his great nephew's chest.

The Tsar's voice was quiet and solemn but seemed to reach the far corners of the square as he offered the benediction: *"Our help is in the name of our Almighty and merciful God, Who made heaven and earth, And in the Immaculate Virgin Mary who worked miracles for the salvation of souls, And in the courage and faith of Saint George who Will always defend Mother Russia!"*

He took the medal from a priest and held it aloft as if to reclaim the very air that was once breathed by Russia's mortal enemy: *"Kindly pour out Your blessing on this medal and on the Grand Duke Nicholas Nikolaevich so that he, who devoutly wears it and reveres it, shall experience the patronage of St George as well as the blessing of the Most Holy and Sacred Mary Mother of God and all of Russia!"*

The Tsar pinned the medal to the Grand Duke as he did so he prayed: *"Take this holy medal; wear it with faith and handle it with due devotion so that the Holy and Immaculate Queen of Heaven and Earth and Russia will protect and defend you. Wear it to honour St George and Russia all the days of your life."*

The orthodox priest closest to the Tsar sang out:
Our Father in heaven hallowed be your name,
Your kingdom come, your will be done,
On earth, as it is in heaven
Give us this day our daily bread
And forgive us our debts
As we also have forgiven our debtors.

Then the priest, swinging the metal thurible on its long chains, moved from the platform down to the humble subjects kneeling in the square.

Gumilyov watched long streams of white incense waft towards the indifferent blue sky.

Then another priest intoned the call of the litany to which the men offered a response:
(Priest): *And lead us not into temptation,*
(Crowd): *But deliver us from evil*

The metal censer on its chains swung clockwise thrice.

(Priest): *Queen conceived without original sin,*
(Crowd): *Pray for us who have recourse to thee*

The thurible swung anti-clockwise and Gumilyov's horse sputtered.

(Priest): *Oh Saint George hear my prayer,*
(Crowd): *And let my cry come unto thee.*

The incense swirled around and around and around in tight circles until it drifted up into the enormous vault of the sky and each man seemed to gaze upward as their pleas were taken into the vast cavity of un-knowing.

Then the choir sent up the resonant *Amen.*

The men stood.

Finally, the Grand Duke was presented with an or-namental golden sword of victory, its hilt and scabbard shimmering with sun encrusted diamonds, his lined face was washed in tears.

Despite the mood of celebration and relief amongst the men who were now lubricated with vodka and filled with sausage, onion and bread stew, Gumilyov felt darkly sober. The afternoon ceremony had done nothing but aggravate his cynicism of Russian imperial leadership. In front of these valiant and patient men, who risked their lives every day in this filthy war, was the Tsar valorising and glorifying another member of the imperial household. The irony was that the Grand Duke had been hundreds of kilometres away in Belarus at Headquarters during the entire siege of Przemyśl.

This oligarchical pantomime must end, thought Gumilyov.

Nepotism ruled supreme and the common man in Russia was always and everywhere expendable.

Gumilyov tried to shake himself out of this black mood as he walked the streets of Przemyśl in the waning twilight. Rad kept pace and not surprisingly had managed to secure a bottle of vodka from Supply.

Most of the shopfronts of Przemyśl had been boarded up and as they passed Gumilyov wondered what made some of the civilians decide to endure the unendurable while others chose to die. They had eaten all the animals within the fortified town and when Russian lines became impenetrable, Przemyśl starved.

The Russians first took control of the town two weeks ago and the Austrian soldiers were the most pathetic prisoners Gumilyov had ever encountered. They did not seem loyal to Emperor Franz Josef and were more interested in whether they could just go home to their own towns or farms with their own way of doing things. They did not even consider the Russians to be their enemy.

At least Gumilyov and his countrymen had an unshakable devotion to Mother Russia and, no matter what their ethnicity, knew themselves to be Russian through and through.

What else could matter?

Even with his own university education at the Sorbonne and his travels abroad, Gumilyov knew that Russia was given to them by God. To be Russian was in the blood. Which only made the incompetence of the imperial leadership utterly untenable.

Gumilyov accepted the bottle Rad offered and took a slug of vodka. His mind warmed.

"Hey, what's up brother?" Rad's voice boomed across the street to two Russian soldiers with freshly bandaged wounds.

One, with an impressive head wound, peeled himself off the wall and responded, "You have a smoke, brother?"

Rad mooched over to where the two soldiers sprawled, both of them in different states of post-surgical recovery.

He passed around his bottle of vodka companionably.

Gumilyov helped light a cigarette for a soldier with a stump where a hand should have been. The bandage was seeping badly. He was young and pale in the fading light.

"Where have you come from?"

As Rad asked the question, Gumilyov stood back and realised they were at the entrance of a small hospital. The smell of blood, vomit and shit eked out towards them as if the stench of human suffering could never be washed away. No wonder these poor bastards were cramped on the sidewalk having a cigarette and avoiding going back into the aggravation of further infection.

"Łupkóv Pass," and with their answer neither of the two soldiers seemed to want to look at Rad or Gumilyov.

"Carpathians?" Rad asked.

"Yeah, up Bieszczady way."

The four men smoked and drank for a moment or two.

Of course, being Hussars neither Rad nor Gumilyov had ever seen these men before but they were obviously attached to the Russian 11th. They must have been in one of the first divisions sent out to face the Hungarian sharpshooters holed up in the mountain pass.

"It was bullshit," said the one with the head wound, quietly. "Fucking bullshit."

Rad passed the bottle across and said, "Lemme guess ... orders were for you to charge machine gunners with only five bullets between you!"

"Worse," he whispered. "Fixed bayonets for those who had guns, no ammunition, you see ..."

"For fuck's sake!" Rad spat. "That's not a fucking war, that's not a fucking battle, that's ..." Rad seemed to be struggling to express what all of them knew. It was no secret that ammunition was dangerously low for every Russian Frontovik.

"They sent us in with nothing." The young pale soldier spoke to no one in particular, the red blood of his bandaged stump flowering before them, "We were told a soldier's breast is Russia's greatest weapon," and he closed his eyes.

The guy with the head wound spoke into the gloaming, "It was slaughter ... they forced us to run up into the enemy line, take hill and ridge and crest ... one by one." He fumbled for the bottle of vodka from Rad,

"We failed ... and the mountainside ran with Russian blood."

They lounged about smoking and drinking. The night slowly washed the sky above them in a bruised indigo.

"Hey," Rad slurred and pointed towards the entrance of the hospital. "What about the nurses? Any pretty ones? I mean there's gotta be nurses here right?" Rad preened his moustache as he spoke.

Gumilyov thought of the lovely Jula, her dimples and hot red hair. A few letters had been exchanged, hers more hopeful than his.

"This one," Rad gestured to Gumilyov with his cigarette, "has had a sweetheart in nurse's uniform!"

Gumilyov turned away and watched an inn across the road light its lamps. He wondered what it would be like to walk into that inn and meet Jula for a drink and something to eat, he wondered what it would be like if there was no war.

Maybe I should see her when I am in Moscow, he thought, but he knew it was dangerous to contemplate a future.

"Nuh," the one in the head bandages answered. "Actually, the nurses are kind of ... they're too young and some are not doing any nursing ..." He tried to rally, "It's disgusting really. They're just there to pleasure the old sergeants and lieutenants — the thing is, well, some of them look as young as eight or nine."

The men sat in the muted light and thought about the travesties of war. The struggle for power took many guises and Russia seemed to know them all. Most days it felt like life had become an imitation of hell.

A commotion just inside the hospital drew the men's attention. They could hear accusations being hurled, a female crying and then some pushing and shoving. Rad stepped up into the entrance and disappeared inside, either ready for a fight or to be an enthusiastic bystander. Gumilyov sighed and followed.

The corridor was poorly lit and pungent with a sweet sickly smell. Towards the end of the corridor, there was a contretemps and Gumilyov could see Rad's large outline squaring up to those involved. To Rad's left stood a doctor wearing spectacles and pointing emphatically at a slouching sour-faced orderly who seemed completely uninterested in the whole incident.

Gumilyov pushed in between the orderly and Rad and saw their own regimental priest standing in the middle of the row, scratching furtively at his groin. The doctor was looking with venomous hatred and speaking in Hungarian while pointing his finger at the priest.

"What's this prick done?" Rad asked, but the doctor ignored him and then began yelling at the orderly.

The priest was flushed with alcohol and rubbed and clawed at his itching body.

Gumilyov decided to repeat Rad's question in French, and when he did the doctor looked at him closely and answered, "Your priest was just been caught molesting one of my nursing aids."

They all looked and there, tucked behind the doctor, was a girl with an apron and headscarf, crying. She could not have been more than ten and had pressed herself against the corridor wall, her face half turned from the commotion and her hands wrapped tightly about her breasts.

"You filthy fucking dick!" yelled Rad at the priest who shook his head half-heartedly and tried to un-make a smile.

"What happened?" Gumilyov didn't know why he was getting involved. There was something shaming about the fact that their own regimental priest had been caught in some sort of compromising position, but on the other hand, everyone in the regiment knew what a revolting drunken low life their priest was, as were so many of the priests who lived off Russia like vermin.

The young doctor with his grey eyes and thick dark hair could not have been older than Gumilyov.

"Your priest has been caught fucking this child." He caught the thick gold chain around the priest's neck and shoved the cross into the priest's face, "He is a degenerate! He has been coming into the clinic to be treated for syphilis." The doctor released the priest and turned his rage back to the gormless shuffler at Rad's side, "This orderly discovered this ... this pestilent cockroach shoving his scabby cock up —"

CRACK! The priest's face flew back from Rad's fist. *THUNK!* The priest's itching body slumped to the ground. For a huge man, Rad could move fast.

A pool of blood poured politely from the priest's mangled nose.

The girl's crying increased and Gumilyov heard her moan, "Oy vey", to which the doctor turned and said softly, "Shalom. Shalom."

Gumilyov had heard Mandelstam speak these words and before he realised, he said, "You're Jewish."

"Yes, I'm Jewish, so what?"

Neither Rad nor Gumilyov was used to this sort of audacity from a Jew and they certainly didn't expect it from someone who was a prisoner of the Russian army.

The doctor looked down at the priest below him and yelled, "*He* is a rapist of little girls!"

Gumilyov saw the doctor's leg flinch and for a moment he thought he was going to kick the unconscious priest who lay sprawling on the ground.

The doctor then straightened his white over-jacket and turned about as if to leave.

Gumilyov's curiosity was peaked, "Why didn't you run when you had the chance? We were told Przemyśl was pretty much evacuated, except for the army."

The doctor looked back at Gumilyov, "Like you said," his voice was flat, "I am Jewish. We are expendable. Besides, they needed doctors to administer to the great Austro-Hungarian military." The last few words were bitter with sarcasm and then the doctor added, "Why did we bother to survive? Only to be killed by disease." He pointed to the priest, "Brought here on the pricks of its brave Russian soldiers."

"This guy has a death wish ..." Rad mumbled but he hesitated, unsure if it was wise to punish the doctor for insubordination.

They watched as the doctor turned aside, put an arm across the young girl's frail shoulders and spoke quietly to her. She then left and walked down to the end of the corridor and entered a room. The doctor spoke sharply to the orderly who loped off towards the basement exit. Finally, the doctor turned his attention back to the two Russian Hussars standing before him.

"When your priest regains consciousness, tell him if he comes back here again, I will personally pour battery acid on his dick." His fearless gaze took in Rad and Gumilyov.

The tension in Rad shifted and he replied, "Let's hope he comes back," and with that, he picked up one of the scrawny arms of the priest and unceremoniously began dragging him towards the entrance.

The doctor was already moving away when Gumilyov found himself asking, whether through idle curiosity or for some other reason he could not tell, "Where did you learn French?"

The doctor eyed Gumilyov suspiciously, "I studied Medicine at the Sorbonne." He hesitated and asked, "And you?"

"I studied Letters at the Sorbonne."

Gumilyov realised they were more or less the same age. How strange to think they could have crossed paths in another life and unexpectedly he found himself putting out his right hand, "Trooper Gumilyov."

The doctor must have been thinking something similar because after a few seconds he shook hands and said, "Dr. Gerde."

"Are all your priests nothing but filthy dogs?" Gerde's contempt for his captors was surprising but also strangely refreshing.

"He's usually harmless," but even as Gumilyov responded he knew that the sly self-preserving cunning of their regimental priest was anything but harmless.

"Harmless! Don't those filthy bastard priests rape your women and run your country?"

So the rumours of Father Rasputin, thought Gumilyov, *have reached this hell hole of Przemyśl.*

"Russia is a wedding cake." Gumilyov smiled across at Dr Gerde as he recalled a poster described in one of his mother's letters, "The cake's base is made up of the peasantry and the industrial working class. The religious and the Cossacks sit on top, and with superstition and the threat of violence, they keep the minions below them in check."

The doctor's eyes squinted through his spectacles trying to figure out what to make of this swaggering Hussar.

"Russia's educated middle class —"

"I take it that's you," Gerde said dryly.

Gumilyov nodded and continued with, "The educated middle class is in the middle and on top is royalty and the aristocracy, who live in isolation away from the lower-class peasants and industrial workers."

Gumilyov realised he was enjoying this conversation with the doctor.

"You see, it's only titles and land that offer privilege in Russia. And think on this — the Tsar owns only ten percent of the most arable parts of the nation while the Orthodox Church pretty much owns the rest!"

"Your system is fucked," Gerde spoke with a small wiry smile.

"Indeed," said Gumilyov without any trace of concern. "But what can you do? The system is what it is."

"You think so? You think there is nothing you can do?" Although slight of build, the young doctor pushed into Gumilyov's space, "Religion is a spiritual booze —"

"I've read Lenin," interrupted Gumilyov, "Those who toil and live in poverty are taught by religion to be submissive and to take comfort in the hope of a heavenly reward."

"Exactly!"

Gumilyov looked at his new acquaintance and considered how many Jews, his friend Mandelstam included, were drawn to what they believed would be a better world via revolutionary socialism. In fact, newspapers had been calling the Tsar to pull back hundreds of thousands of Russian Jews from the Front because they were suspected of collaborating with the enemy.

The same narrative over and over, thought Gumilyov. *No one could trust a Jew.*

And as if reading his mind Dr. Gerde said quietly, "The goyim here in Przemyśl accused the Jews of evasion and profiteering, so we were the only people not permitted to escape." His grey eyes blinked behind his frameless spectacles as he added, "There was even discussion that the Jews should be used as a human shield to make good the escape of everyone else in Przemyśl. *Feh!*" Gerde spat out the expression.

Gumilyov was wondering what he might say when Dr. Gerde said, "I am a man without a country." He continued on passionately, "But I would rather take my chances with the Germans or the Austro-Hungarians any day, over and above the Russians!"

Gumilyov knew that Russia's track record of pogroms and systematic Jewish persecution over the decades was shaming, but it wasn't only his parent's generation who lamented the Jews as a scourge on Russia. Most Russians felt that way. And most Jews, like Mandelstam, who wanted to study or get ahead converted to orthodoxy.

Needless to say, Jews always seemed ambivalent, as if being Russian wasn't enough.

The doctor turned away and moved down the corridor. Shoulders a little stooped and his walk a little tired, yet still he returned to his post in order to care for the sick, the wounded and the dying — be they Austrian or Russian, military or civilian. It was as if his war was somewhere else, ever-present but ever-shifting.

Somewhere deep inside of Gumilyov, despite knowing he was absolutely right about the inviolable state of being Russian, Dr. Gerde's words remained with him … *I am a man without a country.*

Chapter 4

May — June 1915

It wasn't a long walk to the Dog but Mandelstam had insisted on meeting Lidka outside Kolobok's when she finished her shift. They had quickly become lovers after first meeting at Anna Akhmatova's for Christmas dinner.

As she came through the kitchen door, Mandelstam was sitting up on a brick wall watching her with a lazy insouciance, which she found both endearing and irritating. Mandelstam had the good looks of a 17 year old and he also had the sex drive of a 17 year old, with a great deal of pushing and shoving and insatiable desire.

Lidka smiled to herself and pulled the door behind her.

Mandelstam's face lit up in the summer evening sky and he leaned back with his legs spread wide.

"I thought you were taking me to your cabaret club," Lidka said as she sauntered across to him. "But it looks like you're going nowhere fast,"

A slow smile moved over his serious pale face and he said, "Come here."

Sitting up on the brick wall he wrapped his legs around her. No one had ever kissed her as he had. Tender, firm and slow. His lips kissed her mouth and eyes and nose and forehead; his hands travelled across the base of her throat and down beneath her buttoned shirt. He could make her skin tingle and buzz.

It isn't love, she told herself, and ignored his whispered declarations of "You are my destiny ... we are the beginning and the end ... nothing else is."

She didn't let herself believe it, not with her child at home in Odessa and her mother waiting patiently each month for money to tide them over. Lidka didn't believe it, with her future being of no consequence, while he was one of the most significant poets of his day. Or so the critics of St Petersburg claimed: *Dazzling! Iconoclastic! The voice of a new Russia!*

No, hers was another destiny.

"Come on." Lidka pulled herself away from her dark messy-haired lover, "I need to sit down — it's alright for some, sitting on a brick wall all day!"

She laughed as he pushed off the wall and caught her tightly about her thin waist, in the way he always did. She had never felt so secure in the arms of another.

"Pronin got served notice today and the Dog is closing." Mandelstam's voice was neutral but she knew it was a blow.

A number of so-called decadent cabarets had been slapped with higher taxes; a government effort to enforce national sobriety and shut down anti-war discussion.

The Dog had been forced to lay down for good.

Meanwhile, soot from workshop chimneys was still belching across the St Petersburg skyline, despite it being well past 9 pm. This was how it was of late, with the workers expected to toil away at a 12-hour shift every day, or if you were in textiles, 13 hours. The newspapers were full of propaganda saying this was the war effort that every Russian was willing to make. And yet the factories and clubs were full of Russians saying this was the war no one was willing to fight.

"Apparently, the Dog is decadent and a waste of resources. Everyone's guttered." Mandelstam spoke in his usual restrained dispassionate way but she knew his true feelings.

He had been utterly embraced by the milieu at the Stray Dog Café no matter his Jewish background or his lack of money or his vagrant lifestyle of no fixed address. He was one of the founding Acemist members, a group of cutting-edge poets demanding poetry be honest and stripped of artifice.

She looked across at his serious face and thought about this intense boyish lover, who craved her body and soul like it was his drug and the way he rode high in the poetic debate about what constituted great contemporary poetry.

"That's a shame," she said. She didn't mind the club, but despite all the talk of politics and revolution and art and the avant-garde, she felt like the only worker there. People at the Dog seemed to treat her like a novelty as if she was the first worker with whom they'd ever socialised. There was something condescending in the way they would either ignore her or ply her with endless questions.

Mandelstam and Lidka turned down Nevsky Prospect.

St Petersburg was a city of contradictions. On the one hand, there were daily queues for the bare essentials, and on the other hand, there were stores still showcasing Pears Soap, Golden Syrup, Boiled Fruitcake and even Smelling Salts. Such was the city's anglophile fetish.

Not that anyone Lidka knew bought these sorts of items. The fact that she worked each day at the restaurant meant she could take home some of the leftovers and rotting vegetables to contribute to the few shared meals with her aunt. The fact that Yirina often ate at the Putilov Factory, worked in Mandelstam's favour because he was always scrounging for a feed and a sleepover.

"What a city, huh ..." Mandelstam was striding alongside her lost in his own thoughts, as was his way. "It's sacred and festive and ..." He looked about him expansively, "An elegant mirage."

His last image made him smile and he added, "When I first arrived here in my breeches I had this feeling that something was going to happen — that's what St Petersburg does to you, it's a heaving mass of potential." He let go of her hand absently and said "It's a city surrounded by the sprawling chaos of Judaism."

She had gotten used to the way he would excavate ideas in order to understand what was hidden beneath.

"I don't know," he had come to a halt on the Fontanka Bridge and gazed down into the racket of rushing canal water. "Agitation, uncertainty, catastrophe, change, war, revolution ... it's all noise. The noise of our times ..."

Lidka glanced across at him and said, "They've taken down all the flags. Do you see?" She pointed at the long shopfront façade that ran onwards to the Neva.

When she had arrived late last year the city was strewn with flags, bunting and posters declaring *Victory is Russia's! God Save the Father Tsar!* To her, this city was a stage for the Romanovs — their anti-Semitism, limited intelligence and despotic rule.

"Anyone and anything is possible, here in this marvel of a city," said Mandelstam as he seesawed between recondite brooding and luminous bon vivant, but always and everywhere caught up in the idea rather than the thing itself.

At times this made it frustrating for Lidka who would only allow herself to see the world as the thing itself. Her reality was living cheek by jowl with the illiterate masses who were hopelessly poor and slaving away to prop up a war that distracted the revolutionaries, like her aunt and Mayakovsky, from achieving their aims. Mandelstam surprised her: on the one hand he was scathing about the Tsar and the war but on the other hand he was seduced by the grandeur and aesthetic of St Petersburg, which to him, was Russia herself.

At that moment Mandelstam pulled her to him and there, with the oncoming foot traffic, he kissed her again.

People swerved about them and some smiled indulgently.

His kisses were slow and passionate and long.

Lidka eventually pulled away and found herself responding to his love of Russia with, "So ... anyone and anything is possible here in this city — as long as you are not an outsider or ... a Jew?"

He looked away from her incontrovertible truth.

"So long as you are Russian..." he added, but even he didn't seem to be convinced.

At first, Lidka thought they wouldn't be able to get through the crowd gathered outside the Dog, let alone make it inside and find a table, but of course, someone had seen Mandelstam and called out to him and dragged him down the stairs, Lidka in tow. There were so many bodies and so much noise that she could do nothing but push up behind Mandelstam, who kept a fierce hold of her hand.

Within minutes they had achieved the impossible and were cramped in a corner table with Mayakovsky, Anna and others. The brightly coloured checked tablecloths, plates of long demolished caviar and drinks were the mood of the night. The fug of Mahorka tobacco, still fashionable in this basement below the Dashkov mansion, made the evening seem other-worldly. Mandelstam had made sure Lidka was seated as far from Mayakovsky as possible which amused her no end.

The oversized poet was talking loudly to Mandelstam about the Tsar's stupefying indifference to the protests and strikes building over the last few weeks in St Petersburg.

Mayakovsky is all spit and noise, thought Lidka, and she wondered at his unorthodox upbringing, his revolutionary aspirations and stints in jail and whether this was the making of the poet or the man or both.

She could tell Mandelstam was annoyed that Mayakovsky was here, even though he was always at the Dog. She knew Mandelstam would have preferred his evening to be spent across from the smouldering gaze of Anna while hooking his arm over Lidka's shoulders. She sensed he was still in love with Anna, how could anyone not be? All of St Petersburg was in love with Anna Akhmatova.

And Anna knew it.

Mayakovsky interrupted her thoughts and asked, "You know Lourie?"

Lidka shook her head quietly and sipped a beer that someone had spirited across from the bar and placed before her.

"Anna!" Mayakovsky roared across the table. "Introductions, please!"

Anna gracefully disentangled herself from the slow, deliberate and intimate discussion with the man beside her.

"Lidka, darling, this is Artur Sergeyevich Lourie. I've told you about him," Anna's dark blue eyes took in her friend from across the table.

Lourie had thick sensuous lips and the softest skin Lidka had ever seen. He wore a perfectly pressed suit and was already going bald, which made him look more distinguished than the rest of them. Lidka realised with a start that he was gazing at her with deep concentration behind his glasses.

Mandelstam jumped in with, "May I introduce my girlfriend, Lidka Matveyevna Yurkovich," as if making a point to Anna that he, too, had moved on.

Lourie was enchanting. He leaned over the table and instead of shaking Lidka's hand, he kissed it lightly. Anna nursed a small secret smile and lit up a cigarette, then she looked across at Lidka as she exhaled and said, "Artur is working on a musical composition with Pablo Picasso."

Lidka had never heard of that strange name and looked quizzically at Anna. The crowd of people at the Dog were ever threatening to jostle their table.

"The Spaniard. Painter."

"Cubist," Lourie corrected Anna and she promptly rewarded him with a deep kiss.

Lidka leaned across the table and asked, "How is it at the hospital, Anna?"

The last time they spoke, Anna had told Lidka she was volunteering at Tsarskoye Selo, nursing the soldiers who had sustained injuries while at the Front. At the time, Anna seemed to be hinting that Lidka should join her. Lidka had no intention of getting that close to the suffering soldiers, not after her own husband had been blown to a thousand pieces.

Anna seemed reluctant to disentangle herself from her lover, "Oh very sad, some of them are just boys." She had the capacity to convey tragedy in a way that stilled the world around her, "I do what I can, along with the other volunteers. The nurses and doctors are exhausted ..." Anna was not alone in knowing this to be the case.

Everyone in St Petersburg was talking about the endless stream of incoming soldiers arriving daily at the railway stations and being carted off to hospitals, both established and temporary. Even the Tsarina and her daughters were among the glitterati of St Petersburg offering solace to the Frontoviks.

And it wasn't just the multitude of the wounded putting pressure on transport and resources, it was also the countless refugees pouring into the city — desperate to escape famine, war, unemployment, displacement and, in Lidka's case, widowhood.

"It's unsustainable!" Mayakovsky lent into the conversation between the two women.

"The shops have nothing in them," Artur Lourie spoke quietly. "Except for the telegrams in their windows listing the endless names of the dead."

Lidka looked at him closely.

"And the lines for bread and milk begin at four in the morning!" added Anna but Lidka doubted whether Anna stood there herself but rather sent out one of the house-girls she employed.

Lidka wondered whether hardship and suffering, for the intelligentsia of St Petersburg, existed only in their heads and never ever in their bodies.

She turned her attention back to Mayakovsky who was bellowing on about the workers' right to an eight-hour day, universal education and equality before the law.

She had gotten to know him well over the last few months. He was a chameleon but she liked him. Back in the day, when Mayakovsky was a Futurist, life was filled with possibility, and Russia felt as if it was on a radical knife edge that might embrace socialist revolution, youthful experimentation and sexual transgression.

All that seemed like a long time ago.

Now, it was as if she was a completely different person.

In a few grains of time, Lidka had married, had a son, experienced war, lost her husband, travelled to St Petersburg, moved in with her aunt, found a job and, despite her disinclination at first, discovered warmth in bed with Mandelstam.

Mayakovsky was on one of his hobby horses. He was expounding his views on the state of the economy and what Russia needed to do to keep up with the growing pressure seen on the streets. Lidka's aunt was active in the Putilov Factory soviet and often attended its clubhouses for lectures on the war or Marx, and Yirina had even joined the local choir. Lidka was exhausted even thinking about it. She could barely do much else other than wait on tables for 11 hours, six and a half days a week and see Mandelstam every second or third evening.

Lidka felt Mandelstam's arm like a dead weight across her shoulders and knew he was still watching Anna.

"Minimum wage and the end to land tax!" Mayakovsky sculled the remains of his glass. "The Duma is made up of spineless nanny goats — it must be completely overhauled!"

"And how is all this to be achieved, comrade?"

Lidka wondered if she was the only one who heard the sarcasm in Mandelstam's voice.

"Revolution my friend, revolution! You Jews are at the forefront of the movement!"

And there it is, thought Lidka, not ten minutes in before Mayakovsky was outing Mandelstam.

She had spent hours telling Mandelstam that Mayakovsky was not anti-Semitic, it was just the Russian way (*to be anti-Semitic*, interrupted Mandelstam) to openly speak in generalities, Lidka had continued, about people who were outsiders.

"Well, some of us Jews are busy with other things." Everyone looked across at the warm gravelly voice of Artur Lourie who smiled conspiratorially across at Mandelstam and added, "Like composing great poems or, dare I say it, music!"

The table cheered and Mayakovsky took it upon himself to yell for a bottle of vodka.

In a flash the exquisitely dressed Pronin was at their table, tray adorned with a large bottle of black-market vodka and a clutch of fresh glasses.

"Friends! Please! May I?" The proprietor of the Dog deftly distributed the glasses across the table and handed the bottle to Mayakovsky's outstretched hand.

"If I may ask, most sadly but also with great joy —"

"Darling B.P ..." purred Anna and extended her gorgeous pale hand across the heads of others to be kissed by Pronin.

"Yes. Thank you, Anna! My dear — what an honour it has been. Yes, my dear friends, tonight will be the last night we shall be permitted to open our doors —"

"No!" interrupted Mayakovsky as he sloshed vodka into the waiting glass, "I forbid it I tell you! I will stage a protest —"

"Really, my dear friends," Pronin was annoyed at the interruption and Lidka watched on curiously. It wasn't as if the club employed anybody. It was just a basement where poets, dancers, musicians, and artists were allowed in free to drink while others were charged an exorbitant fee. Which, shockingly, they paid.

"Dear friends your talent will live on because of the humble efforts of my little establishment — or that is what I like to think. I flatter myself perhaps ..." Right on cue everyone brayed their praise of Pronin and his bohemian establishment.

"Well then perhaps tonight as the Dog's final swan song ..." he chuckled at his own lame joke. "Dear Anna and company, perhaps I could beg you for a final rendition, an oration, a performance that will live on when the Dog lays down its head."

Lidka actually saw tears in Pronin's dark little almond eyes and realised, from the quiet of those around him, they too were feeling the poignancy of times changing.

"Of course," Mandelstam responded and Lidka turned to face him.

He was utterly sure of his destiny. And she realised at that moment she must peel herself out of their intoxicating love affair. She must shape her own future, somehow. She was a waitress, nothing more. And Mandelstam was one of Russia's most beloved poets.

Pronin grasped Mandelstam's hand and then turned back to the crowd, who were already aware that the deal had been achieved.

"Ladies and Gentlemen, the incredibly talented Osip Mandelstam will read one of his poems tonight!"

The cheer should not have surprised Lidka but each time something like this happened where she was reminded that Mandelstam was not just her own lover but adored by most of St Petersburg, she was slightly unnerved.

She sipped her fresh glass of vodka and noticed Artur Lourie was watching her with an unblinking gaze. He lifted his own glass to his beautiful lips and drank, never once looking away.

Mandelstam took the floor in front of the bar and the crowd fell silent. His recitation needed no copy from his book, published 18 months ago because what he delivered came from the heart.

She turned right round, Oh sorrow,
Towards indifferent onlookers.

The people around their table glanced across at Anna, a poem well known and entitled *Akhmatova*. Lidka stole a look at Lourie who was lighting his cigarette and the flame of the match coruscated off his glasses as he smiled across at her.

Turned stone, from her shoulders
A shawl, quasi-classical, flowed.

Lourie wrapped his arms about himself and smiled indulgently at Mandelstam who was surrounded by a haze of cigarette smoke and saintly adoration.

Ominous voice — drunk with pain —
Rising from heart's depths there.

Anna was transfixed by Mandelstam. She must have heard this poem a thousand times and yet, perhaps because this was the last time they were all gathered at the Dog, she held on to every word as if it might salvage her soul. Lidka had only been a witness on the sidelines to this world but at the same time, she knew this was an ending, a finale to the time they had once known.

Like this — as indignant Phaedra —
She once held the stage.

Lidka felt her skin tingle, she knew Artur Lourie was looking at her once again. Then, she noticed a rustle of surprise from a few people around their table in something Mandelstam had done in his recitation, but she had no clue what it was.

Later he would tell her he used the pronoun *She* in the last line so that Lidka might know it was to *her* he was speaking.

But it was too late by then.

The clapping finished and Mayakovsky's roar led the crowd to call upon Mandelstam for *Stone*. A poem Lidka had heard him read many, many times. A St Petersburg favorite. She took another sip of her vodka and this time saw Lourie glance from Anna, who was spellbound by Mandelstam, to Lidka. And without thinking why, she pressed her middle finger deep into her wide lower lip.

A flame is in my blood.

The crowd broke into spontaneous applause and then settled almost immediately. Lidka's body felt electric and she knew Lourie was watching her finger her mouth.

Burning dry life, to the bone.

Lidka tried to steady her breathing as she felt a hot languid blush push up her neck and face. A blush that could clearly be seen from across the table where Artur Lourie sat.

I do not sing of stone,
Now, I sing of wood.

As Mandelstam paused, Mayakovsky looked from Anna to Lidka and began to smile. Lourie was transfixing the blonde beauty and Mandelstam, the smoking brunette.

It is light and coarse:
Made of a single spar,
The oak's deep heart
And the fisherman's oar.

Lidka turned her head so that she seemed focused on Mandelstam's poetry recitation but her body remained alert to Lourie.

Drive them deep, the piles:
Hammer them in tight,

And then she saw Mandelstam wait, momentarily, and seek out her eyes, a gesture which filled her with such sadness.

Around wooden Paradise,
Where everything is light.

Later she would remember the resounding applause and the love that washed over her darling Mandelstam as the crowd lauded him as the poet of their broken, desperate lives. She would remember Mayakovsky's generosity and the way he made everyone feel it was right to acknowledge the ending so passionately (he too was called upon to read from his latest poem). She would remember the Dog lifting up on its hind legs in ovation when Anna read from *The Rosary* after which people called out to her "Queen of the Neva!" and "Soul of our nation!".

Afterwards, Mandelstam — her own lovely-skinned boy with eyes that drank in the world around him — whispered to her, "*You* are the wood ... Anna is stone ..."

But the wretched thing was, she already knew this would make no difference.

It was not her destiny to be Mandelstam's.

No one would forget that warm summer evening in the middle of May with Pronin crying as he farewelled all his stray pups who had frequented the café. And no one would forget Mandelstam leaping onto a chair, glass raised high as a priest might raise a chalice to his devoted congregation, and intone.

We shall meet again in St Petersburg,
Here in this place where we buried the sun.

2

It was well after 11 am when Anna walked through the thin silvery haze of morning. Her headache was crouched just behind her right eye and not even the small glass of coffee she had procured from her neighbour's dexterous black-market connections eased the pain. When she had left her apartment the streets were busy with trams and buses and pedestrians racing along either side of the Moyka Canal.

It usually only took Anna 30 minutes to walk to the Winter Palace where she then hailed a tram all the way to Tsarskoye Selo, 25 kilometres south of the city. There she volunteered as a nurse's aide for the injured soldiers at the Catherine Palace. It was something she did about twice a week.

The rest of the time she wrote. Gumilyov had his pay sent directly to his mother. Occasionally, and not frequently, her mother-in-law would send her a little money but Anna had a small stipend from her own family and didn't want for much.

At 26 she remained a magnet for artistic men who wanted to shower her with gifts while exercising a greedy desire to make her theirs. These connections helped her top up her food stocks and as for clothes, Anna had a winsome beauty that allowed her to wear a scarf or hat or coat in such a way as to indicate St Petersburg was still in the height of fashion.

She caught the 213 Tram just as it was pulling out of Dvortsovaya Square and found a seat towards the back against the window. She had eaten nothing since yesterday. In the end, Anna had stayed longer last night at the Dog than she had intended.

Everyone was drunk.

And dear Pronin was so insistent she stay till closing. It was, after all, the club's final night.

Anna hated farewells of any kind. It was better to hold loosely and without too much intent, otherwise, the leave-taking was painful. She had said goodbye to so much and so many already. But in the end, she snuck out with Artur Lourie, on the promise she would return after a bout of fresh air.

Of course, they took a cab and fled.

The tram pulled swiftly across the yellow Pevchesky Bridge and scooted south towards Sennaya

Ploshchad. From her mucky window she could see a long patient queue winding its way around the corner and along the road, across side streets, until it finally ended at a small grocery store and a customer, gripping a basket, shot out from its doors and scurried off with, Anna imagined, a small loaf of bread or a packet of semolina or tea or powdered milk or butter made of lard or sausages filled with starch and waste meat.

Just before they crossed Obukhovsky Bridge, Anna's attention was drawn to a poster stuck hastily on the bridge's stone entrance. She had seen such crudities before. She turned back for a second look: a stencilled cartoon of the Tsarina, nude from the waist up with the lascivious Rasputin groping her from behind, one huge hand pawing her right breast and the other inserting his enormous phallus into her rear.

They were both smiling.

Meanwhile, the tram rattled onwards.

Anna had spent some of her childhood in Tsarskoye Selo, the Tsar's village. Then it was the summer resort for the aristocracy. Although her family had aristocratic blood, they lived a fairly modest life with her father's gambling and incapacity to support his family. In her memory, the cellar of their dark green wooden house on Shirokaya Street in Tsarskoye Selo smelt of milk and old books. Beyond her home, tossed about

in the uncertainty of infidelity and marital loveless-
ness, she wandered the park behind the palace where
Pushkin once frequented, and she dreamed that one
day her juvenilia would morph into great writing. In
this same park, Anna had often seen the young Tsar
and his German wife riding about in their open carriage
during the summer months. She had thought them
central to her deep devotion and love of Russia.

But as the years passed, and with such discontent
pervading her cityscape as ordinary Russians demanded civil rights and better pay, Anna was beginning to think that her dear friend Mayakovsky was
right.

A drastic change to the Tsarist regime was needed.

Less than half an hour later, Anna arrived at the
south entrance of the Catherine Palace where nursing
staff and registered volunteers were bustling about and
changing into their uniforms; in her case, an apron and
headscarf to cover her own street clothes. She then
went to report to the supervisor on the wards.

The Palace was converted into a military hospital
after nursing had become the Tsarina's passion. Indeed, most days she and her two oldest daughters the
Grand Duchesses Olga and Tatiana would move among
the wounded. Anna had seen them nursing with her
own eyes, much to the hilarity of her friends back
in the city. Anna, who had always thought the Tsa-

rina shy and imperious, wondered if this experience of nursing the soldiers might force the royal family to reconsider its archaic and despotic hold over Russia.

Anna made her way to the makeshift ward, awkwardly ensconced in the gilt-edged palace interior with its staggering collection of Rembrandt, Jordaens, Snyders, van Dyck, Botticelli, Raphael, Titian, Caravaggio, da Vinci, van der Weyden, Giorgione, El Greco, Veronese, Tintoretto, Velazquez, de Ribera, Breughel and so it continued, up the swirling staircase and across rooms now appropriated for the care of the wounded or dying.

Her friend Valentina approached and with a mischievous look in her eye, asked "Did you hear? The Grand Duchesses went shopping for the first time, yesterday — but didn't know how to actually *buy* anything!" Valentina let out a soft peel of laughter and added, "So they want us to join them for their second attempt this afternoon!"

Anna had enjoyed her friendship with some of the Red Cross nurses but her favourite was definitely Valentina, who had made firm friends with the two Grand Duchesses.

"Oh, I am sure you can manage that alone with the young princesses," said Anna who was older than Olga, the eldest princess, by four or five years and found her forthright manner and moodiness a little irritating.

"No! It will be great fun." Valentina picked up a bundle of freshly laundered bed linen. The servants had been railroaded by the Tsarina to do the hospital laundry and cleaning.

"But won't the villagers know and there will be a scene ..." Despite Anna's reluctance she was actually starting to think it could be a bit of a lark.

"6 pm!" called Valentina over her shoulder as she moved off down the west corridor. "Besides, they wore their uniforms and no one recognised them yesterday — Olga specifically asked me to bring you along ..." And then she disappeared through a doorway.

Anna had no time to think about Valentina's proposal because her shift had already started and there was little respite. Unlike the nurses, which included the Tsarina and her two eldest daughters who had completed a nursing course, Anna was a volunteer and, as such, was directed to wash and bandage the gaping wounds and mangled body parts of the soldiers in the makeshift wards. She did not venture into the operating room but knew Valentina did and had to sort the ether cones, sterilize instruments and dispose of the amputated limbs handed to her by the surgeon. The entire so-called hospital was fug with the pungent odour of sickness and death.

For the most part, Anna noted that the soldiers were often stoic in their suffering and asked little of her other than water or for her to write a letter or read aloud from one of the books in the bookcase.

She often saw the Tsarina walk between the beds of the men. It was strangely moving how these hardened men would weep as they reached out to touch the hand of the Tsarina. They would then fall silent when she knelt in the ward and prayed for them.

Anna watched all this from a distance and tried to reconcile it with the hateful accusations that were spinning around St Petersburg that the Tsarina was a German spy and a whore to Rasputin. But what was indisputably evident was that, while the Tsar was in Stavka, the Tsarina and Rasputin were driving the country into ruin.

But here, in this threshold world of suffering and dying under the canopied ceilings of the Catherine Palace, Anna saw how some would believe the Tsarina was Mother Russia herself.

Anna busied herself with a patient.

He was so young she wondered whether he was more than 12. When she asked him as she unravelled the putrid bandage from around his thigh and knee he said 16, but he was pale and perspiring and, they both knew, lying.

She bathed his lacerated thigh and groin, danger-ously dark in colour, and gently brushed iodine across what she could.

Anna steeled against the rising bile in her throat. She took a jar of Vaseline and smeared it over the top of his wound and then with fresh cotton strips ban-daged the boy's leg as best she could.

He was so quiet and still that at one point she won-dered if he was dead, but, glancing quickly, she noticed his dark brown eyes watching her.

"Where are you from?" Anna asked as she gently placed a sheet over the ruined section of his body.

"Vilnius," he whispered.

"Ah, Lithuania." She paused because she was not usually comfortable speaking to children and yet there was something so profoundly adult about this brave boy, "You are not too far from home then." She took a sponge from the tray she had brought and began to lightly mop his fine face.

"Would you like me to write to your parents? They would be glad to know you are here in St Petersburg."

At first, she thought he had not heard or was too unwell to answer with the infection gathering around his wound, but as she packed her tray she heard him say, "They do not read."

It was an acknowledgment of one of Russia's great-est shames.

"It won't matter. I can write and tell them you are getting better and I can send it off to the local priest." She hesitated when she thought of the high illiteracy amongst the clergy, "Or a local doctor." Her offer was sounding more and more improbable but there must be, she thought with exasperation, someone who could get news to his parents.

She looked down at her patient who had now closed his eyes as if completely withdrawing into some dark cave of his own, where he might drift away for good or drag himself back to what was left of the living. This was how it was for so many of the men and boys she had come across in these last few months of volunteering.

"At last!" It had only just gone 6 pm but Valentina was waiting for Anna just outside the Palace where the staff from the military hospital usually exited. "Quickly, they are over there in that carriage! No — keep your apron and headscarf on, we are all in disguise!"

She followed Valentina and scrambled into the carriage. Within minutes, the four women were chatting excitedly under the tree-lined road leading into the village, the clopping of the two horses drowning their plans.

Of course, Anna had met the princesses before, but it was the elder, Olga, with her nurse's headdress framing her astonishing wide Slavic cheekbones and deep grey eyes that made people notice her rather than Tatiana, her younger sister. Olga was smart and a reader who leaned over conspiratorially towards Anna in their ride to the village and told her she had read *The Rosary*, one of Anna's published books of poetry. She loved poetry she said, and then added a surprising addendum *and politics*.

Anna wondered how this could be true, considering her family had never shown interest in the rising disquiet amongst the Russian soldiers and civilians.

"Here we are!" Tatiana was two years younger than Olga but looked more like the Tsarina, with whom she was close.

To Anna's dismay, she recognised the shop as the same place where she had met Gumilyov, nearly ten years ago. She was just a schoolgirl at the time when he had approached her and asked her name while she shopped on Christmas Eve. She remembered feeling enthralled and repelled at the same time by his slow steady gaze.

"Now girls — let's run through the plan," said Valentina and Anna smiled across at her because she was always in charge, even if it included members of the Royal family. Valentina continued, "Now I will amble about with Tatiana and, Anna, you loop arms with Olga and remember — no giggling!" Valentina was already bubbling over with titters.

Once inside the brightly lit shop, Anna and Olga strolled about looking at whatever was on the display shelves and only really stopping to examine the small bottles of perfume and then the stationery.

Olga tugged at Anna's arm, "But how do you *buy* these things — if you want them?"

So, it is true, thought Anna, but without any hesitation, she said, "Follow me and watch what I do."

With that, Anna selected a small box of crème coloured writing paper with matching envelopes. She walked briskly across to the counter and placed it into the hands of the attendant.

"Is it a gift, Miss? Would you like it gift-wrapped?" The attendant was probably in his sixties with a clean woollen brown suit that had seen better days.

"No. Not a gift," Anna responded and placed a rubble note next to the box of stationery.

She then turned her back on the attendant who wrote something swiftly on a docket and popped it, with Anna's money, into a small dish above his head. He then rang a bell and way up behind on the mezzanine level Olga watched, wide-eyed, as the dish was trolleyed along a wire contraption to the cashier who sat up there above them. The cashier assiduously emptied the contents of the small dish, examined the docket closely, counted out some coinage, spilled it ostentatiously into the dish, rang his own little bell and away it flew on the wire until it reached the counter.

Anna couldn't help but laugh out loud at the astonishment on Olga's face. Luckily the shop attendant was too busy wrapping her box of stationery in brown paper and string to notice. To him, they were simply two young nurses shopping after their shift had ended up at the Palace Hospital.

"Thank you, Miss," he said bowing respectfully and handing Anna her parcel. He then placed her change on a tiny silver tray which Anna collected, then she linked arms with Olga and sauntered away.

"Gosh! How wonderful! Let's do that again!" Olga was riven with delight.

"What about some perfume?" suggested Anna.

"Yes! Perfume! Great idea." Then she added quickly, "I have my own money, you know."

"That's good — because I wasn't going to give you any of mine." Olga turned swiftly and saw Anna attempting to hide a smile.

"How selfish," was Olga's swift riposte and they laughed easily.

Some of the small corks were too difficult to unplug but the two women managed to lean into a number of different scents and discuss which was most appropriate for attracting an admirer or attending a dance or even working in the hospital.

Anna was finding the Grand Duchess quite good fun. She was surprisingly well-read and high-spirited but what was more compelling, she was disarmingly honest in her opinions.

She told Anna, as she had several times already to her own housemaids and nurses, that she despised *Our Friend*. She explained that the Tsarina invited *Our Friend* most evenings to the private Royal quarters in the Palace. It took only Anna a moment to realise she was referring to the starets himself, Father Grigori Rasputin.

"I mean, I know exactly what people say about him!" Olga sniffed cautiously at one small bottle she had just uncorked, "And my darling nurse, Maria, who looked after us in the nursery, fell to his rapacious advances one night when he was prowling about our rooms!" She put the perfume back and chose another.

Anna watched on a little aghast at the younger women's alarming openness.

"Anyway, Mamma dismissed her and Anya Vyrubova told me later that Maria was impregnated by one of the Cossacks but I know it was Father Grigori …" Olga seemed set on the small violet glass of perfume that she had originally examined, "And he is still allowed to come into our rooms late at night."

Anna's face must have shown her horror, indeed, her own body felt like it was sinking in the quicksand of the most vicious of all rumours, because Olga added hastily, "Father Grigori says it is to pray for us." She lowered her voice, "Particularly when our courses are heavy."

Anna thought about her friends back in the city and how they spoke of Rasputin as a toxin crawling about the Palace.

Olga pushed on, "My sisters and I, we bleed very heavily each month and …" She paused and Anna saw Olga's skin wan. "Well … he says he comes in to comfort us and place his healing blessings upon us."

The two women stood at the wooden display cabinet of perfume.

The younger woman's voice sounded quiet and lost as she said, "But I told Mumma I didn't like him stroking my younger sisters to sleep — I mean, I am nearly 20 but they are too young to understand ...”

Anna knew she needed to steer her young companion over to the counter to make her first purchase, a vial of perfume, but somehow the joy had gone out of their playful evening. Anna felt the heavy weight of Olga's shared confidence and wondered what was happening to her beloved Russia.

“Let's buy my perfume and find Tatiana and Valentina,” said Olga as if there had been nothing untoward in what she had shared with Anna.

As the purchase was made, without mishap, Anna thought about the sheltered reality in which the princesses lived. Despite its high stone walls and a score of Cossack guards surrounding the Palace, two intruders had stolen into their protected world. One had entered their daily lives and was the sordid horror of the war-wounded soldiers who had been desperately fighting to protect Mother Russia. The other had entered their bedroom and this was the holiest of all depraved beasts in Russia.

Anna wondered to herself whether this was one of the reasons why Rasputin had been recently banished by the Tsar to Pokrovskoe, Western Siberia.

But everyone knew, including Anna, that the Tsar was weak and such an exile would not last long, especially as the Tsar was now at military Headquarters.

3

Aysen heard the piano accordion well before he saw the performer. He was a young soldier sitting on the railway platform in Moscow, oblivious to the oncoming foot traffic that surged about him. The old piano accordion moved about on his lap and within his expansive arms. The soldier was legless. Both legs were gone and the stumps protruded like some half-forgotten limbs.

His playing was slow and plaintive.

Aysen paused. He dropped his bag at his feet and shut his eyes. His back was to the sun and he stayed there on the platform just metres away from the musician, listening. Not thinking about the train that he must board or the hospital's discharge papers in his pocket. He stood in that moment on the Belorusskaya Railway Station and thought about the music.

The soldier was good. He compressed and expanded the bellows effortlessly and the melodic notes rang sweet, like birdsong hopping alongside a spring stream.

The music dipped then rose up and up and up, faster and more urgently; then around a corner, the music flew and plummeted downwards, and upwards and upwards, nearly disappearing, then it fluttered and flew, again up and up and up and up, until finally the music was caught in Aysen's throat and he thought he must move on otherwise he would be that man who started crying on the platform and no one could stop him.

He opened his eyes and gathered up his kit and then he heard the pace of the music shift and change. It moved to a folksy melody and although he may have been imagining it, he thought the pedestrians on the platform slowed.

Russia, O My Russia, Hail!

The soldier's voice was rich and deep. It rose over the accordion, about the crowd and above the unintelligible rail announcements.

Steeds as tempests flying,
Howling of the distant wolves,

Eagles high, shrill crying!

His singing seemed to charge the very air about him and Aysen saw that indeed, some people had stopped and were gathered about the soldier.

Hail, my Russia, hail!

The voices of the crowd joined him, and their song soared to the high steel rafters of the train station — startling the pigeons, which, on cue, took flight.

Hail high! Hail thy green forests proud,

It seemed the entire railway station was singing with all its might.

Hail thy silvery nightingales,

The very lungs of its people expanding in and out and in and out with love.

Hail Steppes and wind and cloud!

The arms of Russia stretched out to all.

Russia, O My Russia, Hail!
Hail, my Russia, hail!

And in that instant, blinking back tears and standing shoulder to shoulder with his fellow countrymen and women, Aysen saw, in this cathedral of transport signalling progress, might and power, that Russia still believed in a Tolstoian romance, serenaded to them by a broken and ruined troubadour.

Then as quickly as it had gathered the crowd dispersed and Aysen was hauled along onto the platform marked for Minsk.

He pulled along his kit bag. Although he had his orders to return to his regiment, he was still weak from battling typhus. But he was one of the lucky ones — so many others had not survived. Meanwhile, he had spent time recovering in a sun-chair in a Moscow military hospital.

And then Sayaana had visited.
Did she come? At first, Aysen didn't quite know if she was an apparition or real. One day he was sitting in the garden of the hospital listening to the birdcall and the next moment his beautiful Sayaana was walking towards him.
Her hair was liquid black like a moonless night sky, thick and wondrous. She knelt right there in the grass with the other patients and staff looking on curiously

and laid her warm scarfless head on his lap. When eventually she looked up at him her eyes smiled with their old mischief and he knew she was a force with which to be reckoned. As it turned out, her father had escorted her all the way to Moscow.

Later, when he was strong enough to move to the convalescent wing of the hospital, Aysen shared his letters from Kaskil with Sayaana. His cousin wrote they had been redeployed to the Siberian 12th Division, somewhere down south in Polish Russia. They were supporting the Russian 3rd Army and, according to Kaskil, had every intention of just kicking back there in the vineyards and orchards until it was time to pack up and go home to celebrate victory.

Sayaana had told him then that she hoped it would be soon because she was pregnant.

Aysen was sure that's what she told him.

Kaskil wrote that the boy who had led them to Grodno had been picked up by some Brit, an official military observer, and was now working for him as a sort of junior orderly. This amused Aysen no end, considering there was nothing subservient about that boy, whatsoever.

Sayaana had not stayed long and left with her father the day before Aysen himself was to join the Siberian 12th. She didn't cry but he did, there on the grounds of the Moscow hospital after she had walked away. He could still feel her lips, warm and sure, against his ear, *Don't forget to come back to us*, she had whispered, and her eyes tried hard to smile.

A day later instead of heading east and following her home, which every bone in his body insisted, he boarded the train heading west, southwest.

At the very moment when Aysen was boarding the train along with thousands of other soldiers, the seasoned and grim with their furlough ended or the rookies eager and terrified with their wide-eyed watchfulness, his cousin Kaskil was being buried alive.

4

Kaskil had woken that beautiful May morning, just before dawn. It wasn't that he was getting used to being away from his home in the Yakutia, with its startling velveteen blue irises running riot about the valley floor, it was that southern Polish Russia, with its ripening vines of heavy grapes and peach laden trees, made for rather a nice sojourn. Well, it certainly was an improvement on everywhere else he had been since answering the call to fight for the Motherland.

Kaskil pushed out of his shallow dugout and decided it would be a good plan to mosey back to the forest and smell his way to the Supply wagons, for the purpose of finding out if there was anything on offer. It would be at least another 40 or 50 minutes before they would be called to relieve the platoons hunkering down on the closest defence lines to the enemy. Kaskil fancied himself a bit of a raconteur when it came to the Supply crew, charming his way into a spare chunk of bread or a few vegetables or even some corned meat.

He moved quietly, enjoying the peace of a morning that was still dozing with only one eye open.

What Kaskil didn't know, and what the entire Russian 3rd Army had no suspicion of, was that the Germans had decided that today, and for every other day that followed, their first and foremost aim was to knock Russia out of the ring.

Soberly, discretely and methodically, the German 9th Army was massing along the 130 kilometre Front, from Gorlice to Tarnow, southeast of Krakow. This was the Front that the Russian 3rd had been protecting with a certain level of indifference.

Meanwhile, what Kaskil believed, along with all his fellow countrymen, was that when Russia took the Fort of Przemyśl, less than six weeks ago, the tide had at last turned in their favour. It would now only be a matter of days before their troops would be over the Carpathian Mountains and into Hungary. After that, as every Russian knew, it would all be over. The Germans would then be released of their obligation to protect an annihilated Austro-Hungarian Empire and, as there really wasn't an issue between the Russians and the Germans, the Tsar and the Kaiser being look-alike cousins, then they could all just simply go home.

There was one Russian who knew that today's attack was coming. Grand Duke Nicholas Nikolaevich had received intelligence a few days beforehand that the German 9th was facing off the Russian 3rd along the Gorlice-Tarnow Front and that an attack was imminent; Germany had eight divisions, Russia five. But the Grand Duke sat and waited and then decided he would not make a counter move.

What Kaskil was thinking, as he sauntered off to Supply, was that the thick undergrowth beneath his boots promised the lush warmth of spring and summer and even a furlough home. To think that all his life he had a wanderlust to leave the top end of Siberia and travel Russia and perhaps even the world. It was this desire, to see more than just the Yakutia, that led him to eagerly take up arms against Russia's invaders.

The irony was that as soon as he left home, all he wanted to do was return.

He walked on contemplating this strange turn of events.

Just as Kaskil got to the Supply wagons, he looked skyward and noticed the sun spearheading the pine tops above him and it was then, like a giant slow-motion wave, that the ground rose up and his knees gave way beneath him and he tumbled backward. The roiling earth bucked up and down and up and down until the air in Kaskil's lungs was dragged out of him. Wave after wave after wave the forest tossed him about like a paper boat on a giant ocean. And somewhere in the distance, he heard the most appalling noise, as if the world was imploding.

Then Kaskil remembered nothing.

Time passed.

It was dark and warm and the taste of woodsy mulch and crunchy soil was in his mouth.

He lay still.

Time passed.

The weight of the earth above held him hard and fast, the stench of loamy petrichor filled his nostrils.

Kaskil had been buried alive.

Maybe the Yakut died or lost consciousness or left to go home to the Lena Basin where wildflowers littered the valley floor and the only prints were those of newborn cubs.

Time passed.

Somewhere overhead, a ghastly muffled pounding throbbed.

Gradually, the belly of the earth stopped churning and land remembered it was not a sea, swirling in a storm of augury and portent, but fixed and solid ground.

Kaskil's skin awoke to hearing.

His short-haired grandmother, with her skin cross-hatched in lines, laughed and said without speaking, *Get going now little one!*

Kaskil's fingertips twitched at the earth's rhythmic pounding. It moved like a heartbeat up through his shoulders and into his chest.

His grandmother called out his skin name, *Brave-Fortune!*

Kaskil shuddered and the caul of soil decorticated off him and shucked him out.

Eyes clenched, like a mewling newborn, he crawled up from under clods of soil and tree roots and branches. He was trying to get somewhere, anywhere. All the while his pulse smashed in rhythm with the bombardment. He propped himself against a large tree and wiped away dirt and debris from his face and eyes.

He tried to get his bearings.

Chaos ran around him as soldiers sought the shelter of any kind. The Supply wagons were all but abandoned and he could see officers shouting orders and attempting to whip some order into the hell that had launched itself upon them.

He remembered he had left his dugout earlier that morning which was about 300 meters from the enemy.

He had gone in search of a feed.

He hadn't reached the Supply, he was sure of that fact.

Somewhere, in the back of his mind, he wondered what that meant for the Russian defence lines.

The hammering of the enemy's big guns was then followed by heavy howitzers. The mortar shells were blasting men as far back as 50 metres from detonation. Kaskil felt his heart explode again and again and again as the bombardment continued.

It was then that he realised the defence lines he left this morning were no longer defence lines. They were mass graves.

Kaskil wanted to tuck himself, fetal-like, inside the enormous exposed roots of the trees. There was no way he could stay on his feet let alone join the throng of Russian soldiers staggering this way and that before another round of bombardment hit them.

The sound was deafening and Kaskil knew his ears would burst and bleed before long.

In the end, he clung to the soil and tried to wait out the cacophony of hell.

But it went on and on and less and less frequently he saw bedraggled Russians moving out of the shelter of the forest.

Two or three hours in, with the relentless shelling smashing the world around him, Kaskil had drifted back to the Lena Valley in the Yakutia.

The long cool quiet fields of spring opened up, and he and his brother and cousin hunted with stealth and patience. Elk and moose made them dismount and leave their horses a long way off and walk for hours. They caught squirrels or hares in the hushed meadows, they fished for salmon and mundu in the river gurgling over rocky turns and twists. The jays fluttered about the pines, muted, fussy and alert. Across Yakutia, the sky stretched like a tight drum. It was infinitely tranquil and ever watchful.

I will stay here forever, thought Kaskil, as he was rocked to and fro, nestling in the never-ending offensive.

At some point he found himself thinking about those poor bastards he had left that morning. Although the platoon was at least three or four lines back in the defence, he knew they would have been completely annihilated. He tried not to think of who they were and was glad no name or face came to mind.

There would be no hope for survival.

He heard a couple of Fokkers fly over the forest top and listened to the rattle of their machine guns as they picked off the moving wounded exposed on the Front lines.

Kaskil, like most Russians, never dug deep trenches, but rather opted for shallow dugouts; digging trenches inevitably led to uncovering the dead and no Russian in their right mind was prepared to bring that omen upon himself.

Eventually, he realised there was little to no return fire from the Russian Front lines.

We are dead men, he thought and hunkered down in the wooden arms of the tree's roots on the forest floor for all he was worth.

By early afternoon, the pieces of sky through the forest roof were now just a grey smoky haze. Once again, some officers were moving troops through the forest towards the Front. Kaskil decided he needed to scramble up, somehow, and join the fracas. The bombardment had quietened, mercifully, for the last 20 or 30 minutes but in its place, he could hear cries and gunshots from what must be skirmishes between the forest edge and the Front line.

Then out of nowhere, he saw his lieutenant, who was attempting to stride about upright, like some other officers, despite the fact that they still had sea legs.

"Sir!" called Kaskil and young Lieutenant Gusev looked across at the dirt-covered Yakut struggling to stand up against a tree.

The lieutenant looked dazed, "The enemy has given us a hammering!" cried Gusev who seemed to be struggling to breathe. "How did you manage to crawl out of your position?"

Kaskil hesitated, "Woke up before the whizz-bangs, and ... just so happened to walk this way ..."

"Well done. Well done," Gusev looked distracted. "Look we have heard the Germans took out our defences and are pushing us back. My orders are to get my mob and retreat but I'm afraid it might just be you and me, for the time being ..."

The young lieutenant paused and again looked about as if he was unsure where he was, "Our Front defence lines have been wiped out."

Kaskil didn't know whether Gusev was repeating this for his own benefit or for Kaskil's. Then the young lieutenant leaned over and vomited, resting one hand up against the tree trunk that was steadying Kaskil.

The Yakut waited.

"Right." The lieutenant pulled away from the tree and took stock, "Let's pull back and help these reinforcements get through. They've been in a fix because of this bloody heavy fire we have been under all morning. C'mon, grab your rifle!"

Kaskil didn't need to be told twice and moved as best he could behind Gusev, as they made their way deeper into the forest.

There he saw hundreds of wounded and dying that must have been brought past him while he was buried alive earlier that morning.

He was glad for Gusev and his decisive presence.

They walked and rested with more and more Russians who had also been ordered to retreat. *What a monstrous blow,* thought Kaskil.

Every so often he would wait as the young lieutenant stopped to talk to a fellow infantry officer and gather whatever information he could. Afterward, the lieutenant talked quietly to Kaskil about how the Germans would have been preparing this calmly and efficiently for some time. It was a diabolically well thought out plan, to drive them away from the Carpathian Mountains and Galicia.

Gusev estimated there were only a few hundred survivors out of the 17,000 men who had made up the Russian 3rd.

Kaskil and Gusev moved off the forest road to allow soldiers from the Caucasus to replace them at the Front. They gazed on these strange Moslems, in their cherkeska caftans, with blatant curiosity. The young lieutenant pointed out the Tartar Regiment in their red straps and burgundy cowls, then the Chechen, and after that the Daghestan, all in different colours and many bearing dark facial features that were more Arabic than Slavic.

Kaskil and others standing by heard what sounded to them like gibberish spoken by these ferocious Russian warriors. And their fearlessness was indisputable.

Later Kaskil would read it was 40,000 soldiers from the Caucasus who marched forward to fill the breach.

Kaskil looked over the heads of the new recruits, moving on towards what had once been the Russian Front line, and to his astonishment, he saw his cousin.

"LANCE CORPORAL!" he yelled.

Aysen peeled off and saluted Gusev and then caught Kaskil in a bear hug.

"Alright you two," smiled the lieutenant. "I take it you know each other. Where are you headed, Lance Corporal?"

"My orders from Moscow were to find my platoon, sir, and report to my commanding officer."

Aysen looked better than he had when Kaskil last saw him, which would have been six weeks back at the Red Cross base alongside the Minsk railway station. Of course, he had written and even received news from Aysen while he was recovering from typhus in Moscow, but he never thought today, of all days, he would see his cousin's familiar face.

Kaskil gave him a friendly thump.

"Well let's get on men," said Gusev, whose spirits seemed to have lifted in seeing another platoon member.

They moved off in the opposite direction to the Caucasian Corp and Kaskil took the opportunity to catch Aysen up on what had happened. Kaskil was a tireless talker and Aysen, a good listener. Even as boyhood pals they were good company but thoughts of Kaskil's brother, Tuyaara, who had died at the battle of Łódź late last year, remained heavy between them. They had promised their family that all three of them would return when the war was won. This was not to be.

"What about the others?" asked Aysen quietly.

"I never saw anything like it. You couldn't stand up, shrapnel was landing 30 or 40 metres from where the bombs exploded. Everyone was lost ... I was back in the forest, they were in the dugouts ... it was ... they were ..."

They walked on together in silence for a while and then Aysen jostled his cousin and asked po-faced, "Bet you were off taking a shit somewhere — or scrounging a feed."

Both of them chuckled and kept pace behind the lieutenant.

After a moment Aysen asked, "And the boy?"

"Valentin! No, he set off a while ago with the biggest Cossack you've ever seen. Supposed to be driving about with some important Tommy — but I feel sorry for the Cossack, that kid takes no prisoners!"

They laughed again, in their quiet companionable way.

5

Valentin Gavrilov had no intention of once again waiting back at the hotel for Professor Bernard Pares and that filthy Cossack to return from their daily reconnaissance. Initially, Valentin was grateful Kaskil had volunteered him to be Pares' batman, only to realise later it was a fancy word for servant. For the last two days they had been in a town formerly known by its German sounding title of Lemberg but now renamed, Lemberik. This was only confused further by the locals — half were Polish Russian who referred to their town as Lwow, while the other half were Ukrainian Russians, referring to it as Lviv.

Things were far less complicated for Valentin back in his hometown of Augustovo.

Valentin made his way down the stairs of the Metropolitan Hotel and waited outside the breakfast room. He was rehearsing his argument as to why the Professor should take him on his trip this morning, when the overfed Cossack fool, hat tilted at a ridiculous perky angle, appeared in front of him. He wore a semi-permanent sneer fastened beneath his over coiffured moustache.

"What do you want, small-fry?"

"I'm here to see Professor Pares." Valentin held the Cossack's icy stare.

"Piss off." His moustache never moved when he spoke, Valentin noted, only when he stuffed his gob with food.

Then Pares exited the breakfast room with the leather satchel he always carried and called out, "Valentin bring my binoculars, would you? I must have left them in my room."

Valentin held the Cossack's gaze a moment longer and then moved swiftly up the staircase.

Pares' spoke Russian with a Russian accent. Apparently, he had been a great historian and teacher back in England. He said he was from Cambridge but when Valentin asked if that was one of England's provinces Pares had quickly sketched out a detailed map and patiently explained the counties and cities and just when Valentin thought he could not stifle the yawns any longer, the Professor continued on, marking out the universities and significant castles and major ports.

Valentin wasn't interested in going to England, why would anyone live anywhere but Russia?

But Valentin admitted to himself he was impressed with Pares who could not only speak Russian but could also read and write it.

Valentin suspected the arrogant Cossack he had to put up with could neither read nor write. Only yesterday he had been thumped hard in the stomach by that brute when Valentin pointed out that the Cossack was merely a driver for the Professor.

Valentin flew back down to the Professor who was clambering into the Charron.

"Sir, I could come with you this morning, in case you need —"

"Goddamnit!" hissed the Cossack who was, once again, having trouble with the hand crank at the front of the vehicle, a daily occurrence that Pares chose to ignore.

"Sir, I know I could be helpful to you and —"

Chutter, chutter, chutter spluttered the car. The Cossack swung himself behind the steering wheel and leaned out through the open window to release the handbrake.

"Kuznetsov," called Pares over the bubble and hiss of the engine. "Valentin is joining us today. Climb up front, boy!"

And that was that.

Valentin felt his face split in a grin as he deftly hauled himself in beside the Cossack who was already picking up speed as they coasted down the outer streets of Lemberik *heading hopefully*, thought Valentin, *to the Front!*

It was the third week in May and according to the Professor, since the start of the month the Germans had been pushing Russia out of south-eastern Polish Russia.

Some were calling it *The Great Retreat*.

How could this be possible? Valentin thought miserably.

Today he had heard the Professor and the Cossack, Kuznetsov, discuss the best route to Radymno, just north of the fortress Przemyśl. Valentin would have like to have seen this so-called impenetrable fortress the Russians had recently taken from the enemy but considering this was the first day he was allowed to join the reconnaissance team, he wasn't going to jeopardise a second trip by suggesting visits to this place and that along the way.

Valentin hunkered down enjoying the spring breeze in his face. The roads were consistently potholed and the Cossack made a show of swerving dramatically at the last minute to avoid a broken axle. The sun was heating up and its thick warmth soon filled the cabin. The countryside flew by on either side of the vehicle, mostly farmlands with rustic homesteads and small ruins of stone fences.

The morning drove on.

After a while, Valentin realised he was watching dark columns of smoke rising a long way off in the distance to their right. Kuznetsov reached out his arm and pointed, in case the Professor had not seen, but when Valentin looked over his shoulder, he could see the Englishman peering through the binoculars in the direction of the smoke.

As the vehicle made its way to Radymno the blue and yellow ink sky began to smudge into dirty grey.

Meanwhile, the Charron rattled closer and closer to their destination and the daylight bruised darker with tawdry browns, dusky violet and steely ash.

By the time Kuznetsov pulled up behind some shrubs, the entire sky beyond the ridge was a smouldering gloom. The smell of burning hit the back of Valentin's nostrils and throat.

Beyond the parked vehicle was a rise and past that, obvious to everyone in the vehicle, was a battle underway. The crash and smash of distance artillery reverberated beneath them.

"Valentin, stay by the car and if you see Kuznetsov and me scrambling back down that hill, start up the Charron immediately," said the Professor as he scrambled out of the vehicle. He then asked as an afterthought, "Can you use the crank starter?"

He didn't wait for Valentin's answer as he hurriedly strapped on his satchel, like some late schoolboy. Pares was also juggling his binoculars in one hand and a notepad and pencil in another. Valentin slung a canteen across the Professor's chest and finished off the satchel straps.

The Cossack was already striding up the slope when the sound of two monumental crashes shook the very earth upon which they stood; both the Professor and Valentin ducked instinctively but Kuznetsov strode on.

Knob-head, thought Valentin.

The acrid pungent smell rose up from the other side of the hill and belched into the air above them.

The Professor gathered himself together and moved swiftly up the hill.

The young batman waited a few minutes, then began his own ascent. There was no way he was going to wait by the vehicle when he might defend Mother Russia.

At the rise of the hill Professor Pares and the Cossack stood and looked down at the valley below them, hugged by undulating hills to the left and right. For approximately 400 metres, the valley floor was littered with Russian soldiers moving this way and that under enemy attack. Fiery explosions shot up spasmodically, devouring this church or that barn or this homestead or that tree along the burning valley. Meanwhile, from the safety of their eyrie, the British observer, his Cossack, and, a little further back, the young batman watched on.

The whole atmosphere was tight with smoke, but every so often the most extraordinary thing would happen; as the bright sunshine pierced through the smoke-laden sky it would reach out like a blessing or a curse and touch the vulnerable pockets of Russian soldiers seeking both visibility in order to find the enemy, and invisibility so they might hide from them.

Valentin stood a few metres behind the Professor and Kuznetsov. The young batman saw what they saw but couldn't comprehend what he was seeing. He watched as scrambling insects, unaware of the nearness of their enemy or their own fellow soldiers, moved this way and that, seemingly without rhyme or reason. On and on the Russian soldiers were being pushed back out of the valley and up into the exposed hillsides where the three of them were standing. The Russians were being systematically annihilated by an array of howitzers or, in the more wooded areas, machine gunners.

This wasn't the noble battle that his brothers had told him would be his destiny, as was theirs and their father's.

Shells and shrapnel began crashing closer to where Valentin stood, and a Russian soldier dragged himself up the ridge to the Professor and the Cossack. The soldier had been sent by his commanding officer to see if more ammunition was arriving.

To Valentin's shock, the young soldier had nothing on his feet.

"No — the telephones are giving no answers. We are waiting for reinforcements, sir, or ammunition or ..." The soldier was exhausted and seemed unable to finish his sentence.

The Professor handed his own canteen to the soldier who thanked him, distractedly, and drank and drank and drank and, without shame, handed back an empty canteen.

As if revived the soldier explained, "The trenches were destroyed and the Austrians have taken our line."

Another explosion shook the four of them at the top of the rise and they all looked down into the valley and saw a hut burst into flames. They could see ants of men scurrying about trying to avoid falling wood and burning debris.

"We can't get contact with the other Frontoviks," the soldier said. "Down there in the valley ..."

Valentin didn't know why the soldier was telling the Professor all this, maybe he thought he could bring help but it was obvious from the road they had travelled that no support or supplies were coming.

"We're basically in retreat, sir. The last order was to retire at nightfall but that's hours away," the soldier looked desperate and if the Professor offered to drive him out there and then, Valentin suspected the soldier would have agreed.

If only I could shoot some of those filthy Germans, thought Valentin savagely. *I would never turn and run!*

At that moment they espied movement in the valley close to the ascent of the hill. Russian officers on horseback could be seen galloping forward towards

Russian battalions that crouched 300 metres from the enemy. The officers must be either delivering orders to retreat or charge.

Meanwhile, another soldier was making his way, hand over fist, up the hill before them. When he arrived at their feet, he seemed to be in a worse condition than the first. He announced without preamble the dreaded words: "We are surrounded!"

They all looked at the Professor who was watching the passage of the wounded now crawling up the hill towards them.

"Have you been ordered to retreat?" Kuznetsov spat incredulously.

The soldier ignored him because he was looking down the hill, as was the Professor, at the retreating Russian army. Maybe a couple of thousand darting and scampering Russian figures were making their way out of the valley floor and up the hill towards them.

Suddenly, they noticed a column of blue figures coming up behind the Russians as they swarmed the wooded hillside.

Then Valentin saw the Cossack point to a couple of Russians rapidly setting up two machine guns mid-way on the hillside. They were more or less out of sight in some brushwood 30 or so metres from the approaching enemy.

Valentin looked down into the valley and didn't know whether he imagined it or not, but he saw the enemy come on, with their fair hair glinting in the momentary sunlight and their pale young faces peering anxiously forward.

Where were their officers?

At least, Valentin thought hotly, *Russian officers lead from the front!*

From where they stood, they heard the tattoo of machine-gun fire thundering all over the valley and the Austrian column disappeared into the forested floor.

And Valentin wondered if the pale-faced enemy, the fair-haired youths, were lost.

The barefooted soldier who had first come upon the Professor pushed past the observers and rushed down the other side of the hill towards their parked vehicle. As he pounded on Valentin noticed he had no rifle. Somehow, his retreating back with his grimy threadbare uniform whipping about him galvanised Valentin who flew down the hill towards the vehicle and the awaiting crankshaft.

And it was at that very point that the retreating Russian army poured over the hill.

Valentin's thumping heart felt as if it might explode, as he slipped and scrambled down the rough descent, the sweat of desperation blinding his sight. All he knew was that there was no way the Charron could save anyone other than himself, the Professor and the Cossack.

Valentin grabbed the crankshaft.

The Charron was their ark against the flood of Russian soldiers.

"HURRY!" he heard the Professor roar as he and the Cossack surged down amongst the retreating soldiers.

"Pack in some of the worst of the wounded, Kuznetsov!"

Valentin had the vehicle chugging and ready to go.

He was wretchedly anxious to be on the road as soon as possible. And he couldn't seem to get the pale-faced, fair-haired youths out of his mind. They couldn't have all been killed by the machine gunners.

Kuznetsov had managed somehow to shove in three wounded Russians on the back seat and someone was propped on the floor. At the last moment a young Frontovik desperately pleading for his older comrade to be taken, was successful, and the ancient soldier was passed in across the laps of the seated wounded.

There were no groans.

Valentin slung himself quickly in between Kuznetsov and the Professor on the front seat and as the Cossack released the outside handbrake he heard him yell at the young fellow who had been so grateful that they had taken his older friend to, "GET THE HELL ON BOARD!" and Valentin saw this young soldier jump the running board alongside the Professor and hold on tight.

The vehicle thundered along the road and Valentin was grateful for the Cossack's heavy foot on the accelerator. He glanced into the back seat. The men had been bandaged haphazardly in the field, but he was sure the fellow curled up on the back floor was unconscious or dead.

The old soldier who lay across the laps of those on the back seat was saying, "Thanks be to Thee, Oh Lord! Eternal gratitude to you, Oh Lord!"

The young fellow riding on the running board kept ducking his head through the back window and calling out, "Nearly there Harchin, nearly there!"

He was like a loving son as he tugged at the old soldier's leg or foot, readjusting his position as if it would make all the difference to his comfort.

One of the wounded explained to the Professor what had happened to them.

"We had come down from Jaslo," the wounded soldier in the back clarified. "We were being bombed by the aeroplanes ..." There was the sound of wonder in his voice, despite the horror of a battle gone terribly wrong. "We were driven out. No living man could have driven us from our position, but shells fell night and day till our trenches were levelled. I crawled out afterwards, but most were gone ..."

Valentin didn't know whether the soldier in the back was referring to the oncoming enemy or to his fellow platoon members.

"Thanks be to the Lord! Eternal praise and glory unto him," murmured Harchin.

And Valentin heard the young lad on the running board call, "Nearly there, good friend, nearly there."

As they charged through the roads towards Lemberik, Valentin saw the hordes of retreating Russian soldiers moving east away from the Front line. There was no panic or hurry in the great throng. Soldiers more erect and mobile seemed to help their neighbour as they moved on with the sun setting at their backs. There was something strange and disturbing about their silent shuffle east.

No one seemed to speak or stop, the retreating army just moved on without a word and their long dark shadows lengthening before them.

It was then that Valentin realised he was witnessing something profoundly noble in this moment of Russia's abject failure. These men from across the eternal expanse of the Motherland had come to do their best, to risk their lives, to protect their country.

Many without boots, without rifles, without training.

All the while the Professor asked questions to those inside the vehicle, nodding and taking notes in his notebook. This was his way. Kind and considerate but somehow detached. *He may speak Russian as a Russian, he may write Russian as a Russian, and he may read Russian as a Russian — but he would never be Russian,* concluded Valentin.

By dusk, they had arrived back in Lemberik and Kuznetsov, with Valentin, helped the wounded from the vehicle and into the hospital. The elderly Harchin offered thanks and praise to the Lord as his young comrade assisted the nurses with his litter. The soldier on the floor of the vehicle was alive, after all, and he uncurled himself from his foetal position and was carried in also.

The hospital was a Polish monastery, a whitewashed building in amongst fields of gently sloping vineyards and orchards. As Valentin helped the last of the wounded they had brought back from the attack near Radymno he pressed his palms against the cool stone of the cloister as they passed through to the Red Cross station.

He needed to assure his body that they had made it to safety.

On the walls of the cloister were mosaics depicting the Stations of the Cross. Valentin slowed as he passed the small tiles that swirled in colours of skin and blood and thorns. *Jesus condemned to death ... Jesus carrying his cross ... Jesus falling the first time ... Jesus meeting his mother ... Simeon of Cyrene helps Jesus to carry his cross ...*

Valentin knew the rest of the stations off by heart and felt strangely consoled by this familiar tale of human suffering. The vulnerabilities of the human body, the courage of the human spirit.

Valentin felt overwhelmed with fatigue and just wanted to lay down, there and then, in one of the cots a nurse was preparing. He heard her cluck gently to a wounded soldier who was crying as he was lowered down into the cot. She pulled and tucked and smoothed and fussed about the blanket as if that action itself would right the terrible unspeakable wrongs he had seen and done.

Eventually, her efforts calmed him, and the soldier closed his eyes.

Valentin watched as she stroked his dirt-encrusted hair across his forehead and hummed a tune. The soldier smiled, faintly, and didn't open his eyes again.

Later when he was dressing the Professor for his evening meal, the Englishman uncharacteristically talked aloud, not to Valentin and yet besides the young batman, there was no one else in the small tidy room.

"It was all for nothing. The line so desperately defended by the courageous Russians has been taken from them in a blink of an eye ... what was it all for? What was it all for?"

The Professor looked past the looking glass, where Valentin was reflected attaching his ivory cuff links and remained still for some time.

"One hundred thousand Russians taken as prisoners and 80 guns captured."

The Professor's voice was calm, but it belied his despair, "Poorly trained and poorly shod Russians are being sent out to the Front without guns."

Valentin tried not to listen, he was tired and wanted to get to his own cot.

"We will not be able to hold the line. Russia will be pushed back and back and where will it end?"

Valentin gathered up the Professor's uniform to run it down to the laundry girls.

"Przemyśl will fall back into the hands of the enemy."

Valentin closed the Professor's bedroom door on these last words.

But the Professor, alone in his room, spoke on to the darkling mirror that flickered in candlelight, "Russia is drowning in its own blood."

Valentin eventually got to his own bed and as he fell asleep he dreamed of a nurse stroking his forehead, all the while she was humming a tune that his mother once hummed, long ago in his childhood. The nurse's touch was like silk and softly, slowly, he saw beneath her touch, his own pale face and fair-haired youth.

6

Gumilyov lent against the doorjamb and smoked his last cigarette.

He had just sat through a quick update delivered to the squadron by Lieutenant Zheleznyak about a final stand at Przemyśl.
Gumilyov was having none of it.

He dragged deeply on the cigarette.

For the start of June, it still wasn't warm enough. He had come to hate this broken-down old fortress that was as much a prison as it was an outpost. He thought about summer in St Petersburg and his son, Lev who would be three years old soon. He wished he had another cigarette and wondered whether Rad was around so he could scrounge one.

Gumilyov found himself thinking about the past and those times when he would smoke in bed with Anna, his dark willowy wife, who was as cold-hearted as she was beautiful.

Bitterly, he stubbed out the finished cigarette. The command handed down to Zheleznyak was that they take a stand for this godforsaken fortress; the enemy was circling and an attack was imminent.

And Gumilyov thought, *Another bloodbath, that's what it will be.*

Later, he pushed himself out into the dusty street and decided to go for a walk before blackout at 9 pm. They had been stationed at Przemyśl for just over two months. His original regiment, the 8th Hussars, had been reassigned to the Kiev Hussar Division of the 11th Army under General Selivanov.

As Gumilyov strolled about the town he noted, not for the first time, that Przemyśl was a rundown dive of a place and most of the taverns and shops had closed long ago. He was sick and tired of the whole debacle and wanted to be home in St Petersburg or more deliciously in Moscow with Jula, his one-time lover and nurse who wrote faithfully to him.

He moseyed along the broken pavement, under shopfronts and the occasional awning.

The Old House Bar was doing business and when Gumilyov slipped inside he noticed Rad was amongst the clientele. This bar on Jagiellonska Street over-looked the River San. It was always open. Its Jewish owners served good dumplings, mushroom soup and, very occasionally, borscht. It was early evening and Rad was already tucking into a serve of the dumplings and sucking back a large glass of beer.

Watered down, no doubt, thought Gumilyov but he ordered a beer regardless and sat in the wooden booth alongside Rad.

"Hungry?" enquired Gumilyov laconically.

"Fucking starving," answered Rad and wiped his mouth with his sleeve. He added, "What about the bullshit Zheleznyak was spinning! Defend Przemyśl!"

The scorn in his voice made Gumilyov smile as he looked around at the other people in the bar, mostly military.

"I'm not doing it — I'm done." Gumilyov hadn't re-alised he had made up his mind until he opened his mouth to Rad, "I haven't been home since we joined this circus and ..." He reached for the beer placed before him and took his first swig without finishing his sentence.

Rad pushed his plate away and said companionably, "You already had your furlough, mate! Two weeks in the arms of your sweetheart nurse back in Warsaw!"

They looked at each other and chuckled.

"Don't you bastards get fed at your own refectory?"
The Hussars looked up at Dr. Gerde.

"You gotta come down and take food from the few decent places that serve civilians!" said the Hungarian as he shoved himself into the booth where Rad and Gumilyov sat, all the while trying to catch the eye of the long-suffering waitress.

"How are *you* a civilian!? You're not civilised!" Rad said, laughing at his own joke

The doctor and the two Hussars had shared the occasional drink and meal on and off for the past few months. War made unlikely comrades: a Hungarian Jewish doctor and two Russian Hussars, one who was a university educated poet and the other, a son, grandson and great-grandson of a well-known St Petersburg military family. Gumilyov admitted to himself he enjoyed the moments he caught up with the doctor with their discussions about poetry, philosophy and, of course, the war.

Gumilyov said evenly, "Have you heard the rumours?"

Gerde often knew what was happening before the Russians did.

"Ahh, so the Russians think the Germans are coming to Przemyśl ..." Gerde didn't sound at all concerned and then he asked, "How long before your commanders think they might arrive?"

The men drank in silence and Gumilyov said quietly, "One, maybe two, days."

Rad lit a cigarette and dumped the packet on the table indicating to the others to go ahead and take one.

"What are you guys going to do? You know you're fucked." Gerde had a way of speaking that seemed brutal and uncaring but the two Russians had learned that this was not the case.

All three smoked with studied indifference.

The usual ease with which they normally shared a drink had vanished. Gumilyov realised that in many ways he hadn't thought further than the daily boredom of holding the captured Przemyśl. In his mind, it was as if the Russian 11th and their 120,000 prisoners, were going to live on together, here, for the rest of their lives.

It was strange how quickly life as prisoners or guards took on the semblance of normality. Many of the so-called soldiers of the Austro-Hungarian Empire were Slavs and therefore more Russian than Austrian — hence those they guarded seemed hardly the enemy.

But it wasn't just that which bothered Gumilyov. He had personally met and talked to different Russian combat units who were either coming through Przemyśl en route to the Carpathians or staggering back from a failed attempt to get through the mountainous pass in order to reach Hungary. While everyone back in Przemyśl hoped they were making headway not a single Russian soldier doubted it was a catastrophic failure.

More significantly, they all blamed the incompetence of those giving orders for the untold Russian fatalities.

The groundswell of anger was unnerving.

"So, what are you going to do?" When Gerde repeated his question Gumilyov knew, at that very moment, what he was going to do, but despite the friendship between him and the doctor, Gumilyov hesitated.

Gerde, after all, was Hungarian, and a Jew and not Russian. *Can he be trusted?* he wondered momentarily.

Gumilyov put down his glass and said quietly, "I know what's going to happen. We will be told to mount our horses, then wait in the wings."

Gerde had heard both Gumilyov and Rad express their frustration in the way Hussars were often sidelined, despite being highly skilled cavalry. Meanwhile, the moment there was a parade, the Hussars were lined up like the valued collection of Carl Faberge soldiers.

Gumilyov stubbed out his cigarette butt and continued, "We will watch on while the Germans come for us. Those of us who are lucky will be slaughtered before our horses are shot and for those less lucky, well, we will be taken, prisoner."

Gumilyov spat out the word *prisoner* like it was a curse.

"Besides," Gumilyov added sarcastically, "by the time the enemy arrive there will be different orders sent down — such as *Strategic Withdrawal!*"

Rad snorted in derision.

Gumilyov finished with a bomb, "So I am going to get out ahead of the bullshit. I joined up last August to fight for the Motherland and when I get out of this godforsaken Przemyśl I am going to make my way back to Warsaw, to do just that!"

The three men sat in the booth, surrounded by the debris of empty plates, dirty ashtrays and drained glasses.

Gerde dropped two cigarettes on the table from his pocket and lit up his own. Rad and Gumilyov picked up his offer, took a match and did the same.

It occurred to Gumilyov that this could be the last meal, drink and cigarette they might share.

After a while, Gerde lent into the table and fastidiously tapped his cigarette against the ashtray, "The northeast gate is not locked."

Gumilyov waited and without looking at Gerde asked, "Are you sure?"

"Absolutely. The gatekeeper is recovering in the hospital." The doctor sucked on his cigarette, "Drunken brawl. Lacerations. Nothing serious."

"But how do you know someone else won't lock the gate —"

"Because I have the key," and Gerde patted his coat pocket.

Gumilyov didn't know why Gerde had taken the key of one of the more obscure egress points of the town. Unless it was to help the Germans enter, but he didn't want to think about that now. Besides, it could mean the end was coming sooner than Gumilyov realised.

He thought quickly then said as nonchalantly as possible, "Maybe tomorrow morning or tomorrow night …"

Gerde inhaled deeply and then blew the smoke out across the mess in front of them, "If you are going, it needs to be tonight."

His voice was barely audible.

The men finished their cigarettes then Gerde insisted that he be the one to leave a few bills behind to pay for their food and drink.

They pushed outside into the summery darkness and Gumilyov was filled with sudden optimism.

He hugged Gerde and said, "Come with us brother."

Up until that point he hadn't even checked with Rad but he knew the huge Hussar would be in lockstep with him.

When he pulled back out of the embrace Gumilyov was surprised to see the doctor blink back tears behind his rimless spectacles.

"It is not my destiny," was his hoarse reply. "But I will read your poetry in years to come and say — this was my friend."

Rad hugged the small dark-haired, grey-eyed doctor and kissing him on both his cheeks asked, "You still got that battery acid for the priest's dick?"

The doctor's soft laugh could be heard long after he moved off towards the hospital.

Later that night, a pair of horses were led out of the stables by two Hussars. To any observer, it looked nothing more than a nightly reconnaissance. They moved quietly through the streets, past the dilapidated buildings, the ragged curtains drawn to suggest sleep and out towards the northeast exit of Przemyśl.

One of the horses nickered impatiently as the bigger of the two Hussars shoved the heavy wooden gate open.

There was no gatekeeper checking papers.

The horsemen passed through the egress and melted into the great night sky.

Chapter 5

July — August 1915

The small round pebbles were smooth and warm underfoot. The Black Sea rippled in and out and in and out and in and out of the shoreline. On it ran up and alongside Mandelstam as he pushed his bare feet into the beach and mooched along, with the gently sloping headland beside him.

He had arrived about an hour ago and was glad to dump his luggage in his room and take off to the beach in order to wash off his travel weariness.

Some would say the journey getting to the Crimea was a vagrant folly when troops and supplies desperately needed to occupy the trains, but so much had gone wrong in such a short time for Mandelstam that he had accepted Max's invite to the seaside resort of

Koktebel. And even though it took more than a week to get there from St Petersburg, it was worth it the moment he smelled the thick luxuriant salt of the sea. Max's mother had greeted Mandelstam and insisted he take the guest room on the first floor that overlooked the great expanse of watery blue. Saxe, cerulean and ultramarine rinsed the sky and the hills of this small forgotten village.

Mandelstam pushed onto the end of the beach and felt the familiar rumble of hunger deep in his stomach.

He was surprised when Max Kirienkov-Voloshin had invited him to stay for the summer months and write. By the time Mandelstam accepted the invitation he discovered his host had moved to Switzerland for the duration of the war but insisted the poet travel to Koktebel and be the guest at his house in the Crimea, which his mother had bought for a song years ago.

Mandelstam turned around at the end of the beach and began his retreat which would eventually lead back to the queer two-storey house overlooking the sweeping bay and pebbled shoreline.

St Petersburg was too much during summer and overcrowded with desperate refugees and maimed soldiers. Mandelstam shuddered. But it wasn't this alone which prompted him to long for escape.

He had not heard from his friend Gumilyov since he was stationed in the southeast of Polish Russia. Meanwhile, Mandelstam had read in the newspapers that the long-awaited success of taking Przemyśl had recently been overturned. Mandelstam worried that Gumilyov might have been caught up in this battle.

Despite all of his bravado about being a Hussar and fighting for Mother Russia, he knew Gumilyov's faith in the war was slipping. Initially, when he first went off to East Prussia and then Polish Russia, Gumilyov's letters were filled with exhilarating and noble declarations about the war. Gradually, this was replaced with cynicism and despair. Gumilyov had told Mandelstam that the chain of command was hopeless. Russian officers often made themselves sick on plum brandy and stuffed themselves senseless with goose and chicken while their men awaited certain death in the trenches. But while Mandelstam harboured grave doubts about the value of the war, it wasn't this that pushed him to travel over 2,000 kilometres in the last week.

Mandelstam let the warm water lap over his pale feet as he stood and looked at the village, his back to the expansive sea and, somewhere off in the distance, the Ottoman Empire.

He wanted to leave St Petersburg as soon as heard Anna Akhmatova was sick with tuberculosis. She had left for Slepnyovo, a forested village in Bezhetsk where

Gumilyov's mother cared for their son. He could not understand why he had to hear this news second hand.

He longed to go to Anna and hold her in his arms. His whole body still wanted to feel her bone-hard certainties, but most importantly he wanted to sup on the fierce passion she had for poetry. This love affair with verse was her strength and weakness. It attracted poets and writers and musicians who were already partly in love with themselves and thus saw their own reflection in her lust.

He knew that Anna still loved him and was hoping to persuade her to travel south and take up the sun and rest here in Koktebel with him at Max's place. But she had replied to his letter with an absolute *No!* And so he borrowed money from Mayakovsky for the train fare in order to come here, alone.

As Mandelstam pushed on back to Max's house, he noticed a softer palette washing over the late afternoon.

I don't understand women, thought Mandelstam. They took to him with such vehement desire only to move on to someone else.

Lidka had told him, the morning after their last night together at the Dog, that she didn't want to be with him anymore. She had said something vague about still mourning her dead husband, but Mandelstam knew it was more than that or less. She had just shut herself off from him as if her mind was a steel door that could be slammed against him.

Mandelstam left the beach and forgot to put his shoes back on. They dangled languidly in his right hand. His eyes blinked back tears at the memory of that breakup. He walked slowly up the steep footpath to Max's house on the cliff.

I will never love again, he thought to himself and pushed his weight against the front door. It opened with protest because of the years of sea salt, ocean rain and intense heat warping the doorframe.

When she looked up, Marina saw the tousled good looks of a young man whose skin was too pale for his large dark melancholic eyes. Her teacup was poised midway between her saucer and her lips. She couldn't remember whether she was about to sip her tea or had already done so. The young man stood still, looking across at her, but Marina had the strangest feeling he was not seeing her.

She was in luck because Sofia was deeply entrenched in a conversation with Max's mother, who insisted everyone use her pet name, Pra. Her grey hair was swept back in a dramatic coiffure and she wore a white kaftan with silver and blue trimming. She and Sofia were sharing news from abroad and the war.

Always the war! thought Marina as she placed her cup quietly on the saucer and smiled carefully at the spellbound windswept man who held his shoes distractedly.

"Good afternoon, Mr. Mandelstam, how was your stroll?" Without waiting for an answer Pra stood up and gestured to the two women seated on the settee alongside her, "May I introduce the journalist and translator, Sofia Parnok, and the poet, Marina Tsvetaeva, they have been our guests for the past two weeks."

Mandelstam continued to stand in the hallway but bowed to the two young women.

"Ladies, may I present Osip Mandelstam the talented poet from St Petersburg, who arrived today." Pra glowed with the wonder of all this youth and talent in her living room.

"How do you do?" Sofia put out her hand for Mandelstam to shake and he moved immediately to do so but did not look at Marina.

"Please join us, Mr. Mandelstam." Pra glanced at his bare feet but pushed on regardless, "For tea."

She rang a small bell and when the maid appeared Pra promptly requested fresh tea and more blinis with jam.

Mandelstam, who was always hungry and often had no idea where his next meal was coming from, dropped down into an overstuffed armchair that seemed to be covered in dog hair.

As if by way of excusing the lackadaisical house-keeping Pra murmured, "My son took his Crimean sheepdogs with him. Wolves!"

Marina watched as Mandelstam placed his shoes beside him on the floor. *Oh ... he must be Jewish*, Marina thought, and then quickly shook her head with her silliness.

"Are you on a sabbatical, Mr. Mandelstam?" Sofia was always gathering data, which made Marina's fluster all the more intense as she watched the poet eat the pancakes and drink hot tea from a porcelain cup which he cradled in his beautiful hands.

Eventually, he cleared his mouth and answered with as little interest as etiquette would allow, "Not exactly ... I work for the Union of Cities, an organisation providing war relief. It's not much of a job, really ..." Then he added with far more conviction, "I'm taking a break from the St Petersburg literary scene."

The truth, of course, was that the literary scene seemed to have cleared out for the summer. Sickness, food shortages, bad news from the Front and the on-going strikes in the city had rattled Mandelstam.

"Oh really?" *Why did Sofia have to take control of every conversation*, Marina wondered mournfully. "We were there a few months ago, weren't we Marina, and we found it somewhat claustrophobic."

Pra laughed, "Well Muscovites are well known for not liking anywhere except their beloved Moscow." Her motherly observation was light-hearted and meant to diffuse Sofia's opinionated chatter.

"Not at all," said Sofia.

Marina groaned inwardly as she placed her saucer and cup on the small coffee table between herself and Mandelstam.

"What we found was a very particular clique who seemed disinterested in anything other than what the literati of St Petersburg had to say —"

"Sofia that's just not true," interrupted Marina.

"Well, they were not falling over themselves to hear *your* poetry," snapped Sofia and Marina was mortified.

"Well," Mandelstam said and all eyes were on him as he finished his tea, "I have read your poetry."

Marina felt heat rise up her neck and along her ears. She realised then that Mandelstam was looking at her as if there was no one else in the room. She glanced away and asked for more tea, despite it being far too strong. Pra busied around the samovar and Sofia resumed her conversation about the Tsar's disastrous decision-making at Stavka.

Marina couldn't care less about the Tsar or the army or even the tea Pra was handing her. Marina wanted the room to be cleared so that she could be alone with this wondrous creature.

Then through the quiet background chat between Sofia and Pra, Mandelstam recited:

These my poems, written so early,

His voice was soft and intimate because there was no one else in the room.

That I did not know then I was a poet,

Marina held her breath and watched his face sharp with concentration.

Which having tore, like ... like ...

"Droplets" Marina offered.

Which having tore, like droplets from a fountain,

Pra was quiet and Sofia sat on the knife-edge of the settee.

Like sparks from a rocket.

When Mandelstam concluded the recitation of Marina's poem, he offered her an impossible smile. The world was made up of only Osip Mandelstam, the great lauded poet from St Petersburg and Marina Tsvetaeva, a self-published poet from Moscow. A man who would always think of himself as a raznochinetz, an outcast, an outsider. A woman who would always feel herself to be trapped, confined and restricted.

"Shall we retire and read before supper, Marina?" Sofia stood and brushed down her long skirt.

Pra rose as well and said, "Supper is served at 8 pm, Mr. Mandelstam."

Marina could not believe her own audacity, "I think I would prefer a stroll before supper."

She knew Sofia would be furious but she also knew Sofia would want to seem unconcerned.

"I am happy to accompany you on a short walk," Mandelstam stepped back into the hall and Marina wondered whether he could feel the tension crackling about their heads as he laced his shoes.

"Yes, thank you," said Marina as she moved swiftly to the hallway.

Pra fluttered behind them saying something about other guests expected later. And, not for the first time, Marina wondered why Pra kept the identity of her impending guests a secret.

When Mandelstam and Marina stepped out through the front door, she made the mistake of looking back. In that glance she saw Sofia, glittering hard and furious in the hallway behind their hostess.

Instead of returning to the seashore, Mandelstam took the pathway towards the small village marketplace.

"I think your friend would have preferred you to retire and read," he said.

Marina checked Mandelstam's face. She thought she could hear laughter in his voice but she couldn't be sure. She was aware of Sofia's ire at her decision to leave her and go for a walk with Mandelstam. *Anyway,* thought Marina, *I have stayed here at Max's house many times and walking inspires my writing.*

As if reading her mind Mandelstam asked, "Have you been here before?"

"Oh yes."

They walked on past a few wooden houses painted long ago in what once would have been bright colours.

"I actually met my husband here." *God, why am I telling him this?* "On that beach down there," and she pointed past Mandelstam's shoulder to the beach which he had walked earlier that afternoon.

He stood a moment and looked in the direction she pointed as if waiting for her husband to emerge.

"You see, Max invited me here when I published my first book of poems and he was so terribly supportive and interested and encouraging ..." *Stop talking so much!* "... And then I came back again the next year and met Alexander Blok and ... I don't know whether you have met Blok?"

They moved unhurriedly past a few houses that gave way to a small road that twisted up into the village marketplace. Mandelstam had ignored her question about Blok, he seemed caught up in his own thoughts.

"I met Efron. Sergei. My husband here." *Oh shut up!*

Mandelstam walked on steadily next to her and looked with no interest whatsoever at the dilapidated market stalls, abandoned by their owners who had returned home to their supper.

"Anyway. You see I was walking along the beach and Efron was walking towards me and without a word, he picked up a pebble and handed it to me and ..." She saw the corners of Mandelstam's mouth begin to smile.

"Actually when I looked at it I saw it wasn't a pebble, after all, it was a cornelian ... and I thought, fancy that. You see, cornelian is my favourite stone."

Then she heard Mandelstam repeat her phrase, *fancy that*, but so quietly that she decided she had imagined it.

"Efron is in the army. My husband. Reserves, actually. He had to go east with some German POWs."

They pushed on past the marketplace and took the windy street towards the church spire which stuck up ahead out of the village skyline.

"He's very talented ..." *Why am I still talking!?* "I ... we ... he's away." She sighed and added, "And then there's Sofia ..."

They had arrived at the church and Mandelstam led the way around the outside walls. He was neither looking at the structure nor at Marina but somehow, she knew he was intensely absorbed by her.

"Sofia ... I don't know of her," his vague response made her feel embarrassed and thrilled at the same time.

"She's a wonderful writer," Marina's comeback lacked any shred of enthusiasm.

They came to stand still and from where they stood the village looked as if it was tumbling into the sea below them.

The aromas of fried fish and onions washed about the early evening in all its supper preparations.

Mandelstam stopped looking at the sea and turned his dark grey eyes on her. He stepped towards her and Marina found her back against the sun-heated stone wall of the church.

Slowly and deliberately he bent his tight body against hers so that she felt his shoulders and chest and erection pressing her into the church wall.

His lips found hers and he was rapacious as he kissed her and kissed her and kissed her until she thought she would never breathe again.

He pulled back and brushed her fringe upwards with his thumb and smiled into her eyes and then lent in again to kiss and kiss and kiss some more.

And an ache of such tender love rose up within her and she thought she would break down and cry. Right here against the stone church wall with this beautiful, beautiful boy kissing her.

On the hurried walk back, anxious not to appear too late for supper, Mandelstam hooked Marina about the waist and held her close. She felt as if she was in a wild dream. Marina knew Sofia would be in a pout because Marina had chosen to slink off with the new guest for an early evening stroll. Marina realised she would have to unravel herself from Mandelstam's warm hard chest and arms just as soon as she regained her senses. And definitely, before she reached Lilacskya Ploshchad where Max's house stood overlooking the Black Sea.

Why do I get myself entangled in these situations? Marina tried to scold herself, but she felt completely filled up with the possibility of Mandelstam.

She blushed at her own boldness and Mandelstam pushed his hand up into the back of her thick hair and slowed his pace. They were only minutes from Max's home.

He stopped and kissed her neck, "I'm in the front guest room on the first floor," he murmured.

Marina felt an electric current run from her groin down to her legs and then to the tips of her toes.

"I will leave my door unlocked." He kissed her again and Marina thought, *I'm going to die.*

Eventually, he pulled away and Marina looked into his soft eyes and the mess of wavy curls falling this way and that.

"Come to me. Tonight."

They both knew it was an impossibility and an absolute certainty.

Marina lent her body into his and hoped to hell Sofia wasn't watching from their small window high above on the second floor.

She replied feebly, "I will try to get away. Sofia is not well and is often going to bed early. So maybe ... but I don't know."

"You must come to me," and then he pulled away and moved swiftly towards the house without holding her waist or hand or fingers. An action so cruel and sudden that she felt her knees buckle.

She couldn't understand why Mandelstam was a magnet drawing her towards her own destruction. Or at least the destruction of her and Sofia. There was something about him that she found irresistible. He was a coil of sex and appetite and she was hot liquid and heresy.

Just as she ascended the front steps to Max's house, Mandelstam turned around and looked at her.

She stopped.

He pressed two fingers up against her top lip.

She couldn't move.

Then slowly, teasingly he dropped one finger into her mouth until she opened it and sucked him.

She still couldn't move when he opened the door.

"The evening post has arrived, Ms. Tsvetaeva, and there is a letter for you," announced Pra who must have been waiting in the hallway for them to return.

Marina picked up the letter on the stand and immediately recognised her husband's handwriting.

"I, too, have received a letter. From Sergei Efron, your husband." Pra seemed to place emphasis on the word *husband*. "He is arriving earlier than expected. Tonight, in fact by the 10 pm coach. So, I assume you would like to be moved into the room I have allocated for your husband. Ms. Parnok may remain where she is on the second floor."

Marina's head was spinning. She had no idea Efron was even back from Perm, let alone heading to the Crimea. *Goddamnit! His sister must have told him I was travelling with Sofia!*

She looked down at her own unopened letter from her husband and felt tears fill her eyes because she knew what she had to do.

"I must speak to Sofia. She mentioned earlier that we might have to return sooner than expected to Odessa." Marina was already moving to the staircase, "I must see her." She turned back to Pra and the beautiful exquisite Mandelstam below, "I might have to travel with her — she is not well as you know — just to make sure she arrives safely. I'll just go to her now, check on her, and I will let you know if we have to leave tonight."

She could hear how ridiculous and unconvincing she sounded but she had no other choice. She bounded up the stairs towards the second floor.

They had to get out tonight.

Sofia would know what to do and she would see this flight from Efron as a declaration of Marina's love for her. When in fact, she was escaping one gaoler for another.

Deep down, her greatest concern was wondering how long it would be before she would have Mandelstam's fingers deep within her once again.

2

When Lidka got off the train at Bezhetsk she was greeted above by a murmuration of starlings sweeping and swooping in the summery noon sky.

What a spectacle, she thought, as she strode towards an awaiting horse-drawn cab. Anna had said it would be easy to hail a cab at the station and to remember to get off at the sleepy village of Slepnyovo, alongside the forested lake.

This was the first time in just under a year that Lidka had travelled. She had come to like St Petersburg and her newfound friends, of which Anna was probably the most important, although she wasn't too sure why the great poet found her company so amusing.

The cabbie clicked his tongue and his old horse pulled out of the railway station and skirted about, what appeared to be, the main part of the town.

Even though she was only staying for two days, Lidka wished she was stepping off at Odessa railway station at Pushkinska Ploshchad to visit her own son, Dimitri, and her mother. Anna was lucky, of course. Her son, Lev, was with her mother in law who lived in Slepnyovo, where Anna had come after her affair with the great musician Artur Lourie had cooled.

Lidka shifted uncomfortably on the hard cab seat and tried not to think about her own illicit dalliance with Lourie which had meant she had to chase Mandelstam off to the Crimea.

Anyway, her focus was on Anna over the next few days. Lidka was surprised to receive a letter from the poet asking her to visit Slepnyovo. She had wondered at the time whether Anna had found out about her fling with Lourie but when she had read on, she realised Anna had tuberculosis. This must have been the real reason she had left St Petersburg for the countryside, all those weeks ago.

The cabbie urged his reluctant horse across the first of many wooden bridges.

Mayakovsky had told Lidka that Anna went through bouts of ill health, mother guilt and hypochondria. He was generous to a fault and insisted on paying her fare so that Lidka could visit *their friend*, as Mayakovsky referred to Anna. But really Lidka knew he was, in his own way, trying to untangle both Lidka and Anna from Lourie. Mayakovsky had his own sexual proclivities but was protective of his women friends when it came to other men. Meanwhile, he was caught up in his own love affair at the moment. And to Lidka's great surprise it was a woman! *Ce la vie.* She liked the sound of this phrase that she had picked up before the closing of the Dog.

The cabbie pulled off into a forested area and Lidka could smell timberworks close by. Then she saw the road open up ahead and she spied the first of a few gaily painted houses, some of which seemed to be dachas.

This must be Slepnyovo.

The cabbie gave a curt nod when Lidka indicated she wanted the house of L'vova, Anna's mother-in-law. Minutes later he drew up beside a neatly kept white house with a pretty dark wood gable-board.

By the time Lidka had climbed down, paid the cabbie and picked up her string bags there was a small elderly woman at the front door and clinging to her was a chubby three year old boy.

"Did you bring French Brandy?" The woman's voice was strong despite her thin-lined face.

Lidka was unsurprised at the greeting, "Yes." She held up the string bags as she walked towards the door.

The old woman's expression softened as she took them and fossicked inside and saw, besides the brandy, a number of leftovers that Lidka had managed to collect from her waitressing shift yesterday: kholodets, salted herring and cabbage varenikis. The kholodets were the cook's signature dish, as he seemed to have no trouble sourcing cow's feet — out of which he made an exceptional jellied texture.

The old lady gave Lidka a smile and beckoned her indoors. The little boy was tall for his age and strangely incurious about this newcomer. Lidka followed the old woman into the house with her grandson calling out ahead, "Visitor! Visitor!"

The living room was littered with rugs and blankets and pillows and throw-overs and doilies and table clothes of every colour and design imaginable. There was a small fire burning in the fireplace, despite the warmth of summer outside. Along the mantelpiece was a crowd of glass trinkets that glittered and winked in the sunlight streaming through the front window. The walls were covered in paintings, photographs, decorated plates, maps and icons of the Holy Virgin and St Stanislaus. And there inside this Aladdin's cave, in the supine position, was Anna.

Lidka tried to show her delight and not her shock. She had no idea Anna was this ill.

"Lidka," Anna moved her hand listlessly towards her friend and coughed.

Lidka went swiftly and knelt beside her. Anna was a bird stranded, her bones thin, her pulse quick and her skin feverish.

"You poor thing! I didn't realise you were this bad ... has the doctor seen you?" Lidka's words sounded too loud in the overcrowded room.

Anna seemed to ignore her friend's question as she looked beyond her tall blonde figure to her son pressed against his grandmother in the doorway, "My darling. This is Lidka Matveyevna Yurkovich. Come and shake her hand."

Lidka remained kneeling and turned about as the young boy moved hesitantly towards her, hand extended.

She pumped his little fist, "How do you do?"

"I'm nearly three," he answered.

"Yes! Look at you. How lovely and tall you are!" She longed to hug him and push her face into his warm hair as if he was Dimitri.

"Your friend has brought brandy and St Petersburg fare," said Anna's mother-in-law brusquely and promptly disappeared down the hallway clutching the string bags.

When Anna wrote and asked her to come and visit, she had also requested she go to the home of Andrey Antonovich Gorenko, Anna's father in St Petersburg, and deliver the enclosed note. He would respond with a bottle of something to help his daughter sleep when she was feverish.

Lidka had done as instructed and found Anna's father and stepmother nicely ensconced in a well-decorated apartment. After Gorenko had read the letter and fetched the brandy he also stuffed two bars of dark chocolate into Lidka's hand for his grandson, Lev, who he had met once. Gorenko was a tall man whose handsome features had long since left him. Anna had told her once that he was a squanderer of money and women's hearts; she also believed divorce was one of the great gifts to Russian women — indeed, Anna's poetic lines that carved their first impression on Lidka had to be:

Forgive me for so often mistaking
Other people for you ...

Lidka collected the chocolate from her purse and solemnly handed it to Anna's son. He took it and retreated to a threadbare couch opposite his mother.

As she settled onto the worn armchair Lidka asked, "What has the doctor told you?" She could hear the quiet mousey nibbling of chocolate behind her.

Anna held a stained handkerchief to her mouth and coughed for some time. After she finished, she dropped back onto her pillow, "Artur took me to his doctor in St Petersburg. TB. Nothing to be done."

Lidka knew this was a death sentence for many, and Anna's thin frame and vapid skin were disconcerting. Her friend was swathed in rugs and furs as she lay upon the settee near the small fire. She was struggling to keep her eyes open. Lidka tried not to look at the blood on the handkerchief.

"Gumilyov visited. My husband. I don't think you have met him ..." Anna's voice faded into the room.

Lidka had heard a great deal about the poet Nikolay Gumilyov. Mandelstam regaled stories about their time at the Sorbonne and how Gumilyov was a great womaniser and had therefore joined the Hussars.

Lidka had found that both amusing and annoying. She had met men like this who felt it their life's work to seduce then throw over as many women as possible. Mandelstam never contradicted this perspective of hers but did try to persuade her that Gumilyov was a great poet. Lidka was sceptical. If that was the case, then why did no one ever talk about Gumilyov's poetry at the Dog or even at Kolobok's where she waitressed.

She thought Anna must be sleeping, her long slender hands crossed at her heart. On her right middle finger, she wore her enormous black ring with gold enamel and a small diamond. It had once been her grandmother's. Anna had told her that when her father accused her of being a decadent poetess who was threatening the reputation of the family name, she had promptly reinvented herself as a descendent of a Tatar princess, on her maternal side. The ring was her talisman. Besides, her father had already brought great shame to the family name of Gorenko and thus she had chosen a fresh start and a new name: Akhmatova.

The afternoon light was thinning, and Lidka heard the sound of water and the chink of glasses coming from the kitchen.

Russia was filled with men who believed themselves to be utterly entitled, like Anna's father and husband. And then there was the marvellous Mayakovsky who gossiped about everyone including Gumilyov, saying no man who married the goddess Anna Akhmatova had a right to abandon her. Mayakovsky went on to say, to anybody who would listen, that Gumilyov was not man enough for Anna.

Anna's breathing seemed laboured and almost painful. Her eyelids were so pale Lidka imagined she could see tiny spidery capillaries at work.

"He stayed here for a night or two, didn't he, my little one? Papa came to visit ..." Anna's voice was deep and throaty, as it always was, and Lidka heard Lev chuckle in between mouthfuls of chocolate.

Then Anna's mother-in-law appeared with a generous glass of brandy.

For someone seemingly gruff, the mother-in-law stooped low over Anna and made her drink from the glass with such tenderness that Lidka felt a stab of loneliness in her own brittle life. The elderly woman's hand was a claw about the glass and she pressed an arm around Anna's neck to steady her upturned head.

As in all Russian households, where private conversations were treated as the business of everyone, Anna's mother-in-law chimed in, "My son has been decorated twice! The Order of St George. He is with the 3rd Hussar Regiment."

She let Anna rest her head back down on the lumpy cushion and stepped back.

"My son, the poet."

Lidka didn't know whether she was expected to reply. She couldn't quite read the tone of the older woman. It was somewhere between pride and irony.

Then Anna said, "Gumilyov was on leave. He had been in Polish Russia ... down south ... After that a few days off in Moscow ... then visited us here. Isn't that right, darling?"

Again, the three year old kept himself busy on the couch, not aware that his mother was speaking to him.

"But he had to go to St Petersburg!" The elderly woman crossed her arms over her chest and continued with her disappointment, "Even though he only had a few days left of his leave! No. He couldn't stay to look after his mother and sick wife."

Lidka held her head a fraction higher knowing her own mother would never speak of her in this way. When Lidka was wealthy enough she would bring them to St Petersburg. She knew that meant marrying someone in order to be secure — but how was that possible with so many men of her generation marching off to be killed at war?

The old woman took Lev by the hand and walked out to the kitchen. Next thing Lidka smelt was the aroma of hissing onions.

God help me, thought Lidka, *all over Russia women are frying onions.*

It was a good thing she herself ate infrequently and with little interest.

Anna began coughing again and her thin body shivered beneath the mountain of coverings. Eventually,

Anna indicated for Lidka to sit at the end of the settee, probably so she wouldn't have to turn her head too much.

"How is it here, Anna?"

Anna loved her friend Lidka and the way she would just cut to the essence of things. She was more surprised than anyone that she had struck up a friendship with another woman. Anna was usually wary of women, especially those who might be jealous of their men wandering out of the confines of their marriage and into her bed.

It is only sex, Anna thought, *why do they place such significance on bodies pleasuring bodies?*

Anna shifted under the weight of the blankets and rugs on top of her. The chatter of pans and voices could be heard from the kitchen.

"Are you comfortable, my friend? Do you need anything?"

Lidka is different, thought Anna, *she enjoys sex.* Anna knew this because they had talked about it many times and both women agreed that sex could actually be delicious, although some of the men became very needy.

It is a Russian thing, Lidka had argued one night at the Dog in front of Mayakovsky and Artur (was Mandelstam there?). *All men in Russia want you to be en-*

thralled by them and when you aren't, they feel compelled to manipulate your emotions with the grand gesture of threatening suicide or, more boringly, actually kill themselves. Anna always found Lidka amusing. There was something flinty about her that Anna loved.

"You should meet my husband." Anna paused, "When you return to St Petersburg ... He is an attentive lover — but you have to hurry — because he is ... travelling up the country ... having affairs with as many ... woman as his leave will permit."

Both women laughed and Anna coughed and closed her eyes.

Chatter between grandmother and grandson wandered up the hallway from the kitchen and spilled into the living room.

Lidka had to admit she had wondered about this strange marriage of Anna's. But wasn't everything strange these days? At least that's what it had felt ever since the war began, less than a year ago. Less than a year ago? How was that possible? She had lost her husband, her life in Odessa and the future she had imagined for herself. Now she lived in some half-life in St Petersburg, sleeping in the same bed with her aunt.

Lidka could smell the distinct aroma of kholodets being fried down in the kitchen and Anna opened her eyes.

"We married when I was 20 ..." It took Lidka a moment before she realised Anna was talking about Gumilyov, "He had pursued me ... from when I was 13 ... can you imagine?"

Lidka had never heard her friend speak of her marriage and she often suspected Gumilyov had caused her deep pain. *Perhaps that is why I have never liked him much*, thought Lidka to herself.

"For seven years ... he begged me to marry him ... He wore me down."

Lidka felt she already knew how the tale would end.

"But as soon as we married ... he lost interest ..." Anna sounded as if she was telling the failed love story of someone else. "He never forgave me ... for loving poetry more passionately ... than him ... *Love me with that same intensity, that same passion* ... he would say ... I tried ..." She closed her eyes, "But I could not."

A few months ago, such ideas would have been ridiculous to Lidka.

Now, listening to Anna and many of her new friends in St Petersburg, Lidka had come to realise different truths. That their bodies belonged to themselves and not the marriage market. That art was not a decorative element to one's life. That war need not be the epicentre of their lives.

"Gumilyov plucked me out of the wasteland of the provinces ... parochial Russia is the most indigent, the most disease-ridden ... the most cruel." Anna coughed weakly, "He took me to St Petersburg."

Lidka leaned over and wiped her friend's fevered brow.

"So I was in the very heart of writing ... art ... music — everything that I had ever wanted ... you see I was poor when I met him ... living with my mother ... My parents were divorced ... My father is a Gorenko ... my mother, a Stogova ..."

Since coming to St Petersburg, Lidka had met more of the impoverished Russian nobility than ever before, it sometimes made her wonder if there were any Russian nobles, besides the Tsar and his family, who were actually solvent. Regardless of their penurious circumstances, they always let you know they were of noble birth.

One time, Lidka had actually gone to a pawn shop with Anna — one that the poet obviously frequented — to exchange heirlooms. Pearls, ruby rings, a red-gold necklace and a Faberge egg in exchange for grocery money. This was the same woman who had been hailed as the *Soul of the Neva* and recognised, even as they were en route to the pawnshop, as *The great poet of Russia!* The irony was not lost on Lidka.

A child's burst of laughter rose above the cooking and the women looked towards the hallway.

"You see ... I was longing for love ... longing for a mentor ..." Anna murmured.

Mandelstam had told Lidka that back then his friend, Gumilyov, had assured Anna of her centrality to him, nothing else mattered except Anna and everything that concerned Anna. It had been a truth. At least, right up until the wedding.

"Osip told me a little about him — your husband."

Anna smiled at Lidka, "Dear Osip ... He wrote to tell me ... he was travelling to the Black Sea ... staying at Max's home ... I think he misses you ..." She kept her eyes on her friend.

Lidka suddenly felt she could turn to Anna and confess her affair with Lourie — but what would be the point? Besides, Lidka was finished with both men. Mandelstam had no prospects to haul her into a possible future and Artur Lourie had a penchant for married women, all the while being married himself. Besides, he, along with every other man, was attempting to court the stunning Olga Sudeikin, the wife of the muralist who had painted the ceiling at the Dog. Yes. Lidka was definitely done with both men — she must look to another if she was to find marriage.

"You are beautiful Lidka ... any man would want to make you his wife," Anna knew that Lidka's destiny was different from her own. Anna had no intention of returning to the fate that had been hers and her mother's: marriage, childbearing and struggling to make ends meet.

Meanwhile, Lidka was under no illusions that her friendships with these young artists living a bohemian lifestyle and funded by other people's money was of any use to her, and yet she couldn't help but be drawn into its glittering circle. These talented people in turn loved her because she suspected, she was not competing with them for fame, accolade and immortality.

The kitchen had quietened and Lidka thought about the satisfaction one got when seeing a child eat his fill.

"I was a wife once — I am still Gumilyov's wife ... but ..." Anna plucked the frayed sable fur thrown across her shoulders and coughed, handkerchief clenched against her mouth, "I do not think I will ever marry again ... It's difficult because we have a son."

It was silly, probably even mean-spirited, but it occurred to Lidka that perhaps Anna had forgotten the name of her son, the three year old who never seemed to hear his mother when she spoke to him. The child who had been raised by the mother-in-law, the boy whose parents either reluctantly visited while travelling to St Petersburg or came when they needed to convalesce.

"Gumilyov visited ... because we had to sort out some financials ... He misses his son ... but he was hoping to get across ... to Vilnius ... Tatyana Adamovicha." Anna shrugged and breathed deeply, "She wants him to divorce me ... so she can be ... his wife."

After that Anna really did seem to sleep, fitfully and without peace. The light in the living room faded and Lidka realised that the noise in the kitchen had ceased. She wondered whether the grandmother and grandson were also taking the opportunity for an afternoon nap.

Country living was slow in comparison to the city.

The most noticeable difference, as she travelled down from St Petersburg and into this region, was that most people seemed to have their own vegetable patch, a few scrawny hens and even some livestock. Lidka had read in the newspapers that the war was having a terrible impact on these rural areas because the workers on the farms and lumberyards were now fighting for Russia. So, there was no one left to generate the resources desperately needed.

Lidka looked at the eclectic conglomeration of trinkets and fabrics and wall hangings about the room. All of them lovingly dusted and preserved. As the summer evening spilt its quietude into the room a realisation came slowly to her that these very items that decorated his mother's house could, in fact, be the memorabilia Gumilyov had brought back from his travels to the East before the war began. Mandelstam had proudly listed the names of the countries Gumilyov had travelled, she barely had heard of any of them.

Lidka was wondering about what sort of man needed such trophies when she noticed Anna watching her.

With her face chalky, her eyes shining and her voice thin, Anna recited:

He loved three things in this world:
White peacocks, evensong.
And faded maps of America.
He hated it when children cried.

And there it was — a framed map of the Americas on the wall above the fireplace and his long-forgotten son asleep somewhere down the hall in the arms of his mother.

He hated tea with raspberry jam and
Any female hysteria in his life.
Now imagine it: I was his wife.

Somehow, Lidka knew they were supposed to laugh at the irony of Anna's verse but she couldn't even rally herself to smile. Instead, she looked at her friend who seemed utterly bereft as she closed her eyes, once again.

3

Gumilyov's eyes were wide open. It seemed like a lifetime since he had been in a cabaret club and this dive that Sergei and Olga Sudeikin had brought him to was fabulously decadent.

The patrons sat about in alcoves with thick red velvet curtains drawn loosely back so that they might look out and observe the painted harlequins, semi-naked tightrope walkers and masked musicians gadding about the club's stage, that had been positioned in the centre of the establishment.

Olga Sudeikin fancied herself as one of Anna's greatest fans and desperately wanted to become her closest confidant and friend. The fact that she had met Anna infrequently and openly lusted for Artur Lourie, Anna's most recent lover, meant Olga's chances were slim. Gumilyov didn't have the heart to tell Olga that his wife preferred males to females and had very few women friends if any.

Sergei Sudeikin managed to attract a wait staff who was either a beautiful-looking boy or a very handsome girl and ordered a couple of bottles of beer and vodka for their table. Sudeikin had just sold his latest painting and was eager to celebrate.

"Gumilyov, how long are you in St Petersburg?" Sudeikin's voice rose above the chatter, "When do you think it will be over? The war I mean!"

The number of times people asked Gumilyov this question made his shoulders slump.

When will they ever get it? he wondered. While military Headquarters continued to send ridiculous orders to those fighting at the Front there will never be an end to the war until the entire Russian army was dead.

"Who knows, my friend," replied Gumilyov as he watched Olga bow to his match. She lit her cigarette and, in that instance, Gumilyov had to concede that his friend, Sergei Yurievich Sudeikin, the *greatest* artist and set designer for Ballets Russes, had surely married the *greatest* beauty of their Age.

Olga Sudeikin was a strikingly handsome woman with her aristocratic features, dewy skin, auburn hair and see-through pale blue eyes. And with all this Sudeikin still had a roving eye for men.

"We have been coming to the Comedian's Hat ever since the Dog closed down! Not exactly the same crowd but ..." Sudeikin paused as the exquisite boy-girl wait staff returned and bent low over the table with the tray, heart-shaped face turned upwards, and cleared their space of any talk. Sudeikin somehow kept his pince-nez in place, mouth open, and watched every move as glasses were distributed and alcohol poured.

Well of course the rumours are true about Sudeikin's peccadillos, thought Gumilyov as he turned his attention back to Olga, who was as luscious as she was aloof.

"Have you heard from Anna?" asked Olga and her lips formed a perfect pout as she exhaled cigarette smoke. "I believe she has left St Petersburg for the summer."

Gumilyov held her gaze a fraction more than expected and she glanced furtively across at her husband who was still watching the boy-girl with intense concupiscence.

"Actually, yes. I have just come from visiting her at my mother's. In Slepnyovo," and then he added as her beautiful face clouded, "Bezhetsk." Still, the great beauty looked troubled, "Between Moscow and St Petersburg."

Maybe it is true what they say about her, thought Gumilyov. *But I am in pursuit of her body, not her brain.*

He smiled across at her smile — *Ahh*, thought Gumilyov, *now she's getting it.*

"Is Anna writing? She is the most wonderful poet and has even inspired me to write."

God help us, thought Gumilyov as he took her hand and kissed it saying, "Please, I must read your poetry."

The flush was divine as it travelled up her impossibly long neck, "Oh how sweet ..."

"Look!" Sudeikin merged back into the picture, "It's Mayakovsky!"

Gumilyov was momentarily annoyed. Mayakovsky had an uncanny ability to draw women and all points of conversation towards himself.

"Friends!" boomed Mayakovsky. "Wait — is that Gumilyov?! My dear, dear Gumilyov — look at you! Nearly as handsome as me, you old bastard!"

There was laughter and kissing and handshakes and hugs between the Sudeikins, Gumilyov and Mayakovsky and then a petite dark woman, who had been standing behind the huge poet all along, stepped forward and Mayakovsky added, "May I introduce Lilya Brik."

There was something in Mayakovsky's voice that made the raucous joy of the friends quieten.

"How do you do?" Gumilyov pulled her ungloved hand towards him and offered it a kiss.

This set the table off laughing all over again but Gumilyov had achieved his goal in pulling Lilya Brik alongside next to him, while keeping the lovely Olga on his other side. Lilya settled in between Gumilyov and Mayakovsky, as Sudeikin called for fresh glasses.

Mayakovsky leaned in and spoke to Gumilyov, "Seriously man, how long before you have to go back to this bloody mess of a war?"

In Slepnyovo, Anna had told him that Mayakovsky, once a great patriot awaiting his call-up papers, was now lobbying people in high places to have him exempted from service. To be honest, Gumilyov couldn't blame him. Sure, there was a time early on when he was a great believer in the war and fighting for Mother Russia but now, he realised they were all fighting for the egotistical pride of a bunch of ignoramuses at Headquarters. Maybe if Russians refused to fight then the Tsar and his motley lot of generals would have to make a separate peace with Germany.

"My leave ends in a few days," said Gumilyov, enjoying the two lovely women on either side. "I was hoping to get up to Vilnius but I am not sure ..."

"Ahh, I believe Tatyana Adamovicha is in Vilnius ... and I hear Nurse Jula is still in Warsaw." The table laughed good-humouredly at Mayakovsky's prattle.

"I see you have been speaking to Mandelstam," replied Gumilyov hoping that Olga was ignoring Mayakovsky.

"Gumilyov is a poet and a Hussar!" Mayakovsky announced across the table. "And ladies," he looked dramatically at Lilya then Olga, "beware!"

Just then the music rose dramatically and all five were distracted by the bodies writhing on the dance floor before them. Women and a few men with rouged cheeks and heavily kohled eyes laughed and chatted and preened each other's need to be seen and to be alive as they gyrated and whirled in a way that had nothing to do with their ordinary lives.

Lilya Brik spoke softly to Gumilyov, "I think I have read one of your poems." Her body leaned towards him coquettishly, "And you are an adventurer as well, I hear!"

"In so many ways," his reply was smooth, as was his eye-line that dropped from her eyes to her lips to her ample breasts.

"Tell me, Lilya Brik, how does that lout interest you?" He tried to make his comment light-hearted but there was jealousy in Gumilyov towards Mayakovsky. How could such undisciplined talent have such luck? Women, in particular, were drawn to his tall well-built physique and, Gumilyov suspected, his booming bass voice.

But what an overstuffed testosterone bore, he thought.

"Oh ... I don't know." Her smile was charming, "Looks like a labourer, imprisoned once, a member of the Bolshevik party, jubilantly impatient for the Revolution — I'd say those are some of his stronger attributes, for starters!" As she laughed she revealed her perfectly white teeth.

Gumilyov was finding Lilya Brik difficult to navigate and it only flustered him further when Mayakovsky interrupted the table with an extract from a poem he was working on:

God plucked a woman before whom the mountain
will tremble and shudder,

Gumilyov stole a glance at Lilya Brik and her face was upturned in reverence to the annoying Mayakovsky as he continued the recitation:

He brought her forth and commanded:
love her!

The table applauded and Gumilyov thought to himself, *have I missed something?*

Typically, Mayakovsky was unrestrained in the face of such collective love and so yelled, "There's more!"

The table quietened:

Where the earth fades into tundra,
where the river bargains with the North wind,
there I'll scratch Lilya's name on my fetters!

As the cheering subsided Gumilyov drank heavily and wondered whether he could push his luck and jump a train for Vilnius.

Lilya Brik cocked her head at Gumilyov, "You are Anna Akhmatova's husband. The St Petersburg poet. Aren't you?" Despite her high cheekbones and sassy eyes, Gumilyov felt a sudden dislike towards her.

He replied, "And *you* are Osip Brik's wife. The literary critic. Aren't you?"

"Osip Brik is my greatest fan," interrupted Mayakovsky, as if dating the wife of the critic who had praised his work was acceptable.

"No. *I'm* your greatest fan." And right there in amongst people who had met her for the first time Lilya Brik opened her pert mouth and kissed Mayakovsky, long and hard.

Sudeikin clapped and Gumilyov turned his attention to Olga.

As the night rattled on Gumilyov longed for a break from what would have to be the worst cabaret he had ever witnessed.

Drunken old men wearing make-up cavorted with underage semi-dressed dancers. Meanwhile, the band was playing some strange concoction of, according to Sudeikin, *jazz*. Its propulsive rhythm, as the musicians interacted and improvised with each other, sent Gumilyov's head spinning, or maybe it was the alcohol.

The audience was mostly soldiers on leave and the way they were carrying on made Gumilyov wonder if any of them would ever be returning to the Front.

Meanwhile, Mayakovsky had asked about Anna and confirmed Mandelstam was presently sunbathing in the Crimea. Gumilyov missed his friend. Mandelstam was someone he could talk to and never expected Gumilyov to be better than the sum of who he was. Besides, Gumilyov was sick of the war and no one had more ambivalence about Russia's participation in the war than Mandelstam.

Sitting here amongst his friends in the heart of St Petersburg at the Comedian's Hat made Gumilyov feel strangely disconnected and lonely. For so many months, he had longed to do just this — sit and drink and talk with friends about nothing and everything.

The escape from Przemyśl with Rad seemed like someone else's tale to tell, and so when he was asked by those at the table whether he was there when the fortress fell, he simply said no.

This provided the perfect segue for Lilya Brik, "The war is unconscionable! None of us can justify the brutality in the battlefields — what has it all been for?"

She really is one of the most annoying women, thought Gumilyov, and he wondered whether Olga would join him on the dance floor.

"The Bolsheviks argue that this is a war of imperialism and it has nothing to do with the workers!" Mayakovsky barged on, "There are strikers being shot in the streets of Kostroma — for nothing other than demanding wages that will allow them to feed their families!"

Sudeikin smoked on and tried to catch the attention of the boy-girl wait staff who had re-emerged from the bar. Olga did not seem the slightest bit interested in the topic that Lilya and Mayakovsky had embarked upon and so it fell upon Gumilyov to respond.

"Yes, but wasn't that strike out east to do with the manufacturing of garments? I mean to say, men are desperately in need of uniforms and coats and — well just about everything at the Front."

"You are not getting it." Lilya turned her head away from Gumilyov and looked at the others as she spoke, "It was a spinning factory, actually. And the point is the Bolsheviks have called on *all* workers to strike because the conditions have worsened since the start of the war. Workers are suffering from chronic food shortages! What happened in Kostroma has generated waves of protests throughout Russia! It is happening as we speak."

Gumilyov felt tired. He had forgotten why he had come here tonight and even why he had stayed so long. Of course, he didn't want to go back to the Front but at the same time, he didn't want to be here amid this political stoush.

"Those particular strikers in Kostroma took their demands in an orderly peaceful manner to the Zotov Brothers' Mill ..."

She is infuriating, thought Gumilyov as he poured himself another glass of vodka.

"But those protestors were met by police, who opened fire and mowed them down!"

Gumilyov held a match to his cigarette and promised himself that this would be the last and he noticed Olga looking mournfully at the dance floor.

"You know, my friend," Mayakovsky was leaning across Lilya towards Gumilyov, "the Bolsheviks have also called on the soldiers to strike."

"I see," Gumilyov's voice was tight. "So you would rather the German barbarians enter Russia and take whatever they want, without a fight?"

"They already have entered Russia!" Lilya answered disdainfully. "In this last year, we have gained *nothing* except the annihilation of a generation of Russians!" And her eyes glistened with the drama of her declaration.

Gumilyov looked at her mouth and realised he wanted to kiss Lilya Brik passionately while scooping up her soft full breasts.

Then he said to her quietly, "You know nothing."

And the hatred for her and for everyone at this ridiculous club and for those striking rather than helping the war effort rose up in him like vomit. He stubbed out his cigarette and swallowed the remains of his drink.

"You have been away for so long, my friend." Mayakovsky was just making it worse, "St Petersburg is a different place to the one you left behind. Gumilyov, how can I make you see?" Mayakovsky gestured expansively behind him as if the degenerates, cabaret performers and guests still cavorting were the reason Gumilyov couldn't grasp what had ended and what had begun.

Mayakovsky continued passionately, "Man! You should see the queues each day! For bread, eggs, milk, flour, vegetables — forget meat, there is no meat! The queues alone will bring that ridiculous yellow-bellied Tsar down and everything he represents! It is a different world here now, comrade ..."

Gumilyov wondered how long it would take him to get to the train station.

"You've done your bit, old man," Mayakovsky said effusively. "The whole system is rotten to the core! The bankers are corrupt! So are the industrialists! And the factory owners! And as for the fucking Romanovs! I say — we need a REVOLUTION!"

Lilya raised her right fist high above her head and shook it with fierce agreement.

Olga took out a small compact and, with the care of a professional, powdered her perfectly upturned nose.

Gumilyov gently tapped Olga's elbow closest to him and said to the table, "Well that's me done ..." and he leant his weight a little more into her side until she realised, he wanted her and Sudeikin to shuffle along their seat so that he could escape.

To the protests of all, Gumilyov pushed his way out of the booth and began his farewells.

He explained that he had to catch up with other friends as well as attend to some business matters before reporting for duty.

Everyone knew it wasn't so, but even he himself would have found it hard to explain why he felt so much fury and so much sadness.

It was as if *his* Russia was slipping away.

After the second then third then the fourth embrace from Mayakovsky with his huge wet kisses hitting the sides of Gumilyov's face, again and again, he was finally released to leave the Comedian's Hat that had supposedly replaced the Dog. As the door swung shut behind him and he stood opposite the Griboyedov Canal, Gumilyov thought with disdain that this cabaret was nothing like Pronin's place.

He missed the old days.

Gumilyov walked across the bridge and leant over the old stone walls and looked into the grey rush of water below. It was probably one in the morning now and he might as well head towards the train station. Even if he had to doss down for a few hours it would be better than heading back to the apartment he had once shared with Anna.

Too many memories.

Gumilyov knew in his heart it was ridiculous to try to get to Vilnius ... a train to Sumilino then another to Molodechno and then another to Vilnius. Besides, it was only a matter of time before the Germans marched into Vilnius.

It felt like the whole world was shifting into something strangely unfamiliar and remotely threatening. Gumilyov knew he really should return to Minsk and, as planned with Rad, report for duty.

Like someone lost and unsure, he stepped on into the silvery night that held nothing but the dreams of a time long ago.

4

Throughout the summer, Pasternak had been following the newspaper coverage of the strikes from St Petersburg to Vladivostok.

Workers had been so hard hit by the war shortages and longer working hours that they were demanding food and pay increases. It was a matter of survival. Moreover, the crushing of the strikers in Ivanovo and Kostroma triggered more and more walkouts; resulting in police brutality and violent suppression, as ordered by the Tsar.

Pasternak had read that even in Perm, and the surrounding areas, the agitators in the factory soviets were forcing the owners of production to hear their demands for better conditions, meals and pay. In the heat of summer, there had been over 1000 strikes with more than 500,000 participants.

Moreover, there was talk, once again, that the Tsar was about to dissolve the Duma just as the living conditions were worsening. This, coupled with the bewildering failure of the Russian army to rout the enemy, intensified discontent.

It was all coming to a head.

Pasternak was a firm believer in supporting the war effort, primarily because of his love of Russia but also because he felt guilty. He had not passed the medical in order to be sent to the Front.

Recently, he had requested to travel back down to Perm from Vsevolodov-Vilve because his parents had sent a chest of books, which he wanted to collect and use in the classes he was offering at the factory's soviet at Vsevolodov-Vilve. He also wanted to send a hamper to his family because the prices had skyrocketed in Moscow and he knew Perm would be considerably cheaper.

Manager Zbarsky usually ran a tight ship and no worker or staff member would have been granted the luxury of leave, not to mention the time and cost in securing travel documents, but the manager was not from the same class as the prestigious Pasternak family and it was an honour to have their son work for him at the factory as well as to accommodate him in his own home.

So, during the first week of August, with the forested Ural Mountains constantly to their east, Pasternak was transported by a craggy sexagenarian called Vassya down the River Karma on a small steamer carting timber. Two hundred kilometres they travelled down the deep flowing river, seemingly without effort.

Vassya had been working as a bargeman for the chemical company in Vsevolodov-Vilve long before Zbarsky and his wife had arrived. At 62 years of age, Vassya sported a long unruly grey beard and head of untamed hair. He was a gnarly figure, with bow legs and thick olive skin, who knew the waterways and rivers better than anyone. If it had mattered, he would have calculated just how long he had worked the waterways where he took the logging and the occasional repairs to Perm and brought back supplies. And if he could write more than the first letter of his name, he would have been able to have read the telegram informing him that his son and grandson had been killed in the battle of Galicia. It was Zbarsky himself who had to read the grief aloud to the old bargeman. Like Zbarsky, Vassya was a member of the Socialist Revolutionary Party and unlike Zbarsky, he was hell-bent on proselytising.

Keeping his eye on the endless run of water below them, Vassya had asked, "Is it true, comrade Pasternak, that the workers in St Petersburg and Moscow dine at restaurants and send their children to school?"

He never looked at Pasternak when he struck up one of the many conversations about politics that they had on their 200 kilometre journey south.

"Well I'm not sure whether anyone is dining out in restaurants at the moment ..." Pasternak knew his answer was inadequate but he felt thrown in this new world where peasants used the word *comrade* rather than the traditional obsequious term *Master* or *Lord*.

Theoretically, Pasternak didn't mind being referred to in a more egalitarian way, but after enduring days of questions from Vassya, who truly believed in the Bolshevik's vision for a new Russia, Pasternak felt deeply unsure about everything he had hitherto thought was right and true.

"I ask, comrade because until all Russians join together and fight for equal pay and education, we will never eliminate the Imperialist's stranglehold on our beloved nation."

Pasternak admired how the Bolshevik's axioms had been committed to the old man's memory, no doubt from the lectures given at the very soviet in which Pasternak himself was a staff member.

"I agree my friend. For every Russian to be educated and to never die of starvation would be a future in which we could all be proud."

But the old captain was not convinced this well-dressed educated Muscovite really understood the call to revolution. Earlier, he had asked Pasternak what he contributed to Russia prior to the war and the handsome youngster had said *poetry*.

"The Bolsheviks will take Russia out of the war."

Pasternak had been hearing Vassya assert this for most of the journey.

"And their petitions for peace will be accepted gratefully by Germany."

Like all Russians, Pasternak had been alarmed then disturbed and finally horrified by the ongoing losses and retreats at the Front.

"The Bolsheviks will then redistribute land to the peasants."

It all seemed so simple and Pasternak could see that this was quintessentially why such views had captured the imagination of Russia.

"And they will ensure all soviets are effectively running the factories, food supply and education."

Despite his old-world patriotism Pasternak could not help but marvel at this new world edict that had ignited the minds of many.

Perm, let alone Vsevolodov-Vilve, was so remote, emotionally, mentally and geographically to all that was going on in the world of Russia. Working at the chemical factory had offered him perspective, solitude to think, time to play the piano, write some short stories and the occasional poem.

As the sharp craggy mountains of the Urals receded, Pasternak moved about the rustic innards of the steamer until he found a quiet corner up against the *chug chug chug* of the steam-driven engine. He decided to pen an afternoon letter to accompany the hamper he would send to his family on arrival in Perm:

Dearest Papa

Both you and cousin Olga write to me about the growing disquiet in Moscow drowning out all noise of war. But, as you say, the noise of revolution is as bloody as that of war. So, to all of this, we must listen carefully.

I have had much time to think about the messages of hope from the Bolsheviks that come to us, even here, in our secluded world of the mineral-rich Urals. Promises of a new tomorrow. A new Russia.

He paused and watched the sunlight flicker across the river and patinate the window, casting indiscernible shadows across his letter.

It seems to me that the future of Russia already resides in the Russian mind. In other words, the idea is about to arrive. People want the absurdity of war to end and yet absurdity will only end when meaning begins.

He thought of his preliminary training in the philosophy of Kant in those few early years at Marburg University in Germany — a country he couldn't help but love, at the time.

The beginning of meaning is the only way absurdity can be annulled. Perhaps they are right ... meaning could be in the great intellect of Vladimir Ilyich Lenin and the so-called enlightenment offered by the Bolsheviks ...

Pasternak wondered where he was going with this, but his thoughts on the future of Russia had been forming, slowly, over the past few months.

The thing is, I think there will be no gleam of light in what we have been buried under — a tunnel of darkness — but rather — there will be immediate light.

Then he knew what it was that he thought. His pen shot on.

I believe the light is seeking us and tomorrow or the next day it will flood us with illumination.

He thought about the nakedness of wealth in Russia which only intensified the poverty. Vsevolodov-Vilve was in many ways a medieval village where the mail was delivered on horse-drawn sleighs from Kazan, 350 kilometres away. A village like so many others: filled with superstition, isolation, and dire cruelty — the Janus face of poverty. Even in his own home city of Moscow Pasternak knew only too well how palaces and cathedrals of breathtaking beauty, the treasure trove of the country, stood cheek-by-jowl alongside wooden huts, dark alleyways and rotting apartments. The great leveller was that all of Russia stank of loamy black earth. Pasternak knew the centuries of mismanagement meant that this schizophrenia, that constituted his nation, was imploding.

The next morning, Pasternak pointed to a spire that could be seen from their barge as they manoeuvred between vessels coming into port. Vassya supplied the name, the Church of the Ascension, and Pasternak knew soon he would be leaving his sea legs behind. He had plans to explore Perm and maybe take in some evening entertainment at the Opera House as his arrival coincided with the production of Stravinsky's *The Nightingale*.

His cousin, Olga had written in one of her lovely long letters to him about this magnificent production that had premiered in Paris last year. It was his petite dark haired cousin who had told him Stravinsky's opera would be playing in Perm and how she longed for him to attend as she was sure he would be missing the arts! Music and reading were the lifeblood of his and her family.

As innocent childhood sweethearts, he and Olga had exchanged vows of everlasting love. He, like everyone in their family, knew it would have been a perfectly companionable match.

That was before he had met Anna Akhmatova.

So, he had been grateful that Olga pretended their exchange of love had been nothing more than a childish fancy. Unlike him, his cousin was not driven by the grand obsessions of the heart, she was less mercurial, more refined in her appetites.

Vassya pulled the barge up to the docks and, after agreeing on a meet time the next day, Pasternak stepped gingerly ashore with his small overnight bag, amidst dockworkers, porters, shipmen, cargo haulers and POWs who were stacking timber on waiting barges. Pasternak decided he would collect the chest of books at Perm Post Office tomorrow morning and send off a letter and hamper to his family just before he re-boarded the steamer. Meanwhile, Vassya was to sort out the supplies waiting for them in the docks and attend to the innumerable tasks Zbarsky had assigned.

This afternoon shall be my oyster, thought Pasternak happily.

He strolled up the main street lined with willow trees and decided to purchase a ticket for that evening's performance of Stravinsky's *The Nightingale* before he booked into one of the more salubrious boarding houses he had seen on the main drag.

After this is done, he thought to himself, *I will find a café in the park behind the Opera House until the sunshine runs out.*

Pasternak found the ticket office just outside the impressive façade of the Perm Opera House.

"Miss, I would like to purchase a ticket for tonight's performance," Pasternak looked across the counter at the young woman.

She had the most startling green eyes.

"*The Nightingale?*" She held his gaze and Pasternak drank in her flawless skin, bow-shaped mouth, and delicate collarbone rising above her blouse.

"Yes. Yes, just one ticket please."

Pasternak watched as she flicked leisurely through a book of tickets, checking them against the names on a list, presumably for those who had already sent through their reservations.

She turned up her face to him and said, "I'm afraid there are no available tickets tonight, sir."

Pasternak stared at her soft blonde hair tucked neatly behind her ears.

"Perhaps, sir, you would like to purchase a ticket for tomorrow night? I could check the — "

"No, that's not possible. I have come all the way down from Vsevolodov-Vilve to see the performance. I return tomorrow morning ..."

How could I be so stupid! he thought to himself. *I should have written and reserved a ticket.*

Pasternak knew it was slightly disingenuous to say that he had come down especially for the opera but staring into those eyes compelled him to speak in absolutes.

The young woman in the ticket box watched him and wondered why this Muscovite was living in the backwaters of Vsevolodov-Vilve.

Perhaps he is a doctor, she mused and blushed when he caught her staring.

"Could you possibly look again?" Pasternak was desperate, both he and she knew it.

"Maybe one of those names on the reserve list is from Perm and they mean to attend tomorrow night's performance ..."

He seems so nice, she thought to herself. *And hand-some.*

But she didn't look back at the list because she already knew that the paperwork for the tickets was impeccably executed, besides, he was probably married.

Pasternak looked at her perfect lips and impulsively leaned across the counter and touched the small wooden nameplate propped there: *K. Tiverzina.*

"What does the K stand for?"

She was flustered by his question and then realised what he meant, "Oh ... no ... that's not me, I mean, this is not my office." Actually, he really was the most lovely young man, "This is the manager's office." She longed for a sweetheart but there were so many men gone to war, "I am only the assistant manager. That is the manager's nameplate." *Maybe he's not married after all*, she thought.

Her smile across at him was completely disarming and Pasternak thought of a poem he had recently begun work on:

My boat throbbed in the drowsy depths,
Willows bowed, kissing collarbones,
Elbows and rowlocks ...

"Ahh ..." he smiled. "So what's *your* name?" All of a sudden getting in to see the opera seemed less of an emergency.

He had looked right into her heart when he had asked her name, so she had no other option but to answer, "Lara."

5

It was mid-afternoon before Walter and the other POWs had finished loading the barges with stripped and stacked birch trees. They had steadily been clearing the forest at the back of the farm, just outside of Perm. Russia was a strange world with exotic onion domes atop various buildings and dark-skinned women with their slanty eyed husbands.

He couldn't remember his geography lessons from school but Walter wondered if China was actually somewhere inside Russia.

In the last few months, he had learnt a little Russian from some of the more enterprising guards who were willing to trade the POW's rations to the POWs for the potatoes or beets they had smuggled out of the farm. Walter and the logging crew collected forest mushrooms and armloads of firewood to use as barter for their daily rations.

Russians were the hungriest people Walter had ever met.

In these last three or four months of captivity, he was stunned by the contradictions of this strange Slavic race. On the one hand, they were illiterate and ignorant peasants, but on the other hand, many of the Russian guards and soldiers could speak more than one language, recite poetry, sing long classical ballads, play instruments and make their own uniforms and boots if and when materials were supplied.

Russians puzzled Walter.

Today, the prisoners were marshalled to take their food break away from the busy docks. The guards carried rifles, but the prisoners were far too thin and weak to make a run for it, and besides, where would they go? Walter imagined himself in the middle of some strange purgatorial ring from which there was no escape. Some of the German officers who had been taken prisoner with Walter had explained it would be unconscionable to try to escape, as Germany would soon march into Russia, triumphantly, and then the POWs role would be to take German control of the centre of Russia. No one seemed to know the length and breadth of this strange inhospitable country, not even the educated German officers. Needless to say, these same German officers in the POW camp were exempt from labour and had the best accommodation and received monthly salaries.

The world makes no sense, thought Walter as he trudged behind the other POWs up Pokrovskaya Ploshchad to the park behind the Opera House.

In the park, they were given a bean and potato stew. As usual, there was one bowl between four or five men. Apparently, this was customary in the Russian army and probably throughout many Russian households, but the Germans found this trait particularly backwards. Having said that, the POWs either quickly scooped their stew up or waited patiently for a bowl to become available. There was also the dry black bread, served daily, and as much water as any man would want to drink.

One by one the POWs finished their meal and then slunk down into the grassy afternoon sunshine of the park. The guards seemed in no hurry to move them back to the docks or to push on back to the prison camp. It was a traitorous thought, but Walter admitted to himself that this was a much better life than being shot at by Russians in some freezing battlefield.

Walter stretched out his limbs and took in the sights of the park, thick with flowering colours and smells. He noticed the café positioned at the other side of the park and a single patron who seemed to be writing in a small notebook and eating a meal of something or other. He wondered if he would ever be free again to sit in a café one summer afternoon.

Walter looked harder at the café patron and felt there was something familiar about the tall dark young man.

And then it dawned on him that it was the same Russian who had been outside the Railway Square reading Rilke when Walter first arrived in Perm. He would never forget those high Slavic cheekbones and square jawline.

From where the POWs were situated in the park it was impossible for Walter to see what he was writing, but he was intrigued by this young Russian. He seemed to be so intense, so caught up in the world within his head. *He is a free man, living in his own country*, thought Walter wistfully.

An unbidden image of Heike filled Walter's mind, her thick blonde hair, hazel eyes and warm brown skin. He would tease her saying she must be careful not to leave her bare arms near him when he was hungry, should he accidentally think them loaves of *landbrot* fresh out of the oven. Her giggle was as dependable as her love.

Walter closed his eyes so no one would see his homesickness.

6

Meanwhile, Aurelia Dobrovolska had begun her afternoon voice exercises with her coach, conductor and orchestra. She noted that the Opera House, all the way out here in Perm, was surprisingly grandiose.

Of course, she was the darling of Moscow and St Petersburg, and yes, the stage had been littered with bouquets after their performance last year in Paris but if she was honest, which she hardly had any cause to be, she would have had to admit that preparing for this particular opera had been trying.

At one point the strange, gangly composer, Igor Stravinsky, had burst into their rehearsals demanding that she sing the soprano in a *more coloratura manner*.

The ignorance of the man!

She was the Bel Canto who sang coloratura soprano — there was no one else in Russia, or across Europe, who could match her.

Indeed, it was her agile runs, impossible leaps and titillating trills over the vocal landscape that made Aurelia Dobrovolska the icon of her age.

Igor Stravinsky obviously had never read her reviews.

Today, she had wanted to run through the final act.

Her job as the nightingale was to rise above the exhortations of the Emperor, sung by the fabulous bass singer Pjotr Pavel Andrejev. According to the Hans Christian Andersen folktale, upon which this opera was based, the Emperor could not live without the nightingale's song and, here in the end scene, he had promised never to cage her again if only she would visit and sing.

Pjotr was 51 to Aurelia's 20 years and took every opportunity to drown out her astonishing flights of multiple octaves, as a reminder that he was the greatest opera legend and had been well before she was born.

These were only some of her challenges. Another was to cajole Death, played by the tricky, conceited and, it had to be said, less talented soprano Elisabeth Petrenko, to leave the room. Death haunted the Emperor and refused to be defeated by the nightingale's song of freedom and love — until Aurelia's final aria.

It was to be her song, and her song alone, that would save the day. Like all talented and beautiful 20 year olds, upon whom fame shone gloriously, Aurelia believed it was just a matter of will for her to triumphantly outperform these two stage rivals.

The diva was facing the empty red velvet seats that would soon be completely filled. The oak parquet floor beneath her small silk shoes was soft and firm. As per her request, the porters had opened some of the windows at the back of the stage so that the fragrance of camomile, lavender and crocuses tumbled in from the gardens behind the Opera House. The perfume filled Aurelia's lungs and made her heady with the deliverance she, and only she, was about to offer the Emperor.

The orchestra began to play, and she let the music enter her body and swell her lungs.

She opened her mouth and the nightingale swept into the Emperor's chamber, quietly and unexpectedly, defying the imperial edict that if she did so, she would be captured. All the while that Aurelia sang the nightingale refused to see or hear Death looming large at the end of the Emperor's bed. The tiny bird's melody was so fragile, so exquisite, it took the conductor's breath away. Little by little the nightingale's voice grew and as it did the Emperor stirred and looked beyond Death to the fanciful flights of this darling bird, this songster!

Up and up and up she trilled, darting this way and that with a voice that was unearthly.

Aurelia closed her eyes and as she sang, she imagined Death, trying unsuccessfully to lure the Emperor away from the nightingale. The coloratura soprano leapt effortlessly beyond the Opera House walls and ceilings, and all who listened lifted up and soared along with her into the very reaches of hope. On and on the nightingale trilled and flitted above what was humanly possible, and the drama of the orchestra gave power to her wings.

Finally, when the music told her the Emperor was weeping Aurelia gave her greatest performance. She sang and sang and sang until the musicians in the orchestra shed tears because her song was the song of freedom for which each of them longed and it could only be theirs while the great diva, the coloratura soprano, Aurelia Dobrovolska, the nightingale, sang!

When she finished, it was silent for an impossibly long moment, and while she breathed deeply to regain her composure she smelt again the summery floral afternoon falling like stardust about her.

Aurelia looked down into the orchestra pit and to her surprise, the musicians were looking up, their faces awash with tears.

She glanced at the conductor. He too had been crying.

Aurelia squinted across to the wings of the stage and there was her coach with his face in his hands, shaking with sobs ... the porters and stagehands stood open-mouthed.

Quietly at first, and then with rising power, she heard cheering beyond the windows at the back of the stage — it was coming from the park behind the Opera House!

The applause and ovation grew louder and louder and instinctively she moved slowly towards the audience, all the time hearing the cries of *Viva La Diva! Brava! Encore!* And even *Dobrovolska!*

Aurelia stood at the windows and looked out.

There was a roar from the park below and to her astonishment, she saw the strangest reception she had ever encountered in her life.

Hundreds of citizens and workers and soldiers had gathered to listen to her rehearse. They cheered and cheered and cheered. Ceaselessly, uninterruptedly.

One tall dark-haired young Russian with astonishing Slavic features, bent down and broke off some carnations and threw them to her, which she caught, and the crowd went crazy.

She held out her arms to the throng.

Her audience! Her beloved! Her Russia!

It was then that she caught sight of a gang of prisoners loosely corralled by their guards. They too stood amazed, and thundered their applause and in amongst it all, she noticed one young blonde POW, his face upturned, weeping openly.

7

At that moment, Father Marian-Josef was thinking it best to snuff out the two burning candles on either side of the altar and pack them away securely. If rumours were right, and the endless scurrying past the church across the Vistula River and ever eastwards suggested they were, then the Germans would be in Warsaw by nightfall.

The Carmelite monk took his time to reach the old marble altar and took some pleasure in the hot start on his thumb and forefinger as he snubbed out the flame.

Last week he had caught two urchins, probably parishioners, attempting to nick the melted wax off the brass candles sticks. It wouldn't be the first time his Polish people had tried to stave off hunger by eating the inedible.

As Father Marian-Josef wrapped the half-used candles in an old newspaper he could hear the rumble of carts, the bellow of donkeys, the squawk of hens, the prattle of children and the urgent commands of husbands to wives and wives to their children as they moved along the road in front of his church. Like everyone, he knew where they were headed. The enemy would soon be at the city gates. But he was sanguine about this truth because, while his people had endured the great partition of their nation into Prussian-Poland, Russian-Poland and Austrian-Poland, Father Marian-Josef believed in the power of prayer (and Piłsudski's Legions) knowing that one day they would have a united Poland.

It just so happened that the long exit out of the city passed his Carmelite Church, Our Lady of the Assumption. He had always been proud of its 17th Century Neo-Classical façade with its Baroque interior.

Father Marian-Josef stepped away from the altar and looked up at the organ.

How many churches could boast Chopin got his start playing here? thought the monk to himself.

He wondered whether he had mumbled the last of his thoughts out loud because a pale face bobbed up from the centre pew.

"Ahh ... Mrs. Kukiel."

Her lace mantilla was tied beneath her chin.

"Shouldn't you be leaving Warsaw? The edict is for the entire city to evacuate ..." He didn't want to alarm her but surely she would have known. "The Germans are coming." His final statement was uttered softly, and he stood leaning his thin body towards her as if to help her from her knees.

The young woman didn't move, and for a moment her eyes closed and she seemed to slump. The monk thought she might have fainted but as he awkwardly manoeuvred his way between the wooden benches and the kneeler, she opened her eyes and looked past him to the altar.

"I cannot go," her reply was quiet but determined.

Father Marian-Josef had noticed this young pregnant woman a few weeks ago when she had waited back after mass for a blessing. Father Marian-Josef remembered her husband had joined one of Piłsudski's Legions, outlawed in Polish-Russia as it ultimately fought for an independent Poland. He couldn't remember the husband's first name, but he saw at the time she was scared.

"It will all work out. God has a plan." Father Marian-Josef paused and wondered at the veracity of this statement, "And, well, I have faith that your husband

will be happy you left to seek sanctuary in ..." He realised he couldn't finish the sentence because they
both knew, as did every fleeing Pole, that the road to
Russia was a long, long haul.

The ground beneath them shook and Father Marian-Josef hoped he didn't look as terrified as the young
woman kneeling.

"Good Lord!" he spluttered as he charged off down
the aisle, brown scapular flying and sandaled feet slap-
ping the tiled floor. At the doorway, he paused and
looked out at the endless stream of human traffic that
had not faltered.

One wizened Polish grandfather hauling a cart with
what must have been his three grandchildren said by
way of comment, "It's the factories, Father ... the workers were told to blow up their factories."

His gnarly old wife had caught up with him by this
stage and miraculously dug out her rosary beads from
her apron and held them up to Father Marian-Josef. He
blessed them with a quick gesture — a cross drawn in
the air.

"They don't want the Germans getting the factories," and with that explanation, the grandfather, his
wife and their grandchildren moved on.

The monk stood there for some time and watched
the haul of human misery pass on by. So, despite sur-

viving unemployment, malnutrition, inflation, the lack of fuel, the spread of infectious diseases and forced food contributions to the Russian army, the Poles had been ordered to flee their ancient city and take only what they could carry. He knew those attempting to take out whatever livestock was left would be stopped and robbed along the way by the Russians who were offering them sanctuary.

Here was the great exit of Warsaw by his Polish con-frères who were just about ruined — *but not ruined yet*, he thought, as he drew himself up and extended a sign of the cross over those scurrying towards their new Jerusalem.

Father Marian-Josef turned back into the cool of his church and he heard the murmuring of the young woman reciting her rosary: "... *full of grace ... blessed art thou ... blessed is the fruit*," he waited, "... *for us sinners ... hour of our death ...*"

Father Marian-Josef began, "Mrs. Kukiel." Then he remembered, "Zofia."

She looked up at the monk who was probably as old as her parents, should they have lived.

The monk sat down on the bench next to her, "Please Zofia, you need to leave. Your husband is a brave man."

He wondered whether he in fact lay dead out there in the merciless summer heat of some terrible battle-field.

She looked down at her tired wooden beads and bowed her head:

Glory be to the Father, and to the Son and to the Holy Spirit.

The monk sighed but his voice joined hers.

As it was in the beginning, is now and ever shall be, world without end.

They seemed to balance uncertainly on this last phrase. He wondered whether she would pray another decade of the rosary, but instead, she lowered her beads and pushed herself up onto the hard wooden pew.

Far off to the west they heard another explosion and then another. He realised he hadn't told this young pregnant woman it was the Poles blowing up their own factories, he wondered if it was wrong to let her think it was the Germans entering their city. Then again, maybe she needed to be scared in order to survive.

"Mrs. Kukiel, I have to insist once again that you join the others and leave —"

"I cannot leave my son."

For a moment he felt confused and looked from her pregnant belly to her determined profile.

She added quietly, "I will not leave him ..."

He followed her eye-line as it skidded to the holy icon framed above the altar: the Blessed Virgin Mary holding the child Jesus in her arms.

The clacking of carts crunched by outside. A dusty warm breeze scooped about the church and he remembered, "You buried your son here, in the graveyard outside. Last year? Last summer ..."

The monk saw the young woman close her eyes on the grief.

She stayed like that for some time.

The explosions continued to the west and he could smell acidic chemicals in the air.

Finally, Father Marian-Josef bent towards the young woman and said, "I am staying here with Our Lady ... with our church. I will be staying." He was surprised by his decision, considering he had told the other monks that he would collect the last of the valuables, the candles and ciborium, then lock the church and be on his way.

Zofia Kukiel looked at the monk and the pain in her throat lessened, "You are staying?"

"Yes. Of course, I am staying." He felt expansive, "Someone has to be here when the Germans arrive ... many of them are Catholic and besides," his avuncular tonsured head dipped towards her, "someone has to hear their confessions!"

She smiled as she looked at Father Marian-Josef. Yet still, her reluctance held her back. She thought about the tiny grave her husband had dug. She remembered the weight of her dead infant son before she eventually handed him into the grave. She would never forget the sound of dirt falling over her son as he lay snugly between her buried mother and father. The monk had prayed and blessed the soil but all she wanted was to lay in the dirt of her homeland and suckle her baby.

Father Marian-Josef spoke, "I will not leave him." She looked up into the old monk's earnest expression. He added, "I will be with Our Lady and together we will keep vigil." Then he stood up, walked towards the altar, and took down the icon.

When he returned, he handed it to her and said, "Take this and give it to the Carmelite Church in Gatchina, near St Petersburg. Tell them I sent you and you will be taken in and the nuns will care for you. Until your husband comes ..."

He stood up and hoped he wouldn't lose courage, "Go now, the icon will protect you and your unborn child. Hurry now!"

The young pregnant woman stood shakily, hesitated momentarily, and then took the icon from the monk.

"Hurry! Hurry now!"

He watched her move swiftly down the aisle to the open door.

Hail, holy Queen, Mother of Mercy ...

He prayed to her small retreating back.

Our life, our sweetness, and our hope ...

He saw her being swallowed up in the great retreat.

To thee do we cry, poor banished children of Eve ...

He felt his own hands begin to shake.

To thee do we send up our sighs, mourning and weeping in this valley of tears ...

His voice filled the church.

Turn, then, most gracious Advocate, thine eyes of mercy towards us ...

He thought of Zofia Kukiel's young anxious face.

And after this our exile show unto us the blessed fruit of thy womb, Jesus ...

And he surveyed the only place that had offered him and his fellow Poles sanctuary.

Oh clement, Oh loving, Oh sweet Virgin Mary ...

Father Marian-Josef stood there lost, alone and be-wildered, knowing he should prepare himself to meet his maker.

8

Aysen surveyed the last of the stragglers crossing the Kierbedzia Bridge. The official Russian-Polish name of this salient, Aleksandryjskiego Bridge given in honour of Tsar Alexander II, was unsurprisingly ignored by the locals who called it after its designer.

Along with his platoon Aysen had been incorporated into the 12th Division of the Siberian Riflemen, and now observed the evacuation of Warsaw. They were supposed to be stripping the evacuees of their possessions, as per their orders, to ensure a quick exit from the city, but no Russian soldier manning the bridge seemed to be bothered anymore. There had been some efforts earlier, but the resistance from the Russian-Poles was so pathetic that it was shameful. Most of the infantry simply turned a blind eye to the few bony livestock, hand-pushed carts and old sheets bundled on the backs of young and old.

Aysen watched quietly.

They needed to get off the bridge by 5 pm. There were no trains coming and there was no plan to save these poor pathetic souls. Somehow the 12th Division was supposed to guide these refugees fleeing on foot all the way to Russia. His cousin Kaskil, Lieutenant Gusev and others had already crossed over and moved on. Aysen was supposed to let the sappers know the bridge was cleared. They were still busy climbing about under the steel spans of the bridge, strapping dynamite to its belly in readiness to offer an explosive welcome to the incoming Germans.

Aysen squinted across the bridge as the sun fell in the west. They had about three hours of daylight left.

I need to get going, he thought to himself, and then he saw a small woman moving out of the Maryenstadt area towards him. This old area of Warsaw was filled with National Democrats, anti-Russian sentiment and militant Catholic monks who were radicalising young men to join any number of Polish legions fighting to free their country of occupation.

Aysen had no opinion on this matter. He himself was a Yakut, first and foremost, and had endured discrimination whenever he had come down from the Lena Basin to trade furs throughout Siberia and elsewhere in Russia. But come the war, when every Russian officer wanted a Siberian Rifleman, particularly a Yakut shooter, he had felt a shift in attitude. Aysen had seen his comrades warily embrace him as a fellow Russian.

He peered closer and realised that the woman striding towards the bridge was younger than he expected and significantly pregnant.

Aysen gestured to her to hurry and she seemed to grip something small at her breast as she came across the first span of the bridge.

Aysen could hear her panting and yelled out, "Hurry!"

She wore a lace mantilla tied under her chin, a red shawl, a wide brown skirt and dark tights with a pair of men's shoes. As she passed, he saw she clutched an icon of Holy Mother Russia.

"Am I the last?"

He ignored her question and shouted down to the sappers, "Right! That's it! We're pulling out!"

He glanced once more at the western side of the bridge and then trotted off behind the young woman who was huffing and puffing to the other side of the Vistula River.

No one would be permitted to enter Warsaw via the Kierbedzia Bridge.

It didn't take Aysen long to realise the young pregnant woman was travelling alone as he followed her out on the dirt road that would eventually take them to Minsk. *And it won't take her long*, Aysen thought grimly to himself, *to realise she is in peril of rape, theft and murder.*

And that's not even taking into account what the enemy might do.

Aysen had seen enough dishonour amongst his own countrymen, with their appalling treatment of women, to know that she was prey. This had been aggravated by the fact that so many Russian soldiers had melted into the tidal wave of refugees heading east in order to avoid doing their duty and fighting the enemy coming west.

He watched the small young pregnant woman trudge anxiously away from the city and begin the ten-day walk to Minsk.

Aysen kept a distance behind her and thought about the war. She was keeping up a steady pace as the shadows lengthened. Vilnius and Riga had already fallen. Warsaw was expected to be in the hands of the Germans by this evening.

The ongoing rhythmic trek folded him into his own thoughts. Russia was losing, this ultimately meant that the death of Tuyaara, back in the battle at Łódź, was utterly pointless.

Once or twice up ahead he saw the young woman pause to stretch the small of her back.

He too paused, momentarily, and noted that she wore her red shawl, like most Polish women, wrapped about her neck, crossed tightly over her breasts and tied behind her back.

WHOMP! POOM! BOOSH!
Aysen turned sharply and looked back at Warsaw, the city of churches. A pillar of black smoke shot up like an avenging angel. And at that moment, he thought about the brave sappers left behind putting the finishing touches to the intricate strapping of the explosives, beneath the Kierbedzia Bridge.

Aysen's heart raced and with steely determination, he called out to three or four older, frailer Poles, "That's the Germans! They're on our heels! C'mon, we must go! Hurry!"
He said this last word in Polish then in Russian and then in Yakut, for himself and everything he would lose if they didn't get a move on. But he knew that no

matter what he said the Poles thought this was an ethnic war between the Teutonic Germans and the Slavic Russians. In these last few days, when he had been ordered to assist with the evacuation of Warsaw, many Poles had told him in their heavily accentuated Russian that their friends and relatives in Prussia and Austria had been promised a united Poland when Russia was defeated. In other words, they had nothing to gain in cooperating with the Russians.

Aysen estimated he had been walking for around three hours. The light was leaving the sky and a tired grey wash began to paint the evening. He was satisfied there was no one behind him as he came up, what he hoped, would be the last hill and skirted its forested tuft. Soon the Polish refugees ahead would be instructed to sort out their makeshift sleeping arrangements because everyone would be moving at dawn.

It had been a while since Aysen had seen the young pregnant woman, so when he saw her, snarling and hissing at two teenage boys he thought of a doe encircled by a pair of filthy hunting dogs.

Then Aysen saw her shoes, dark tights and red scarf discarded in the dirt. Her blouse was torn and her hair was a tangled hot mess. Her mantilla was nowhere to be seen.

And sure enough, both teenage predators wore the tunic of the Russian infantry.

Deserters, thought Aysen bitterly.

He slung his rifle lazily about in front of him and spoke to the youngest deserter in a low and menacing voice, "Move on lad."

The teenager pointed a knife unconvincingly in Aysen's direction, "This doesn't concern you, *chinaman*, move on yourself or —"

Aysen's rifle butt smashed into the deserter's face. The boy staggered and then stumbled after his fleeing pal into the oncoming night.

Aysen moved to the pregnant woman and saw that she was still gripping the icon. He didn't know whether they had already raped her and he wasn't going to ask.

"It might be best if we sit down."

She ignored him and slowly began to shove her little feet into what must have been her husband's shoes. He watched as she tied her tights into her shawl. Her face was pale against the soft summer sky.

"You need to travel with a group of people. You are not safe on your own ..."

She stumbled a little and instinctively he moved to her and gently lent her against himself. Her face was a smear of tears and snot and dirt.

"You are alright now, little one ..." He felt the hard belly of her pregnancy against his side and knew she was close to her time. "My post is at the rear of the retreat to Minsk, so ... look for me."

The young woman pulled away from him suddenly so he tried to reassure her with, "My wife is expecting ... like you." Although wary, she seemed to soften and he added, "Soon your baby will come." She nodded and Aysen thought of Sayaana.

"I am Aysen Manchari, if you cannot find me, tell one of the other riflemen and they will help you." He had no idea if this was true or not but he needed to believe that there were others who would defend a vulnerable pregnant woman on her own.

She began moving away from him and then she said over her shoulder, "I carry the holy icon of the Blessed Virgin Mary and the Infant Jesus."

Aysen didn't really know why Russian-Poles used these sorts of appellations for Mother Russia.

"She will protect me," her voice sounded even younger than what she looked.

It was on the tip of his tongue to say, "Don't be so sure," but instead he followed close behind and they made their way to where his platoon was setting up camp.

It was August 5.

Figuring they had a better chance of surviving if they stuck close to the Russian soldiers, there was a number of refugees asleep at the edges of the platoon's camp.

Zofia found a place to lay down amongst the other tattered Polish refugees.

"Are you travelling alone?" The old man who asked seemed to be more curious than concerned.

"Yes." Zofia's back and legs ached and her pregnant belly felt heavy.

The old man's wife made a space for her to drop into and Zofia thought, *If I can survive this day, I can survive anything.* She tried not to think of the young Russian teenagers who had attacked her.

When she shut her eyes, she was still hugging the icon of the Blessed Virgin Mary and the Infant Jesus that Father Marian Josef had given her, and she knew this would be her passport to a Carmelite sanctuary in Gatchina.

The nuns will help me when the baby comes, she thought.

"Where is your husband?"

The old man's question was met with his wife hissing *shh!*

Zofia didn't realise she was going to answer until she did, "Wincenty, my husband, went with Piłsudski's Legion to fight," she paused. She had found that this piece of information had an impact on all Poles who heard, but she had no faith he was alive.

"The Piłsudski's Legions! Ahh, it will be *those* boys who will bring back a united Poland to us all!" The old man was on a roll and a few other refugees close by stirred as he sat up and spoke boldly into the night, "My nephews are in Prussia-Poland and her sister's family," Zofia realised he was speaking about his wife, "are in Galicia ... Austria-Poland." The old man laid back down as if he had made his point.

Zofia shuffled to her other side then she heard him talk on into the sleeping night, "This is not a war between the Russians and the Germans. No."

Again, she thought he was done and falling asleep, but she waited anyway and then she heard a final quiet statement, "No. This is a civil war. Poles against Poles. And each battle has been fought on Polish soil."

Zofia heard the old woman pat her husband's back and hush him. After some time she heard the old man snore.

Eventually, the old woman turned to Zofia and said, "You must walk with us. Don't let the Russian soldiers see your face. Cover it." The old woman's bony finger touched Zofia's cheek, "They are animals. Not even the baby in your belly will protect you from them. Keep your head down when they are near."

Zofia felt the baby kick inside her and she shuffled again onto her back.

Just when she thought everyone was sleeping, she heard the old woman murmur, "In the morning ... rub dirt in your hair and on your face ..."

Then she heard the old woman begin to snore, *pah ... pah ... pah ... pah ... pah*, and all was quiet.

Zofia hugged the icon to her belly and hoped it would protect her.

An hour before dawn the camp broke.

Aysen's platoon, assigned to bring up the rear of the refugee march to Minsk, had been told trains would meet them there and transport them all to Moscow. They moved along dusty dirt roads, across dry fields and on and on as the sun rose high above them.

No one believed there would be trains, but Aysen and his platoon yelled they would miss the train whenever a refugee began to fall behind. There were few breaks. Information had been carried up that Warsaw had fallen, and the Germans were intent on reaching Brest-Litovsk before they did.

They still had another nine days of marching but, as most of the refugees were elderly or very young, the going was tough.

The sun fell in the west behind them and still, they hauled forward. Another division had been assigned to burn whatever crops and stores had been left behind as the Warsaw exodus moved towards Minsk. The sunset began to fill the sky which, at the same time, was daubed with grey and brown smoke. It made no sense, not only to the refugees who looked disgustedly upon the burning devastation but to the soldiers themselves. All of them had suffered the hard gnaw of starvation deep in the pit of their stomachs.

They marched on into the night. There was little talk amongst the refugees and soldiers, just the occasional hushing of a child crying.

By nightfall of the second day, Zofia knew she wouldn't make it. She had to find a burnt-out farmhouse and pray that the Germans be Catholic and recognise the power of the icon she carried.

Her back throbbed, she could no longer feel her feet and her belly was drum tight. She couldn't let herself think about the Russian deserters roaming the countryside raping and murdering women.

It was another month before her time, but at the back of her mind, she worried the baby might come early. All she could hope was that the Germans might take her back to Warsaw or leave her in the countryside with some farmer's wife. Zofia had nothing else in which to believe.

When she nestled in behind the old woman to sleep that night those around them were already snoring.

So, it was slightly bewildering when the old woman stretched her arm back and laid it on Zofia's hip, "We will stay with you."

At first, Zofia thought she must have voiced her plan out loud but she knew deep down she had not.

Despite this, there was no point lying, "I have to wait behind. It is too much ... with the baby coming ..." and she didn't know whether it was the old woman's warm hand patting her hip or if it was the fact that this elderly couple, whom she had only known for a day, would sacrifice their escape to stay with her, but she started to sob. Although she tried to cover her mouth, the gulps of anguish and fear punctured the night.

The old woman kept patting her hip and then, after a while, she began to sing a hymn they had sung so often in the Carmelite church.

Hail, Queen of Heav'n, the ocean Star,
Guide of the wand'rer here below ...

Zofia had never seen the sea before and she wondered, not for the first time, what this miracle must be like.

Thrown on life's surge we claim thy care,
Save us from peril and from woe ...

Zofia hugged the icon and knew she might be saved.

Mother of Christ, Star of the sea,
Pray for the wanderer, pray for me ...

Zofia laid her hand on the old woman's shoulder and soon her sobbing eased.

Virgin most pure, Star of the sea,
Pray for the sinner, pray for me ...

Zofia closed her eyes and steadied her breathing to assure her baby all would be well.

Pity our sorrows, calm our fears,
And soothe with hope our misery.

The old woman's voice sailed on and Zofia curled her legs up under her belly and fell asleep.

Refuge in grief, Star of the sea,
Pray for the mourner, pray for me.

It was raining the next morning when the refugees awoke to the clatter of the soldiers decamping.

Aysen knew there were deserters mingling amongst the refugees, taking cover in the pack. After what he came across the other night, two teenagers — once Russian soldiers — assaulting that pregnant woman, he knew he had to be vigilant. He and Kaskil were part of the rear-guard of the hundreds and hundreds of refugees heading to Minsk, ensuring no one was left behind.

For the most part, no one had food except for what could be scrounged along the route and gleaned from the fields and roadside shrubs as they passed.

The summer rain was changing to a steamy drizzle and with eyes, on the backs of the last of the refugees, Kaskil handed Aysen some leaflets that he had collected in the trenches before his timely departure along the Gorlice-Tarnow line.

As he trekked on, Aysen read the leaflets quietly:

Why are you fighting the Germans?
Because a Serb shot an Austrian a year ago?
Does that make any sense?

He unfolded another and read on:

Do you still support the Duma
and the Tsar who sent you to fight?
The war is a year old with nothing to show!

And then the final one:

The Russian Army is torching their own country
just to survive!
It makes no sense!
Don't you want to be in control of your future?

Aysen had heard about these leaflets that the Bolsheviks distributed at the Front but he hadn't actually read one, until now.

Just two days ago his cousin had suggested they should think about taking control of their own destiny. Like Kaskil, Aysen longed for Yakutia and was bitterly sick of this war that seemed to have forgotten its objectives. To make matters worse, most soldiers had been granted a furlough home, but not for those as far afield as Siberia, let alone the Yakuts from the Lena Basin.

Aysen handed the soggy leaflets back to Kaskil and kept trudging forward, all the while keeping his eyes on the bent backs of the Poles in forced exile up ahead.

"I can't go home without you, cousin," Kaskil sounded as if he had made up his mind. "There's nothing left for us here ..."

Aysen saw the road dip ahead and thought there might be a creek or rivulet where he could fill his canteen.

"Remember when we joined?" Kaskil never tired, "We were the chosen ones! We thought we were going to see Russia and the rest of Europe and ..."

They marched on together quietly inside their own memories, each recalling the sense of adventure and pride. They were going to make something of their lives ... they were going to see the world and live.

"Then Tuyaara ..." Although Kaskil's brother was never forgotten this had been the first time either one of them had said his name, "I mean — you gotta ask yourself — what the hell has it all been for?"

Aysen could hear the tears in his cousin's voice. The road was dipping now, and sure enough, ahead of them was a creek where the last of the refugees — an old man and his wife — were scooping up mouthfuls of water.

"If not us, then who?" Aysen asked and his words stayed between them as they walked on.

When they had just about reached the creek Aysen noticed that the young pregnant woman was there with the old man and woman, splashing water on her pale face.

Aysen frowned. When he told her to travel with a group of people in order to be safe, he didn't mean for her to choose the oldest and most infirm Poles she could find.

"But we *have* stepped up. We *have* done our part," Kaskil had never sounded so serious, "I have seen enough of the world. I have seen too much ..."

Aysen laid his hand on Kaskil's shoulder, "I don't want some other man to have to do my job. I will finish this job and —"

"Hey, what are they up to?" Kaskil pointed to the three figures at the creek scurrying upstream and away from the tail end of the marching refugees and soldiers.

"Dedushka!" Kaskil bellowed to the fleeing grandfatherly figure.

The old man didn't look back but the young pregnant woman did. She saw Aysen and stopped. The old woman said something to her, perhaps urging her to follow the old man but the younger woman stood her ground.

Aysen and Kaskil stumbled over the large smooth rocks alongside the creek bed.

"What's going on? Come on, this is the wrong way to Minsk." Kaskil's tone was hearty and reassuring until he added, "That direction is back to the bayonets of the bastard Fritz!"

The old woman and man peered with open distrust at the two Yakut men with their rifles slung casually across their backs.

"Dedushka, you need to come with us," Kaskil said to the old man who ignored him. He then decided to appeal to the old woman, "Babushka, you have put yourself and your ..." Kaskil looked closely at the heavily pregnant young woman, "granddaughter in great peril."

It was to Aysen that the young woman spoke and when she did everyone turned to her, astounded at the warmth and respect in her voice.

"Aysen Manchuria this is the way I must go. Please do not stop me."

She had wound her red scarf across her breast and tied it tightly at the back. Her pale face was gleaming with perspiration and her light brown hair, short and feathery, stuck to her head in the steamy mist at the end of the morning shower.

Surely, she could be no more than 18, thought Aysen.

"It is too dangerous," said Kaskil. "The Germans are close behind."

The old man and his wife turned and looked back towards the way they had come, as if, at any moment, they would see the distinct pickelhaube bobbing up over the rise.

The young woman kept her deep brown eyes on Aysen but said to Kaskil, "I am not afraid of those men." And it occurred to this strange posse of Yakut and Poles that it wasn't an ethnicity she feared.

"She cannot keep going!" said the old woman to Aysen and Kaskil as if they were ignorant boys who needed reprimanding. "She will be a mother soon and she needs a quiet place so I can help deliver her baby."

The men, including the old man, seemed immediately unsure of themselves.

"So, you boys be on your way." The old woman took the elbow of her young charge and added, "We will be safe enough." Then with a final jut of her wrinkled chin, she added, "Besides, this is our country, invaders come and go but *Poland has not yet perished.*"

The old man nodded at his wife's truth and her cleverness in quoting the anthem sung by Polish freedom fighters.

But at that moment Aysen gestured quickly to stop speaking and crouched low. He had heard the drone of an approaching vehicle and Kaskil hurriedly began moving the Poles away from the creek and into the low shrubs. The rumble grew louder and Aysen scrambled up the small rise away from the creek bed and towards the dusty road. In a few swift movements, his rifle was loaded and ready.

The roar of the vehicle could be heard as it crested the hill and swung into view. Aysen stood against a tree, with a stillness that somehow made him part of the tattered countryside, and looked through the scope of his rifle at the driver's head, which was now 20 meters away. The vehicle sputtered as the driver changed down the gears and Aysen heard the crunch of metal on metal as it came towards the creek crossing.

He gently squeezed the trigger then abruptly stopped — he recognised the papakha on the driver's head.

A Cossack!

He pulled up his rifle but the irony wasn't lost on him — if there was to be any Russian shot by a Yakut it might as well be a Cossack. A payback for invading Yakut country a few short centuries ago.

The vehicle drew up at the creek crossing and with a *putter putter putter putter* it eventually hissed and jolted to an abrupt stop.

The Cossack leaned out the driver's door and wrenched the brake.

Both Aysen and Kaskil ambled towards the vehicle where the Cossack and one of his passengers were clambering out. The Yakut riflemen had no intention of saluting the Cossack, which was good because the Cossack had no intention of acknowledging the filthy Siberians.

It was a strange soft-looking foreigner, stepping towards them, who saluted and fixed them with his determined eye. Aysen and Kaskil returned the military show of respect and gave their name, rank and division.

"How long have you been marching the refugees forward, Lance Corporal?"

"Two days, sir."

"You have come this far from Warsaw, in two days?"

"Yes, sir."

"That's rather surprising ... You're headed for Minsk you say? Will there be trains for the refugees waiting?"

"That's what we are told, sir."

The foreigner's Russian was outstanding but he seemed to be asking the wrong questions and in the confusion of it all, there was a shout of joy when the other passenger ejected himself from the vehicle and rushed into Kaskil and Aysen with the slathering love of a puppy.

"Valentin!" yelled Kaskil and pummelled the young boy with a flurry of feints.

The Cossack flushed with irritation and thought to himself, *Am I the only one here who is a true and dignified Russian?*

Valentin turned to the foreign officer and said, "These are the two Siberian riflemen I told you about. I showed them how to get through the German lines in the Masurian Lakes." The young teenager looked at the Cossack and added, "I took them to Grodno Headquarters."

Aysen couldn't help but ruffle the dirty blonde hair of this fearless, bragging Pole.

Professor Bernard Pares turned to the two Yakuts and, to their surprise, shook their hands with genuine warmth and asked for as much detail as possible about Warsaw.

The Cossack was looking put out at this stage, which seemed to please Valentin no end.

As Aysen offered up the facts of what he knew and the impressions of what he had observed, Kaskil and Valentin pushed and shoved each other, and the young lad told his older pal about their escape from Lemberik, which had now fallen to the enemy, and their subsequent race to Minsk.

Aysen learned in his quick discussion with Pares that he was English and an official war observer for Russia.

Meanwhile, probably as a display of irritation, the Cossack wandered down to the creek bed to stretch his legs and it was then that he spied the three Polish refugees taking cover just a few hundred metres from where he stood.

"Come out where I can see you," he barked and Pares, Aysen, Kaskil and Valentin all looked at the old couple and the pregnant young woman who gingerly moved towards the Cossack.

Aysen turned to Pares and took a gamble, "Sir. This woman is my cousin's wife and she is about to deliver their baby."

Kaskil looked confused.

"Could I beseech you, sir," Aysen continued, "to drive her with you on to Minsk, where she might be assisted?"

He decided it was best to look only at the Professor who was sizing up the situation. Aysen had no idea what Zofia might do or say, let alone the old couple with whom she had attached herself. Out of the corner of his eye, he could see Valentin looking askance at open-mouthed Kaskil, it was obvious that the teenager thought Kaskil had made a huge mistake.

"Well, Lance Corporal, if we picked up every woman about to give birth along the way we would be a veritable ambulance service and I'm afraid —"

"*Arghh uh uh uh uh!*"

Zofia was either giving a stellar performance or she actually was going into labour as she doubled up in agony. After a moment she tried to straighten but could only manage to lean heavily on the old woman.

"Sir. Just to Minsk. My cousin and I have been fighting at the Front since November last year and if his wife could just be taken to safety ..."

Aysen wondered whether his tale was going to add up but right on cue Zofia again let out a deep guttural groan.

"Right." Pares went into action, "Kuznetsov, get that woman in the back. I will ride in the front with you, Valentin —"

"My parents are coming with me!"

They all turned to the young woman who seemed perfectly able to confront a high-ranking British officer, a fierce Cossack and two Siberian riflemen, without a moment's hesitation.

"You've got your hands full with that one, Chink," muttered the Cossack as he pushed past Kaskil and started cranking up the vehicle.

Without hesitating the old man scrambled into the back seat before anyone could change their minds, followed by his elderly wife helping the lumbering Zofia.

The *chug chug chug* of the engine turned over and the Cossack held the passenger door open for Pares. Valentin hugged Kaskil, then Aysen and ignored the scornful snort from the Cossack as he strode back to the driver's seat.

"Keep safe little brother," Kaskil said and pushed him towards the vehicle.

The Cossack fiddled with the brake on the outside of his driver seat and said under the grumble of the engine, "I'll take good care of your whore, Chink."

"Prick," was Kaskil reply and in two strides he had mounted the running board of the moving vehicle so that the Cossack drew back, surprise and alarm on his face.

But to the astonishment of everyone, the Yakut leaned deep into the back seat and kissed Zofia on her soft full lips.

"Good luck, my love!" He pulled himself away and cried, "I will see you soon, I promise!"

He then threw himself off the running board.

Aysen and Kaskil heard those in the vehicle cheer and the two Yakut men threw their caps in the summer air as the vehicle chugged across the creek bed and up the road, ever eastward, to Minsk.

Chapter 6

September — October 1915

Behind the clutter of dishes, the 11 year old boy was quietly assembling his black bread pellets on the thick linen tablecloth.

Meanwhile, the grown-ups were engrossed in talk about the Front.

Carefully, shielding his operation, the boy rolled the pellets in salt from the cellar he had surreptitiously up-ended.

To his right sat his father who was deep in conversation with an Englishman who had been impressed earlier with the young boy's rendition of Tennyson's

Charge of the Light Brigade. It was the boy's favourite English poem.

The young boy chuckled quietly when he noticed his target was eating his way through a second helping of zakouska, roast beef and Yorkshire pudding.

Ahh, the young boy thought, *victory is mine!*

He glanced, once again, across the table at his target — the larger than life, garrulous Belgian General.

"TAKE COVER!" yelled the 11 year old across the imperial glassware and bone china.

A shower of black bread pellets flew through the air, raining down on the unsuspecting General who was, at that very moment, using a large gulp of claret as a mouthwash.

The dining room erupted in laughter, protest and calls for *More Bread!* to the servants.

For a fat man, the General moved swiftly. From what little bread was left on his side of the table he deftly rolled his own pellets. The boy squealed with delight and his grey tabby shot out from under the table in a caterwaul of irritation.

The General's chair shrieked as his huge bulk shunted forward and yelled "I TAKE NO PRISONERS!"

and let loose a flurry of bread pellet artillery across the table at his young enemy.

In the fracas, it was difficult for any serious conversation to persist but the father of the young boy smiled indulgently and continued his discussion with the English gentleman.

The young boy's mayhem was infectious and soon the table of 20 or so military advisors and guests were throwing whatever food they could grab from the leftovers.

Pierre Gillard, the boy's Swiss tutor, implored his charge to desist but no one could hear his pleas.

The boy ducked and dived behind his father's chair, shielding himself from the onslaught. He was tall for his age, fine-featured and with startling blue eyes; his khaki uniform and long Russian boots suggested he was a private soldier, a fancy the entire Russian Army permitted him.

"Maybe, that's the end of it," the boy's father said evenly. "I think you have got him, my darling one. No more hijinks, son." The affection was evident in the father's eyes and voice.

The 11 year old calmed, perspiration on his upper lip and forehead, but he kept his eyes on the General, who, with studied indifference, was beckoning a servant to replenish his glass.

The father looked across at the dark-haired naval seaman standing near the doorway and quietly said his name: "Derevenko." The boy's moustachioed nanny nodded, then murmured something to the lad about enjoying the afternoon before the autumn insisted they all remain indoors.

Meanwhile, the servants worked invisibly to bring order back to the dining room table. Topping up glasses of wine or vodka, sweeping away the various food pellets and restoring dignity to the adult's luncheon.

Just as the 11 year old left the dining room with Derevenko, a thick damp napkin flew through the air and landed on the boy's head, followed by a Belgian accent: "So long, Tsarevitch Napkin Head."
The room erupted in further merriment.

Even the Imperial Highness, Tsar Nicholas Romanov, was laughing as his son swaggered out, beaming at his own success in attacking his favourite General, whom he called, Papa de Ricquel.

The heart of Russian Military Headquarters, Stavka, had recently moved to Mogilev in the forested area of Belarus. A governor's residence was selected to accommodate the Tsar and his entourage, a modest place of only three floors with a smallish dining room.

It had been a month since Grand Duke Nicholas Nikolaevich had been notified that the Tsar wished to command the Russian Army himself. The Grand Duke was to depart that day and take up his new post as commander in chief of Russia's efforts in the Caucasus.

Over the past few months the Tsar had spent time on and off at Stavka but as the Tsarina had so often pointed out in her loving letters, all of Russia looked to him, not the Grand Duke, to bring their nation to victory. Besides, the Grand Duke was too popular by half, despite the army being in tatters. Well, at least that's how the Tsarina, the Imperial Highness Alexandra Feodorovna, saw the matter.

That her husband had absolutely no military experience or training was neither here nor there, what mattered to her and to all of Russia was that the Tsar fulfil his God-given destiny. She decided not to write to her husband that many members of the Duma were appalled by this decision nor did she write that the students from the universities were rioting, as a result of this decision to replace the Grand Duke. God how she hated this man, who had not only openly shunned Father Grigori Rasputin but had declared that a single bullet to Rasputin's head would please Russia no end.

At least her darling husband had had the grace to never mention the malicious gossip that she was both a German spy and Rasputin's whore. Her letters never referred to these wicked rumours which dogged her at every turn as she tried to do God's work. Only yesterday she had written to her husband about how each day she prayed that she would prove herself worthy of running the country while she remained in St Petersburg (she didn't mention Rasputin was her guide night and day) so that Russia's Imperial Highness, her beloved husband, was free to run the Russian Army.

All is as it should be, wrote the Tsarina, *and with God's help, soon the enemy will be conquered and our family nest, with its warmth and affection, can continue on without further interruption.*

The Tsar turned back to the Englishman's recount of what he had seen across the Gorlice-Tarnow Front and the latest attack by the Austro-Hungarian forces on the Russian Army in Galicia and Volhynia. The Englishman's Russian was impeccable and his measured intonation made the Tsar feel he was in the company of a friend. It was such a relief after so many alarmist discussions with various advisors. The Tsar knew that he alone would be able to offer the Russian military the boost in morale that it so desperately needed.

The Tsar gestured for cognac. How he longed to be out in the fresh afternoon sunshine with his darling son.

"The early rain has churned the battlefield into a mud bath, Your Highness, but I would have to say the troops are hunkering down and —"

"You're not trying the cognac?" asked the Tsar of Professor Bernard Pares. "It is excellent. Gaston Camus keeps us in supply — even during the war. He is a wonderfully clever Frenchman."

The Tsar sipped the rich ochre digestif then added, "Do you know him?"

Pares blinked behind his rimless glasses, "Gaston Camus? No, your Highness, I can't say I have had the pleasure." He paused. "What we saw as we came up through Volhynia was primarily mud and when the bombardment was over the enemy could only plod forwards to the Russian lines, cutting through the barbed wire. Meanwhile, the Russian machine gunners could do nothing other than reducing numbers. There seemed to be utterly no strategy —"

"Jolly good show, from our chaps then!" responded the Tsar in English.

Pares smiled thinly and continued in Russian, "Well that's right, Your Highness."

Pares looked across at the Belgium General who had been at the centre of the young Tsarevitch's antics earlier and noted the rotund man was itching for the Tsar's attention.

Pares pushed on, "I spoke to many of the officers, Your Highness, and they reported an increase in desertion, a lack of discipline and the terrible spread of typhoid. Of course, there is little to no medication getting out to the troops, let alone food —"

"Swollen rivers."

Pares looked closely at the Tsar in puzzlement, "I beg your pardon, Your Highness?"

The Tsar placed his crystal wobble snifter on the table and lit a cigarette from the exquisitely carved silver box sitting in front of him.

Eventually, he clarified, "The rains would have resulted in swollen rivers which, of course, brings typhoid."

The Belgian General quickly chimed in from across the table, "Quite right Your Imperial Highness. Well said."

The Tsar looked kindly across the table and murmured, "My dear brave soldiers ..."

Pares calculated that he had about as long as it might take for the Tsar to complete his cigarette before some other guest would catch the Tsar's attention, or before he withdrew, as was his custom, after luncheon.

"I agree, Your Highness, they are very brave." Pares wondered if the Tsar needed reminding, once again, of the terrible losses Russia was sustaining, the deteriorating quality of artillery and the tactical insistence on counterattack which was affecting the morale to an all-time low.

Does he realise, thought Pares, *that the Grand Duke's crippling logistical failures and Stavka's lack of strategy are going to continue to generate discontent and war-weariness for Russians everywhere?*

As if reading the Englishman's mind, the Tsar, tapping ash from his cigarette, said firstly in English, "The thing is, old man ..."

Pares noticed how lined the Tsar's face was and his beard was more grey than brown.

"The thing is ..." The Tsar had switched back to Russian, believing that the entire table needed to hear, "No one loves his country like a Russian. No soldier from the German or the Austro-Hungarian Empire has the devotion for their country in the same way that a Frontovik has for Holy Mother Russia."

Pares ignored the hearty cheer and table-thumping from his fellow diners, what he did notice was how the 48 year old Tsar was immediately warming to his topic.

"And our policy is to kill as many of the enemy while suffering minimum losses." The Tsar held his snifter aloft, "We will be the last man standing!"

"TO RUSSIA!" cried the well-upholstered Belgian General from across the table, and every man was on his feet.

"And to the TSAR!"

Pares re-seated and, undeterred, said quietly to the Tsar, "But not only has Russia had to abandon all conquered regions, but Your Highness has also lost considerable amounts of land that has always been Russia's. All of Poland is now in the hands of the Central Powers."

The Tsar sighed and looked away from the Englishman, whom he had clearly misjudged, and spoke tiredly, "Yes I am well aware and in due course, this will be righted. What you have to realise is that we have more and more recruits each day. And they are desperate to get out there and fight for Imperial Russia!"

Pares reflected grimly on the fact that these very recruits were now entering the fray without training or weapons. Fodder, they were.

"Also," the Tsar was stubbing out his cigarette and the conversation with the Englishman, "I have the best and most experienced military personnel out there on the ground."

Pares nodded his head to the supreme ruler of Russia and knew, then and there, that the country would haemorrhage itself to death.

After luncheon, the Tsar took the opportunity to retire to his private rooms on the second floor of Stavka, to write a few letters and read before the afternoon's engagements got into full swing. He had every intention of getting out to his son Alexei to enjoy his playful mischief and uncomplicated company.

Sitting in his comfortable cane chair with the window facing northward he heard the excited voice and laughter of his son, as well as the quiet patient tones of Derevenko, and some other young boy whom he did not recognise.

With his gold nibbed enamelled fountain pen, he began today's letter to his wife, the Tsarina:

My Darling Sunny,
As I write I can hear Baby playing happily in the warm sunshine. I can only presume it is at the fountain.

How I miss you, my darling, and your quiet smile, which I imagine as I gaze from my window and look down upon this happy scene.

He knew Petty Officer Derevenko would be watching Alexei like a hawk, but all the same, he wanted the boy to be upstairs with him, reading his books on the cot he had insisted be brought in and placed beside his own bed.

Would you believe it, I noticed today at luncheon our darling Baby has a sunburnt nose! And a penchant for mischief and mayhem (I know that will not surprise you!). He is doing splendidly and lifting the spirits of all those around him, especially your dear husband.

He rubbed his face and thought about the tyranny of distance. He needed his wife like oxygen. No one understood him in the way she did. Only she nurtured the hopes he had in all he wanted to become and smothered the fears he harboured in all he could never be.

I had the Englishman, Bernard Pares, with me today at luncheon. It was very interesting talking to him about Tennyson and Cambridge University and hot toasted muffins served at afternoon tea. He was quite charmed by Baby's recitation of the Light Brigade. He is a good fellow, but I must say, and I can hear you agree, his obser-

vations are merely those of an outsider. What does he really know of Russian courage and tenacity and heart?

The Tsar cleared his throat and massaged his breast bone where he imagined he felt physical pain for his anchor, his light, his wife who loved him devotedly, jealously and without end.

Papa de Ricquel talked to us about a Miss Cavell who has been arrested by the Germans in Belgium. I can't remember her first name, and she is a foreigner. A nurse (like you and my darling daughters!). Somehow Miss Cavell had managed to funnel 80 or so soldiers from the Entente Powers out of Belgium into the Netherlands! Remarkable! This is what war does, it makes heroes of the best of us. Especially you, my sweet one. Apparently, Miss Cavell is to be tried for treason — but she isn't actually a German or Belgian — so the charges are just dastardly.

He gazed at the framed photo he had on his writing desk. His dear wife and his four beautiful girls.

I long to be with you, my most beloved, and to have your arms around me and your soft ear pressed against my cheek. Give kisses to my beauties and tell them I will be home soon.

The Tsar realised he had written this inky longing without any real plans of how he could make his exit from Headquarters. He dashed off a few more lines:

This afternoon, we are to watch a display by a regiment of the Caucasian cavalry — I am told there will be Kuban and Terek Cossacks, so it is sure to be a great show! Then after supper, there is another meeting I must attend but I will scribble a few words before bed, my darling Sunny, so please forgive me if my handwriting is poor by that stage!

He thought back to the letter he had received from his wife yesterday and decided he must again repeat his cautious advice.

Please, my beloved, I ask you to go slowly with your appointments to the Duma. We do have an honourable and efficient group of men there and while I sympathise with your concern that 'Our Friend' has been offended by so many of them, it is paramount our government does not degenerate into a rapidly changing succession of appointees.

He stopped himself adding *made by Father Grigori Rasputin* and settled for an early full stop. It was said that Rasputin valued only those politicians who were sufficiently sycophantic towards him. Many had warned him of Rasputin's influence, even his great uncle, the Grand Duke held no punches when it came to expressing his pathological hatred of the man, but deep down the Tsar knew it was his wife's devotion to her son that compelled her to keep the mystic healer close by. The Grand Duke had gone so far as to accuse the priest of using military secrets to control the Church and the State of Russia — *Which is ridiculous,* thought the Tsar, *because Sunny knows the importance of keeping all matters I share with her utterly confidential.*

How he hated conflict.

2

Valentin had seen the Tsarevitch yesterday when everyone was gathered at the Mogilev Cathedral. Professor Pares had tried to interest his young batman in the building, which was a combination of Folk Art and Old Russian architecture, a sanctuary of orthodoxy dedicated to Saint Basil the Great, Gregory the Theologian, and John Chrysostom.

Valentin didn't even bother stifling his yawns.

As far as he was concerned, the Tsar was too pious and the religious ritual, too tedious. After what he had seen over the past months driving about the countryside with Kuznetsov and the English Professor he was convinced that the Tsar needed to open his eyes and *do something* about the massacre of his men. Even at 12-going-on-13 years of age, Valentin could see that those making decisions at Headquarters were utterly blind to the truth of the Russian Army. He had seen the diabolical slaughter of the Russians while standing alongside the Professor in the various battles, and retreats, across Polish Russia.

At the Cathedral yesterday, the Tsar had been blessed as the new commander of the Russian Army and Pares had told Valentin that they were watching history in the making. By the faces of the thousands of soldiers who were rallied to form the guard down Pervomaiskaya Ploshchad to honour the Tsar, there was not a great deal of hope evident in their new commander in chief.

Valentin had watched on as the Tsar addressed these men, saying something about building up their spirit and leading them to conquer Germany.

The soldiers waited impassively.

Towards the end when the Tsar asked who among them had served since the start of the war, only a few raised their hands. Indeed, there were entire companies where not one single hand was raised and Valentin heard the Professor sigh.

Valentin had been preparing the Professor's luggage for their departure. Tomorrow they needed to be on the road if they were to make the Professor's appointments in St Petersburg. Valentin had to admit he loved this new itinerate lifestyle and had seen more of the world in the last few months than he had ever imagined.

When he had done all he could and secured the straps around the leather suitcases he heard a deep-throated meow from the courtyard.

Time for a break, Valentin thought to himself and left the Professor's room and made his way outside.

The pint-size grey tabby saw him as soon as he stepped outside. With a show of affected nonchalance, it mooched over the cobblestone courtyard to where Valentin crouched.

Quietly Valentin made kissing noises and then, "Here puss, puss, puss, puss."

The tabby stopped just out of Valentin's reach and made a great performance of stretching her back, then flipping over onto her side so that he could see the perfect whiteness of her belly. Valentin scooted closer and rubbed her soft white fur.

Eventually, she purred.

He saw her pale grey eyes narrow against the thin slabs of sunlight. Valentin shucked her under her jaw and she writhed against his hand.

"Mythie!"

Valentin swung around and scrambled to his feet as the mealy-faced son of the Tsar appeared in the courtyard. The grey tabby responded immediately and charged towards the Tsarevitch who lowered himself carefully until he offered a morsel of something to the cat that had seconds before shown so much love to Valentin.

Sullen with irritation, Valentin lowered his head, knelt before the Imperial Prince, and hoped he could skulk away just as soon as he was dismissed. Meanwhile, and without shame, the young heir crooned and smooched the cat whose tolerance was coming to an end.

"Are you a son of one of the military advisors to the Imperial Highness?"

Valentin was surprised at the Tsarevitch's direct manner.

"No." Valentin was urged to add more when he looked up and saw the watchfulness of the Prince's bodyguard, "I am Valentin Gavrilov, the batman to the Englishman, Professor Pares, an observer for your ... for the Imperial Highness," he stood up gingerly.

"Ahh ... do you like cats?"

Again, Valentin was thrown by the Prince's curiosity.

"Well, I suppose so ... I don't know many," Valentin blushed.

It was a stupid answer to a stupid indulged royal child. What he really wanted to say was that he had witnessed war and killing and had been with real men and was very much a man himself. Not some namby-pamby baby!

"This is Mithridates," said the Tsarevitch as he tried to scoop up the cat but to Valentin's delight she darted off into the shrubbery.

The Prince then turned his intense light blue eyes on Valentin as if waiting for something, so the young batman said, "That's an interesting name," but thought to himself, *Only a smart arse would choose such a ridiculous name for a cat.*

"I was reading about Ancient Rome and my tutor suggested I call her after one of the great kings —"

The grey tabby tore out of the shrubbery with fierce determination and then just as suddenly rolled to its left and plonked down on the warm cobblestones. Giving a name of a king to a female cat confirmed Valentin's sense of superiority over the boy.

The bodyguard moved quietly across to the Tsarevitch and slipped a short khaki jacket over his ward's gymnastika. As he did this, Valentin noticed the large moustachioed man spoke quietly and with immense tenderness to the Prince.

As if prompted, the Prince asked, "Would you like to play?"

At first, Valentin didn't understand what the Tsarevitch meant. He looked around the courtyard and then at the tabby with the idiotic name and eventually back to the Prince.

"Come on! I'll race you to the fountain!" Then with the steady pace of an elderly invalid, the Tsarevitch moved past Valentin and out of the courtyard to the well-manicured garden at the front of the mansion.

Sure enough, there sat a squat fountain that Valentin had not even noticed before. Around the sides of the fountain were porpoises in bronze relief facing each other with water shooting out from their eyes and smiling mouths.

Valentin groaned inwardly and thought, *If Kuznetsov sees me playing in this fountain, I will never hear the end of it!*

The Tsarevitch scrambled up the back of one of the porpoises and the bodyguard moved immediately behind him as if the overgrown infant might fall backwards at any moment.

I've got to get out of here, despaired Valentin.

"Climb up on that one, Valentin Gavrilov!" The young Prince pointed to the porpoise directly opposite the one upon which he sat but all the young batman could think was, *The heir to the Holy Russian Romanov Dynasty has just said my name!*

He scrambled up dutifully.

Even before Valentin had secured a position on the bronze marine mammal — a jet of cold water smashed his face and shoulders, pushing him off balance and tumbling him into the fountain below. Spluttering with indignation he looked up and saw the young Prince laughing his head off like a maniac at a carnival.

"Get up!" yelled his young assailant. "See if you can knock me off!"

As Valentin scrambled back up the now slippery porpoise, his mind's eye recalled how the young Prince had jammed his two fists into the eye sockets of the porpoise. As Valentin dragged his sodden self up onto the curving bronze back he realised that was how the Prince redirected the water surge — through the short smiling beak of the mammal.

Valentin took his time and the Prince, with royal graciousness, waited patiently, believing his new-found playmate had no idea how to win the aquatic battle.

"Are you ready —"

Before the Tsarevitch finished his question, Valentin hauled his fists into the eye sockets of his porpoise and a hard fume of water charged into the head and upper body of his royal annoyance. In a blur of squeals and rushing water, the bodyguard swooped in like a falcon and caught his chick effortlessly. The young Tsarevitch was a mess of wet clothes and wide open laughter as he was hauled to safety.

The Prince didn't seem to be embarrassed, Valentin realised, as he watched the bodyguard cradle him to dry ground.

If it had been Kuznetsov he would have held my head under the water till I drowned, thought Valentin.

"Well done, my friend," called the Prince. "Let's now make Derevenko our invigilator!"

Valentin had no idea what the Tsarevitch was talking about but realised it had something to do with the bodyguard. Regardless, the afternoon was shaping out to be far more compelling than he had first thought.

Hours later, while he was assisting Professor Pares dress for the Caucasian cavalry parade commencing at 16:00 hours, a messenger arrived from the Tsar inviting Valentin to be the young Tsarevitch's company during this upcoming event. Pares was momentarily baffled and thought there had been some mistake in requesting his young taciturn batman, but Valentin managed to convince the Englishman that he had spent the early part of the afternoon dousing the young royal in the fountain. So, Pares gave his consent.

Pares, Kuznetsov and Valentin entered the royal marquee that was surrounded by spectators on a large open field, flanked by hills. At one time the field must have been part of a farm but ever since Stavka had moved into Mogilev it had been used for military parades or morale-boosting speeches delivered by the Tsar — the ones that would go on for far too long with great complex deviations into Russian history and Orthodoxy.

Twelve months ago, the average soldier would have knelt and wept before the great Imperial Highness of Holy Mother Russia. Nowadays, soldiers were grateful if their commanding officers relieved them of such pomp and ceremony. Besides, it was harder and harder for those in command to ensure their men demonstrated due respect, what with the Bolshevik influences and despair felt amongst the troops that this war was unwinnable.

Valentin found himself to the left of Derevenko, the bodyguard, who stood behind the Tsarevitch and the Tsar. If Valentin had ever bothered to write to his mother, this would have been the moment he would have liked to recount, but as it was, he scanned the faces behind him till he lighted upon the sour mouthed Kuznetsov, who, sure enough, had his evil eye on Valentin. The young batman smiled generously back at the Cossack driver.

After the priests blessed the mounted Caucasian cavalry, the population of Mogilev who had turned out in their hundreds and was clustered on either side of the royal marquee, sent up cheers to the leaden skies:

"LONG LIVE THE TSAR!"

"HOLY IS HIS NAME!"

"THE TSAR AND SAVIOUR OF RUSSIA!"

The Tsar smiled benevolently like some divine effigy who neither saw nor heard his people.

"LONG LIVE THE HEIR! THE ANGEL! THE PRETTY BOY!"

At this last appellation, the Tsarevitch saluted the crowd and then to the mounted Cossacks, who hollered their love more devotedly than the townsfolk.

Valentin had heard stories about the Imperial family but he had never, in all his life, realised their power. They were somehow more sacred and powerful than the holiest of all icons. More disarmingly, he had been playing with the young Tsarevitch just hours beforehand and, if truth be told, it had been one of the best afternoons ever. Yes, of course, he thought the young Prince was mollycoddled but that was more the bodyguard's fault.

When the Cossack regiment drew back into a formation ready to perform for the Tsar, Derevenko grumbled something at Valentin, and then, because the young batman had no idea what he had said, the bodyguard manhandled him across to stand next to the Prince. Professor Pares followed and looked very pleased with himself as he stood between the bodyguard and Valentin, up close to the action of the Cossacks.

The young Prince turned to Valentin and grinned, "Look! There — you see? Kuban and Terek Cossacks! They're my favourite because they are the fiercest!"

Valentin nodded and tried to look like he was well and truly acquainted with these particular Caucasian warriors, but he wasn't actually sure he was even looking at the right squadrons.

But it didn't take long before Valentin and all of Mogilev were in the thrall of the Kuban and Terek Cossacks. Both wore black kaftans — one with red shoulder straps, braiding and waistcoat — the other with blue. Both had ornamental gaziri, containers on the breast of their kaftans which held the single measure of gunpowder for their muzzle-loading muskets. Both wore grey trousers tucked into black leather boots and perched on their grizzly heads were black fur hats.

With precision and exactitude, the Kuban and Terek Cossacks began to wheel this way and that on their wild-eyed steeds. The crowd was captivated. Everyone watched the circular formation they made as horseman and warrior became one; trotting in and out of the complex pattern that expanded ever outward, as if they was one giant writhing Dinniki viper from Russia's subalpine. Then the Kuban and Terek Cossacks gathered speed and galloped in and out of the intricate serpentine shape they had formed.

Valentin noticed that some of them were standing high in their stirrups, holding their black whips aloft. Moments passed and the drumming of the hooves got louder and louder, until, with all their strength the horsemen swung their whips heavenward and CRACK! CRACK! CRACK! CRACK!

It raised the very hair on Valentin's head!

Then with increasing ferocity the Kuban and Terek Cossacks rode even faster in and out of this ever-moving, ever-changing ring.

The cacophony of hooves and whip cracks was deafening but despite this, the young Prince turned to him and yelled something, but Valentine only caught "... greatest!"

Then the snaking spiral pulled apart and each Kuban and Terek horseman broke into a canter and tore up the surrounding hills in the most ear-splitting ascent, followed by the other Cossacks.

The crowd cheered and Valentin heard the Tsare-vitch shout, or maybe it was himself because the power of the mounted Cossacks was infectious and all around them resounded the *HAW! GEE! YAIR! HUHUHU!* of the legendary horsemen.

As they pounded along the crest of the hills the young Prince leaned across to the Professor standing on the other side of Valentin and recited passionately:

Half a league, half a league,
Half a league onward!

And to Valentin's irritation, the Professor re-sponded with similar enthusiasm,

All in the valley of Death
Rode the six hundred!

Valentin ignored them because now the ferocious warriors had turned the heads of their chomping horses to face the crowd, which waited at the bottom of the small hillside.

The horses stomped and thrust their heads up and down.

Theirs not to make reply
Theirs not to reason why

Theirs but to do and die ...

Called the Professor, and Valentin was pleased the young Prince was so spellbound by the spectacle on the hill that he had failed to hear the Professor.

At that moment the horsemen stood high in their stirrups and yelled *HI!HI!HI!HI!* and charged down the sweeping banks of the hills.
An utterly unconquerable force.

Cannon to the right of them
Cannon to the left of them
Cannon in front of them!

Shouted the Prince over the fracas but only Valentin heard without understanding because thundering towards them was the great crashing of hooves, equine bodies and silver sabres held aloft as riders and horses charged for the bystanders.

Stormed at with shot and shell,
Boldly they rode and well!

Cried the Prince as the agrestal warriors pounded ever closer and the crowd pulled inward as one and no one heard the Professor respond:

Into the Jaws of Death
Into the mouth of hell ...

And a hair's breadth from where the screaming crowd clung to each other the horsemen brought their steeds to a halt.

A heart-stopping theatre of terror.

The crowd remembered it was only a performance, after all, and cheered wildly.

And then the tallest Russian war hero Valentin had ever seen in the saddle, rode up slow and stately, and took the lead position.

There he was flanked by the fierce Caucasian horsemen, his innumerable medals across his breast glittered in the tumbling dusk.

He was a gaunt figure, almost skeletal, and his grey whiskered face and colourless eyes looked straight ahead.

Then Valentin heard the shouts of soldiers everywhere:

"VICTORY TO THE GRAND DUKE!"

"HIS GLORY WILL NOT FADE!"

"THE NOBLE GRAND DUKE NICHOLAS NIKOLAEVICH!"

But the entourage surrounding the Tsar, his son and his military advisors, remained strangely quiet.

Valentin's heart raced on and he found it hard to catch his breath as he thought to himself, *What an astounding spectacle! What exceptional warriors!* His own hair was mattered in sweat because this was what he had hoped for all along — to witness the glory of those fighting for Mother Russia.

He knew then and there he was going to slip away, the first chance he got, to join these wild horsemen. He had never ridden a horse before but that only made him more determined. When these warriors met him and heard his tales of courage and endurance, he knew they would take him in a heartbeat.

Yes, that's what he would do, he realised, as he craned his neck to see the last of the great Cossacks wheel their horses out of sight behind the Grand Duke.

And then it occurred to him that the young Prince and he could join together! Yes! He knew this was a great idea because the Prince had told Valentin, just a few hours earlier, that his father wished for him to see that war was not all fun and games.

Valentin looked across, expecting his young friend to be there with eyes ablaze but instead, there was a crush of grown-ups milling about under the marquee.

Valentin just had to reach the Prince before anything else got in the way. He knew that when he shared his plan, the Prince would call for horses to be saddled immediately.

Valentin shoved his way through the mess of dignitaries busy congratulating themselves and military officers readjusting their belts over well-fed bellies. On the other side of the marquee, he saw the back of the Prince's bodyguard striding towards the mansion.

Valentin propelled his way through the dispersing crowd, all the while gaining on Derevenko.

Valentin was just about to call out the bodyguard's name when he realised he was carrying a small boy whose head hung limply across his left arm with two thin legs dangling across the right.

Valentin stumbled and heard Derevenko croon bits and pieces of some old folk song as if he was lost in the labour of his day.

Valentin slowed and followed like a sleepwalker, telling himself he was going to ask the bodyguard the whereabouts of the young Prince just as soon as he put down the poor idiot kid who had obviously been trampled by one of the horses.

But even as he said this to himself, it made no sense.

He tripped along and as they got closer to the mansion Valentin realised that his were the only footsteps behind the bodyguard.

It was as Derevenko turned around that Valentin heard his friend's soft voice pleading "Don't let them touch me ... I cannot have them touch me ... Don't ..."

"The Tsarevitch must rest," Derevenko spoke surprisingly softly to Valentin who remained slack-jawed before his friend who was now cradled like a mewling infant in the arms of the Petty Officer.

Valentin stared at the young Prince whose skin had turned grey and eyes were fluttering backwards.

"What's happened? I mean — is he hurt? What ..." Valentin knew he was jabbering but nothing made sense.

"He must rest." And with that, the bodyguard swung around and moved swiftly towards the mansion.

3

The next day, on the other side of Mogilev, Gumilyov was saddling his horse and thinking it was only a year since the war had begun ... back then they all believed victory would be theirs.

And now Russia had lost so much.

These days there were no cadets and Hussars were expected to wash and brush and feed and saddle their own horses.

He was tightening the strap around his horse's girth when he heard Rad come into the stables calling, "Hey Gumilyov, did you stay and watch those wankers yesterday afternoon? Fucking circus monkeys on the backs of their inbred horses!"

Gumilyov didn't bother looking up, "You must be referring to the final parade ... the one we were ordered to attend. The one where we were instructed to wear parade uniform. The one you absented yourself from, is that the one you mean?"

Satisfied the strap was snug against the belly of his Piebald, a poor replacement for his Orlov gelding that he had lost at the battle of Bolimów, Gumilyov began looping the strap through the large metal ring on the side of the saddle.

"You know what your problem is?" asked Gumilyov. Rad ignored his friend.

"You won't take instruction from your superiors."

Saddling his own horse Rad chuckled and said, "Actually, I was giving instruction last night ..."

Gumilyov lit a cigarette and leaned against the low wall dividing his stable from Rad's and asked, with a note of irritation, "Is that right?"

Rad grunted as his Bay deliberately puffed out its belly, stubbornly refusing to be strapped tightly. Gumilyov watched, as his friend elbowed the horse hard in the gut, it ambled sideways and farted. Rad pulled tight and got the strap sorted.

"Yes. First, I instructed Mogilev's finest to take it in the mouth, then in the arse, then in the —"

"When you say, Mogilev's finest, I take it you are referring to some fat military officer at Stavka?" Gumilyov inhaled with satisfaction at his own comeback.

"Seriously, you should have come with me. The whores were well-fed —"

"I guess you'd know!"

Rad laughed quietly, finished off the saddling and took a cigarette from Gumilyov's offered packet.

When they eventually reported to military command, after taking a month off in Moscow and St Petersburg, their unofficial furlough after Przemyśl, they were sent down to Belarus to join the cavalry moving out into the Caucasus.

By then both Gumilyov and Rad were ready to return to war because their time in Moscow and St Petersburg had been so confusing. Once the toast of Russia, they were now treated as traitors fighting a war that no one wanted.

In the end, they returned to their squadron because both men felt it was better to be charging the enemy and led by a worthy commander, the Grand Duke, than to flop and flounder under the impotency of the Tsar. And to not return was, still, inconceivable.

The Kuban and Terek Cossacks had been assigned to escort the Grand Duke, all the way to Tiflis, where military Headquarters would be established. The regiment to which Rad and Gumilyov had been attached was instructed to follow and ensure that the Supply wagons, these days a mere euphemism, got through the mountain passes.

It was a grunt job but the two Hussars were happy enough to be back in the saddle, especially as it gave them an opportunity to earn a wage of sorts while killing the two-faced Muslims who made up the Ottoman Empire.

No one hates Muslims like a Russian, Rad had recently commented, but then he corrected himself and added, *Actually no one hates Muslims and Jews and all non-Russians, like a Russian.*

Cigarettes finished, both Rad and Gumilyov led their horses out of the stables and into the changeable September morning. It was time to leave, high time in fact, but something pulled at the edges of Gumilyov's heart.

He rechecked the left, then right hoof of his horse's rear legs.

Rad adjusted his cloak and said nothing.

Gumilyov softly felt the hocks and ran a warm hand up the horse's buttock. He then gripped the pommel of the saddle in one hand and tugged the cantle with his other; all secure and ready to mount.

Still, he waited.

Rad mounted his Bay and squinted into the distance as if contemplating their future. The other Hussars of their squadron were walking towards the road that would lead them out of Mogilev where they were to assemble for inspection and departure.

At last, Gumilyov swung himself up into his saddle, all the while keeping the reins in his right gloved hand. He adjusted his cloak and nodded to Rad, who did his palatal clucking that set their horses walking from the stable courtyard out towards the road.

"Anna sent a poem," Gumilyov patted his breast pocket. Tucked therein was the crumpled letter with her own black sharp handwriting slicing up the page.

Rad's Bay moved in pace with the friskier Piebald.

"Just when I thought I was over her ..."

"You'll never be over her." Rad had never met Anna Akhmatova but her beauty and promiscuity were legendary. He also knew Gumilyov never forgave her for the poet she had become.

"She wrote a poem in response to *my* poem."

Rad made no reply. The Bay and Piebald clopped onto the dirt rutted pathway that wound its way around the town. Rad had no interest whatsoever in poetry. Gumilyov, on the other hand, was always trying to get him to read his verse or somebody else's. Sure,

Rad could recite a bit of Pushkin, but what Hussar couldn't? It was part of the troubadour skills of any moustachioed swashbuckler, and the ladies loved it.

With building exasperation, at Rad's complete disinterest in his poem, Gumilyov recited by heart:

> *I know her, her bitter silence,*
> *The tiredness of her words and cries*
> *Her heart is opened with craving*
> *Only to the music of the verse,*
> *Before the life of joy and playing,*
> *She stands aloof and won't converse.*

The Hussars' horses walked on and the Piebald nickered when he smelt the gathering of many horses up ahead, where the regiment's cavalry assembled. Gumilyov pushed his left hand into his breast pocket and pulled out her letter.

Meanwhile, Rad, po-faced, considered how Gumilyov would never extricate himself from this goddess-witch who lived somewhere in St Petersburg. So much for courting her at 13 in the hope he would shape her into his muse and long-suffering wife.

No need for a wife when the brothels are infection-free, thought Rad, *for the most part.*

Gumilyov shook the letter at Rad and cried, "So, while I wrote those lines, she has the temerity to write:

As a white stone in the well's cool deepness,
There lays in me one wonderful remembrance.
I am not able and don't want to miss this:
It is my torture and my utter gladness.
You've been turned into my reminiscences
To make eternal the unearthly sadness.

Actually, Rad didn't mind Akhmatova's poem, especially the bit about the stone which laid in her like a memory, or whatever it was.

He realised Gumilyov was looking at him waiting for a reaction that would mirror his own outrage.

"Bitch," spat Rad.

The two Hussars pulled up their horses and fell in line with their gathering regiment.

Rad had seen this time and time again, the way his friend would be at ease and relaxed but then boil over in frustration with a letter or memory that connected him to his wife.

The one he had no interest in despite constantly thinking about her.

The Bay bit the Piebald's mane, and both men twitched their reins accordingly.

"Whatever happened to that red-haired nurse you had down in Warsaw?" Rad asked.

Gumilyov lent his right elbow on the pommel of his saddle and seemed to visibly relax, "Jula ... now she was a honey. I caught up with her in Moscow. Just before we headed out here."

Rad was glad to see a wistful look of lust pass across his friend's face.

"Unlike some," Gumilyov looked askance at Rad, "Jula actually reads my poetry. Yes, she's a regular fan of mine, that's for sure."

Rad chortled, "Well I'm not trying to fuck you — so there's no need for me to read your poetry."

Despite himself, Gumilyov found he was smiling, as he stuffed the scrap of paper back into his breast pocket.

And it occurred to him, as his Piebald jostled against the Bay, that war changes nothing.

4

Aloft a truck bed, parked outside the yawning mouth of the Putilov Works in St Petersburg, stood a Bolshevik shouting into a bullhorn.

"FACTORY AND MILL WORKERS ACROSS RUSSIA ARE NOW ON STRIKE! LEAVE YOUR WORKSTATIONS AND MARCH WITH US TO THE WINTER PALACE!"

The workers cheered and Lidka's aunt downed tools.

"WE WILL MARCH BECAUSE OUR WAGES MUST BE INCREASED AND THE PRICE OF BREAD, LOWERED!"

Yirina joined her comrades surging out of the factory.

"WE WILL MARCH IN SUPPORT OF FELLOW STRIKERS IN IVANOVO-VOZNESENSK WHO WERE MERCILESSLY SHOT DOWN!"

The crowd booed and hissed.

"TO THE WINTER PALACE! THE TSARINA AND THE MEMBERS OF THE DUMA MUST RECEIVE OUR PETITIONS — THEY MUST HEAR OUR VOICES!"

The workers yelled their approval.

"WITHOUT THE PEOPLE, THE ROMANOVS ARE POWERLESS! WITHOUT THE PEOPLE, THE DUMA IS NOTHING!"

Empowered by what it meant to be a worker ridden by generations of grievances and vexations that had never ever been addressed, the crowd lifted their banners — its head chanting slogans and its tail singing songs of revolution to the tune of La Marseilles.

Yirina felt the fire of revolution in her belly. She tightened her grey woollen scarf around her head and across her chest.

The crowd began to move out of the Putilov gates and Yirina was swept along with the tide of times turning. All around her moved the other women with whom she spent each and every day assembling artillery gun barrels.

As they moved down the streets, strangely devoid of trams and trucks, they began to sing.

Rise sisters, sunward to freedom!
Up, brothers, up to the light!

Yirina thought about her blistering workstation near the furnaces, her ears ringing with the clanging of hot steel being beaten into submission.

Out of the dark past behind us,
March for the future is bright.

Politicized workers from the Putilov Soviet had been talking openly about the injustice of this war, about the Russian men who were slaughtered daily so that the Tsar could maintain autocratic rule and align Russia with the foreign British government — all in an effort to secure gas and oil from the Turks. The voices of those around Yirina rose.

Slowly the life of millions,
Out of the night comes birth.

Yirina marched with her head high. On and on through the streets towards their final destiny: Nevsky Prospect and then the Winter Palace.

Till all the surge of your longing,
Whelms o'er the Heavens and the Earth.

Yirina was striking with her fellow workers for so many reasons. They now worked 12 hours a day, seven days a week, with only two short breaks a day in which they could sit. It was torture. Meanwhile, as their hours increased, their wages remained fixed, despite inflation soaring. Unlike the rich, the workers had no servants to stand in food lines for them and so they were unable to find bread, meat and vegetables.

Now, brothers, hands clasped together,
Death with a laugh we put by!

Yirina was 34 and had the thin bent body of an aged woman. The crowd surged around her and she joined her voice with tens of thousands who had stopped work for this protest against the rulers of Russia.

Holy is this, our last struggle,
Ending our slavery for aye.

Arm in arm she marched.

The crowd was swelling with more and more work-ers. Yirina could feel the power of liberation and change because it was like an electric current through her body.

Nothing could stop them now.

They would have to be heard. The whole world would have to listen to their cry for peace, justice and food.

Despite the weariness that never seemed to leave her, Yirina felt alive, as if her whole life had been head-ing towards this point. This was Russia in the making and she, Yirina Matveyevna Sokolova who owned noth-ing except the beginnings of an education, acquired at the free lectures organised by the Putilov Soviet, was part of it.

Mayakovsky had been at Kolobok's when he heard the Putilov was on strike — so he had grabbed Lidka and the two of them pushed their way into the march and eventually found Yirina.

The poet bellowed out the revolutionary songs and chants along with the best of them. Even though the sky was bleak for late September, hope rose up and he almost imagined he saw the lightest blue patches ap-pearing above.

Mayakovsky strode on and knew that he and his fellow Russians would change the course of history.

The crowd steamrollered down Akademika Lebedeva towards the bridge that spanned the Neva. On either side of the protestors were onlookers lounging in various states of commitment. Some smoked, others jeered at the protestors which only provoked them to urge their fellow Russians to join them.

One bystander, a wounded soldier, spat out, "YOU BOLSHEVIKS ARE LIMITED TO THE CITY! YOU ARE NOTHING — YOU DON'T SPEAK FOR RUSSIA!"

Mayakovsky shouted back, "ENOUGH IS ENOUGH! BROTHER, JOIN US!" No longer did the poet remember that he, himself, had volunteered for the Front at the start of the war and that because he was deemed politically unreliable, he was rejected.

The flow of human bodies pushed on and Mayakovsky heard another anti-demonstrator, an overfed and overpaid official, cry out from a window above street level, "PERSONAL FREEDOM AND HUMAN RIGHTS ARE UNKNOWN TO LENIN AND TROTSKY! YOU ARE ALL FOOLS — GO BACK TO WORK AND HELP RUSSIAN SOLDIERS WIN THE WAR!"

Mayakovsky yelled up at the jowly face, "JOIN US BROTHER! BUILD A BRIDGE BETWEEN THE WORKER AND THE POWER HOLDERS! THEY ARE FEW. WE ARE MANY!"

People around the big poet cheered and called out their own messages: "EDUCATION AND LITERACY TO THE WORKERS!", "FOOD AND PAY FOR AN HONEST DAY'S WORK!", "NATIONALISE BANKS AND RAIL-ROADS AND OIL!"

The crowd squeezed across the bridge and Mayakovsky saw how the sky and the Neva looked the same steely colour of resistance.

As he stepped off the bridge, an old soldier along-side the crowd called out, "BOLSHEVIKS ARE TRAF-FICKERS ON THE GERMAN PAYROLL!"

Then Yirina responded with, "ROLLING, ROLLING, ROLLING! OUR TRAIN IS UNSTOPPABLE! THE WORKER IS THE FUTURE!"

The crowd around them cheered and repeated the mantra *Rolling, rolling, rolling* and Yirina shouted, "OUR TRAIN IS UNSTOPPABLE!" They responded

Rolling, rolling, rolling to which Yirina and Lidka yelled, "THE WORKER IS THE FUTURE!"

This continued and Mayakovsky joined the call and response which fuelled the engine of the crowd as they marched down Liteyny Prospect that would turn left into Nevsky.

By now Lidka could see swarms of people surging out of buildings and off the sidewalks. No longer were they bystanders but becoming the shape of a new tomorrow. She held on to her aunt and the charismatic Mayakovsky and wondered when she had started caring, once again, for her country.

The banners and ribbons along Nevsky Prospect were becoming more and more vivid. A huge red banner, draping from a window several stories above, had the shock of white paint announcing: *DOWN WITH THE TSAR! DOWN WITH THE DUMA!*

The protestors surged on and Lidka knew there was no turning back.

From the sidelines, a detractor yelled, "WORKERS CAN'T EVEN MANAGE THEIR OWN FACTORY! HOW THE HELL CAN THEY MANAGE RUSSIA?!"

Mayakovsky boomed, "JOIN US BROTHER! WE ARE BUILDING ON TRUTH — NO MORE LIES!" He lithely swung his enormous self onto a street bollard and cried out across the sea of upturned revolutionaries, "THE REVOLUTION IS THE HOLY WASHERWOMAN AND SHE WILL WASH AWAY THE FILTH FROM THE FACE OF THE EARTH!"

The crowd cheered and he swung back down into their unstoppable current.

Lidka squeezed her aunt's arm and knew this was what it felt to be alive. To be actively building a better future so that her son, Dimitri, would never have to live a life of uncertainty. This was what she was always meant to do. To fight for a better Russia where education was a right, not a privilege. Where poverty, crime and abuse were something of the past.

The voices surged around her and up ahead she saw another banner flutter and sway in the pewter skyline: *REVOLUTION WILL CLEANSE US OF THE WAR AND THE ROMANOVS!*

Lidka moved with the crowd past the Cathedral of Our Lady of Kazan. Its impressive stone colonnade that encircled the garden was littered with hundreds and hundreds of people cheering on the protestors.

This will be a victory, Lidka thought, as she strode on and on with the chants of those around her demanding *JUSTICE FOR ALL WORKERS! BETTER WAGES! CHEAPER BREAD!*

The crowd was heaving forward but the sheer force of numbers caused a bottleneck at the entrance of the Dvortsovaya Square that sprawled in front of the Winter Palace.

The guards were ready with rifles and even Cossacks had been called to protect the outer rim of the palace itself.

The front of the crowd pushed inside the square and chanted their slogans and sang their songs of revolution, knowing they must be heard. *Because how could such a voice, from 50,000, not be heard*, thought Lidka and she trembled with the wondrous anticipation of this moment that would change Russia forever.

Again, she heard nay-sayers calling from balconies and sidelines: "LENIN AND HIS BOLSHEVIKS ARE COLLABORATING WITH ENEMIES! TRAITORS ALL! LENIN AND HIS BOLSHEVIKS ARE PARASITES AND COCKROACHES!"

Lidka ignored them but she heard Mayakovsky shout back to the misinformed to join them. She felt larger than life. She was part of something good, and despite the power holders spreading lies about their protest, she was utterly surrounded by her countrymen and women who knew the truth and were willing to march into the palace to force the Tsarina and the government to listen.

All of this would reach the ears of the Tsar who was now commander in chief at Stavka.

The crowd had stopped.

Lidka heard protestors around her saying ... *the Tsarina herself has come out to meet the crowd ... Prime Minister Sturmer is speaking to the leaders of the protest right now ... the Palace Guards have downed weapons and are joining the demonstration.*

But she had an uneasy feeling and knew she needed to listen to her instincts.

The crowd tried to jostle forward but to no avail and their chants rose up around her: *WORKERS RIGHTS! IT'S HAPPENING NOW! WORKERS UNITE! IT'S HAPPENING NOW!*

Lidka felt the shift in the crowd and knew something was wrong.

Mayakovsky's giant head bent towards her and said, "Guards ahead! Armed and ready!"

She strained to see above those in front but she only saw snatches of Cossacks with sabres drawn. There was also palace guards in offence formation. Rifles aimed and loaded.

It's going to be another Bloody Sunday, she thought and her breathing tightened.

She looked across at Yirina who was proudly calling to anyone who'd listen that it was the Putilov workers who carried a petition to the Tsar at this same palace in 1905. And every worker at her factory bore the history of protest with pride.

Oh my God, panicked Lidka, *it's going to be a massacre.*

She wanted to grab her aunt and leave. She wanted Mayakovsky to come with her, but with or without him she wasn't staying.

Then before she knew it the crowd around her pulled forward because, impossibly, they were trying to pour through the various arterial roads that opened out into Dvortsovaya Square.

Lidka didn't know when she was no longer gripping on to Mayakovsky but she realised as the crowd contorted and pushed its way forward, that she needed to extricate herself and Yirina from this roiling mass of humanity.

It was then that she heard the sharp crack of gunshot fire and the crowd rose up in fright. Lidka tried to move off the road with Yirina and onto the pavement where she thought they might escape down a side street and away from the vicinity of the Winter Palace, but she had no strength to move against the crowd.

Then Lidka's feet no longer seemed to touch the ground and she bobbed and swirled and shunted against this one and that as she was carried backwards then forwards, wretchedly aware she had lost Yirina.

Lidka shoved and pushed and elbowed until she thought all she could do was keep her head above the sea of retreating demonstrators. Like a drowning sailor, she felt herself begin to slip under as she desperately grabbed the flotsam of limbs and clothing about her.

Meanwhile, the relentless snap and pop of rifle fire ricocheted off stone buildings and soft body parts; until the streets filled with the screams and cries of those who, minutes ago, were singing songs of hope and freedom.

Then she felt her aunt's vice grip and Lidka found landfall. She knew she should look back for Mayakovsky but she also knew the brutal truth: the unarmed peaceful protestors were being mowed down by the Tsarina's guards and no one was listening.

Ducking and weaving with grim determination Lidka and Yirina pushed their way past the Cathedral of Our Lady of Kazan, then turned left and ran down the Griboyedov embankment, across the Bank Bridge with its winged lions guarding the abutments, on and on and on down the never-ending Lomonosova Ulitsa, gulping for air, staggering, running, staggering, until finally, they arrived at the Fontanka Canal.

A dirty pamphlet scooped up in the greying twilight and pressed against Lidka's long skirt then fluttered off.

She never saw its message: *THIS IS THE BEGINNING OF THE END! BOLSHEVISM AND NATIONALISM WILL TEAR RUSSIA APART!*

5

Earlier that day the Yakut cousins had stood on the corner of Liteyny and Nevsky Prospect and watched in wonder at the spectacle of ten thousand protestors bringing the dirty city to a halt.

Neither had been to St Petersburg before and both vowed they would never return. After their odyssey west from Warsaw to Minsk to Moscow, they were finally granted a three-day furlough. Instead of heading against the tide of refugees to Siberia, the two had finally agreed to take in the sights of the northern city of St Petersburg.

What they saw on arrival were lines and lines of people waiting patiently to buy soap, sugar, flour, milk, meat and bread. In the shop windows stood wooden replicas of the food items that, for the most part, could no longer be purchased but remained there anyway, like a longing for better days.

They had travelled on a sluggish overcrowded train, where soldiers and refugees and regular passengers and luggage and weaponry and produce had been strapped haphazardly, inside and out.

They had walked the cold cobble streets of the soggy city: murky canals from the soupy Neva, reddish-brown buildings pushed out to the sidewalk, soot everywhere, no sewerage and the stomach-churning stench of huge cesspools.

Kaskil had commented sardonically to his cousin that he felt right at home after months at the Front.

Following their one and only night at a flea-bitten inn, they had a breakfast of black bread and cheese washed down with a small glass of something pretending to be coffee at a café that had known better days. They decided to head towards Nevsky Prospect which they imagined was aflutter with ribbons, banners and flags celebrating the national fortitude of Russia and the Romanov's mighty rule.

It wasn't as they expected.

Just after the Nicholaevsky Railway Station, at the commencement of St Petersburg's main thoroughfare, they noticed Lubki cartoons plastered over abandoned shopfronts depicting Russia's war effort: a giant Cossack effortlessly lancing a German zeppelin, Russian nurses with wings and halos, Russian peasants fighting off marauding Germans and a caricature of Kaiser Wilhelm with his left arm ridiculously diminutive.

But Aysen and Kaskil also pointed out to each other a few other Lubki posters glued uneasily alongside these patriotic thought bubbles: Russian aristocracy avoiding military duty, Jewish industrialists prospering, Russian soldiers dying at the Front and a goatish Rasputin penetrating the naked Tsarina with his giant phallus.

As the two Yakuts walked down the wide street they heard the call and response of marchers before they saw them pouring down Liteyny Prospect and turning into Nevsky.

Such civil disobedience was both fascinating and disturbing.

Neither had ever seen a public display of defiance nor did they know there was animosity towards people like themselves. Soldiers who, according to the protestors, had been fighting for a lost cause. But Aysen and Kaskil could make no sense of this because surely there was no greater cause than defence of one's country, one's land and one's home.

A moiling river of people flowed past Kaskil and Aysen. The Yakut cousins stood with their backpacks to the walls of a boarded-up bakery on the corner of Liteyny and Nevsky Prospect and watched dumbfounded.

It was a carnival of jostling and singing and cheers. There were banners and ribbons and flags unfurled with painted messages of *REVOLUTION! BETTER WAGES & CHEAPER BREAD! END ROMANOV TYRANNY!* and *NO MORE WAR!*

Every woman, man and child marching believed passionately in the cause that would benefit all. This was not about the individual but rather about the community and how it was desperate to sustain itself. Here were ethnic Russians sticking together, caring more for the collective than for the self, believing in the commonweal of man.

The Yakuts were astounded.

They must have stood there for the good part of the day, with many demonstrators calling them to join but, eventually, they peeled themselves away from the spectacle and headed back towards the railway station where they had seen buses to Gatchina.

"Maybe I should take her a gift. A newspaper or ..." Kaskil said with rising anticipation as he and Aysen made their way out of the city on a trolley bus, beyond Pushkin, where they had heard was a summer palace of the Tsar, now converted into a hospital, and arriving an hour and a half later at the small sleepy town of Gatchina.

Aysen stepped off the bus first and surveyed the cold greying afternoon. Above the thinning birch, he could see the spire of a church. He leaned back inside the warmth of the bus and asked the red-faced driver where they would find the Carmelite Church and Hospice. The driver chewed on his cud for a few seconds eyeing Aysen's small Asiatic features and, deciding he wasn't a German or a Bolshevik, pointed in the direction of the spire.

"Brother ..." Whenever Kaskil used this appellation Aysen knew what was coming. "Give us a few kopeks would you? I need to go get her a gift. I can't just walk in there empty-handed."

Their footsteps crunched over the gravel road as they tramped towards the church spire. The small closed shops and drab homes were huddled down against the brittle October afternoon.

"Look!" Kaskil was pointing towards a small park that had been recommissioned for growing cabbages. There were thousands of olive heads. Rows and rows of cabbages nestled leafy and well-rested in their red soil beds.

The two small men stopped and looked at such beauty.

The edges of their thick leaves were the colour of dark chocolate while their lemony veins ran to their sunny centres.

Kaskil and Aysen stood there thinking of home and the way their women would dance at harvest time, festooned in the colours of life.

It did not take long for the cousins to find the entrance to the hospice, tucked behind the neo-gothic Our Lady of Mount Carmel Church. Inside, the nuns whisked about this way and that down the various short corridors that led off from the front desk. The smell of sweat and sour milk twitched in Aysen's nostrils.

They waited as the elderly nun in a thick brown habit, long white apron and wimple scratched out something in a ledger with her fountain pen. At last her quiet face lifted and her eyebrow arched in question.

Kaskil spoke, "We have come to visit a patient here."

The nun looked slowly at Kaskil and then at Aysen, her lined skin was paper-thin.

"Her name is Zofia Kukiel." Kaskil pronounced her name carefully as if it was something new and uncertain.

At last, the old nun responded, "She has delivered a child."

Kaskil bounded in with "Yes! Yes, that's right. She was having a child. Well, she was pregnant. She was about to have a … that's right, yes. Pregnant."

If the nun thought Kaskil a nutcase, Aysen would have had to agree. He had counselled his cousin on the train journey up to St Petersburg that visiting the young woman they had met momentarily on the exodus from Warsaw to Minsk was an impetuous action and one where his cousin needed to consider the consequences.

Kaskil had no idea why he wanted to visit Zofia but he was sure as hell he wasn't going to admit to Aysen it had something to do with the feel of her warm full lips when he had kissed her in the back seat of the military vehicle.

Aysen looked above the nun and saw an icon attached to the wall. It was the same icon Zofia had clutched to her swollen belly when he first met her on the Kierbedzia Bridge. The nun saw the other man, the silent one, looking at the icon behind her.

"Where are you men from?"

Although she had addressed her words to Aysen, it was Kaskil who answered, "The Front. We are with the Siberian Riflemen." Then perhaps to counter her look of suspicion he added, "We are Yakut."

As it happened, Sister Mary Charitina did know that in northern Siberia lived the strange Turik speakers of the Yakut people. She had never met one before but she had read about these indigenous fur traders living up above the Lena Basin.

"Mrs. Kukiel is not well enough for visitors."

The nun returned to her ledger as if expecting the Yakut men to return to the Front or the Lena Basin and leave her in peace.

Aysen stood there thinking about Sayaana. Her long silky black hair, her cheeky eyes and the wonder of her own belly swelling with their child intensified his resolve to help Zofia.

Meanwhile, Kaskil was making a last-ditch effort, "But — the thing is, well you see, the thing is ..."

Aysen watched Kaskil run out of steam. Neither of them had really discussed what would happen when they got to the hospital.

"She is his wife," Aysen spoke calmly and addressed his remark to the icon above the nun.

Sister Mary Charitina lifted her eyes to the Yakut who seemed completely unruffled by her authority which usually had the effect of reducing men to a stuttering mess. She then looked across at the other Yakut whose face was all smile.

"My wife." Kaskil repeated to no one in particular, "Yes. And I have brought her a gift."

Slowly, the nun made a show of capping her pen and placing it with great deliberation next to the ledger.

She then folded her arms and looked up at him with strained disbelief, "A gift ..."

When Kaskil and Aysen passed through the corridor and a pair of swinging doors they found themselves in a narrow ward where small beds contained women of various ages in white headscarves and housecoats.

The two men stood still and waited until Sister Mary Charitina instructed a younger nun to take the husband of Zofia Kukiel to her bedside. Everyone, including Aysen, paused at such improbability — a Polish-Russian marrying an indigenous Yakut from Siberia — well, after all, there was a war on.

The entire ward fell silent as the two Yakuts walked quietly towards a bed in the corner, where, sitting upright, was the pale 18 year old Zofia.

"Hello, Zofia," Kaskil's voice trembled with unexpected emotion.

Zofia did not respond but looked from Kaskil to Aysen and then back again at Kaskil.

"How is the baby?" Kaskil asked. "Are you feeling better?"

The young mother had her fists planted on either side of the bed and her body seemed rigid with pain.

From the doorway, where Sister Mary Charitina stood sentry, she commanded the younger nun to take the baby from the crib at the foot of the bed and hand it to Mr. Kukiel.

Swiftly, a small infant package was placed in Kaskil's arms to which he bent and examined.

All the while Zofia watched on as if from a distance, grinding her teeth.

Aysen watched his cousin — infinitely curious, infinitely gentle — rock the baby in his arms and hum a tune that flittered about the hard narrow ward; it had come all the way from the Yakut summer tents and smelled of heather and clear water.

"Are you in pain, sister?" Aysen asked Zofia, almost inaudibly.

Her large brown eyes filled with tears and she looked away from her newborn daughter and Kaskil, whose kiss she had not forgotten. Her small frame shuddered with the fever that had accompanied the unbearable pain in her breasts.

"Mrs. Kukiel is suffering from mastitis," said the formidable Sister Mary Charitina. "It is common for new mothers and she will bear it for the suffering of Christ."

Kaskil looked from Aysen to Zofia and then back to the baby who held on to his finger with her own impossibly small hand.

At that point, the other younger nun was instructed to deposit the baby back in the crib and remove the two men from the ward, but Aysen was going nowhere.

While Kaskil continued to coo and hum and cradle the bundle of love he could never give up, Aysen unlatched his cousin's backpack and pulled out a large leafy cabbage and placed it carefully on Zofia's blanketed lap.

A slight smile quivered around her mouth.

Kaskil looked over at her and said joyously, "That's for you, my love! For you and the baby!"
No one heard the clipped efficiency of Sister Mary Charitina's footsteps as she moved towards the offending gift. The other women in the ward, the younger nun and Zofia herself were all marvelling at the cabbage.

"As I said, this woman is unwell, and she needs her rest!"

Aysen ignored Sister Mary Charitina and said tenderly to Zofia, "Wrap the leaves of the cabbage around your breasts. Bind them to you. It will stop the pain."
Aysen broke off some of the outer leaves of the cabbage and pushed them towards Zofia's fist, which she eventually opened.
Slowly, she placed the other hand protectively over the large cabbage and gave an imperceptible nod.

With that Aysen indicated they should be leaving and Kaskil handed back the baby to the young nun hovering in the shadows. He then made a great show of walking up to the top of the bed and leaning down — touching nothing but Zofia's soft full mouth — and kissing her in such a way that would sustain the onlookers for quite some time.

"You kept your promise," was all Zofia could manage as she clutched the cool smooth texture of the waxy cabbage leaves.

"Yes." Kaskil's heart expanded with love, "And to-morrow, Zofia, my wife, I will visit again, and we will talk about you and the baby coming home with us."

6

"If it wasn't for Pavel Tretyakov, Ladies and Gentlemen, I would not have been born."

The crowd tittered with appreciation as they clustered about the handsome son of Leonid Pasternak whose handful of paintings filled the small atrium of the Moscow gallery.

"When Tretyakov bought *Letter from Home* in 1889 from my father, a struggling artist who had just completed his military service, it gave an immediate boost to his career."

Some random art lover cried out spontaneously, *Hear! Hear!* and others followed suit with the accompanying chink of champagne-filled glasses.

The Pasternak family had footed the bill for finger food and champagne in celebration of the newly purchased half dozen Leonid Pasternak paintings.

"So, you may be wondering why the indefatigable visionary, Pavel Tretyakov was responsible for my existence?"

Anna Akhmatova watched as the majestic Boris Pasternak, ex-lover, friend and confidante drew the crowd back to him.

He really is art, she thought as she gazed at his deep-set eyes, wide forehead and high cheekbones.

"Tretyakov was responsible because when he bought *Letter from Home* it allowed my *extraordinary* father ..." Pasternak's gaze fell admiringly on his father, a smaller, greyer version of his son and far less iconic, who was batting away the word *extraordinary* with his hand. "To marry the *extraordinary* pianist, Rosalia Kaufman," Pasternak looked with great tenderness at his mother standing alongside her artist husband. She returned a steady gaze from her handsome face — in a way that only a woman whose beauty has been a point of fascination, can. "And a year later — I was born!"

The crowd clapped happily and some used the opportunity to replenish their plates with warm blinis with mushrooms or jam from the sideboards. Pasternak knew it wasn't the time or place to reminisce on the struggle his father and mother had experienced in order to get where they were now.

Once: Jews from Odessa. Now: Living comfortably, tastefully, in the apartment given to his father because he was, eventually, made the Director of the Moscow University School of Painting, Sculpture and Architecture.

"And so, Ladies and Gentlemen, it is a great honour to welcome you all on behalf of my family and, more importantly, Igor Grabar the head trustee, of the Tretyakov Gallery."

Pasternak nodded to a small neatly dressed bald-headed man who was beaming with satisfaction.

"What a privilege it is for me to see my father's works hang alongside Rublev, Bryullov, Levitan, Repin and our dear Serov, who was a wonderful friend of father's and supported his ongoing experimentation and journey from realism to impressionism."

Anna pulled away from the crowd, which was snug in their enjoyment of free food and drink at the gallery. It was as if all that was outside, the October mist and rain, not to mention the war that raged on and on and on, had nothing to do with them. She thought of the lines she had written a year ago:

Frightening times are approaching
Soon fresh graves will cover the land.

And although this had come true, it seemed to fill her compatriots with nothing but dried-out despair.

As she moved away Anna was aware of the crowd being lulled by Pasternak's amble through the development of his father's artistic career ... *his study of art overseas ... his eventual homecoming like a true Odysseus ... joining the Polenov, a circle of artists which included Serov, Levitan, Nesterov and Korovin ... all unremarkable guests to his childhood home* (the crowd chuckled appreciatively) ... *Tolstoy's warm friendship and his father's notable illustrations of War and Peace, not to mention Resurrection ...* (a polite smattering of applause).

Alone now in the atrium of the gallery where Leonid Pasternak's newly acquired paintings hung, Anna leaned into *Letter from Home*. It was an oil, a portrayal of Russian army life, a traditional genre scene and one that took on a new and compelling impact now that it felt God had forsaken them at the Front.

The deep resonate voice of Boris Pasternak played on in the background, interspersed occasionally by a responsive murmur or laugh or comment from the crowd.

She peered closer at this first painting Tretyakov had bought from Leonid Pasternak. Anna felt herself tumble inside *Letter from Home* where the three soldiers gathered about a bed in order to hear one of them — the literate one, she guessed — read the letter from home. Anna could nearly hear the letter.

God knows she had received enough letters from Pasternak and others. Letters filled with messages that should never have been sent, with iterations of love or abandonment or hope or despair that should never have to be borne by the reader.

Anna scrutinized the painting. A small tight room set the scene of *Letter from Home*. In the background of the composition was an army cot, upon which lay a soldier smoking pensively. In the foreground was another soldier bent in concentration as he listened to the letter being read by the third soldier in the midground. The letter reader was leaning into the window light, jacketless and his face filled with the drama of the letter's contents.

As she watched the soldier in the painting read the letter out loud, Anna realised it did not belong to him. There was not enough personal investment. There was not enough truth in his expression. It was the soldier in the foreground, bent low and looking beyond the canvas, the one who held the envelope with the torn seal, whose letter it was.

His face was broken with grief or realisation or homesickness.

No tears, no open-mouthed anguish, no fists clenched.

Just a quiet end to something.

Anna leaned in closer. No longer aware of the crowd behind her or Pasternak's appreciation and pride in the achievements of his father.

Perhaps the letter read: *My darling I can no longer go on without you. I cannot wait till this war is over, this war which you had no right to leave me for, this war which ...* Perhaps the letter read: *My son, it is difficult for me to write to you about the death of your darling mother. I know, son, this will come as a shock but you must not let it destroy you ...* Perhaps the letter read: *My beloved husband, our baby daughter has not survived. I write to you with a heavy bitter heart. She was too small and weak to endure the fever and when she took her last breath, I have to tell you, I was relieved she would not suffer more ...* Perhaps the letter read ...

Anna felt warm fingertips touch her hand. She turned suddenly and there was Osip Mandelstam's beautiful face.

"Anna," he kissed her in greeting and she was surprised at the gush of love she felt.

"Osip! I am so glad you are here. Have you just arrived?"

Anna realised Pasternak's speech was over and people were milling around talking about Leonid Pasternak's small collection of paintings and the ever-frustrating news of the war.

"More or less." Mandelstam looked back at Boris Pasternak flanked by his family and friends, "I knew you would be here." Mandelstam turned his brooding eyes back on her and added, "Where are you staying? Did you come down from St Petersburg?"

The thing about Osip, thought Anna, *there's nowhere to run or hide.*

"No. I was staying in Bezhetsk with my mother-in-law, so I came down from there." She took the glass from which Mandelstam was drinking and sipped his warm bubbly champagne, "Now, I am staying with the Pasternak's."

Mandelstam took back his glass, face shifting beneath a scurry of clouds.

"It's not like that," Anna said and wondered why she always felt compelled to protect Mandelstam as if he was more a son than an ex-lover or friend.

"Of course, it's not," he said dryly. Then after scanning the room he asked, "Have you met Marina Tsvetaeva? The Muscovite poet."

Anna wrinkled her nose which made Mandelstam laugh.

Then he added, "I had a fling with her at Koktebel on the Black Sea."

"Max's house?" asked Anna.

"Yes, that's the one. I met her there. Marina Tsvetaeva. We had a luscious moment together and I am hoping to catch up with her again and turn it into something longer."

He smiled lasciviously at Anna and she jutted her hip towards him as she reached out for his glass of champagne and downed the rest of its contents.

"How nice," her honeyed voice dripped in sarcasm and Mandelstam thought about the taste of French champagne on Anna's lips.

At that moment there was a jostle of people around them vying to get a closer look at *Letter from Home*, much to the annoyance of Anna and Mandelstam. They bumped about each other until they had moved to the doorway of the atrium.

There Pasternak found them, their heads bent in the memory of their bodies and minds.

"Dear Mandelstam! So, you got my invitation!"

The two men embraced as if the competition for Anna, the dark willowy goddess, had belonged to other combatants.

"It was hard to know where to address the invite. You have been such a nomad!" Pasternak added.

Mandelstam, dwarfed by Anna on one side and Pasternak on the other, sensed his desire for anarchy surfacing, "I have never been here, to the Tretyakov Gallery, not coming from money or culture so ... when I received your invite I thought — why not!" He smiled at both Anna and Pasternak and added, "I thought the gallery might help me understand how Russia had come from such greatness," his hand swept generously about the room filled with wonderous paintings, "to such madness," he pointed to the back of a guest, dressed in the uniform of an army officer.

Instead of feeling slighted, both Pasternak and Anna nodded sagely.

"Osip is right," Anna spoke to Pasternak and her hand moved languidly until it rested on Mandelstam's lapel. "Russia has forgotten itself. Its art. Its civilisation. Its beauty. What are we fighting for? If all of this ..." She lifted her hand from Mandelstam's electrified chest and gestured vaguely about the room, "Is forgotten? What are we left with? Nothing but blood-soaked fields —"

"Not to mention the blood-soaked streets of our cities," interrupted Pasternak with such gravitas that even Anna faltered.

"Yes. Indeed. I heard about the protest last month in St Petersburg. It was a tragedy." Anna murmured and she looked at Mandelstam wondering whether he knew Lidka and Yirina had been involved.

"Well even in Perm, the factory workers have been striking," said Pasternak. "It has been a ghastly business." And then he abruptly looked over his shoulder and stepped aside.

A young woman with flawless skin and soft blonde hair tucked behind her ears appeared.

Pasternak abandoned their discussion and placed a protective arm around her, saying to Anna and Mandelstam, "May I introduce Lara Fyodorovna Guishar. We met at the Perm Opera House."

Mandelstam drank in her stunning eyes and open trusting expression.

Anna turned her interest across the crowded room to two women, obviously Sapphists, caught up in a strange contretemps played out in a dumb show.

Then Mandelstam commented that he didn't realise chemical factory workers got to go to the opera, Pasternak laughed good-humouredly.

That is what is so annoying about Pasternak, thought Mandelstam as he had his glass refilled by the one and only roving waiter, *he is someone who always rises above petty jealousies.*

That is what is so annoying about Pasternak, thought Anna as she accepted her own glass of champagne from the waiter, *he expresses his undying love for me, and the next time I see him he is with some 16 year old ingénue.*

But Pasternak had no thoughts for either Anna or Mandelstam, rather he looked down at Lara's smiling face and thought, *What a pity Lara had to stay with her seamstress aunt in Moscow despite being my guest at Father's opening.* Lara had insisted she was unworthy of such an event but had eventually accepted his persistent invitation.

And Pasternak saw the way Anna looked down her nose at the cotton dress Lara wore (the one her aunt must have sewn in haste), its soft floral pattern and excessive flounces worked in stark contrast to Anna's figure-hugging blood-red velvet dress.

"What was the opera?" Anna's voice curled lazily about in a question directed at Pasternak as if the fresh-faced, bow-shaped mouthed Lara was nowhere to be seen.

"*The Nightingale.* It had come to Perm. My cousin Olga had written and told me it was something I just had to attend," Pasternak twisted about and looked towards his family's huddle where a small bright-eyed Olga, whom Anna had met once and found tiresome, threw a dazzling smile.

"Any good?" Mandelstam asked. He never assumed high art was worthy. Art must be tested constantly by the audience in order to ascertain its greatness.

Pasternak smiled expansively and looked down at Lara as if they had some sort of secret and replied, "Wondrous ..."

Anna looked away. And then, never being one who felt compelled to excuse herself, Anna turned and left the animated conversation between her two ex-lovers, and the newly arrived but underwhelming Lara.

As she walked through the room Anna took a few minutes to take in Leonid Pasternak's other paintings and it was a small endlessly moving depiction of the *Island of Rügen* that made her pause. Everything was wrong in terms of colour and perspective yet the painting quivered with life and breath: a sky in a flurry of gold, a stippled green sea, a breeze blowing across a yellowy landscape, reapers at rest with their shadows wavering. She thought about the night before at the dinner table with the gracious and cultured Pasternak family, and the way they persuaded her to recite one of her poems:

> *There are such days before the spring*
> *When meadows rest beneath the snow,*
> *And dry and cheerful branches swing,*
> *And gentle warm winds blow.*

She looked over her shoulder and noticed one of the two Sapphists looking straight at her. Anna moved out through the doorway and turned to her right and found the rest of the poem step into her head as she climbed a wooden staircase that creaked beneath her insubstantial weight.

You marvel at your body's lightness
And do not recognise your home,
And sing again with new excitement
The song that once seemed tiresome.

Everything about her felt wistful and unresolved. She wandered through the gallery towards a Marc Chagall.

No one was around.

Anna cut a dark blood silhouette as she stood against Chagall's romantic folly of *Flying Lovers Over the Town*.

She had loved it the first time she had set on eyes on its childish dream of a man flying his woman away from ordinary life. As a child, she had been a sleepwalker and often dreamed she was flying and so it was that she came to recognise herself and her first love up in the stratosphere of sad paint.

Anna felt her heart fill up with tears.

Chagall had painted her. There was no need to look closer at the tall dark-haired woman enfolded in Gumilyov's arms at the centre of the composition. It was this very abduction that had shaped her lonely heart. She knew why Chagall had painted Gumilyov's face looking elsewhere, because the moment he caught her, was the very moment he had left. In winning her, he was done.

Chagall had painted Anna's face as if she was startled at the realisation that art was the only thing worthy of love.

Anna left the painting and walked back down the staircase. She found herself taking an unexpected turn away from the atrium to a side room that contained the most recent acquisitions. She was drawn into its quiet and walked slowly to the back wall.

She stood in front of a black square, backgrounded and framed in white, realising she must be viewing the controversial painting that the Pasternaks had discussed last night.

Anna inclined towards the neatly printed card propped alongside the painting and read: *Black Square by Kazimir Malevich*. She thought to herself, *Mayakovsky would rave about this*, and smiled.

It was as if all the world had been reduced to nothing but darkness, magnificently framed in such a way as to suggest that the void mattered. The imploding emptiness disturbed Anna.

Have we reached the end of Art, she wondered. *Is there nothing else to create, to say, to make sense of? Has everything been done?*

But at the same time, strangely, she found the painting of the black square, liberating.

Anna turned back and recrossed the room with the intent of returning to Mandelstam, Pasternak and the crowd that would be in full swing.

That was when she saw it.

There on the wall.

It was a modern icon — glorious, powerful, terrifying and full of promise.

Anna stood rooted before the gigantic red horse filling the foreground — a naked youth mounted its back, a mass of swirling blues and greens formed the background where other riders and horses cavorted in the waves.
Bathing the Red Horse by Petrov-Vodkin.

It sucked the air out of the room.

It was a portal into a future that she, prophetess and poet, could make no sense of. And yet the roaring red of the horse that filled the canvas reminded her of the Bolsheviks and at that moment she knew that this painting was Russia hoisting its own petard.

The crowd in the atrium of the Tretyakov Gallery seemed to have doubled in size when at last Anna glided back.

She manoeuvred her way about the chatty throng till she reached Mandelstam, who immediately caught her about her waist and said, "Pasternak was wanting you to recite a poem for the masses."

She laughed at his sass and ever-hungry hands.

"Where is he? Did he have to drop his girlfriend back to the babysitter?" She reached for the glass in Mandelstam's hand which, this time, he moved teasingly out of her reach.

"Come on Anna. You can't have every man waste away because of you — he's over there but he did want you to recite a poem and so do I."

She looked into Mandelstam's face and saw the boy who would always be from out of town and thought how much she loved the way he just didn't care. Mandelstam would not be caught up in fashion or politics or better judgment.

Anna looked at his mess of curly dark hair, his shabby necktie, shirt and trousers and realised no one was more worthy of adulation and commendation than this darling man with whom she shared a deep friendship, all the while knowing he would never let her forget that once upon a time theirs was the most passionate of all affairs.

With her heart full she said, "I want to hear you recite one of *your* poems. Please. Do it for me."

Pasternak burst in on them with, "There you are Anna, I was worried you had left! Now my father and mother would be very pleased if the *Queen of the Neva*," Pasternak smiled without a hint of irony, "would recite one of her latest or even oldest poems!"

Anna looked at his face and then she turned her eyes on Mandelstam and said, "I know your parents and the crowd would be astounded to hear Osip Mandelstam recite."

The missed beat was almost undetectable and then Pasternak agreed, "Absolutely. Would you do us the honour, Mandelstam?"

She watched Mandelstam step away from her and secure a space that would allow him a platform of sorts, from which he would recite one of his poems with his signature intensity.

The crowd fell silent as Osip Mandelstam unfolded his notebook. The circle of space widened about him and someone cleared their throat.

Quiet.

Insomnia. Homer. The sails — stretched out.
I've read the catalogue of the ships halfway:
This lengthy brood, this train of cranes
That soared from Hellas up into the clouds.

As soon as Marina heard his voice, she knew it was him.

The beautiful boy poet who had kissed her in Koktebel, a kiss that was like sex. Sofia bristled alongside her and knew that her girlfriend recognised the lodger at Max's house. Marina had confessed what had happened between herself and Mandelstam on the hurried escape from the Black Sea hours before Efron arrived. Sofia had been spitting mad, but Marina could do nothing but feel Mandelstam itch under her skin.

A wedge of cranes towards a foreign land —
The heads of kings sprayed by the foam of heaven —
What's Troy to you, if not the home of Helen,
Where are you sailing, Archaean men?

His recitation was slow, and Marina watched the way he kept the crowd in a trance. This wasn't about the iconic Helen of Troy and the battle that raged in her name; this was about Germany's war against Russia.

Ivangorod fallen, Kovno fallen, Brest-Litovsk fallen, Bialystok fallen, Grodno fallen, Vilna fallen, Warsaw fallen.

Marina wondered if this litany would soon include Moscow and St Petersburg — until all of Russia was gone!

The sea and Homer — all are moved by love.
Whom should I heed? Now Homer has grown mute,
Black sea

Mandelstam paused and looked across at Marina, without seeing.

She held her breath.

The crowd waited.

And the statuesque dark-haired poet who Marina thought, *must be Anna Akhmatova*, stepped quietly towards Mandelstam but he regained his composure, blinked and continued his recitation.

Black sea, orating, nears me, resolute
And thunders by my headboard, loud and rough.

The crowd loved it and applauded and the shock of the intimacy between Mandelstam and the legendary Akhmatova filled Marina with grave uncertainty. As recently as last year, Marina had been the toast of the Muscovite writing scene. She was well acclaimed by the critics, especially Max Kirienkov-Voloshin, yet all she ever wanted was to be part of this set.

Anna Akhmatova, Osip Mandelstam and the handsome Boris Pasternak.

She watched the triumvirate laughing and hugging each other.

Pasternak and Mandelstam are utterly in love with her, Marina thought as she saw them feast on Akhmatova's every gesture, every move.

The room filled with noise and the tinkle of glasses and Marina heard a uniformed officer next to her say, *The war can no longer continue.*

She heard Sofia say, *I must ask Leonid Pasternak for an interview.*

She heard a bright-eyed woman ask another, *How did you meet my cousin, Boris Pasternak.*

Marina realised she was at sea, one filled with the discordant colours of sounds, and she wondered whether poetry could ever make sense of it all.

She wanted to approach Boris Pasternak, the adored Muscovite poet, whom she hadn't met till now on account of the fact that he had been working somewhere in the Urals. She looked across at this tall handsome Adonis. She, like Pasternak, had emerged from Moscow. This was their city. A place of cloisters, towers and churches with gold-domed cupolas. Their fathers, for goodness sake, had both been on staff together at the School of Painting, Sculpture and Architecture; their mothers had both been great pianists ... the only difference really was that the Pasternaks were Jews and Tsvetaevas, ardently anti-Semitic.

Marina saw Osip Mandelstam say something that made Pasternak laugh. She longed to press her body against Mandelstam and remind him of their clandestine tryst that had literally taken her breath away, she had not known intimacy like that before or after.

But more than anything she wanted to know Anna Akhmatova.

Marina stopped.

She looked harder at Anna and realised that it must be, it had to be, the same woman she had seen run out of the Stray Dog the first night they had arrived in St Petersburg, last November.

Marina gazed across the room and saw the poetess glance over at her as if sensing she was being watched.

Marina stood there desperate to move towards them.

She told herself this was what she wanted, to be part of this inner sanctum, this sacred quartet of Russia's poets.

This was what she wanted.

Postscript

One and a half thousand kilometres away, in a POW camp nestled in the Ural Mountains northeast of Perm, Walter sat on his bunk.

Beyond the small square window, the light from the grey sky was thinning.

Walter's hands were hardened with callouses that had come from chopping and stripping pine trees in a forest so dense a man could wander in and never ever return. One or two of the prisoners had done just that but by the time the guards had realised a POW had gone AWOL, they merely shrugged, saying the wolves would finish him off.

Walter found himself looking pensively at the dense mountain range that, according to a fellow prisoner, formed the spine that divided western Russia from Asiatic Russia.

Walter had ruminated upon this fact for some time. There had been little else to do when they were not working. Besides, it was only recently that the Red Cross had forced the Russian authorities to supply books, medication, mail and correct rations to each and every prisoner.

Walter stared out of the bunkhouse window and re-alised soon it would be winter, and although the older prisoners encouraged the younger ones to keep busy and not lose heart, Walter knew that his was lost a long time ago.

Each day the POWs carried their dinner in large shared pannikins out into the forest where they worked. They ate around midday. Mostly stew with mushrooms and turnips and very occasionally meat of some kind with soft doughy dumplings or hard black bread. Their evening supper was tea with pancakes and those lucky enough to have a bit of a racket on the side, supplying firewood, mushrooms, squirrels, martens and chipmunks to the guards, could enjoy cig-arettes. After supper, most of the prisoners, like Wal-ter, usually found their own little space amongst the thousands of prisoners, where they might be quiet or play skat or smoke or read one of the books supplied by the Red Cross, inevitably written in English or French or Russian.

Never German.

Walter realised that he had been a prisoner of war longer than he had been a soldier for the German Empire. He had no memory of why he had been fighting in the first place. Schmidt, an accountant from Dusseldorf, had told him that was what the prison camp would do to them — erase their identity, numb their patriotism and mould them into Russians.

But Meyer had scoffed and explained that unless you were Slavic, Russians had no interest in you — all non-Russians were simply beasts. Walter was watchful of Meyer, who had once let slip he was from Wehlau, East Prussia. Meyer's name marked him as a Jew and he often pointed out that here in the POW camp there were Jews from every corner of Europe and as such this was an anti-Semite war and not a war against the French and Russians who threatened the boundaries that secured Germany for the Germans.

It was a late afternoon October sky and Walter's spirits dropped with the thought of the oncoming all-consuming darkness.

So, when Ebbe stretched out on the cot, where Walter sat, in order to finish off his cigarette and chew the fat — Walter brightened.

There was a curl of a smile forming beneath Ebbe's dark moustache as he said, "Hey Walt, you left supper early."

Walter could feel Ebbe's worn boots against his back as he sat looking at the sawdust that covered the pressed dirt floor.

"One of those Red Cross matrons handed out the first batch of mail." Ebbe was grinning and held his cigarette aloft as he spoke, "You should have been there …"

Walter thought about the men sitting at the rows and rows of trestle tables that the prisoners themselves had made, and the wonder of letters from home that had somehow, miraculously, made their way from houses filled with the light of German love all the way to the autumnal shadows of Russia.

Walter looked back at Ebbe who laid in the exhalation of cigarette smoke that whisked and shimmered above him.

"Anyone we know get a letter?" Walter asked.

He was surprised at his own question. He had lost hope in anyone ever knowing his whereabouts, despite the rigmarole of registering as a POW in Łódź, then Minsk, then Moscow, then Perm.

What did it matter? He had asked himself again and again. Unlike his confreres, Walter felt no sense of purpose in consuming resources that would otherwise be redirected to the Tsar's soldiers. Moreover, he did not believe he would be repatriated or rescued.

He had no faith left.

Nothing.

"You," said Ebbe.

Walter lifted his head up slowly and looked back at Ebbe who was sucking in the last of his cigarette.

"What?" asked Walter.

Ebbe exhaled and smiled his secret smile and said, "*You* received a letter. Meyer collected it for you because you had already left."

Walter knew this wouldn't be a prank. These more experienced men had taken him under their wing. Walter's despair was something he tried to keep hidden but he suspected they knew. It filled Walter's chest, caught in his throat and slid down his face during the dark of night.

"A letter ...?" Walter whispered and at that moment Meyer appeared and plonked himself down on a small wooden stool.

Meyer held up the letter and looked at Walter, "This came for you."

Walter's mouth was dry and his pulse pounded.

"So, I took it and said I would deliver it to my friend," said Meyer as he handed the letter to Walter who touched the already broken seal.

"Censorship." Meyer offered the perfunctory explanation.

The envelope shook as Walter pushed his hand inside and pulled out a letter as thin as onion skin. He tried to hold the letter still but it quivered and trembled.

"Read aloud so we can all hear," said Ebbe as he lit another precious cigarette, marking the moment that one of theirs had, at last, a letter home.

Ebbe nestled one hand behind his head and looked towards his countrymen. He thought of his wife and her unruly chocolate brown hair and plump belly that shook with giggles when he would horse around with her and their two young sons in the back garden on Sunday after church. He would act the fool pretending to be a dog devouring the young boys and attacking his wife's ample bosom until she would call the game to a halt.

What I would give, Ebbe thought, *for one more indolent Sunday afternoon with my beloved.*

Meyer gently took the letter from Walter, scraped his stool closer, saying quietly, "May I read it for you, Walter?"

Meyer had heard, not long after he had left for the Front, that his mother, wife and children had been relocated somewhere west. That was more than six months ago and he had no idea where they had gone. It haunted him day and night. His mother was old and still mourned the death of his father. He wondered what, if anything, they had taken with them. He knew his wife would make the best of it, with her quick brown eyes and wiry body that could send an electric shock, through his in the tumble of their bed. His wife was smart and resourceful, and his three little dark-haired girls were sassy. He just hoped they had somehow made their way to Berlin, where they would be safe from the Russian barbarians.

Meyer crossed his legs and lent into Walter.

Letter poised.

The sticky-sweet aroma of Ebbe's cigarette corkscrewed the air.

Meyer cleared his throat and began:

My darling
I am writing to you on your mother's kitchen table. The afternoon sunlight is pouring through the window. The cooking is done and the dishes washed and put away. This week we managed to make our rations last with the help of extra potatoes — it was payment for staying back on the farm to help with the harvest.

In the quiet corner of their POW bunkhouse, Walter was listening to Heike. He felt the warm autumn sunshine buttering his mother's old kitchen table, he saw the yellow tiles along the kitchen bench and beyond the window (that was always clean), he smelt the chicken pen and then the lemon trees and when he squinted he could see the old stone fence he had helped mend that divided their small cottage from the farm.

Walter didn't see Meyer pause and look across at him nor did he see him glance at Ebbe, who nodded and blinked back his own homesickness.

Walter was watching the fall of Heike's thick blonde hair, her hazel eyes bent in concentration and her hand move the pen across the paper. She had always been so sure Walter loved her and that their future was bright, despite the sudden eruption of war and his call up papers.

Mama sends her love and says we are not worried now that you are a POW because the Red Cross will make sure you will be sent home when the war is over. I must tell you Walter when we first got the news, we both cried with relief knowing you were out of harm's way.
It won't be long now, my love.
Everyone here says the war will be over before Christmas! Can you imagine, my darling, all of us around a Christmas tree singing carols and thinking about that poor un-fattened goose we had to roast!

Ebbe started to chuckle and Meyer paused to think about Hanukkah and the way his mother and wife would bake challah until every room filled with the mouth-watering fragrance of warm bread.

Walter needed Heike's voice to go on and on and on. He needed her to help him make sense of a world that had lost its meaning.

So, you are not to lose heart, my beloved. We always knew this would be a difficult time, being separated and not in each other's arms, as we should be.

The bunkhouse waited.

Meyer cleared his throat, then coughed and then cleared his throat again before he read on:

You are not to lose heart, Walter. You are to keep well and come home to me so that we can trim the Christmas tree and get married in the New Year, as we always planned.

I pray every night that the angels will protect you and although there are no longer candles to light at the church, your mother and I always kneel and pray for you at the Blessed Virgin's grotto. You know the one, just beyond the side door of the church.

Because as Mama says, no mother — and especially not the Mother of Our Lord — would abandon her son. She will protect you, Walter.

She must.

The last finger of sunlight stretched in through the window, past Ebbe on the bed and Meyer bent over the letter, and pointed its frail and insignificant hope at Walter.

I tuck your photograph under my pillow every night, my darling, my Walter. I am waiting for you, my love.
Kisses and kisses and kisses
Heike

The three men sat in the stillness of the early evening as the light fell away from the window and the shadows of the bunkhouse somehow took on the familiar shapes of home: A soft cotton pillow beneath a sweetheart's sleeping head ... a backyard with the tumble of boys ... a table laid with the braided challah beneath the menorah.

Around them, their fellow prisoners from the German and Austro-Hungarian Empires made ready their cots.

But Ebbe, Meyer and Walter remained where they were.

Straining for the smell and touch and taste of family, remembering the way the light had fallen through a window, and having nothing to believe in but this letter from home.

Glossary

Adzhika — Russian red spicy sauce

Al lukh mas — the largest tree in Yakutia

Bashlyk — a protective hood with long ends, for use as a scarf, worn especially by the Russian military

Blinis — Russian pancakes

Buryat — a group of Indigenous Siberians

Challah — a plaited loaf of white leavened bread, traditionally baked to celebrate the Jewish sabbath

Cherkeska — a caftan with a single, unfastened opening down the front and no collar worn by men in the Caucasus

Dinniki's viper — a venomous snake endemic to the Caucasus

Durak — a popular Russian card game

Feldgrau — the greenish-grey colour of military uniforms of the German armed forces from the early 20th Century

Fokkers — German aircraft

Frontoviks — the Russian infantry

Gaziri — ornamental containers that had originally contained single loading measures of gunpowder for muzzle-loading muskets, and worn on the breasts of the kaftans

Gefreiter — a rank used in the German infantry

Goyim — a name for a non-Jew

Gymnastyorka — a Russian military smock comprising of a pullover-style garment with a standing collar with double button closure

Ichchi — spirits of the Yakut totem

Khinkali — Russian dumplings

Kholodets — a jellied meat dish made from cow's feet

Kumys — fermented mare's milk

Landbrot — German sourdough bread

Lavash — unleavened flatbread

Lubki — popular prints with simple graphics and narratives

Menorah — a candelabrum, especially one with eight branches and a central socket used at Hanukkah

Mundu — fish in the Yakutia

Papakha — a woollen hat worn by Russian men

Pickelhaube — the spiked helmet worn in the 19th and 20th centuries by Prussian and German military, firefighters and police

Raznochinetz — a Russian term given to those considered an outcast or outsider

Rusalka — a virgin who was drowned but resurfaces to entice men to their watery grave, according to Slavic mythology

Solyanka — Russian salty soup

Starets — is an elder of an Eastern Orthodox monastery who functions as a venerated adviser and teacher

Stavka — Russian Headquarters

Tochka — a popular euphemism for an outdoor market or meeting point for prostitutes

Urasy — conical tents used by Yakuts

Ushanka — a Russian fur hat

Varenikis — dessert dumplings filled with fruit

Yakut — Turkic ethnic group of people living in north-eastern Siberia

Yakutia — a region in Siberia, also known as the Republic of Sakha

Yakutsk — capital of Yakutia

Zakouska — hors d'oeuvres with caviar or sausage

Zbeetyn — a Russian honeyed spiced drink served at Christmas

Zemlyankas — a dugout or earth-house which was used to provide shelter for humans or domestic animals

Acknowledgements

This book owes its existence to the encouragement of my husband, Roger Murray, and my daughter, Madelaine Rose Guy-Moore.

To all the editors and those involved in getting *Take Ink & Weep* ready at First Rider Publishing, my heartfelt thanks.

For as long as I can remember I have loved Russian history and its literature. When I first started teaching the Silver Age Poets, Anna Akhmatova, Boris Pasternak, Osip Mandelstam and Marina Tsvetaeva, I knew that their work and lives reached across all temporalities. This novel contains these and many other real historical people and it also described actual historical events – but being a fictional text I have taken liberties in order to tell a story.

I have travelled through Russia a number of times with my husband, whose passion for Russia equals mine, and once with my daughter and son in law, James, who helped me see this extraordinary country with new eyes.

Finally, it is with much joy that I dedicate this book to my daughter whose love and generosity continue to teach me what really matters.

www.ingramcontent.com/pod-product-compliance
Lightning Source LLC
Chambersburg PA
CBHW060808120726
47909CB00006B/1834